Praise for Re[illegible]

A Touch of Scarlet

"Renee Ryan's second book in her Gilded Promises series, with its emotional depth and wonderful sense of time and place, is another thoroughly engaging and sigh-worthy read."

—Winnie Griggs, award-winning author of inspirational historical romance

Journey's End

"Utterly charming and not to be forgotten, *Journey's End* is Gilded Age delight."

—Victoria Alexander, #1 *New York Times* bestselling author

"Powerful and inspiring. *Journey's End* is a wonderfully rich and rewarding book."

—Gerri Russell, bestselling author of *Flirting with Felicity*

"Renee Ryan's heart-tugging story set in New York's Gilded Age kept me turning the pages well past my bedtime!"

—Winnie Griggs, award-winning author of inspirational historical romance

"Ryan's written a touching story of family, forgiveness, and a forever sort of love."

—Holly Jacobs, award-winning author of *These Three Words*

The Marriage Agreement, an RT Top Pick

"Fanny cares for Jonathon deeply, but she won't marry him without his love. At a crossroads, Jonathon will have to choose whether to walk away or be the man that Fanny believes him to be. The elements of Christian faith are superbly woven into the story, and fans of this delightful series will surely enjoy this sweet tale of forgiveness, hope, and redeeming love."

—Susannah Balch, RT Book Reviews

Hannah's Beau

"With book two in her Charity House series, Ryan writes with passion and love, as always. She knows what readers expect and never disappoints."

—Patsy Glans, RT Book Reviews

The Marshal Takes a Bride

"Don't miss this wonderful story about redemption and forgiveness. The characters are lovable, and likable, even at times when they're not nice, and the faith message is interwoven without being overbearing and preachy."

—Patsy Glans, RT Book Reviews

The Outlaw's Redemption, an RT Top Pick

"This sixth in the Charity House series is filled with complex characters and many endearing, familiar faces. It's a fascinating addition to this delightful series."

—Susan Mobley, RT Book Reviews

Dangerous Allies

"Ryan outdoes herself with this latest offering—a mix of romance, intrigue, and spies. She writes her characters with strong feelings and heart."

—Patsy Glans, RT Book Reviews

Finally a Bride

"I absolutely love books where the two main characters previously had a relationship that ended badly. Watching them work through past issues and forge a new, stronger relationship is so enjoyable. Garrett and Molly are great characters . . . Watching them open up their hearts and seeing them learn to trust each other was so sweet. *Finally a Bride* was such a great book and I definitely recommend it to fans of Christian romantic fiction (5 stars)."

—*Britt Reads Fiction*

223 ORCHARD STREET

ALSO BY RENEE RYAN

Gilded Promises historical romance series

Journey's End
A Touch of Scarlet
Once an Heiress

Charity House historical romance series

The Marshal Takes a Bride
Hannah's Beau
Loving Bella
The Lawman Claims His Bride
Charity House Courtship
The Outlaw's Redemption
Finally a Bride
His Most Suitable Bride
The Marriage Agreement

World War II historical series

Dangerous Allies
Courting the Enemy

Village Green contemporary romance series

Claiming the Doctor's Heart
The Doctor's Christmas Wish

Stand-alone works

Heartland Wedding
Homecoming Hero
Mistaken Bride
"New Year's Date" in A Recipe for Romance
Wagon Train Proposal
"Yuletide Lawman" in A Western Christmas
Stand-In Rancher Daddy

Published as Renee Halverson

Extreme Measures

RENEE RYAN

This is a work of fiction. Names, characters, organizations, places, events, and incidents are either products of the author's imagination or are used fictitiously.

Published by Waterfall Press, Grand Haven, MI

www.brilliancepublishing.com

ISBN-13: 9781542046701
ISBN-10: 154204670X

Cover design by Kirk DouPonce, DogEared Design

Printed in the United States of America

To Winnie Griggs, my fellow author and dear friend. There aren't enough words in the English language to convey how much I appreciate your loyalty, love, and support. You are the sister of my heart and the writer I hope to become one day. Thank you, Winnie, for being you, and for inspiring me to be more me.

Chapter One

Ellis Island, March 1905

Time had become her greatest enemy, the one obstacle Katie O'Connor hadn't anticipated. She'd meant to arrive at Ellis Island by noon, *not* a scant hour before the immigration station closed for the night.

How could she have known her request to leave the factory floor early would be denied? Or that the storm looming on the horizon would move in so quickly, tossing the ferryboat dangerously off course?

The vessel had bucked across the churning waters, listing to port, swinging over to starboard, dipping low, jerking back up, then repeating the process again and again. Katie had clung desperately to the boat's rail, her stomach lurching with every countermaneuver the sea captain attempted.

What a wretched crossing.

Well, she was here now, and would reunite with her sister soon. That's what mattered, Katie told herself. What didn't matter, what *couldn't* matter, was the nausea that still plagued her even now that they'd docked and she, along with the other passengers, had been given permission to disembark.

At least the rain had halted its merciless attack on New York Harbor. For now.

Lifting the heavy drenched edges of her cloak away from the sodden deck, Katie allowed herself a tight smile of satisfaction. More than happy to put the miserable boat ride behind her, she descended the gangplank.

Thunder boomed in the distance, an ominous warning the storm wasn't finished spewing its wrath. The seasickness reared, took hold, but Katie refused to let it linger. Placing the tips of her cold, wet fingers on the back of her neck, she forced air into her lungs.

Breathe, she ordered herself. In and out. In and out.

In. Out.

Katie wanted to blame the queasiness on the journey over from the Battery, but she knew that wasn't the sole cause. Nerves played a role, as did the flutter of unwanted memories of her previous visit to Ellis Island and how close she'd come to deportation.

The sun chose that moment to peer from behind a slit in the dark, grubby clouds. The lone shaft of light beamed over the Statue of Liberty, exposing her in sharp relief. A green patina had nearly overtaken the dull copper color, but did nothing to hide the sculpture's majestic beauty.

When Katie had first arrived in America, that impressive robed figure had seemed the very symbol of hope. Like the Lady herself, the promise of a better life was a bit tarnished now.

What would Shannon think of her new country?

It was a question Katie hadn't allowed herself to consider as she'd scrimped and saved for her sister's passage from Ireland. Much had changed since Katie had gone through the registration process.

Much had not.

She was no closer to her goal of independence. Would she ever break free of the poverty and daily struggle to survive?

There were days when she wondered.

A year after landing in New York, she was still scratching out a meager existence, living in a crowded tenement house on the Lower East Side of Manhattan.

Newly arrived immigrants staggered past her. Some hopeful, others nervous, most weighted down by the weariness of their travels and bulging pieces of luggage. Children, ever resilient, darted headlong past the slower-moving adults. One of the taller boys clipped Katie's shoulder, sending her toppling into a pushcart overflowing with suitcases.

"Watch where you're going, ye bloody strumpet!" A man with shoulders the size of a plough horse, and a face to match, made a shooing motion with his hands as if he were a farmer scattering chickens.

"Sorry." Katie stepped out of the way just in time to avoid being run over. The smell of wet wool, cheap worn leather, and human sweat assaulted her senses. Ellis Island smelled no better now than it had a year ago.

She covered her nose and moved toward the one building she'd hoped never to enter again. She had little choice but to do so today. Not yet nineteen years old, a full five years younger than Katie, Shannon was an unmarried woman traveling alone. As such, she'd been denied entry into the country, and would be held indefinitely until a family member could promise she wouldn't become a "public charge."

A new determination reared up and, hoisting her head a fraction higher, Katie continued toward the immigration station.

Her plan was simple. She would work her way backward through the registration process, starting at the infamous Kissing Post.

Dozens of unfamiliar languages spoken in foreign tongues mingled with the sounds of a mournful ship's horn, wailing babies, and screeching seagulls. Katie scanned the dense crowd. So many had come to America looking for a better life. Would they find it?

Katie hadn't. Not yet.

But she would. One day. Someday.

Breathing slowly, and so very, very carefully, she glanced up at the massive building that had nearly been her undoing a year ago. Now, her sister would go through the rigorous process of registering as a legal immigrant.

Katie's stomach swooped with conflicting emotions, from thrill to trepidation in a single instant.

The wind screamed to life, whipping strands of her red-gold hair across her face. She hardly noticed the damp chill of the air. She was too busy staring up at the oblong brick and stone building with its square turrets flanking each of the four corners.

Thunder quivered. Then smacked.

Katie jolted at the sound.

The world seemed to pause in eerie silence. Waiting. Holding. A band of low-flying clouds swallowed the last patch of sunlight.

Big, fat drops of rain hit the ground.

More followed, coming faster, harder, a relentless and unforgiving assault, stippling puddles left from the previous downpour.

The smells hit her again, magnified by the damp, pungent sea air. The foul odors were far too similar to the ones Katie lived with daily, and her stomach rebelled all over again.

Refusing to give in to weakness, she took in a gulp of air. And another. One more. And . . .

At last. *At last.* Her stomach calmed.

A high-pitched feminine squeal of delight lifted above the tangled web of voices. Heart in her throat, Katie spun in the direction of the unbridled joy just as a young girl tugged an impossibly old woman into her arms.

One of the lucky ones, Katie thought as she circled the area near the Kissing Post, where families reunited after a long separation.

Out of the corner of her eye, she spotted an official watching the crowds, scanning faces in a probing, spine-chilling way. He was big, his face dark and menacing, his manner callous. He wore the requisite uniform of the Ellis Island inspectors: black pants, a dark peacoat that had shiny gold buttons running down the middle, and a hat with a thick leather bill.

Catching sight of Katie, his face scrunched in a scowl, an ugly, fearsome sight she'd seen once before. A year ago. On this very island.

Panic clawed up her throat, freezing her in place. Dark, terrifying memories nipped at her like pointed little bird beaks. She couldn't draw a single decent breath. Her eyes watered. Her lungs burned. And still, the memories came.

She'd been so seasick when she'd arrived at Ellis Island, hardly able to walk on her own. Had Katie not clung to a fellow immigrant's arm, she would have fallen to the ground and possibly been trampled to death.

Just when she'd thought all was well, seemingly out of nowhere, a hand had closed around her arm and she'd been plucked out of the crowd.

Caught off guard, and too weak to fight, she'd been dragged away, down seemingly infinite corridors. At the end of one especially long hallway, she'd been given a card with the letters *S.I.*, and ushered into a dank dark room for a special inquiry. She'd answered a set of rapid-fire questions, then had been sent on to a rigorous medical examination.

As the horror of that day returned, the world seemed to stop and wait. Even the rain slowed to a patter, as if that most ruthless of elements grasped the gravity of the dreadful memory.

Katie was wasting precious time.

She looked away from the scowling official and focused on putting one foot in front of the other. Chin up, shoulders back, she entered the building. And immediately felt the stares from a pack of male immigrants waiting their turn at the money exchange booth.

Dressed in ill-fitting, crumpled suits, they watched her like stray dogs eyeing a forbidden morsel. Suspicion was there as well, thick and throbbing from shadowed faces that had witnessed too much of life's underbelly.

Head down, Katie moved quickly past them, toward a long row of desks. Surely, one of the inspectors would direct her to her sister.

A hand clamped on her arm, and she was yanked to a halt.

It took precious seconds for reality to crash into her. *No!* The word echoed in her head. She opened her mouth to protest, but nothing came out. Her mind traveled back to another time, a dreadful day, one of the worst in her life. She barely had the wherewithal to shove aside a renewed bout of fear before she was spun around.

The beady-eyed official had followed her inside the building. His gaze roamed with calculated purpose from her head to her toes, then back up, stopping at various spots along the way, eventually landing once again on her face.

"How did you make it past the medical examination?"

Katie gulped in a breath. Suddenly, there wasn't enough air in the building to feed her starving lungs.

No, wait, she had no reason to panic and every reason to stand her ground. She belonged here. She'd been officially summoned.

Drawing in a fast, steadying breath, she said, "I"—she swallowed—"I am *not* a new arrival. I took the ferry over from the Battery." She gave a brief nod in the direction of New York Harbor. "I have come to retrieve my sister."

"Your . . . sister?" Skepticism dripped from his voice.

Katie nodded, doing her best to look confident. "I received a telegram yesterday afternoon stating that she'd arrived on the SS *Helena*, and I was required to come for her at my earliest convenience."

"Let me see the telegram."

When she merely stared at him, he made an impatient gesture with his hand.

"Oh, right. Of course." She dug in the pocket of her cloak, drew out the document.

He snatched the paper from her trembling fingertips.

For several heart-pounding seconds, he held her gaze. Finally, he looked down. Katie was still debating whether to give further explanation when he thrust the telegram back into her hand.

"You'll find your sister in the women's area on the north corner of the building." He gave her directions, then sent her on her way with a hard push.

Katie staggered forward, managing to catch her balance only after a wild flailing of her arms. Were all the workers on this island so angry and uncaring?

No. Not all. Dr. Brentwood had been kindness itself. The handsome young physician had stamped her medical inspection card with one life-altering word: *Passed.*

Bolstered by the pleasant mental image, Katie hurried down a labyrinth of corridors. She turned right, then left, left again, right, and then, there, up ahead, her destination beckoned.

Dizzy with expectation, Katie joined the queue in front of yet another tall desk, where an immigration official sat guarding the anteroom's entryway.

"Are you meeting a family member?" The question came from the young woman ahead of Katie, spoken in an Irish accent much like her own. But the voice was younger, freer.

Less encumbered by life's challenges.

"My sister," she said, forcing a smile she didn't quite feel. Katie attributed her lack of enthusiasm to her previous experience on this island, nothing more. The nagging sense of foreboding? It simply wasn't worth acknowledging. At least that's what she told herself.

"How lovely." The young woman smiled. "I have come for my cousin."

Briefly, Katie saw something in the pretty gaze, a shadow in the shape of worry. But then it was gone, replaced with a happy expression. Innocence personified.

Katie had once been that carefree, that eager to see her new country as a place where dreams came true.

For a moment, just one, she mourned the woman she'd been. Sweet, thoughtful Katie O'Connor, the girl never without a smile or word of encouragement for others.

The line shifted and everyone moved two steps forward. A moment later, the young woman turned around again. "I'm Briana."

"Katie."

"Pleased to meet you."

Katie returned the sentiment with a smile.

"Tell me, Katie." Briana grinned, cocking her head to one side. "How long have you been in America?"

"I left Ireland just over a year ago. What about you?"

"I arrived but two months ago."

Which explained much. Reality had yet to set in for Briana. Katie hoped it never did. She hoped the young immigrant achieved every one of the yet-to-be-realized dreams swirling in her gaze.

They moved another two steps.

"It's your turn," Katie told the other woman, pointing to the desk behind her.

"Splendid." Briana swung around, stated her own name and that of the family member she'd come to meet.

A rustling of papers followed, and, after a short conversation, the official directed Briana to a waiting area where her cousin would join her momentarily.

Katie exchanged a brief smile with the young woman and then took her place at the front of the line. *This is it.* The moment she'd been waiting for since her teary goodbye with Shannon.

Her muscles tensed as the foreboding returned, then eased up when the man behind the desk smiled at her. He had a kindly look about him. His brown hair, ordinary features, and wire-rimmed glasses spoke of a patient nature.

"Good afternoon, Miss . . . ?"

"O'Connor."

His responding nod was as pleasant as his smile, if a bit distant. "How may I assist you, Miss O'Connor?"

"I have come for my sister. Her name is Shannon. Shannon O'Connor. She arrived on the SS *Helena* yesterday afternoon."

"The SS *Helena*," he repeated, reaching for one of the neat, organized piles atop his desk. He shuffled through the stack, then pulled out a page with hand-scribbled notations.

Katie leaned forward and took note of the typed words that spread across the top of the page: *LIST OR MANIFEST OF ALIEN PASSENGERS FOR THE COMMISSIONER OF IMMIGRATION.*

She drew in a sharp breath as he set the paper on the desk and ran his finger down the left column.

"Ah, here we go. O'Connor, Shannon. Boarded the SS *Helena* in"—his finger swept to the right of the page—"Cork, Ireland."

Relief nearly buckled Katie's knees. "Yes, that's her. That's my sister."

A long pause ensued as the man quietly studied the page beneath his hand. More seconds passed, and still more.

Cold from the inside out, Katie stared at the inspector's bent head, silently begging him to look up, smile patiently, and send her to the waiting area where Briana now stood.

Katie did not receive such an order. He sighed instead.

Something was wrong.

"Sir, is there a problem?"

He lifted his head and, eyes perfectly blank, uttered the words Katie most feared in the world. "I'm sorry, Miss O'Connor. Your sister has been detained until further notice."

Chapter Two

Detained? Until further notice?

Katie staggered back a step. Her brain refused to comprehend the situation.

Shannon had been . . . detained?

No. It couldn't be true. Surely, Katie had misunderstood the official's words. Flustered, she scanned the immediate area.

People shifted away from her. Shoulders turned. Eyes were quickly averted. Even Briana pretended grave interest in the tiled floor at her feet, as if Katie's sudden misfortune would somehow rub off on her if she showed too much interest or compassion.

Panic came then, fast, obscene, and painful, like sharp, burning ice shards stabbing at her heart.

Katie returned her attention to the official. "Why was my sister"—she paused to gather a portion of her fading composure—"*why* was Shannon detained?"

"She failed the medical exam." No longer meeting her gaze, he set aside the manifest. "You'll receive word once she's well enough to leave the island."

He didn't need to add any more information for Katie to understand the situation fully. Her sister was fighting some undisclosed illness and could be—*probably would be*—deported if she didn't recover from whatever ailed her.

If only Katie knew specifically what had led to Shannon's detainment, she would know better how to proceed or, at the very least, what arguments to make to have Shannon released into her care.

"Please, sir. May I see my sister? I have some medical training. Not much, but some." As Katie spoke, her panic dug deeper, making her words come faster, more strained, matching the chaotic race of her pulse. "I served as a midwife's assistant back in Ireland. If I could just take a look at Shannon, I might be able to determine—"

"I'm sorry, Miss O'Connor. That's all the information I am at liberty to share with you at this time. I'm afraid you must leave the area immediately."

"But—"

"The station is closing for the night."

The next few moments went by in a blur.

A large man with a shock of wiry black hair and mean, flat features took her arm and escorted her out of the building. Ignoring her pleas to slow down, he dragged her all the way to the waiting ferryboat and practically tossed her onto the gangplank.

Tears threatened, but Katie fought them back. To cry, here and now, was an indulgence she couldn't afford. But, oh. The situation seemed so unnatural, unreal even. Except it was real, so terribly, painfully real.

Stinging droplets of rain struck Katie's face, obstructing her vision. The weight of her disappointment made her steps slow and awkward. Unable to watch Ellis Island disappear from view, she searched for a seat far away from the boat's rail. She spoke to no one, looked at no one.

Shivering inside her wet cloak, she felt wretched grief well up. Every time she thought about her sister, how scared and alone she must be, Katie's heart shattered. Poor, dear Shannon. How ill was she?

How badly did she suffer?

So caught up in her sorrow, Katie didn't think much of it when someone settled on the bench directly across from her. She vaguely registered a pleasant, deep masculine voice engaging another passenger in conversation. The rich baritone was familiar, as if she'd heard it in a dream that had faded long ago, like morning mist over the Irish countryside.

"I was the last to board," he said in a clear, perfectly articulated American accent. "We'll set sail soon."

On cue, the mooring lines were dropped and the ferryboat pulled away from the docks with a jarring metallic groan. As Ellis Island gave way to open waters, Katie braced for another bout of seasickness. When it came, she accepted it as her due.

Your sister has been detained until further notice.

A dark emptiness filled Katie's heart. She'd let Shannon down. Again. Would she ever do right by her sister?

Would she ever be able to fulfill her promise to their mother?

It would be so easy to find fault with the immigration inspector who'd delivered the awful news, but that would be placing blame where it wasn't warranted. He hadn't been cruel. He'd merely been doing his job.

Katie had recognized the tempered impatience behind the wire-rimmed spectacles, the pity, and, sadly, the resolve to follow the stringent rules set by his government.

Your sister has been detained.

The worst possible news.

No, Katie silently amended, not the worst. Shannon could have been deported. *She still could be.*

A sob caught in Katie's throat. It hurt to hear the uninhibited happiness from her fellow passengers as they performed the intimate rituals of coming together after a lengthy separation.

There would be no reunion for Katie and Shannon. No laughter. No excited talking over one another as they caught up with each other's lives.

Tears gathered in Katie's eyes, guilt and grief combined. She attempted to blink them away. It helped to focus on things that made her happy. The green hills of Ireland, the satisfaction that came from helping someone in need, her sister's smile . . .

A small commotion had her opening her eyes.

Katie looked up and saw an elderly woman. The man who'd claimed to be the last to board must have given up his seat. Where had he gone?

Katie searched for him, spotted a likely candidate working his way through the crowd. He moved with methodical grace, his tall, lithe form heading for an empty spot at the railing.

There was something about him. Something familiar. Something that tugged at her very core. Katie couldn't tear her gaze away. He had broad shoulders and lean hips and wore a heavy frock coat made from fine fabric. In his left hand, he carried a black medical bag.

The thumping of her heart drummed out all other sound.

Could it be?

Dare she hope?

Katie placed her hand on her forehead, pushed away the wet strands of hair, and continued watching the stranger, willing him to turn around and face her.

As if hearing her silent call, he shifted his stance and, slowly, pivoted in her direction. Feeling shy, and maybe a bit foolish, Katie quickly lowered her head before he could catch her watching him.

She waged a silent argument with herself, torn between embarrassment and a sudden wish to discover if the stranger was the same man who'd rescued her from certain deportation. She couldn't bear the disappointment if she was wrong.

Clasping her hands in her lap, she kept her head down and forced her mind on her sister. Katie should have tried harder to convince the inspector to let her see Shannon.

Instead, her words had been meaningless, impotent, sliding off his oiled hair like water off a duck's back.

What am I going to do?

Katie didn't realize she'd lost the battle with her tears until a man's hand moved into her line of vision, offering a snowy-white handkerchief.

Out of reflex, she reached for the cloth, took it, and swiped at her eyes. Emotions better under control, she looked up and stared into a familiar pair of piercing blue eyes.

Hope, delicious, star-spangled hope, clogged in her throat.

Him. It was *him.* Her savior from a year ago.

The wind had played havoc with his dark hair, and, at this late hour in the day, he had beard stubble shadowing his strong jaw, making his intense light eyes even more compelling.

He was not a man who needed to be more compelling.

"We meet again," he said, in a deep, hypnotic tone that had appeared in her dreams more than she cared to admit.

Oh, but he remembered her!

The fact that he looked pleased to see her only added to Katie's confusion. Happiness mixed with shock put a stranglehold on her throat. A slow, steadying breath helped her regain a semblance of control.

"Dr. Brentwood." She attempted to return his handkerchief.

He shook his head. "You keep it."

"Thank you." Their hands brushed as she pulled the cloth back toward her lap. Her heart took a fast, extra hard beat.

He felt it, too, that thrilling spark of awareness. She could tell in the way he stiffened ever so slightly, and the brief bemused expression that crossed his face.

Too many thoughts and feelings flooded Katie at once, swarming around her like flies at an afternoon picnic on a hot summer day. This man worked at Ellis Island, performing medical examinations.

Perhaps he'd processed Shannon.

"Dr. Brentwood. I . . . that is . . . did you happen to . . ." She couldn't seem to shove the proper words out of her mouth. She swallowed, tried again. "Please." Katie patted the empty space beside her. "Won't you have a seat?"

A slow smile curved his lips. "Don't mind if I do."

* * *

Ty settled on the bench beside the pretty immigrant he'd encountered a year ago, set his medical bag at his feet, and waited for her to ask her question.

She continued staring at him.

Now that she had his attention, she didn't seem to know how to make her query. Ty gave her another moment to compose herself.

With the unearthly whisper of the wind slipping across the waters playing in his ears, he took the opportunity to study the young woman, this time with the eye of a trained physician. Her clothing was wet. No wonder, that. The rain blown in by an especially relentless storm had been coming down on and off all day, mostly on.

She didn't wear a hat. Or if she had, she'd discarded it, leaving her head bare, which served only to highlight her delicate beauty. Several strands of glorious red-gold hair had come loose from their pins and were now whipping around her face. Her skin was unnaturally pale, the doctor in him noted, and the distress in her expression made her eyes seem entirely too large for her face. She was possibly seasick. No, not possibly, *definitely*, and she was clearly distraught over something that had occurred at the immigration station.

Still, she held silent.

And so Ty continued cataloguing her features. Those large troubled eyes were extraordinary, the light green irises rimmed in the deepest of blues. She gave off a kind of innocence and wisdom combined, and something else, something that soothed. There didn't seem to be a proper definition for it, but Ty could feel her silent pull tugging him closer. Just a bit closer.

He could hardly look at her.

He couldn't look away.

The air dropped a few degrees, causing the girl to shiver beneath her sodden cloak. Without thinking about the ramifications of his actions, Ty removed his own coat and wrapped it around her shoulders. She went still with astonishment, her eyes growing wider. He thought she might try to give the garment back. Instead, she snuggled deeper inside the wool. "Thank you."

Two words. Spoken with such sincerity.

Her gratitude made him feel less . . . numb, more awake, as if he could recapture a part of the man he'd once been. Or, at the very least, as if he could go through the night without reaching for the bottle of brandy he used to stave off the haunting dream that plagued him.

Regret was a cold, lonely bedfellow. And nothing less than he deserved.

Ty's reaction to this woman was much the same as the last time they'd met, when she'd been brought to him for additional medical screening. Even in her fear and confusion, she'd managed to calm his sense of restlessness.

She made him want to be the man he saw in her eyes. Yet a single decision, made out of a selfish need to prove he was equal to his brilliant father, had altered lives forever.

Ty heaved a breath of heavy damp air. The taste of salt and bitterness lingered on his tongue.

With great effort, he tore his gaze away and gave his head a shake. When he looked back at the young woman, he could swear her color had grown paler still. "You're feeling unwell."

She didn't deny the diagnosis. She simply nodded slowly, then swallowed several times. "I have discovered"—another swallow—"I was not made for sea travel."

"I gathered as much."

They shared a smile, though hers came at a cost. The last remnants of color drained from her face. A sudden wish to comfort her had him reaching out, but then he thought better of it and let his hand drop away before touching her.

Lips pressed tightly together, he glanced through the soggy, frigid air toward the Battery. Rain and fog blanketed the waters, blurring visibility. Not a single ray of light shone through the thick cloud cover moving rapidly across the pewter sky.

They were in for a rough ride.

As if to punctuate his silent prediction, the ferryboat bucked over a wave, crested, then slammed down with a hard jolt.

Good God.

"Will this day never end," she muttered.

Ty's heart thundered as he stared at her, absorbing the details of her obvious distress. He turned away again. It wasn't right to look at her so intently, so intimately, as if they were old friends reunited after a prolonged absence.

Something about this woman, with her guileless manner and heart-shaped lips, brought to mind another life, when he'd been a different man, a better one.

This time, when he reached for her, he didn't pull back but, rather, placed his hand over hers.

Her mouth worked through a brief tremor. Yet another lock of hair had come loose, fanning over her face.

Strangely compelled, Ty let go of her hand and reached up to tuck the wayward strand behind her ear. The gesture was overly familiar. They were strangers.

She doesn't feel like a stranger.

He glanced out over the water, silently questioning why he felt such a strong connection to this woman.

"I thought never to see you again." Her Irish lilt, as lyrical as Ty remembered, wafted over him.

"Nor I you," he admitted, swiveling around to face her once again. "That's not to say this isn't a pleasant turn of events."

Her smile returned, sweet and unaffected and full of warmth, like a sunbeam breaking through a slit in the dingy clouds. For several beats of his heart, all Ty could do was stare into those remarkable eyes. He nearly lost himself in their depths.

The wind kicked up, whipping the stubborn strand of hair free. He nearly told her it had come loose again, but she shoved the lock back behind her ear before he could open his mouth.

There was such quiet dignity in that delicate gesture that Ty, exhausted from a long day of examining immigrants and sending more than usual to detention, felt something inside him snap. It wasn't an altogether awful feeling, and was all the more powerful for its unexpected impact on his cold, bleak heart.

For an instant, the groan of the wind, the drone of the ferryboat's engine, and the buzz of muffled conversations tangled into one loud echo. He shifted, stretched out his legs, pulled them back in, then repeated the process twice over.

He was staring again.

He couldn't seem to stop himself.

This woman had stayed in his memory. He'd taken a risk then and had thought of her often since, not sure he'd made the right decision, knowing he wouldn't have changed his mind given the chance.

Why this strong reaction to a stranger? he wondered again. *Why her?* When he'd encountered thousands like her. "I don't even recall your name."

"It's Katie. Katie O'Connor."

"Katie, right, of course. And I'm—"

"Dr. Brentwood," she finished for him.

"Call me Ty." He held her gaze. "Considering our history, it seems appropriate."

"All right, then, I shall call you Ty." His name sounded sweet on her lips. And something deep within him simply . . . let . . . go.

He fought the urge to close his eyes. If he did, he'd be back at New York Hospital, back to a time when he'd been considered the most promising surgeon of his generation, his brilliance exceeded only by his father. Ty had been confident of his skills, convinced he was destined to change the face of modern medicine.

Such certainty was an illusion.

He knew that now. He'd fooled himself into thinking he was a man above the human failings of other, lesser mortals. He'd been ridiculously arrogant. And an innocent young woman had paid the ultimate price for his pride.

A hand touched his sleeve.

The whisper-light contact released Ty from his disturbing thoughts. Rolling his shoulders, he readjusted his position on the bench and forced his mind on the here and now.

Katie appeared to be feeling marginally better and wanting to say something. Yet since she seemed in no hurry to make her query, perhaps now was the time to broach the question that had been on his own mind since sitting down. "What brought you back to Ellis Island in such dismal weather?"

"I . . ." It was her turn to look away.

When her gaze came back to his, Ty noticed she was breathing hard, her chest rising and falling.

"I went to meet my sister," she said, pulling the lapels of his coat tighter around her. "She's only eighteen. I was sent a telegram stating that I'm required to vouch for her before they will release her into the country."

Aware of the restrictions put on young women traveling alone, Ty nodded. He was also aware that Katie's sister was not on the ferryboat. "I take it there was a problem."

She nodded miserably. "Shannon has been detained until further notice."

Detained, not deported. It could have been worse.

Nevertheless, Ty went still a beat, tethered to the spot by the unhappy emotions staring back at him from Katie's pretty face. She reached out with a fluttering motion, as if to sweep away the anxiety that bombarded her.

Realizing the thing she most needed from him was commiseration rather than pity, Ty caught her hand and rubbed the pad of his thumb across her palm in a move meant to instill calm. Though he already suspected the answer, he found himself asking, "Do you know why your sister was detained?"

Katie quivered uneasily. "She was refused entry into the country for . . . for . . ." She drew in a long, tortured breath. "Medical reasons."

Chapter Three

Ty blinked at Katie, her words hanging in the thick salt-infused air. As one of the doctors who signed the order to detain immigrants for medical reasons, he wanted to apologize for her sister's confinement in the Ellis Island Immigrant Hospital. But he couldn't. The rules were in place for everyone's protection.

For the sake of the American citizenry, Shannon O'Connor could not be allowed in the country until she recovered.

"Did the officials tell you what ails your sister?"

Katie shook her head, her expression full of frustration as she absently watched a seagull dive for its supper.

Young boys in floppy cloth hats ran along the boat's railing, splashing in the puddles, their laughter interrupted only by the hiss of the boat slicing through the choppy waters.

"I was told that I would receive word when she was well enough to leave the island."

"I'm sorry." The words sounded empty even to his own ears.

"Dr. Brentwood, I mean . . . Ty," she amended softly, settling her hand on his sleeve. That touch, so light, so tentative. "I have to ask. I have to *know*. Did you perform my sister's medical exam? Were you the doctor who signed the order to detain her?"

Ty would've liked to give her a definitive answer, but he simply didn't know for certain. Although the immigrants were required to wear a card pinned to their clothing with their names written boldly across the top, Ty rarely took notice. He looked past the person, concerned only with searching for clear signs of illness.

"I conduct hundreds of examinations a day. Most last no more than six seconds, a bit longer if I detect a problem." He tried to smile, but it felt disingenuous. "Even if your sister was one of the many people that passed through my station today, I'm not sure I would have remembered her."

"You remembered me."

True. But Ty's memory of this woman was tied up with his past, tangled in the terrible mistake he'd made two weeks prior to meeting her.

"For you"—he lifted a shoulder—"I made an exception."

"Perhaps the same is true of Shannon. Perhaps my sister's symptoms can be attributed to seasickness and she'll be released tomorrow."

The hope that lit her eyes transformed her face, and Ty felt the grip around his throat tighten until he couldn't catch a decent breath. He was seized with a feeling he'd never known, as if an old emotion had been compressed into something new.

"Medical detention is not given lightly."

Another sigh slid out of her, this one full of disappointment. Disappointment in him.

Ty reined in his own frustration.

"Do you have any advice for me when I return to Ellis Island on my next day off?"

Her question had him raising his eyebrows. "You plan to return before you're summoned?"

"I have to find out what's wrong with her."

If it were his family member, Ty would want to know the same.

"There must be something I can do to get more information about my sister's condition. Perhaps if I approach the right person . . ."

The muscles at the back of Ty's neck knotted. Katie planned to approach a specific individual for help. Ty had heard stories of officials misrepresenting themselves to pretty young women like her, making promises that carried certain conditions.

If something happened to Katie . . .

"Stick to well-lit areas," he warned. "Speak only to the officials at their stations. Don't be lured into a private meeting."

Katie tilted her head and looked at him for a seemingly endless moment. "Well, yes. That goes without saying."

It still needed to be said.

"I am not a green immigrant newly arrived in this country." Her voice sounded like a schoolteacher scolding her students. "I have lived in a tenement house on the Lower East Side for a year. I understand the dangers for women like me."

Women like her. The label served only to put him further on edge. The poor weren't always treated with respect or a sense of fairness. Something spread through him. Something more than conviction, more than guilt and bitterness. A renewed desire to aid as many as he could. Not only the immigrants he encountered every day. Right now, in this moment, he wanted—needed—to help this particular woman.

He wasn't sure how. But he *would* help Katie, for the sake of the one he'd failed.

Cold memories pooled inside him. Shep's accusations rang in his ears. Ty had made promises he couldn't keep.

He couldn't go back.

So he would go forward. He would atone for his mistake, the only way he knew how.

The ferryboat slowed, the engine rumbling to a grind as the captain steered the vessel toward the docks. Ty's time with Katie was nearly up.

As if coming to the same conclusion, she clutched his sleeve and spoke in a low, urgent voice, her words tumbling out in a rush. "Please. Won't you give me the name of an official I should approach, one who will give me the information I seek?"

"I only volunteer at the station once a week." The excuse was out of his mouth before he could stop it. "I'm not sure who'll be on duty when you return."

"I understand."

A fresh flood of guilt seared his veins as her dejection swept over him. "Ask for Dr. Wilson—give him my name. Dr. Anderson would be my second choice. Avoid Miller and Seabold, especially Seabold."

The doctor was difficult to work with on a good day.

"Thank you, Ty." A touch of unrepentant happiness curved the edges of her mouth.

Katie O'Connor was a beautiful woman. Her skin was smooth as marble, her face a perfect oval. Her nose was narrow, her eyes large and almond shaped, her lips cut in a cupid's bow.

He'd never been intrigued by a woman like this, not even his former fiancée. Vanessa was equally beautiful, and just as kind, but Katie was . . . different. Special.

They spent the next few minutes discussing her position as a finisher at a garment factory. Like other immigrants, her days were long and filled with hard, grueling work. Yet she didn't complain. She seemed pleased that she'd managed to rise to a coveted position due to her skill and determination. Ty was about to ask what, if anything, she enjoyed about the job when the ferryboat bumped the dock a few times, then settled into a rhythmic bobbing motion.

Distracted, he glanced to the wharf, then to the darkened sky overhead, then back to the wharf. "Let me escort you home."

Katie's eyes widened.

He gave a pointed glance at the streetlamps flickering to life in the gloomy mist. "No woman should be roaming these streets alone after dark."

"I'm well aware of the dangers that lurk in the shadows."

Just how aware?

Ty didn't like the implication of her response. Needing no further encouragement, he gained his feet, then stretched out his hand in silent offering.

Katie stood, her fingers working to remove his coat from her shoulders.

"You can give it back to me when we arrive at your tenement house," he said.

There was a single awkward moment when they both merely stared at one another, Ty's hand still outstretched between them, hers clasped around the lapels of his coat. A slew of words passed between them, entire unspoken sentences written on the air in invisible ink.

"Won't that be out of your way?"

Slowly, he lowered his hand. "I live on the edge of the Bowery." At her shocked expression, he explained, "I work the rest of the week at a small medical clinic on Henry Street."

"Oh." Her shoulders relaxed. "I . . . had no idea."

"No reason you should."

"I suppose not." She smiled. He returned the gesture. Then, feeling lighter than he had in months, he scooped up his medical bag and moved to stand shoulder to shoulder with the pretty immigrant.

As one, they joined the rushing current of disembarking passengers.

* * *

Shannon O'Connor stumbled, would have fallen had the hand on her arm not yanked her forward. "Please, you must slow down. I can't keep up with your fast strides. And, and . . ." She clawed at the hand gripped around her arm. "You're hurting me."

The uniformed official ignored her, his fingers tightening painfully as he dragged her down a dark corridor.

"Where are you taking me?" She'd asked the question twice already.

As before, she was given the same curt answer. "You have been assigned further medical review."

What did that mean, exactly? Would Shannon have to endure another exam? She'd already been poked and prodded by two doctors. Just how much more humiliation must she suffer?

"I'm not sick." *Well, not at this precise moment.* "I'm just a little dizzy from the barge ride over from the ship."

He stopped moving. For one fleeting moment, she thought she might have convinced her jailer—or rather, the immigration official. He was very close, too close, leaning in so she could see that his features had hardened even more, growing stark and dangerous in the shadowed corridor. "Dr. Seabold will decide if you're telling the truth."

There was no more talking after that, not by him or by Shannon. She was too busy trying to keep up with his ground-eating strides. If she didn't know better, she would swear he'd increased his already brutal pace.

What's going to happen to me?

She'd never known such primal fear. The terrible sensation welled up from the pit of her stomach, seeping through every pore, making her sick and weak. Both time and place became distorted in her mind.

Her thoughts spun too quickly, the dizziness a mixture of terror and the ongoing illness that had begun a few hours after boarding the SS *Helena*.

Worry and despair had made her sick. The swaying of the boat had made her condition worse. No part of her body seemed to be under her control anymore. Her heart pounded too hard in her chest, drumming out all coherent thought. Her bones shook. Tears leaked from her gritty, swollen eyes. What if she wasn't admitted into the country?

How would Liam find her then?

How would he know what happened to her?

She yanked on her arm, desperate to be free. The official was stronger than she was and refused to release her. With each step deeper into the bowels of the legendary immigration station on Ellis Island, panic crept into Shannon's limbs, slithering slyly up her spine.

The stench of sweat, urine, and feces had her breath coming in quick, hard pants. The sound echoed off the walls.

"Please, I beg you," she pleaded. "Slow down." Her leaden feet couldn't keep up with his long strides. "You're walking too fast."

"And you're walking too slow." Mouth set in a hard line, he half dragged, half pushed her around the next corner.

Bile rose in Shannon's throat, threatening to make an appearance. She swallowed it back. The nausea returned, but that didn't keep her from struggling against the tight grip on her arm.

She nearly freed herself. But then the official yanked her to a stop, spun her around, and pressed his face inches from hers. "Quit your fighting, you stupid cow. This is for your own good."

His foul breath fell over her in a nauseating cloud of stench.

What could possibly make a man smell that unpleasant?

Accepting momentary defeat, Shannon forced her panic back with a hard swallow, her hundredth since arriving on this terrifying island, and focused on memorizing the twists and curves of their route.

Seven steps, a hard turn to the right, three more steps forward, another quick turn, and one more still.

At last, the official halted in front of a door with a small window. Inside the room stood a man and a woman dressed in white from head to toe, their faces covered with white masks.

The hairs on the back of Shannon's neck prickled with alarm. "You have made a mistake. I'm not sick."

No response.

"I . . . I have family in America. My sister lives at 223 Orchard Street. All you have to do is contact her. She will come for me."

"She was already contacted, and turned away." A gleam of satisfaction lit the official's small ratlike eyes as he opened the door and shoved her into the room.

Shannon stumbled forward, caught sight of the tray of shiny, frightening instruments—*Oh, no, no, no*—and backpedaled toward the hallway as quickly as her feet would take her. Unfortunately, she moved too quickly and tripped over her swirling skirts.

A surprisingly gentle hand took her arm. "Come along, dear. There's nothing to fear." The feminine voice was soft and soothing, and all the more frightening for its calmness. "We'll have a brief look at you, and then you can rest in a soft bed."

Shannon stiffened. "But I'm *not* ill."

In direct contradiction to her words, the contents of her stomach made a grand appearance, all over the nurse's feet.

"Oh, no. I . . ." Shannon covered her mouth with a trembling hand. "I'm so very sorry."

"We've seen worse."

The nurse's kindness proved only to make Shannon more frightened.

"Move closer please." The masculine voice came at her as if from a great distance.

She had no time to obey before large hands reached for her, tugging her forward, dragging her closer to the table of shining instruments.

The medical exam began in earnest then.

What had been mere fear turned into sheer terror. Shannon could hardly obey the orders shot at her in rapid-fire succession from behind the hideous white masks. She was ordered to disrobe to her chemise, and then she was poked, spun around, poked some more, all while being interrogated about her symptoms.

The doctor never introduced himself. With clinical precision, he examined her hair, investigated her scalp, then used a tool that looked like a knitting needle with a hook on the end to pull back her eyelids. Shannon cried out in pain.

"Hold still," he ordered.

The nurse checked Shannon's fingernails and skin. The two muttered to one another. Shannon caught the words *influenza* and *further observation* and, the most dreaded of all, *possibly contagious.*

Until that moment, she'd not allowed herself to entertain the notion that she could be deported. Suddenly, the possibility became real, very real. Fear lanced through her, followed by desperation. "I'm feeling much better now."

"We have seen evidence to the contrary." The response came from the doctor, cold and emotionless.

No point arguing when the nurse wore said evidence on her shoes. "The nausea isn't constant," Shannon offered in a surprisingly calm voice. "It comes and goes."

"Indeed." The doctor shared a look with the nurse.

More questions came at her, faster, some incredibly personal and insulting.

Shannon couldn't explain herself properly. Her fear was too great, and nothing came out but responses that contradicted one another. No matter how hard she worked, she couldn't get her thoughts in order.

After giving her arm a commiserating pat, the nurse crossed the room and opened the door. "Take her to the holding pen for Swinburne Island."

The official returned, eyes glinting with something not quite pleasant, and so began another trip down dark, winding corridors until she stood before another door.

Once again, Shannon was shoved inside a room with murky lighting. For a long heart-pounding moment, she stood motionless, watching as the official stepped back into the hallway. His sneer was the last thing she saw before he slammed the door shut.

Katie must be so worried. But she would come to Ellis Island again, and again, and wouldn't stop coming until Shannon was safely in her care. It was Liam that worried her most.

Liam. Oh, Liam, where are you?

Shannon refused to give up hope. He would find her. Shannon believed it with all her heart. In the meantime, she would do her best to stay calm.

Taking in the room, she realized she wasn't alone. She counted some thirty other women crammed in a space hardly suitable for half that number.

Her fellow detainees appeared indifferent to Shannon, apparently too caught up in their own misery to bother with her. Some appeared truly sick. A few were in the late stages of pregnancy. None looked happy about their situation.

Shannon's sentiments exactly.

All the strain of the day centered into a sharp point of awareness, leaving her unusually alert to every sight, sound, and smell.

The wind moaned shrilly outside the building, whipping and scratching at a pathetically small window on her right. As she worked her way toward a glimpse of the outside world, her clumsy movements sent her skirts swirling around her ankles, nearly tripping her. Shannon seized her lower lip between her teeth and bit so hard she thought she might draw blood.

Oh, Liam, how will you ever find me?

They were supposed to be married by now. Shannon should be happily presenting her new husband to her sister.

Katie would adore Liam.

He was handsome, tall, with a full head of ginger hair and the features of a fallen angel. He had a reputation for hard work and trustworthiness and was beloved by all, especially the women. He had been sought after by nearly every unmarried girl in the village, so it had never occurred to Shannon that Liam Gallagher would give her a second glance.

How wrong she'd been.

The thought brought a smile, as did the memory of the day he'd stopped by her uncle's apothecary shop. After making his purchase of linseed oil, Liam had lingered longer than usual, seeming in no hurry to be on his way. Trained as a carpenter, he'd told Shannon how he used the oil as a preservative for wood and rope.

"Now that I've shared a bit about myself, tell me something about you, lovely Shannon O'Connor."

Intimidated by the man's attention, Shannon had mumbled something, she hardly remembered what. He'd taken pity on her and drew her into an easy conversation about her personal likes and dislikes. He'd been kind and attentive, and Shannon had fallen almost immediately in love with him.

She'd never known anyone like Liam Gallagher—driven, kind, easygoing. He made her feel special, heard. When he'd declared his undying love soon after their first meeting, Shannon had never known such happiness. Or such sorrow.

"I'm leaving for America as soon as my sister arranges my passage." Her throat had cinched around an ache of longing so new and terrible, she'd blurted out the words with very little finesse.

Liam's response had been immediate, his eyes full of sincerity. "Marry me instead and we'll live happily ever after right here in Ireland."

Shock had left Shannon speechless. Surely, he'd been teasing her. Liam was a seasoned, self-assured man six years older than she was. He was large, and yet also kind, luring her to him like a small woodland creature seeking refuge.

It had taken Shannon a full week to realize he'd been serious with his impromptu proposal. He'd courted her with flattering persistence. Remembering all the tiny gestures, the secret rendezvous in the middle of the night, made her stomach feel very light, as if she were falling for him all over again.

His second proposal had been far more romantic than the first, made during one of their secret late-night meetings. The next morning, Shannon had penned a letter to Katie telling her the good news of her impending nuptials.

She'd never sent the letter. Liam's mother had discovered their relationship. Mrs. Gallagher claimed Shannon was too young to understand love. She'd been wrong. Shannon had the example of her parents to teach her about love. So strong was their union that when her father had died, her mother followed him to the grave three months later.

Shannon had dreamed of loving that fully, that completely, with all of her heart, mind, and soul. She'd found that depth of emotion with Liam. He had her heart. And she had his.

"I will always love you," he'd vowed a week before Shannon was scheduled to board the SS *Helena*. "Never doubt it. I will find a way for us to be together."

"Come with me," Shannon had urged him. "We can make a life in America as easily as we can here."

He'd considered, then agreed.

They'd made immediate plans to sneak away to America together. But there'd been such confusion on the docks and they'd gotten separated. Shannon, certain that Liam would meet her on the ship, had boarded without him.

But Liam hadn't boarded ahead of her.

By the time she'd spotted his familiar form hurrying up and down the bulkhead, shouting her name, waving at her frantically, the mooring lines had been dropped and the tugboats had begun pulling the ship away from the docks.

As cheers erupted from her fellow passengers, many of them crowded at the railings and waving their farewells to their family members, Shannon had desperately tried to return to the docks. She'd been denied.

"I'll catch the next boat," Liam had shouted above the noise. Shannon had shouted out her sister's address in America.

"I'll find you," he'd promised.

Not if I'm deported before he arrives.

Renewed panic clogged the breath in her throat. She was sucking for air when the creak of iron hinges heralded the reappearance of the stone-faced official. “Form two lines.”

“Where are you taking us?” a woman in a red shawl asked in an Italian accent.

“To the hospital on Swinburne Island,” he said, the words dark and menacing.

Shannon ignored a pang of nausea and shuffled along with the other women. She couldn’t help but wonder what new form of torture lay ahead.

Chapter Four

Katie was profoundly grateful she had something, or rather *someone* to focus on besides worrying about her sister. She shot Ty a covert glance.

He smiled. Her mouth went dry, her knees wobbled, and her heart chimed a warning.

Have a care, Katie. This man is not a fantasy figure. He comes from a very different world than yours. You know how this ends.

As she took in his broad shoulders, wide chest, and the firm set of his lips, she thought of her sad mother, who had died of grief soon after her father passed. And for the first time in her life understood the power of a handsome face.

She glanced away.

They conquered the gangplank in silence, then battled the slick cobbled streets. Some of the newly arrived immigrants went in the direction of the train station, their journey only half over. Others headed east, toward the neighborhood where Katie lived. If they thought they would find a better life than the one they'd left, many—most—were in for a large disappointment.

Katie had been shocked to discover the overcrowding and dismal living conditions. She'd come to America knowing exactly what she wanted, and what she didn't, but now everything was confused.

Ty fell into step beside her. In silent agreement, they walked in the direction of Orchard Street, where Katie shared a tiny apartment on the top floor of a five-story tenement house with her aunt and cousin.

The rain started up again. In the glow of the streetlamps, the droplets slanted toward the ground in fine silver darts. Grateful for the warmth, Katie huddled deeper inside Ty's coat.

It was strange watching the world pass by through the blur of raindrops. Halos of light and water formed around the streetlamps. People hustled to and fro, either seeking shelter from the rain or hurrying to some unknown destination.

Katie felt somehow apart from the activity. They passed by a lady in a tattered crimson dress. A lanky fellow of indeterminate age staggered out of a building, a straggly dog barking and nipping at his heels.

The poverty was worse down here by the docks, as was the crime. Katie peered at her surroundings through jaded eyes, wise enough to be glad for the man by her side.

They'd nearly reached the end of the block when three bodies slipped out of the shadows and moved into their path. They stood in a straight row, big to biggest, their arms muscular, their faces unreadable. An objectionable scent of stale liquor, refuse, and coal dust wafted off their filthy clothing.

"Stay close," Ty told her, linking Katie's arm through his as he steered her off course at a quick, steady pace. His gaze went from her face to the men. His lips peeled back, baring his teeth in a look meant to intimidate.

Katie felt her heart miss a beat.

The men paused . . . then, seeming to think better of approaching them, slipped back into the shadowed alleyway.

Katie let out a slow breath.

Until that moment, she hadn't thought of Ty as anything but a good, gentle man. But now that she took another look from beneath her lowered lashes, she realized he had a dangerous edge. "You know how to handle yourself on the docks."

He directed her around the corner. Now that the threat was over, he released her arm. "I've broken up a few fights in my tenure at the clinic."

The mention of his clinic had Katie wondering if Ty was a man of wealth with an altruistic desire to serve the poor and needy. Or had he risen from humble beginnings, and now he gave back to his community?

Thrown into confusion, Katie glanced at him. His profile gave nothing away of his thoughts, making it hard to tell what sort of man lay beneath the handsome veneer. In the gloomy air, his eyes were cloaked in shadows, framed by long lashes.

There was so much unknown about him. So much Katie wanted to know. He'd scared off the street thugs with nothing more than a look. And yet, she felt safe in his presence. "Is Ty short for something else?"

Looking amused, he said, "Titus."

"Titus," she repeated.

"My full name is Titus Bartholomew Brentwood."

"That's quite a mouthful."

He laughed, a rumbling sound that surprised her with its warmth. "My friends call me Ty."

He said this in a low, mysterious tone, as if he were letting her in on a secret. The intimacy of the moment was not lost on her. Katie knew she should return the conversation to less personal matters. But Ty's nearness felt like a refuge, and she wanted to burrow inside the haven of his presence as she had in his coat.

"Do you have many?" she asked, then gave a shaky laugh at his raised eyebrows. "Friends, I mean."

His head swiveled away, but not before Katie saw the pain in his eyes. "Not many, no."

There was a story there, a sad tale that made her want to offer him comfort. She didn't take such liberties, of course. They were, after all, strangers.

Feeling oddly nostalgic, and as sad as Ty looked, she wrapped his coat tighter around her. "I was named after my grandmother and her mother before her and so on for several generations back."

"Katie is a pretty name."

"I always thought it rather ordinary, much like me."

He stopped walking, the sudden move forcing her to do the same. He cocked his head and stared at her. A strange expression crossed his face, a mixture of astonishment and wonder, much like she often felt when she finished a garment that had been alive only in her mind and was suddenly surprised to discover she'd made such a lovely creation.

"There is nothing ordinary about you, Katie O'Connor."

Her breath caught in her throat. "I'll try to take that as a compliment."

"It was meant as one."

A slow smile spread across his face, the look solely for her. The light from the streetlamp set off his handsome features. His dark mane hung a little too long, artfully shaggy. She held her breath, enthralled by the bold, patrician face, the square jaw, and chiseled features that declared he was more than a mere man. He was a healer, a scholar, and . . .

Sad.

He had an air of hard-won worldliness about him, a sense that he had seen enough of the ugly side of life to no longer be surprised. What had he endured? With his head tilted down and his eyes looking straight at her, his face was a study in fierce emotion.

She'd seen that look before. In her own mirror, ever since her mother had died and she'd taken on the burden of caring for Shannon.

Shannon.

Katie's mind should be on her sister.

She tore her gaze away from Ty's haunted eyes and resumed walking. He fell into step beside her. They completed the next few blocks in silence.

Questions filled Katie's mind. She wanted to know about Ty's clinic, about his life, everything.

Another block and they were on Orchard Street. Katie tried to see her neighborhood from Ty's point of view. The sky had turned the color of charcoal and granite beneath the heavy drizzle of rain. Pedestrians scattered for shelter. A few held umbrellas, and some vendors continued selling their wares, their cries full of impatience now that the crowds had begun to thin.

What must Ty think of her, that this was the best she could do for living accommodations? Katie thought back to her first glimpse of this street.

Foot traffic had been heavy. She'd been so very tired and weak from the registration process, barely able to put one foot in front of the other. A fight had broken out near the tenement house where she lived now, drawing Katie's attention. She'd never seen anything like it—the brutality, the animal passion, the crowds cheering on the violence.

Oddly compelled, she'd gawked with the others. A well-dressed man had reached into the tangle of people and plucked out a shabbily dressed ruffian, then slammed the man against the building.

The crowd had gone wild after that, their shouts of encouragement echoing off the brick and mortar. Outwardly calm, the gentleman had been in complete control of the situation.

Katie had felt sorry for the ruffian until she'd discovered the supposed victim was the landlord of one of the tenement houses. He'd been stealing from the renters and the owner, who, after discovering his employee's treachery, had come down to deal with the matter personally.

Shoving the scene from her mind, Katie drew to a stop at the base of the steps of 223 Orchard Street, a five-story structure with twenty three-room apartments, arranged four to a floor, two in front and two in back. A poorly lit wooden staircase ran through the center of the building. Her home. For now. "This is where I live."

Ty took in the tenement house that was her home. *Temporary home,* she amended in her mind. She would not live here forever.

The narrow steps leading to the front door were cracked in places, and the wrought-iron railing needed a fresh coat of paint. Rectangular concrete blocks on the first floor gave way to a brick façade that continued to the top. Perfectly spaced windows ran five deep vertically and horizontally along the building. "You live here? Alone?"

She heard the concern in his voice and hurried to relieve it. "I share lodgings with my aunt and cousin."

"No uncle?"

"He died years ago." Katie didn't remember much about Aunt Jane's husband, but she did recall liking Uncle Morgan. He'd had a kind smile, a booming voice, and a belly that jiggled when he laughed. The village's farrier, he'd been exceptional with horses. Which was so terribly tragic since it was a crazed stallion that had killed him. One swift, unexpected kick to the head. He'd never seen it coming.

"Aunt Jane left for America soon after his death, but she kept in contact with her sister, my mother. She and her daughter, Bridget, have lived in tenement houses for more than a decade, this one for about two of those years." To punctuate her words, Katie vaguely gestured toward the structure.

"Ah."

There was so much said in that one word, even more left unsaid. Katie tried to take in the building from Ty's perspective.

"The conditions could be worse," she found herself saying in her defense.

"The building doesn't look safe."

"It's safe enough," she assured him. "The previous owner renovated the building shortly before I moved in." Though much could still be done. Perhaps the new owner would make some much-needed updates.

Ty pivoted slightly, his entire body moving until he faced Katie. He looked at her directly. The air seemed charged with some unknown force. Katie wondered if it was possible to feel both hot and cold at the same moment.

"You deserve better." The gravity of his tone made her heart thump against her ribs.

"I plan to get better. But until Shannon is safely in America, my plans are on hold."

He stepped closer, and she knew, to an outsider, they made a cozy scene, as if they were a couple saying good night.

A yearning so deep shot through Katie that for a moment she couldn't seem to catch her breath. She pulled in a quick gulp of air but stayed right where she was, watching, hoping, praying for something so far out of reach that she couldn't make the image form in her head.

"My aunt will be waiting for news of Shannon."

"Of course."

Katie felt it again, that strange, powerful wish for something . . . *more*. It was the same sensation she'd experienced when she'd taken his handkerchief. She ignored the feeling. Denied it. The process proved far less successful this time around.

Sighing, she removed Ty's coat and thrust it in the space between them.

He took the garment, made to turn, then swung back around. "Remember to ask for Dr. Wilson when you make your return trip to Ellis Island. Tell him you're a friend of mine. He'll help you."

Katie's head was spinning. She could hardly stammer out a reply. "You have no idea how much your help means to me."

His thumb found her jawline and traced around the edge. "You must have hope, Katie."

She tried to swallow the heartbeat that had ascended into her throat, nearly choking her. She couldn't remember a time when a man had made her feel so understood. She wanted to live in the moment, even as she felt something unpleasant twist in her heart. "I hate that I've let Shannon down."

His hand dropped away. "Her detainment isn't your fault."

"A part of me will be devoured by guilt until I can see for myself that she is well."

"She will be in your care in no time."

His confidence made her want to believe. "I'll cling to that hope."

For a span of several heartbeats, their gazes remained locked. "Good night, Katie."

"Good night, Ty."

Neither made a move to leave. They didn't smile, didn't speak. They simply stared into each other's eyes. And then, they stared some more.

One moment stretched into two. Two into three.

Katie lowered her eyelashes, and the odd interaction was over. She opened her mouth to say—something—when, out of the corner of her eye, she caught a movement off to her left. An instant later, her cousin came into view.

She did not look happy.

In fact . . .

Bridget swept cold, shrewd eyes over Ty, glanced briefly at Katie, then resumed glaring at Ty, her displeasure obvious. The corners of her mouth drooped, and Katie felt a sudden need to stand in front of him.

The move served to inflame Bridget's suspicion. "What, dear cousin, is going on here?"

Chapter Five

Katie loved Bridget. Not much older than Katie, her cousin was loyal, hardworking, driven, and ambitious. Unfortunately, those qualities had not led to monetary success but, rather, bitter disappointment. Bridget was jaded and didn't trust easily.

At the moment, Ty stood in the direct path of her suspicious nature. He didn't seem daunted, not by Bridget's scowl or her rude assessment. He simply stood there, allowing her to take him in from her position at the bottom of the stairs with her hard, cynical eyes.

A gust of wind whipped Bridget's cloak behind her with a hard snap, revealing the bright, multicolored, and skimpy costume she wore underneath. With a quick burst of movement, she grabbed the edges of the cloak and wrapped them firmly around her. To complete the ensemble, her dark hair hung in long, loose curls past her shoulders.

Katie sighed.

The sound gave Bridget a start. Ignoring Ty now, she made a grand show of looking around the general area. "Where's Shannon?"

"She's been detained." The word stuck in Katie's throat. "I wasn't able to—"

Bridget cut her off with a quick slash of her hand in the air. "You can tell me the details when we're alone."

She put unnecessary emphasis on the last word as she once again commenced her silent appraisal of Ty. Her narrowed gaze traced across his face, down to his toes, and back up again. "Who are you?"

"This is Dr. Brentwood," Katie answered for him, and she attempted to move between the two. "Ty, this is Bridget Sullivan, my first cousin on my mother's side of the family."

Ty gave Bridget a small nod over Katie's head, a sort of abbreviated bow that could have been interpreted any number of ways. "It's a pleasure to meet you, Miss Sullivan."

"Indeed." A quiet, scoffing breath escaped her. "I have yet to determine if I can say the same."

Mortified, Katie snapped out her cousin's name. "There's no reason to be rude."

"On the contrary, there's every reason. Caution is a virtue," Bridget replied with stilted dignity. "The Bible says so."

"The Bible doesn't say anything of the sort."

Bridget lifted an unrepentant shoulder. "Well, it should."

Dumbstruck by her cousin's behavior, especially after everything Ty had done for her, Katie looked helplessly at him. For one confusing moment, she thought she saw a flicker of amusement in his eyes.

As their gazes caught and held, Katie felt her own lips lift at the edges. "Dr. Brentwood was kind enough to escort me home from the docks."

Bridget lifted a skeptical eyebrow in his direction. "Aren't you the gentleman?"

"Bridget." Katie looked at her cousin intently. "What's gotten into you?"

Her cousin's only answer was to make an unladylike sound deep in her throat. Bridget's protective stance warned Ty that he'd have to go through her to get to Katie.

Oh, honestly.

Her cousin and Ty were caught in a silent contest of wills. Ty's mouth tightened in what looked like humor or perhaps irritation; Katie wasn't quite sure which.

She cleared her throat. "Thank you for seeing me home, Ty."

A beat passed before he turned his head, a smile on his face. "Think nothing of it."

"I'm in your debt."

His smile widened. "Let's call it even, shall we?"

Katie's heart constricted. For a moment, she was too fascinated to speak. It seemed impossible that this handsome and sophisticated man could look at a woman like her with such intensity. She'd seen her father stare at her mother like that and, well, that had not ended well for either of them.

Be smart, Katie.

She tried to think of a response, but Ty was already saying goodbye and advancing down the sidewalk. He paused a few feet away and glanced back over his shoulder. "Remember, Dr. Wilson or Dr. Anderson if he's unavailable. Avoid Seabold. He'll be of little help."

"I'll remember."

He seemed about to say more.

Bridget gave him no chance. "Good evening, Dr. Brentwood."

Eyes twinkling with some private thought, Ty raised a hand in silent farewell. Katie raised hers in return. A moment of solidarity passed between them before he slipped into the shadows, becoming another dark faceless figure moving among the throngs of immigrants.

Staring after his disappearing form, Katie felt an acute, inexplicable sense of loss. He was nothing to her. And she certainly wasn't anyone special in his life. And yet . . .

She shook her head, then turned toward the building, only to run smack into Bridget. Feet planted in a wide stance, eyes narrowed, she stared after Ty, her brow knitted.

"Tell, dear cousin, since when do you keep such fancy company?"

"You have it all wrong." In fast, clipped sentences, she explained how she'd run into Ty on the ferryboat. She kept the story short, glossing over their previous meeting a year ago.

"So, he's the one."

"Yes," Katie said, her voice but a whisper. "He's the one."

A thoughtful expression came into Bridget's eyes as she squinted at the spot where Ty had stood only moments before. "Have a care, Katie. Blokes like the good Dr. Brentwood are nothing but trouble for women like us."

Katie knew Bridget spoke from experience. She hated that her cousin's chosen way to earn money put her in a position to know such things. Katie especially disliked having to lie to her aunt on Bridget's behalf.

Unfortunately, the money her cousin earned was three times what Katie made at the factory. Nothing she said worked to sway her cousin to reconsider a more reputable pursuit.

"You don't need to worry about Ty," Katie said, addressing the more pertinent issue. "I doubt I'll ever see him again."

"I hope you're right. Now." Bridget wove her arm beneath Katie's and pulled her in close. "Let us get out of this miserable weather, and then you can tell me why Shannon isn't with you."

* * *

Ty paused at the corner of Orchard Street where it met East Houston and looked back the way he came. Switching the medical bag to his other hand, his gaze sought and found Katie O'Connor. His heart stumbled in his chest.

As he watched Katie turn her head to respond to something her cousin had said, his first thought was one of relief. At this hour, a delicate woman like the pretty young immigrant shouldn't be alone on the dangerous streets of the Lower East Side.

But then he studied the woman beside her.

Bridget Sullivan couldn't be more than a few years older than Katie, and yet the woman seemed capable of handling herself, though perhaps a bit too capable. For one so young, Katie's cousin had a toughened look about her, as if she'd seen too much of the evils of men. *World-weary* and *suspicious* were the words that came to mind.

Whereas Katie was warmth and light, grace and serenity. She was everything good in their dark world, a breath of fresh air in the acrid, bitter urban winds. He hated the idea that with a few more years of fighting to survive in this neighborhood she, too, could become as jaded as her cousin.

Was her innocence why Ty had been unable to forget her?

The thought of her untouched beauty enduring despite the odds brought a momentary respite from the weight he carried. She was so unlike the broken-down, pain-filled world inside him. A world of his own making.

Ty resumed walking.

His journey took him through the most impoverished neighborhoods of Manhattan—and the most hazardous. Though he never looked for trouble, violence was a way of life in the Bowery. Ty didn't fear what lurked in the shadows, however. He knew how to wield the knife he carried in his boot.

Coiled like a spring, he welcomed the cold heaviness of the blade resting flush against his ankle. Adequate protection, as were the instruments in his medical bag, tools meant to save lives that could be used just as quickly to take one.

The thought struck like a fist, sending his feet in a staggering diagonal. Catching his rhythm again, Ty focused on his surroundings. The streets were transitioning from day to night, reputable businesses and pushcarts giving way to saloons, gaming dens, and bawdy theaters.

Most of the residents were poor. Holed up in the run-down buildings lining the street, they were the hardworking people who'd come to America seeking a better life. The people Ty had chosen to serve.

In contrast, the men and women slipping out to "play" were the very definition of lowlifes looking for a quick, easy buck. Not all of humanity was good, Ty knew.

Which category did he fall into—the good, the bad, or something else entirely? He didn't know anymore.

He rounded the next corner, heart grim.

The streets became wider, dirtier; the buildings grew dilapidated, with shattered windows and disjointed architecture. The noise was incredible: clattering carriages, horses whinnying, the shrill, gay laughter of people forcing themselves to have fun.

Ty was in the heart of the Bowery now, a vast dark cave filled with the stuff of nightmares, of destitution. He sidestepped a puddle with some kind of chunky brown debris floating in its murky depths, then swerved around a pile of horse dung.

The foul odor of raw sewage mingled with the scent of day-old oysters from a street vendor who'd yet to close up shop for the night. Ty had to wonder at the man's tenacity, or perhaps *desperation* was the better word.

Con artists and petty thieves worked the close-packed crowd. In a single block, he passed five music halls, three wine houses, and two saloons with glittering exteriors and expensive fittings. The air was weighted with the odor of sour beer and cheap perfume.

Waste and squalor seemed to ooze out of the very cracks in the buildings, turning the streets into a hotbed of infectious diseases. Ty saw too many cases of cholera, tuberculosis, and typhoid fever, often—usually—when the disease had progressed too far for him to make a difference.

Could one flawed man make a difference? If not Ty, then who would help these people?

Vanessa had tried to understand his work. She'd stood by his side longer than most. In the end, she'd been right to break their engagement. She would never have survived in this world.

Katie lives among this filth and disease.

Ty swallowed against the sudden thickness in his throat. She probably worked in equally inferior conditions.

Unacceptable. Without realizing it, she'd put a personal face on the poverty he witnessed daily, making the people he served seem more real. No longer merely a means to an end, or a way to atone for his own selfish pride, but living, breathing people with hopes and dreams for a future free of suffering.

His work at the clinic and Ellis Island was important. But was he making enough of a difference?

So much need.

So much pain and misery.

Ty set his jaw and increased his pace through the densely packed mass of humanity. The rain had let up, leaving a heavy humid haze in the air. People swarmed the area, spilling from buildings and alleyways, much like rats seeking higher ground on a sinking ship.

Ty crossed the street, his feet taking him beneath the El and into blazing light.

The Bowery had the most well-lit streets in New York, which only illuminated the gaudy and vulgar buildings. Ty suspected Katie's cousin worked in one of these saloons or gaming houses. The costume had given her away. She might be a tambourine girl, the equivalent of the hot-corn girls of decades before, her job to lure men to buy her "wares," which was nothing more than a scam. Or so he hoped, for Bridget's sake.

Impatient to be home, Ty took a shortcut down a side alley between a saloon and a vaudeville theater where a second-rate actress was headlining. The noise, the high-pitched, raucous laughter, told him business was booming.

He increased his pace.

Two women stepped out of the shadows and approached him, one with dark brown hair tangling in a river of knots past her shoulders, and a blonde with unfashionably short hair.

Working as a team, they tracked toward him side by side. The ongoing cycle of sin and degradation was perpetuated in their sulky gaits. The curvy blonde and willowy brunette both had similar expressions on their faces. They were young for this life, too young. But their eyes were old, disillusioned, their expressions blank and distant, making them look slightly separated from the moment.

Ty understood such brokenness. He made to walk around them. But then another, harder-looking woman with less generous curves and straggly orange-red hair edged in front of the other two.

She slinked around the brunette, knocking her competition aside with her bony hip before focusing solely on Ty. "Ain't you a looker?" She gave him a thorough inspection. "You up for some fun, darling?"

"Not tonight." He tried to step around her.

She blocked his retreat.

"We saw him first, Trina."

Trina shot a quick glance over her shoulder, scowled at the ridiculously young girls, then faced Ty once again. "You want experience, you get it from me."

"I'm not looking for that kind of fun." He took a step to his left.

A look of defeat came and went in the hard eyes, not dissimilar to the look he'd seen in Bridget Sullivan's when she'd questioned his motives for walking Katie home.

Ty reached inside an inner pocket of his jacket, pulled out a card, and handed it over to the prostitute. "Get yourself a meal and a good night's sleep."

She scowled at the piece of paper with the Bowery Mission's address scrolled in bold black letters. "I don't take charity from no one."

A flick of her wrist and the card fluttered to the ground.

Message received. Ty handed a similar card to the other two women, then continued on his way without a backward glance. A block later, he bounded up the steps of his medical clinic and shouldered his way inside the darkened building.

The yawning silence told him he was alone.

Exactly the way he preferred to go through life these days. The alternative led only to pain and tragedy. He almost convinced himself that was true. Almost.

Chapter Six

While Ty worked his way home, Katie and Bridget set about accomplishing the five-story climb to the top floor of 223 Orchard Street.

They conquered the first set of stairs in silence. Bridget didn't ask about Shannon, and Katie didn't offer up any information. The stairwell and hallways of the tenement house were not the place for such an important conversation.

Exhausted, footsore, and chilled to the bone, Katie peeked at her cousin from the corner of her eye. Bridget looked especially tired. She seemed to be wearing the day's burdens in the creases of her clothing, her skin, even her manner.

At the second-floor landing, Katie paused, unable to hold silent a moment longer.

"Bridget?" She placed a hand on her cousin's sleeve. "Are you feeling unwell?"

Bridget shrugged out from under the light touch. "Don't fuss, Katie. You know how much I hate it when you mother me."

"I wasn't mothering you. I was—"

A pair of skeptical eyebrows rose.

"Well, yes. Maybe I was mothering you, but only a very, very little. I worry about you, Bridget, and tonight . . ." She eyed her cousin closely, taking note of the fresh lines around her eyes. "You seem more tired than usual."

More downtrodden.

"Some days are tougher than others." Though she spoke calmly, nothing could mask the dejection that seemed part of the young woman's very being.

What had Bridget been forced to endure today? Katie doubted her cousin would answer honestly if she asked.

It was all so frustrating. Bridget used to be a vibrant young woman, quick to laugh, swift to show affection to the people around her. And Katie suspected she knew the source of the change in her cousin.

"I wish you wouldn't work at Morrison's Club House."

"We need the money."

Katie couldn't argue the point, especially now that Aunt Jane was no longer able to work. She'd contracted scarlet fever six months ago, and though she'd recovered, her stamina was practically nonexistent now. The lack of that third income had put added pressure on both Katie and Bridget. Katie had taken on extra sewing jobs.

Bridget had chosen a more drastic route.

She'd become a tambourine girl for a gentlemen's club in the Bowery, nothing more than a gambling den. Bridget was charged with luring patrons inside the building by attracting their attention. The tambourine she carried was used both as a prop and a warning system. If the police arrived for a raid, Bridget was to, quite literally, sound the alarm.

"There are other ways to earn a living, ways that are more"—*reputable*, Katie nearly said but caught herself—"or rather, *less* dangerous."

Glancing left, then right, Bridget pulled Katie away from the light and the remote possibility that anyone inside one of the apartments could hear their conversation. "We've been over this too many times to count," she hissed in a low voice. "What I do for Mr. Morrison is harmless."

"It's *dangerous.*" Katie could not emphasize that point enough.

"Don't be dramatic." Bridget brushed off Katie's concerns with a careless wave of her hand. "I sell a promise that others are more than happy to fulfill. It's all relatively tame."

"That's where we disagree." Katie lowered her voice to match her cousin's. "You open yourself up for attack every day. One of those men you so *harmlessly* lure into the club could get the wrong idea about you."

Bridget's eyebrows slammed together. "While I appreciate your concern—no, Katie, don't give me that scowl. I truly am grateful you care about my well-being. But you have to trust me when I say I know what I'm doing."

Katie wanted to weep in frustration. Instead, she switched tactics. "If it's so safe, then why not tell Aunt Jane you switched jobs?"

"Do not bring my mother into this conversation. I mean it. Don't say another word."

"Hit a bit too close to home, did I?"

Bridget grabbed Katie's arm, her fingernails curling in the fabric of her sodden cloak. "You must never, ever mention my new job to her. It'll only serve to upset her. She's too weak to hear the truth."

"You underestimate her."

"Promise me, Katie." Bridget gave her a little shake. "Promise."

Katie scowled at the vehemence in her cousin's tone.

"You must continue to cover for me. You must." Bridget's whispered words were laced with equal parts anger and fear. "Swear you will, Katie."

Katie was surprised into silence by the violence of Bridget's demand. "I . . . oh, Bridget. How do you explain your situation to yourself? How do you—"

"Swear to me. Swear you will not speak of this to anyone, but especially my mother." Bridget's grip dug deeper into the wool of Katie's cloak, cutting off her circulation. There would be no getting through to her cousin tonight.

"I made a promise to you, Bridget, and I won't go back on my word." Katie glanced at the hand squeezing her arm. "You can let go now."

Bridget blinked at her.

"You're hurting my arm."

"Oh." Eyes going wide, she immediately pulled her hand away, guilt coming off her in waves. "I'm so sorry. I didn't mean to hold on so hard."

For several minutes, they stood staring at one another.

Then, compelled to make matters right between them, Katie yanked her cousin into her arms. "I want you to be safe."

"I know how to take care of myself."

Before Katie could say more, two little girls rushed past them up the stairs, pausing momentarily on the third-floor landing to whisper and laugh before disappearing inside one of the apartments.

Katie marveled at their capacity to find joy in the moment, their ability to take full advantage of a chance to play. She remembered a time when she could recover from hardships that quickly.

The past year had proven far more difficult than she'd ever expected. She'd had dreams once. Now all her energy was put toward scraping out a meager existence. Money was always short.

Katie rubbed her forehead with her palm, which did nothing to relieve the ache growing behind her eyes.

"Let's not argue anymore," she said to Bridget.

"Let's not."

They continued their ascent. The higher they climbed, the hotter the air felt. Stale, sticky, and oppressive, promising to turn unbearable once they reached the top floor. Katie dreaded the hot work that lay ahead of her this evening.

She was proud, however, of her growing reputation as a dressmaker with an eye for detail, even if she didn't particularly enjoy sewing. While Katie was better than most, Shannon was the O'Connor sister with talented fingers. Still, the commissions brought in extra money.

Not enough. It was never enough.

An unexpected image materialized in her head of the doctor who'd so graciously walked her home.

What must Ty's life be like? Helping the poor was a noble calling. The rewards must be massive. Katie had dreamed of one day becoming a nurse or, during her more fanciful moments, a doctor like Ty. Such a life was not available to a woman like her, with no formal education to speak of, or money to acquire the training she needed.

What she wanted out of life didn't matter, Katie reminded herself. She had to focus on getting Shannon in the country. Then, only then, would she reach for something more, something just for herself.

At last, they arrived on the fifth floor. Bridget entered the apartment first. She called out to her mother, "I'm home," then quickly rushed into the bedroom she shared with Katie to change out of her costume.

Understanding her role in her cousin's subterfuge, Katie went in search of her aunt. Even through the thick haze of her frustration, she wanted to protect her cousin from the choices she seemed determined to make. As children, Bridget had been the bolder of the cousins, always looking for adventure or some new way to break the monotony of their days. Her favorite phrase had been, "Won't it be a lark?"

Her job in the Bowery was no lark. It certainly wasn't a game. The stakes were so much higher.

While Bridget changed out of her costume, Katie removed her sodden cloak and stuck it on a hook by the door to air out. She turned, then sighed as she took in the cramped space. There was a communal washroom in the hallway, but no privy or running water in the apartment itself. The layout always reminded Katie of a box. With no real entryway, the threshold spilled into the main living area, which was barely large enough to squeeze in a couch, a tiny table, and a kerosene lamp. Two inner rooms, or rather bedchambers, also square, flanked either side of the apartment.

The scent of inferior meat and boiling potatoes drew Katie forward. With no door to separate the kitchen from the living area, she merely had to walk ten paces straight ahead, shift around a hinged, wood-slatted divider, and enter the room. She found her aunt leaning over a pot on the stove.

Katie saw her mother in the stooped shoulders and slightly labored breathing. A beauty in her youth, Jane Sullivan's mahogany-colored hair was now streaked with thick threads of gray. Her face showed her age in the spiderweb of wrinkles around her eyes and mouth. She seemed so small and fragile. She'd suffered and blessedly survived the scarlet fever she'd contracted, but the disease had done its damage and, due to her advancing age, she'd never fully recovered. The most mundane tasks tired her out now, and she took to her bed often.

An overwhelming sense of helplessness crashed over Katie. She let out a noiseless sigh.

As if sensing her presence, Aunt Jane looked over her shoulder. "Oh, hello, Katie. I thought you might be Bridget."

"She's changing out of her wet clothes."

Aunt Jane's gaze narrowed over Katie's crumpled, saturated dress. "As should you."

"I will in a moment. Sit, please, Aunt Jane."

"I haven't finished cooking."

"Let me do it. No, no arguing, I insist." Katie took the spoon, then guided the older woman to a nearby chair. Her aunt's exhausted sigh sent a jolt of fear through Katie.

She reached out, but her aunt shrugged away her assistance. "I just need a moment."

Katie knelt, placed her palms on the older woman's knees. "Breathe, Aunt Jane. That's it. Nice and slow."

At last, she seemed to regain her strength and looked a little less pale, the color returning to her cheeks. Then, as if something had only just occurred to her, she looked at Katie with a question in her eyes. "Weren't you supposed to go to Ellis Island today?"

"I did."

"But . . . where's Shannon?"

Katie allowed herself one small moment of dejection, then dug deep for calm and relayed the news. "She was detained."

"Oh, no." Aunt Jane's trembling fingers went to her throat. "Were you given a reason?"

In nearly the same words she'd shared with Ty, Katie recited the order of events, leaving nothing out. When she came to the part about being all but forced off the island, her aunt sniffed in outrage.

"Well, that's just terrible."

"It was rather awful. I'm supposed to wait for word before I go back to the immigration station."

"When will that be?"

"I have no idea, nor do I plan to follow the order. I'm going back on Sunday, see what I can find out."

She was forced to repeat the story when Bridget arrived in the kitchen a moment later. As she spoke, Katie noticed her cousin's face was scrubbed clean and free of the cosmetics she'd worn earlier. Her dark blue dress was cut in a modest shirtwaist style, and her hairstyle, pulled tightly against her head, was nearly puritanical in its severity.

The transformation from tambourine girl to innocent Irish lass was so remarkable that Katie gaped at her cousin for three full seconds. In return, she received a stern frown full of silent warning.

Katie sighed as she left the room to change out of her own wet clothing. Over dinner, she discussed Shannon's situation at greater length. "I hope to have more information once I return from my second trip to Ellis Island."

"Would you like me to come with you, dear?" her aunt asked. "Perhaps the two of us will have better luck than you alone."

It wasn't a bad idea, but Katie didn't want to put her aunt's health at risk, and so she said, "I appreciate the offer, but now that I have the name of a doctor I can approach directly, I'm sure I'll have better success next time."

* * *

A sickening dread crept through Shannon's stomach as she entered what looked like a receiving room in the hospital facility on Swinburne Island.

She wasn't sick anymore. Until she was. She couldn't understand why the nausea came and went at such irregular intervals, often laying her low without any warning.

Fighting off the frustrating wave of queasiness, she refused to flinch, not at the startlingly sterile white decor or the putrid odor of antiseptic mingling with the scent of something she couldn't quite name. Some sort of medicine or . . . alcohol, perhaps?

Her temporary home wasn't as bad as she'd expected. It was worse. *Much worse.* The air in the building actually smelled sick.

Much to her shock, and against all effort to the contrary, tears invaded Shannon's eyes. *I want to go home.*

I want Liam.

He would come for her. He'd promised. She would not give up hope that they would reunite in America. Once she was released from this wretched hospital.

If she was released.

Needing comfort, she wrapped her fingers around the locket Liam had given her the night he'd pledged his love. A sense of calm momentarily quieted her nerves.

A winding trek took her and the other female patients down a hallway with a series of doors on either side. Which one would lead Shannon to her temporary home? She had her answer when the official opened the second door on his right.

The smell hit her first. Musty, sour, decaying flesh. In that moment, Shannon actually missed the rancid odors of steerage, urine and all.

A team of white-clad figures took over after the official handed off Shannon and the half dozen other women.

One of the nurses gently took Shannon's arm. She was older than Shannon, somewhere near Katie's age, with big brown eyes the same rich color as her dark hair beneath the white cap. "Do you speak English?" she asked.

"Oh, aye."

"I'm Nurse Bradford." She spoke in an American accent. "I'll be taking care of you during your stay with us."

"I'm Shannon."

"What a pretty name."

Smiling broadly, Nurse Bradford escorted Shannon to a row of empty hospital beds, each neatly and identically made up with white sheets, a thick white blanket, and a lone white pillow.

"Put this on." The nurse handed her a plain muslin nightgown, and Shannon thought, *More white.*

Once Shannon and the rest of the new arrivals were settled in their beds, the nurses huddled in a group at the end of the room. *What are they discussing?* Shannon wondered.

"Did they tell you what's wrong with you?" The ragged question came from the bed on Shannon's left. As she studied the pale, shriveled form, one word came to mind: *tragic.*

It was impossible to determine the woman's age. Her long blonde hair hung in filthy tangles, and her face was pinched with pain. A wave of sympathy coasted over Shannon. She couldn't take her eyes off the pitiful, worn-out face. "No, did they tell you?"

The woman shook her head. The move sent the poor thing into a fit of coughing.

Acting on pure instinct, Shannon left her own bed and moved in behind her. As gently as she could manage, she lifted the woman's head to a less awkward angle.

"There now," she soothed, until she felt someone watching her. A nurse stood in the center aisle, gaze fixed on Shannon.

Without a word, the nurse handed over a clean strip of linen. Shannon placed the cloth against her neighbor's lips and gently wiped.

"I'll take it from here."

Choked with emotion, Shannon stepped aside to let the nurse take her place next to her patient.

"I know things look bleak now," the nurse said to the woman, her voice soft and full of compassion. "But you're safe now."

Oh, how Shannon wanted to claim the words for herself. They were so close to what Katie had told her right before leaving Ireland.

A wave of guilt pushed through her misery. Since meeting Liam, Shannon hadn't thought about Katie, not very often. She did now. Her sister must be so worried about her.

The nurse patted the sick woman's arm. "Before you know it, Megan, you will be released into your family's care."

"That would be lovely," the woman whispered.

Shannon couldn't help but agree with Megan. Though not spoken to her directly, she clung to the nurse's promise, wishing she could wrap it up in a pretty box with a pink bow.

"Rest now."

The suggestion was given more as a request than a command. Shannon found herself crawling into her own bed and relenting right along with Megan.

Shannon couldn't remember ever feeling this tired. She squeezed her eyes shut and tried to capture a sense of peace that eluded her. The day had been long and trying. Every part of her body hurt, resulting in an all-over ache that went far beyond the physical. She took a slow, steadying breath.

The smell of illness that hung in the air reminded her of another time, when she'd been just a girl. She couldn't understand why the scent brought back that dreadful day in such stark relief.

Why did the memory seem so real, so tangible and familiar?

Best to forget, a voice whispered in her head. No need to recall all that death and suffering. Shannon let her mind go blank, let her sense of time and place garble in her head. The nothingness soothed her.

Distant, hollow voices buzzed around her, like annoying mosquitoes. Darkness called to her. She reached out to the void. But then the watery images in her head began to form into clear pictures. *Too real. Too familiar.*

She didn't want them in her head.

And still they came.

She shied away from the memories. But past overlaid present, and Shannon's mind traveled back in time, to the day her mother had breathed her last. Her father had been gone less than three months. His death had devastated Maggie O'Connor, leaving her incapable of caring for her two young daughters.

The drumming noises in Shannon's head became a clear, distinct voice that belonged to Margaret O'Connor.

Love with all your heart, her mother had said as if speaking to a confidante rather than her daughter. *Life isn't worth living if you have to navigate it alone.*

The words played in Shannon's mind, drawing her in, dragging her deeper, deeper. Too tired to care, she squeezed her eyes tighter. Just for this moment, this . . . one . . . soothing moment, she wouldn't fight the memories.

The images came again, fresh and true, seeming so very real as they played across the back of her eyelids. Shannon was twelve again, back in the one-room cottage with the leaky roof.

Harsh, irregular pants wafted through the heavy air. The acrid smell of death filled the room. Both Katie and her mother sat wrapped in their own states of despair, each struggling for answers to unspoken questions. Shannon stood back, not knowing what to say or do.

Another fit of coughing had her jerking open her eyes.

The sound had come from the bed beside her. She stared at the haggard woman battling for each breath.

Shannon released a sorrowful sigh, feeling as helpless as she had when her mother had given up on life.

No, Shannon would not allow the final memory of her mother to ruin the other, happy ones. Her mother had taught her what love looked like. She'd taught Shannon about romance and devotion. Love bonded a man and woman, made them a single unit, until death do them part.

Bolstered, she once again climbed out of bed. Taking the limp hand, Shannon closed her fingers over the thin gray skin. "You're going to be all right, Megan."

With her free hand, Shannon grasped Liam's locket and thought, *We both are.*

Chapter Seven

By the time Katie ducked into the bedroom she shared with Bridget, the rain had begun again in earnest. She stooped to avoid hitting her head on the rafters. The room was on the top floor of the tenement house, directly under the building's eaves. The ceiling sloped down from a center point, making a V shape.

There were two narrow beds on opposite walls, a battered table positioned horizontally in between, a straight-backed chair beside a tiny round table, and finally, a dresser with a chipped porcelain basin of water on top.

With the toe of her right shoe, Katie nudged the already half-full bucket to catch the rain dripping from the ceiling. The added moisture made the air feel even heavier. She had hours of hot, uncomfortable work ahead of her in a dreary room that housed more shadow than light. As she studied the piles of sewing stacked neatly on the table and piled in several baskets on the floor, a sense of quiet despair crept into her usual optimism.

Knowing the source of her dismal mood, she closed her eyes and attempted to gather her fortitude. She should be showing her sister around the tiny apartment, offering her own bed while she slept on the overstuffed sofa in the main living area. Instead, Shannon was confined to a sickbed on Ellis Island.

Worry over her sister's situation was nearly impossible to bear. And so she disregarded all that could go wrong and focused on what could go right.

Shannon would be allowed into the country. Katie would find her a job, perhaps a position at the same factory where she herself worked. The extra money Shannon earned would help them move out of the tenement house sooner.

Katie resisted a sigh. There'd been too much sighing today.

When she'd arrived in America, her dreams had been large, and they'd seemed attainable. How utterly naïve she'd been. Nothing had gone as planned, and now Katie did what any smart woman would. She dreamed smaller.

Not tonight. Tonight, her hope for a better life came stronger. She blamed the longing on her trip to Ellis Island. The Statue of Liberty had reminded her why she'd come to America.

Home, love, family. She'd had but a taste of those things in Ireland, yet never fully experienced them. Her parents had been good people, but their love for each other had eclipsed all else, including their own daughters, who were more burden than joy. Katie's parents had been fixated on each other, their love too volatile and obsessive to have much affection left to give others.

Katie's heart yearned for more than leftover affection. She wanted her own home, a husband who adored both her *and* their children. Children weren't inconveniences. They were tiny blessings to be treasured and loved. And, oh, how Katie wanted . . . she wanted . . .

What did it matter what she wanted?

What mattered was providing a stable home for herself and her family. Never again would she be looked at as an obligation. No, she wanted to be more than a burden on someone's life.

Would she ever fall in love? Did she dare?

She wasn't afraid to love. No, Katie was afraid to love too much. The women in her family fell hard for their men, with a crushing passion that drove out all other hopes and dreams.

Katie didn't want that kind of toxic love, not for herself or her future children.

Thoughts of Ty played across her mind, breaking her concentration as surely as if he'd appeared in the doorway.

She'd seen reliability when she'd looked in his eyes. And strength. He was everything respectable and noble and true.

Giving in to that sigh after all, Katie desperately fought to keep the man out of her mind. She would not allow anyone to consume her the way her father had consumed her mother.

Work, she told herself.

She had much sewing to complete before she could go to sleep. She should attack the basket of mending she'd brought home from work. The piece-rate pay would be added to her regular salary at the end of the week.

But first, she needed, or rather wanted, to modify the bodice on the gown commissioned by the tenement owner's wife.

The woman had discovered Katie's talent with a needle and thread quite by accident. She'd been on a tour of the tenement house when she'd seen Katie's work and had been full of compliments. They'd met two days later and, after praising her skill in flattering detail, she'd commissioned Katie to make her a dress for an upcoming ball.

So pleased with the resulting garment, Mrs. Armstrong, a woman close to Katie's own age, had asked for another three dresses.

More money, Katie reminded herself, picking up one of the three commissioned gowns.

Cutting, sewing, and finishing garments was an honorable way to earn extra money, but it was murder on the eyes. After moving a lantern close, she positioned the silk gown on her lap.

Mrs. Armstrong overpaid her, claiming Katie had far more talent than her counterparts in fancy department stores. Katie doubted the veracity of that statement but didn't argue the point. They needed the money. Accepting the outrageous sum was the closest to charity Katie would accept from anyone.

Tongue caught between her teeth, she made a series of stitches along the hem of the gauzy fabric. Tricky, to be sure, but doable with a steady hand. Once she'd created a neat, straight line from seam to seam, she sat back and eyed her handiwork. Perfect.

Standing, she shook out the garment and studied the embellishments she'd added the night before. The lavender brocade over silvery silk would highlight Mrs. Armstrong's dark hair.

Katie lost herself in her work. The finished product would be beautiful, stunning, while also giving Mrs. Armstrong freedom of movement. As the wife of a successful businessman, the woman led an active life. Even for her evenings out at the theater or dinner parties, she preferred convenience and practicality in place of style.

Katie was determined to give her client both.

Mrs. Armstrong could afford an annual pilgrimage to Paris for her clothing. Katie knew this because the woman had told her herself. However, due to her humble beginnings, she preferred hiring local dressmakers. She claimed Katie was the most talented she'd encountered yet. A fine compliment, indeed.

Her eyes grew heavy, closed. She snapped them open.

So much to do. So little time.

Her head bobbed down to her chest, and just for a moment—only a moment—Katie shut her eyes again.

Sleep. The word echoed in her mind.

So very, very tired.

The sound of rain dripping in the bucket was tinny in her ears. Drip. Drip. Drip.

Her mother's words slipped through her mind, catching the rhythm of the rain: *You must promise you'll take care of your sister.*

A ridiculous request. Katie had already been taking care of Shannon, long before their father had died.

Nevertheless, Katie had given her mother the words she'd craved. *I promise.*

She'd been young, barely seventeen, naïve, and believing surely—surely—she could honor her promise. Even when she and Shannon had been evicted from their small cottage a month after their mother's death, Katie had not given up hope.

Surely, she'd thought, her mother's brother would open his home to them.

She'd been right. And yet so very wrong.

Despite owning the village's only apothecary shop, her uncle already had too many mouths to feed. Determined to minimize the burden she and Shannon put on the household, Katie had accepted an apprenticeship with the local midwife. It had taken her years to earn enough money for passage to America, and only enough for herself.

Forced to travel ahead of her sister, Katie had vowed to send for Shannon as soon as she could. Leaving her behind had been the hardest thing she'd ever done.

It shouldn't be much longer. Katie had written the words week after week, hoping, praying she could make them true. But then Aunt Jane had contracted scarlet fever.

One setback after another. They simply kept coming.

Katie never told Shannon of the hardships she endured. *Opportunities abound at every street corner and jobs are plentiful,* she'd written. *Everything is built on a grand scale in America. Your first glimpse of the Statue of Liberty will leave you in awe.*

Guilt flooded through her, hotter than any emotion she'd ever felt before walking away from her sister. All her life, she'd longed for something . . . more. Not just more work and more money, but a purpose that went beyond herself.

She wanted a calling, wanted to leave a lasting legacy that would serve the higher good. Katie had happily followed her ideals across the ocean, straight to New York City. Straight to a situation worse than the one she'd left.

Her new home had stolen her dreams, but not her dignity.

A knock sounded at the door.

Glad for the interruption, Katie looked up from the garment and called out, "It's open."

The door creaked on its hinges, and soon a head full of silver-streaked hair poked through the tiny opening.

"Well," her aunt said with a smile that added more lines to her weathered face. "You're working late this evening."

"No later than usual."

"I suppose not." She hesitated. "Would you like some company?"

Katie was about to send her aunt away. But the older woman looked as overwrought as she felt, her color magnified to a gray pallor in the dull light from the flickering lantern that also emphasized the purple shadows beneath her eyes.

Poor Aunt Jane, Katie thought. The stale air in the building was only making the woman struggle to maintain her strength. Fresh air would do her wonders. Unfortunately, the polluted stench on Orchard Street wasn't any healthier for Aunt Jane than the lack of ventilation inside the tenement house.

Katie felt the stirrings of despair return. She'd had every intention of bringing Shannon home with her this evening. Another person in the household would add tension to their cramped living conditions, but an extra income would also help them acquire better lodgings far quicker.

How wonderful that would be. *Will be,* she amended in her mind.

They would soon move to a new place, perhaps a cottage in Brooklyn, where the air was cleaner. They would purchase a tiny house of their own, with decent ventilation and no noise from the neighbors.

As if to put a fine point on her musings, a crash-boom-crash sounded from somewhere in the apartment below, followed by the wail of a child and the angry shout of an adult.

The dream of moving out of this building wasn't over, Katie told herself, not by a long shot. Just momentarily set aside.

"I would love a bit of company," she told her aunt. "Do come in."

Only as Jane moved deeper into the room did Katie realize she carried a tray laden with a teapot, two empty cups and saucers, and a plate of hard biscuits.

In the next moment, Katie was on her feet. "Let me carry that for you."

Without waiting for a response, she took the tray. While her aunt went to sit on the lone chair in the room, Katie poured the tea. She handed a cup to Jane, took one for herself, then perched on the edge of the bed.

"Where's Bridget?" she asked, more out of reflex than curiosity. Even after a long day of work, her cousin enjoyed going out on the town with her friends. Katie figured Bridget earned the right to blow off a little steam.

"She went to visit her friend across the hall."

"That's nice." Katie liked Regina Kennedy, more so than most of Bridget's other friends. The young woman had a smile that collapsed into dimples and one of those appealing faces that lit from within, as if she were living a slightly better, healthier lifestyle than the rest of the tenement population.

Regina lived with her brother, Declan, and worked as a sales clerk at Bergdorf Goodman. Best of all, Regina urged Bridget to apply for work at the store. Where Katie had failed, perhaps the other woman would succeed.

Out of the corner of her eye, Katie studied her aunt as covertly as possible. The older woman was staring into her teacup, tracing the chipped rim with a short, cracked fingernail. She didn't complain, but it was evident she felt the persistent ravages of her illness. Or was there something else bothering her?

Katie offered a small sympathetic grimace in Aunt Jane's direction and then added a bit more milk to both their cups. Knowing her aunt would speak her mind eventually, Katie sat back and took a sip of the hot liquid.

At last, the other woman got around to the point of her visit. "I understand a man escorted you home this evening."

Katie nearly choked on her tea. She could hear her own heartbeat thumping in her ears, like the hammer on a clock. The tenement house noise that had sounded so loud moments before now seemed to come at her as if from a far distance.

"Did Bridget also tell you who the man was?"

"She mentioned it, yes. It was the doctor who performed your medical exam during your own registration process."

Katie set aside her cup and, needing something to do with her hands, picked up the dress for Mrs. Armstrong. Caressing its smooth edges, she let her vision glaze. She didn't want to think about Ty. She certainly didn't want to talk about him.

What was the point? She would probably never see him again after tonight. And why was Bridget telling Aunt Jane about Ty?

Hating the need to defend herself, Katie proceeded to do exactly that. She told her aunt about coming across Ty quite by accident on the ferryboat. "He was very kind. Once we arrived at the docks, it was growing dark, and he was good enough to offer to see me home."

Worried eyes fixed on Katie. "And you agreed?"

"It was the sensible thing to do because, as I said, it was getting dark."

After a moment of hesitation, the older woman nodded. "Sensible, indeed."

There was enough light in the room to see Jane's lips twist in concern. Katie felt criticized and prickly, and that wasn't fair to her aunt. Jane loved Katie and had taken her into her home without question.

"Ty, I mean . . . Dr. Brentwood gave me the name of an official at Ellis Island who will help me discover what ails Shannon."

"Then you were fortunate your paths crossed."

"I was."

Aunt Jane held her gaze, one beat, two, her black eyes growing grave by the third. "You trust him."

Though her aunt hadn't actually posed a question, Katie felt the need to respond as if she had. "I do. Implicitly."

As soon as the words left her mouth, she knew them to be true. Thankfully, her response seemed to satisfy her aunt.

They chatted a bit longer about nothing in particular, which brought no small amount of surprise to Katie. Aunt Jane was not one for small talk and never engaged in unnecessary chatter in the evenings. She preferred reading in her room.

Tonight, she appeared in no hurry to return to her latest book. Clearly, the older woman had something on her mind, something that had brought her to Katie.

Katie decided to be blunt. "What's wrong, Aunt Jane? You seem troubled about something."

"Oh, aye, it's troubled I am."

"Are you worried about Shannon?"

"Indeed, I am. But, at the moment, it's my fair Bridget that has me concerned."

Katie felt the color drain from her face. "Oh?"

"She's been acting strangely. She's always kept to herself, but she's been even more secretive than usual. I know she's hiding something from me."

Katie stifled a groan. "What makes you say that?"

"Just now, before she left for her friend's apartment, I asked her if she had something to tell me. She hesitated, and I got the feeling she was working up the courage to tell me the truth. But she seemed to change her mind and"—Aunt Jane set down her cup—"from that caged look on your face, I see I'm right."

Katie's insides began to rearrange themselves as if they'd decided to play a game of hopscotch. "About . . . what?"

"My daughter is lying to me."

Chapter Eight

Ty lifted the brandy snifter in his hand and stared into the amber liquid. His second glass for the night. Or was it his third?

He wanted another sip. He'd already had too much, yet instead of the numbness he craved, guilt assaulted him, threatening to drag him into dark oblivion. One more taste.

Taking a bracing swallow, he allowed the burn to sink deep in his throat. His vision blurred and he blinked furiously, but somehow he was back at the hospital, performing the final surgical procedure of his career. The instruments marched in a neat row on the tray beside him, lined up one inch apart, in the precise order he'd demanded.

Camille lay on the table, a white sheet covering most of her body. She'd gone into labor again. The baby had maneuvered into the breech position. Ty had been unable to turn him. Camille's pulse dipped dangerously low.

He was losing her.

There was a chance to save both mother and son.

Ty reached for the scalpel. The metal felt unnaturally cold in his hand, so cold the tool was white-hot and blistering.

"Please, Ty. I don't care about me. Save my baby."

She wasn't supposed to be awake. Ty's grip slipped. The scalpel clamored to the floor. He bent over, picked it up, but when he straightened, Camille seemed to shrink away, her image becoming a watery blur.

No. *Not again.*

Ty couldn't lose her again. Not after convincing her husband to trust him to perform the operation.

Had Ty been too hasty to attempt a procedure he'd only read about but never performed?

The familiar spasm of panic came fast and hard, paralyzing in its intensity. For a moment, Ty had to fight the horrible urge to let his hand shake, but he knew any loss of control would be Camille's doom.

For the sake of his patient, and that of her baby, he had to ignore the choking sense of defeat rising inside him and continue the procedure. Camille and her baby were out of options.

A nurse moved in beside one of the physicians and picked up Camille's wrist in one hand, then flipped open a pocket watch with the other and silently counted the heartbeats.

She nodded to Ty.

Jaw tight, eyes flat and focused, he dragged the scalpel horizontally across Camille's engorged abdomen, the incision made low across the belly.

Blood spurted, oozing out in a stream of unceasing red.

Too much blood. Coming too fast. A hidden tear in the uterine wall. Too late. He'd discovered it too late. The damaged membrane was beyond repair.

He tried to sop up the blood. The crimson liquid flowed like a swelled river. Ty forced his heartbeat to slow to the same rhythmic cadence as the tick-tick-tick coming from a clock. A clock? Why was there a clock in his operating theater?

The nurse's voice came at him again. "Her heart rate is slowing, Dr. Brentwood."

"How many beats per minute?"

"Thirty-two."

Ty felt his chest heave with panic. Panic? That couldn't be right. He never panicked with a patient under his knife.

He dropped a glance over the woman, no longer Camille, but a nameless, faceless form, her color the pale, sickly gray that indicated death. No.

A dull drumming pounded in his ears. The image of Camille's face bled into a kaleidoscope of chaotic shapes.

Ty heard the wail of a baby. He had to free the child or it would die with his mother. A muscle shifted in his jaw, and he felt his control slip.

Had he been too hasty? The procedure was new to him, untested in his hands, but Ty was an excellent surgeon, better than his peers, second only to his father. And this operation was Camille's only chance.

She stopped breathing.

Forget the baby. Save the mother.

No, he would revive them both. Camille first.

"Stay with me, Camille," Ty shouted, his voice hollow in his own ears.

The shadowy figure of her husband materialized beside him. "You vowed to save my wife. You failed us both."

Shep's accusation rang in Ty's ears, a loud buzzing sound.

Camille, eyes blank, turned to look at her husband. "Not to worry, my love. I'm in a safe place now."

But she wasn't safe. The baby was still breech. And her life's blood spilled out too fast.

Stay with me, Camille!

Ty's hand jerked. Had he said the words or had Shep?

The sound of glass breaking jerked him straight in his chair. He'd dropped the snifter of brandy at his feet. Shards of glass were scattered everywhere.

He ignored the mess and, hand shaking, rubbed his palms over his face. He'd had The Dream again. A full year since his close friend had brought his wife to him, begging Ty to save her from certain death, and he still dreamed of his failure.

He inhaled the pungent odor of his own sweat. Self-disgust and loathing filled his nostrils.

Ty had killed Camille, as surely as if he'd put a gun to her head and pulled the trigger. He'd lost everything—his future, his coveted career as a surgeon, most of his friends—and it was nothing compared to what Shep had lost. His wife and child were gone forever.

Ty felt molten rage at the senseless loss. If only he'd been more cautious, less arrogant, less sure of his skills, less ready to try a surgical procedure he'd never performed.

You were out of options.

Ty shook his head. He couldn't dwell on his mistakes. He'd drive himself mad. He must focus on the future, on atonement. He would save others, for the sake of the one he'd lost.

Yet deep down, in the darkest, basest part of his soul, he knew the scales would never be balanced. He could save a thousand lives and Camille would still be dead. Redemption would always be out of reach.

Growling, Ty shoved to a standing position, fast and decisively despite his liquor-addled brain. The sound of glass crunching beneath his feet had him scowling at the bottle of brandy, half empty now. Enough.

Enough.

He might be a shell of the man he once was; he might never find forgiveness for what he'd done, but he would not give in to defeat. He would use his skills to serve the poor and needy.

And by all that was holy, he would do it clearheaded and sober.

With one fast swoop, he grabbed the bottle of brandy, went to the open window, and poured out the liquid until every drop resided in the dark alley below.

Feeling marginally better, he began cleaning up the shattered glass. A moment of powerlessness overwhelmed him. There were so many in need. Too many. His heart began to beat triple time. Then, as if a claw released its grip, one talon at a time, an idea came to him.

There was one impoverished immigrant he could help right away. Instead of a vague desire to assist a woman in need, he had a concrete plan forming in his mind, one with specific steps he could take first thing in the morning. The thought eased the chill of dread in his gut.

Later that night, when Ty collapsed in bed with a raging headache, it was with a real sense of optimism. For the first time in a year, his slumber was deep, restful, and, mercifully, dreamless.

* * *

Ty left the clinic in the capable hands of Dr. Sebastian Havelock. The Cambridge-trained physician had arrived from England several months ago and, to Ty's immense gratitude, volunteered three mornings a week at the clinic. He also helped out an occasional afternoon or two whenever his schedule allowed.

Although he didn't usually work on Saturdays, Sebastian had made an exception when Ty telephoned the man at his boarding house and informed him he was needed at Ellis Island.

The other doctor hadn't asked any questions, though there'd been several in his gaze when he'd arrived at the clinic. Ty could use Havelock full-time, but the man was committed to a career in infectious diseases.

Now, as the full blaze of midmorning burned through a wall of windows at his back, Ty stood just inside the women's ward on Swinburne Island, Shannon O'Connor's paperwork in his hand. With the head nurse glaring her displeasure at him, he realized just how much he'd misjudged the depths of his desire to ease Katie's worry.

By being here, reviewing another doctor's diagnosis, Ty had overstepped his bounds. He was only a volunteer.

He couldn't find it in him to feel sorry, though, especially after discovering that Dr. Hannibal Seabold had been the admitting physician. How could the man make so many detailed notations and yet miss the obvious diagnosis?

Perhaps Ty was overthinking the matter. Perhaps The Dream had sent his mind down the wrong path.

He reviewed Shannon O'Connor's chart again, then ground his teeth in frustration. Katie's sister had either been misdiagnosed, which happened to be the direction Ty was leaning, or she should have been deported. Without actually examining the young woman himself, he wouldn't know for certain.

The fever, chills, headache, fatigue, confusion, nausea, and vomiting could have been caused by a virus, perhaps influenza, but the sporadic nature of her symptoms signaled a different diagnosis.

Ty looked up from the paperwork. "Which bed was assigned to Miss O'Connor?"

The nurse hesitated. "Dr. Brentwood, you are not authorized to see patients in this section of the hospital—"

"Which one?" He spoke not unkindly but with the firm authority of a man who gave orders and expected them followed to the letter.

Sniffing in indignation, the matronly woman with two double chins ground out, "Follow me."

She led Ty into the ward, her stiff spine as pliant as a steel rod. The room looked much like any other found in a hospital or large clinic. White and sterile, two rows of beds stood on either side of a wide aisle, their metal headboards flush against the walls.

"The patient is over there." She pointed to a bed on Ty's right. "The one with the red hair."

Ty didn't need the description. He would have known Shannon O'Connor after one glance. She was a younger version of her sister. The only difference was the hair. Katie's was a pretty red-gold, while Shannon's was a vibrant mahogany.

Her eyes remained closed, and she seemed to be resting peacefully. In that serene posture, she looked painfully young, more child than woman.

Katie had claimed her sister was eighteen. At the moment, she looked closer to twelve.

Ty thanked the nurse, then said, "I'll take it from here."

"Yes, of course . . . *Doctor.*" Her voice was so dry Ty thought he could almost strike a match off it.

Shaking his head, he strode closer to the patient. Though every bed accommodated a patient with varying degrees of sickness, the ward itself was quiet, save for the labored breathing coming from a woman on Ty's right and the creak of bedsprings as another one shifted in her sleep, moaning softly.

Ty's chest cinched. He never got used to the sound of someone in pain. It was one of the reasons he preferred surgery. On the operating table, he was called to treat the ailment not the patient. He'd liked it that way, not too close, not too personal.

It wasn't that he didn't feel compassion for the sick. He did, more than he could bear. His patients deserved better from him, he knew. He was working on that, trying to be less clinical, more human, though he had a long way to go.

In the meantime, perhaps he would hire a nurse, not like the one he'd just encountered, but a woman who would soothe fears and calm restless souls.

He paused at the foot of Shannon's bed. It wasn't hyperbole to say she was beautiful, nearly as stunning as her sister. Her sculpted features, flawless skin, full lips, and bold red hair showed the promise of a girl on the verge of womanhood.

Her color was high, Ty noted, but he didn't think the cause was a fever. If he was pressed for a word to describe her skin, he would say it . . . glowed. He was even more certain her condition had been misdiagnosed.

He would have to do his own exam. It would not be easy. The memories were already beating on the door, clawing at his composure.

This is for Katie, he reminded himself, and some of the disquiet vanished.

As he moved to the side of the bed, his vision blurred. His pulse picked up speed. Blood rushed in his ears. Memories yanked at him, emptying his mind of everything but a miserable sense of grief and loss and guilt. So much guilt.

He hadn't expected this reaction. Ty saw women in Shannon's condition at the clinic all the time and was able to detach.

Yet here he was, suspended in a state of immobility. He fought the urge to close his eyes. If he did, he'd be back in the operating room, back to a time when he'd thought he could do no wrong.

This wasn't about him. *Not about you.*

The words slowly sank in, releasing him from the grip of his past. Mouth flat, he shoved aside the unwanted memories and focused again on Shannon O'Connor's face. The lines of her sleeping features would have sent artists into raptures.

In that moment, Ty better understood Katie's concern for her sister. There was something compelling about her beauty, something otherworldly.

He was wondering how to wake her when she opened her eyes and stared at him like someone who'd experienced much suffering in her young life.

That ended today. "Good morning, Shannon."

She continued staring at him.

He softened his voice. "How are you feeling?"

The wary eyes searched his face.

"My name is Dr. Brentwood."

"You're new." Her voice was soft, lyrical, and nearly identical to her sister's in tone and pitch. If Ty closed his eyes, he would swear he was speaking with Katie.

"I'm new to this ward, yes, but not to practicing medicine." Ty reached out a hand and laid it on Shannon's forehead. "I'm also a friend of your sister's."

The girl startled under his hand. "You know Katie?"

"She's worried about you."

Tears filled her eyes. A few trickled down her cheeks. "Am I very sick, then?"

"That's what I'm here to discover." Ty leaned closer. "Have you been nauseous this morning?"

"Not yet."

Not yet. A telling answer. "You plan to be sick later?"

"I don't know. It's possible, especially if they serve eggs for breakfast." Making a face, she struggled to a sitting position. "I hate the smell of eggs."

Ty rearranged the pillow behind her back. "Have you always hated that scent?"

"No. It's new." She lifted a graceful small hand and swiped at her cheeks.

"Any other odors make you sick to your stomach?"

"Lots, especially fish." She frowned. "And sea air."

Even more telling, Ty thought, keeping his expression free of reaction. "Before I conduct my physical examination, I need to ask you a few questions."

Her entire manner turned resigned. "If you must."

"Some will be of a sensitive nature, but I need you to be as honest as possible. Do you understand?"

"I understand."

Her answer was clear and to the point, but Ty saw the worry in her eyes, the suspicion. He wanted to relieve her fears, to tell her she had influenza and would soon be well.

He would be lying.

Resolve came fast and hard, reminding Ty he had a chance to redeem his past, to prove he was more than his mistakes. He wouldn't squander this opportunity, no matter how uncomfortable the next few minutes proved for them both.

"Did you travel alone to America?"

The question brought fresh tears to her eyes and more swiping at her cheeks. "Oh, aye. Yes, I did."

Ty felt the girl's sadness on a visceral level. The man who preferred keeping his distance from others wanted to walk away now. *Let Dr. Seabold's diagnosis stand.*

No, that would only put off the inevitable. Shannon's condition would show itself soon, probably in a month or two.

Still, the girl was only eighteen years old, young, if no longer innocent. He proceeded with care. "You weren't supposed to travel alone, were you?"

"No." A sob slid from her lips before she could cover the sound with her hand.

"You were supposed to travel with a . . . family member?"

Shannon shook her head.

There was something tragic to her story. Ty asked his next question in a voice barely above a whisper. "Would it be right for me to assume you were supposed to travel with a friend, a male?"

Shannon turned her head away, but not before Ty saw the grief in her eyes. She remained silent for so long he expected her to brush off his question, but she spoke plainly. "Liam. I was supposed to travel with Liam."

"Who is Liam to you, a friend?"

"My fiancé."

Her fiancé?

Well, that was unexpected. "Katie didn't mention anything about your engagement."

Head still turned away, she lifted one slim shoulder, let it fall. "She doesn't know."

So the girl had kept her relationship a secret from her sister. Had it been Shannon's idea or the boy's? Had he preyed on her youth and innocence?

Ty didn't like the direction his mind took. To think this beautiful young woman had been seduced and then abandoned made him want to hit something. Or rather, someone.

He only prayed he was wrong.

Schooling his expression, Ty waded into deep emotional waters with great care. "Was there a reason you didn't share the happy news of your engagement with your sister?"

Her face went paler still. "I didn't tell Katie because Liam and I only found one another a few months ago, and I . . ." Rebellion swept across her features as she pressed her lips into a tight, thin line. "I don't see how any of this has to do with why I can't keep food in my stomach. Or why I'm so tired all the time?"

"I have a few more tests I'd like to perform," Ty said. "Let's get started, shall we?"

He conducted his exam quickly. He checked the girl's pulse, listened to her heart and lungs, and pressed lightly on her stomach, focusing on the lower right side first, then the upper left.

Though he tried to be gentle, she tensed under his inspection, no doubt unused to a strange man taking such liberties, doctor or not.

In an attempt to distract her from her discomfort, Ty asked, "Other than the nausea, what else have you been feeling?"

She seemed to consider her response before answering. "I've been uncommonly tired, often too exhausted to do much of anything but lie down."

"When did the fatigue start?" he asked, moving his hands to her throat. He searched for swelling a few inches beneath her jawline, then near the thyroid gland.

"I guess it started a few days before I boarded the ship, perhaps a bit longer than that." As she spoke, Shannon gradually stopped straining backward to avoid his touch.

Progress.

"Have you had any pain in unusual places?"

"My lower back."

"Any shortness of breath?"

"No, I . . . wait. Yes." Shannon kept her eyes closed for a long moment, as if thinking back in time. "I sometimes get breathless." She opened her eyes. "I also get light-headed, especially when I smell unpleasant scents."

Mentally, Ty reviewed her list of symptoms, convinced Dr. Seabold had misdiagnosed the girl. But just to be sure . . .

He waded back into more personal territory. "Tell me about your fiancé. How long has he been courting you?"

Shannon chewed on her lower lip, staring at Ty fixedly, almost defiantly. "More than four whole months."

She spoke as though that length of time was an eternity. To an eighteen-year-old girl, it probably seemed that way. Ty removed the earpieces of the stethoscope and wrapped the rubber tubing around the back of his neck. "Where is your fiancé now?"

The girl went perfectly still, her eyes blinking rapidly. "Liam is . . ." Blink. Blink. Blink. "He's . . ."

She choked out a sob.

"He's . . . where, Shannon? Where is Liam?"

The floodgates opened, and tears streamed down her cheeks in a river of agony. "He's still in Ireland."

Chapter Nine

Shannon broke out in a cold sweat, a queasy feeling coming over her. Her stomach burned with a nauseating mix of frustration and desperation, as if some huge curtain had been pulled back to reveal her devastating circumstances in a new, more frightening light.

Taking a breath, she plucked at the frayed edges of the blanket thrown over her legs, then tugged it closer to her chin as she struggled to bring the nausea under control.

Slowly, the sickness retreated.

If only pulling the shreds of her composure around her were so easy.

Liam and I should be married, she thought.

There was a moment of absolute stillness in the doctor before he wiped his features free of all expression and handed her a pristine handkerchief. She dabbed at her eyes in a pointless effort to keep her sorrow at bay.

The tears kept coming, hot and embarrassing. She didn't want to cry in front of this stranger, even if he claimed to know her sister. Shannon willed her eyes dry, to no avail. The source of her sorrow seemed small, yet carried monumental consequences. Liam's luggage had been lost during the initial boarding process.

I should have gone with him to the barge office.

Instead, she'd taken her own small leather case filled with her meager belongings and had gone in search of his missing baggage in the opposite direction.

We shouldn't have separated.

It had seemed the wise thing to do, each covering more ground on their own than they could have together. When the ship's whistle blew, Shannon had given up the hunt and boarded the ship alone, assuming Liam would do the same.

We should have had a better plan in place before we parted ways.

Her eyelashes felt sticky, her throat gritty, and still the tears came. They leaked down her cheeks.

It took several attempts, but finally Shannon swallowed her sadness and watched the doctor—she couldn't remember his name—as he watched her. Did he think if he held silent long enough, she would tell him all her secrets?

The irony was, if he'd used the same tactic when she'd first arrived at Ellis Island, she might have answered all his questions without hesitation. She didn't like that her trust had been sullied within a single day. "You are truly my sister's friend?"

"I am." Something flashed in his eyes as he spoke, something with a mysterious edge. Shannon didn't like that either, but he seemed nice enough.

In some ways, he reminded her of Liam.

Both were handsome men, tall and lean of build, patient with their hands. But where Liam was quick-witted and prone to laughing, this man was more careful with his emotions.

Shannon knew he wasn't like the other doctors on this island, the ones who had sent her to languish in this hospital bed as a ward of the state until she recovered from whatever mysterious illness plagued her. This doctor didn't seem concerned about her illness at all. In fact, he seemed more interested in her relationship with Liam.

"I don't understand why you're here."

"I have come on Katie's behalf." He stuffed his hands in his pockets. "Your sister is worried about you."

The simple words, spoken in that flat American accent with both warmth and kindness, alleviated a portion of Shannon's fear.

"I want to help you, Shannon. But I need you to be honest with me. The more information you give, the more candid you are with your answers, the better I can know how to proceed," he said. "Medically," he added when she scowled at his words.

Shannon was quiet a long moment as she mulled over her options. The problem was fighting her instinct, which screamed at her to hold silent.

"I can trust you?"

"You can."

The knots of worry melted into a sort of tentative need to unburden her heart. This stranger, a friend of Katie's, was a doctor, a man who was supposed to listen to her without judgment.

"Liam and I were separated during the boarding process. I thought he'd gone on ahead of me, so I went up the gangplank with a group of women I'd met on the docks. Once I was on the ship, I searched and searched for him, but—"

"He wasn't there."

"No." For the hundredth time, Shannon wished she'd waited in one spot. "While I hunted for Liam on board, he was conducting his own search for me on the docks. I spotted him weaving through the crowd gathered to send off their loved ones. He saw me at nearly the same moment, but it was too late. The gangplank had been raised, and the ship was pulling away from the harbor."

The worst moment of my life.

The memory came with fresh tears, unwelcome and infuriating. No. No more. Shannon was tired of crying. What good did giving in to her grief do? It couldn't bring Liam to her. That much she knew from the endless days since she'd last seen him.

She noticed how the doctor's lips had twisted in a grimace. That expression made her so outraged that her tears of sadness turned into ones of rage. "I know what you're thinking."

"Do you?"

"You think Liam abandoned me." Shannon saw the truth in his eyes. "Well, he didn't. *He didn't,*" she added with a bit too much vehemence when the doctor simply stared at her with a blank expression. The patience she'd admired moments before made her want to tear at her hair.

Why had she believed him when he'd said she could trust him? Why had she told him so much?

"Shannon." He spoke in a voice meant to soothe but managed to inflame her indignation even further.

"Don't talk to me."

"It wouldn't be the first time a man made promises to a pretty girl such as yourself, promises he had no intention of keeping."

"You're wrong. Do you hear me?" She tried not to raise her voice, but it couldn't be helped. How dare he judge the man she loved? "Liam is good and true. He speaks only truth. He doesn't have the mind of a schemer or a liar. He is incapable of subterfuge."

"You discovered this after four months?"

"He . . . he *loves me*. And I love him." The words spilled from her mouth in an angry rush. "We were separated by accident. It was an unfortunate misunderstanding, nothing more. He will come to America, as he promised. He will find me, and then we'll get married and be together for the rest of our lives."

There were dozens of reasons she could give this man to prove her trust in Liam was warranted. But Shannon wouldn't lower herself to defend her love any more than she'd already done.

Shannon believed in Liam. That's what mattered.

This man's opinion did not.

The doctor moved a step closer. By his alert expression, Shannon could see he wasn't through asking his questions. He retrieved a file of papers and flipped through the pages. Just how many times did he need to consult the other doctor's notes?

Frowning, she leaned her head back against the pillow. Still upset, and unable to prevent herself from holding silent, she muttered, "Liam and I should have married before we left Ireland."

The doctor looked up. "Why didn't you?"

"His mother didn't approve of our relationship."

The truth of that still stung. No matter how often Shannon told herself Mrs. Gallagher's opinion wasn't worth having, deep down, she knew that wasn't completely true. Though she hadn't been the one to insist he make a choice between her and his mother, Shannon hated that he'd been forced to do so. Why couldn't Mrs. Gallagher like her?

Shannon looked up at the doctor's eyes. As he made a notation on her chart, defiance took hold. This American's opinion didn't matter, she told herself again. Mrs. Gallagher didn't matter.

Only Liam mattered.

Only their future mattered.

We aren't even together.

They would be soon.

The doctor, Katie's *friend*, finished poking at her and straightened to his full height. He said something under his breath about "just what I expected" and "how did the others miss something so obvious?"

Shannon didn't mean to hear the words, but with him standing this close, she couldn't avoid it.

What she hadn't expected was the lack of disapproval in his voice, the lack of condemnation. Her mood shifted from outrage to one of tentative hope. She realized that had been happening more and more. She would find herself happy one moment, angry the next, then giving in to tears a second later. There were times when she hardly recognized herself. This was one of them.

"Do you know what's wrong with me?"

He nodded.

"Will you tell me?" she asked softly, not sure she wanted to hear the diagnosis, yet desperate to know if she was dying.

"I have a few more questions." He set aside the stack of papers. "You mentioned your fiancé's mother didn't approve of your relationship. Am I to understand that means you and Liam planned to run away to America and marry once you arrived?"

Again, Shannon wasn't sure how the question had anything to do with her illness. Still, she didn't see the point in withholding the truth. "Liam and I heard that if a man and woman were caught traveling alone together without the benefit of marriage, they would be forced to marry before they were allowed to enter the country."

"You heard correctly."

"Under the circumstances"—a wave of guilt crested, and she looked down, plucking at the sheet covering her—"it seemed the perfect solution."

The doctor's brows shot together. "Am I to assume you and Liam got a little, shall we say"—a pause, a move closer, a quick check to his left, then right, presumably to determine if her neighbors were listening—"ahead of saying your wedding vows?"

"Ahead of our vows?" Shannon blinked at the odd phrasing. "I don't know what that means."

It must be some strange American saying.

He leaned in closer, his voice pitched at a quiet tone meant only for her ears. "Shannon, think very carefully before you answer. Could you be with child?"

"What?" She visibly shrank back. *"No."* It was the same answer she'd given when the other doctors had questioned her similarly.

Were all Americans so blunt?

"No," Shannon insisted again. "Liam and I . . . no. I'm not." She lowered her voice to a whispered hiss. "I'm not pregnant."

Am I?

Surely, she would know if she were carrying Liam's child.

"Did your fiancé talk you into doing something you didn't want to do?"

Embarrassment came hot and fast. A part of Shannon appreciated how he chose his words carefully. Another part was mortified and furious at the implication. "Liam has always been a gentleman."

"You're saying he didn't force himself on you?"

Shannon felt the color drain from her face. "How dare you ask such a foul thing? Liam would never do something so cruel. He loves and respects me. I am his very heart."

He'd said the words the night they'd been together.

"I'm sorry this is uncomfortable for you." The doctor didn't seem sorry. Except, maybe he did. A little. Maybe even more than a little.

Shannon shut her eyes against the heat and humiliation creeping up her neck, straight to her burning cheeks. Although she knew the hope was ridiculous, perhaps even childish, she wished Liam would appear at her bedside and tell this doctor to go to the devil for having such nerve.

"Shannon. Look at me. To avoid further confusion, I'm going to be direct with you."

He hadn't been direct already?

"I mean it. I need you to look at me."

He waited for her to open her eyes.

Almost immediately, he gentled his manner and pitched his voice back to a low whisper. "Were you and your fiancé ever intimate?"

It was the same question he'd asked her already, just worded a different way. The man was certainly persistent. She'd answered him about a possible pregnancy. Why wasn't that enough?

The more he pushed her to respond, the more foolish she felt. Desperate.

Ashamed.

What had been a wonderful, intimate, special moment now seemed cheap and tawdry under this doctor's persistence. He couldn't be right about her condition.

Could he?

Until this man had asked his pointed questions, Shannon hadn't thought such a thing was even possible. Well, maybe *possible.* But not probable. The odds were too great.

The first stirrings of doubt pulled her brows together.

Had this doctor seen something during his examination? Something she was supposed to sense on her own? Something she should have known as a woman.

"Were you and your fiancé intimate?" he asked again.

"I'm *not* with child," she said under her breath, with great fervor and a healthy dose of panic. "It's simply not possible."

You mean probable, she corrected in her mind.

He persevered. "You are absolutely . . . certain?"

She looked away from that penetrating glance. A myriad of emotions crept over her as she contemplated how best to respond. Irritation. Desperation.

Shame.

How dare this man make a beautiful, tender act seem dirty!

"Shannon," he said with a renewed gentleness that chipped away at her resolve. "Are you sure it's not possible? Are you positive you're not"—he lowered his voice to a whisper—"carrying your fiancé's child?"

Lips pursed, she shook her head.

"The evidence suggests otherwise."

She refused to meet his gaze. Nevertheless, her heart pounded in her chest as the most profound night of her life played out in her mind. Liam had pledged his love to her, and she to him, their declarations as true and pure as any wedding vows spoken in front of a priest.

"We were together once." Although every moment of expressing their love to one another had been extraordinary, and every touch worth repeating, they'd agreed to wait until their wedding night to continue having relations. "It was only *once*," she repeated with more force.

"Once is all it takes."

Shannon did not have a ready reply.

Her hand went to her stomach, still flat but churning with renewed queasiness. She'd thought herself seasick, but now . . . this was so much better. So unexpected. She couldn't stop the terrible-wonderful feelings that swamped her. Afraid. Happy. Lonely. Excited.

Love swelled in her heart. She was carrying Liam's baby, a child they had made together during a single act of love.

Tears of joy and wonder formed in her eyes and spilled over in a choking laugh. But then the fear came. What if Liam didn't find her? What if he . . .

No, he would come for her. He'd made a promise, and Liam always kept his promises. It was one of the many things she adored about him.

She was with child.

What would happen to her now?

Would she be forced to stay in this hospital until Liam arrived in America and they were married? Would she be stuck in this sterile, horrible-smelling ward with sick women all around her? That couldn't be healthy for the baby.

Shannon's fingers curled into a fist as an awful thought occurred to her. Would she . . . could she be . . .

Deported?

She was a young, pregnant, unwed girl of eighteen. There had to be rules about that. How would Liam find her?

What if the ship taking her back across the ocean passed the ship carrying Liam to America? Their paths could, quite literally, cross one another's, and they would never know it.

The Good Lord wouldn't be that cruel.

Fear had Shannon's stomach balling into a fist as tight as the one curled in her lap. She suddenly felt alone and frightened and young, too young to face the consequences of what she'd done. She wanted her mother.

No, she wanted Katie.

"Katie," she whispered, missing her sister dreadfully.

Even before their parents' deaths, Katie had been the closest thing to a mother Shannon had ever known. Despite the fact that she was only five years older than Shannon, Katie had cared for her, loving her in ways their mother had never been able to.

"I want my sister."

The doctor patted her arm with quiet compassion. "Then your sister you shall have. Stay put." He turned, hesitated, then veered back to lean over Shannon. "Don't talk to anyone while I'm gone, no matter how long it takes me to return. Say nothing to the nurses or other doctors, and especially not to your fellow patients. Do you understand?"

She nodded.

"Not a word," he reiterated.

Shannon nodded again, and her breathing stalled in her chest. She was too stricken and panicked to hope something wonderful would come from this exam. He was an American. A doctor. And . . . a friend of Katie's.

Her nerves sank into a tangled web in the pit of her stomach. "Wait," she called after his retreating back. "Where are you going?"

He returned to her bedside and gave her a kind smile. "To make arrangements to get you out of here."

"You . . ." She dared not say the words. "Truly?"

"It may take a while," he warned. "Perhaps even hours."

Too relieved to care what this man had to do to free her from her confinement, she said, "There's no hurry. My calendar is rather sparse this afternoon."

He left the area chuckling. Shannon decided to see that as a good sign.

Chapter Ten

Weary and worn to the bone, Katie climbed the first flight of stairs to her apartment with little enthusiasm. She'd had a grueling day at work. Her supervisor had given her another warning, her third and possibly her last. After issuing her threat, the woman had watched over Katie the rest of the day, practically looking for a reason to sack her.

To avoid losing her job, a very real possibility at this point, Katie had given Mrs. Zephyr no cause for complaint. She'd huddled over an endless batch of garments needing hemming and other finishing touches.

She paid the price for her diligence now. The muscles at the back of her neck had tied into hard knots. Her spine throbbed; even her hair hurt. And her eyes felt as though the inner lids had grown a layer of sandpaper.

Her mood sunk even further when she thought back over the conversation she'd had with the woman before leaving for the day. One more late arrival, no matter the reason, and Katie would be looking for a new job.

She'd tried to explain about the little girl who'd been nearly run over by a pushcart. The child had been inconsolable, unable to tell Katie her name or where she lived. Katie couldn't abandon her in the street. She'd stayed with the child until her mother came running around the corner, screeching for her daughter. Unfortunately, that had put Katie ten minutes behind schedule.

Ten. Minutes.

Ten. Stupid. Minutes.

Katie stifled a yawn as she commandeered the second flight of stairs. Unmoved by her explanation, Mrs. Zephyr had issued her warning in front of the other finishers. The supervisor seemed determined to assert her authority by using Katie as the example they should avoid emulating.

You make it too easy for her.

Katie knew she should have more regret. But a child in need was more important than any job. Still, she couldn't afford to lose her position at the factory.

Ignoring the rush of self-pity, she reminded herself that each completed garment represented another step closer to freedom. One day, she promised herself, she and the rest of her family would move out of this tenement house.

Not soon enough.

"Why so glum?"

The question had Katie pulling up short. With her hand clutched around the newel post, she glanced up and felt her mouth form an O of surprise. "Bridget. I didn't hear you descending the stairs."

"I gathered." The other woman joined her on the landing. "You're late. Mrs. Armstrong is waiting for you."

Katie groaned. She'd forgotten about their scheduled consultation. "When did she arrive?"

"About twenty minutes ago."

That long? She hadn't realized she'd left work so late. Katie had left her best customer waiting over a quarter of an hour.

She must have frowned or otherwise shown her inner turmoil, because Bridget bumped her shoulder with her own. "Stop your fretting. Mrs. Armstrong's in good hands with my mother."

Of course she was. Still, Katie started up the stairs at a hurried pace, pausing when Bridget didn't fall into step beside her. "You're not coming?"

"I have a quick errand to run."

She didn't elaborate, and Katie was too rushed to press for more information. "How long will you be gone?"

"Not long." She gave a jaunty little wave over her head and continued on her way without a backward glance.

For three full seconds, Katie stared after her cousin, wondering at the young woman's seemingly endless stores of energy. What she wouldn't give for half that amount of vitality.

Feeling the weight of her day in her bones, Katie completed her climb, then entered apartment 504. She opened her mouth to apologize for her tardiness, but when she saw her aunt laughing over a cup of tea with Mrs. Armstrong, she was too relieved to push out a single word.

Jane looked younger, more carefree, her color not fully restored but almost. *Mrs. Armstrong has that way about her,* Katie thought with a smile. She radiated a casual friendliness that put everyone at ease. The slender young woman was elegant, quite beautiful, really, with gleaming sable hair, fine features, and a contagious smile.

To announce her arrival, Katie shut the door with a soft click. "I'm sorry I'm late." She moved a step deeper into the apartment. "I was held up at the factory."

"It's quite all right," Mrs. Armstrong responded in her American accent that Katie had yet to place. The woman wasn't from New York or Boston. That much was clear by the flat vowels and soft consonants. "Your aunt has been regaling me with stories of her youth in Ireland. I am determined to visit your homeland and see the rolling green hills for myself."

Not sure how to respond to such enthusiasm, Katie blinked at the other woman for seconds past what was polite.

Her silence would have turned awkward had Aunt Jane not saved the moment. "Well, now that you're here, I'm sure you'll want to get started on the fitting." She reached for the empty teacups, then said good night to Mrs. Armstrong. "I'll be in my room if you need me."

Katie nodded.

"Your aunt is a lovely woman," Mrs. Armstrong said once they were alone. "I'm quite smitten with her."

Katie felt a swell of affection. "I am, too. I'm blessed to call her family."

"Indeed you are."

Remembering the reason for her visit, Katie sat beside Mrs. Armstrong and asked, "Would you like to conduct the fitting here, where there's more light, or in the bedroom in front of the mirror?"

"The bedroom, of course. But first, I brought a little something for you." She reached for the large satchel at her feet and handed it over to Katie.

Katie peered inside the bag and found herself unable to hold back a shocked gasp.

"Yes, well. I'm afraid I got a bit carried away."

"I'll say." There were enough pieces of lace, buttons, colorful ribbons, and countless other sewing notions to embellish at least a dozen dresses, maybe more if she economized.

When Katie said as much, the other woman gave a happy, self-satisfied laugh. "I do so love to shop, even if only for buttons and so forth." She gave a pleasant flick of her wrist. "I had entirely too much fun to apologize for my extravagance."

"I'll return what I don't use."

"Don't even think of doing such a thing. Employ whatever pieces you wish on the dresses I've already ordered, and save the rest for yourself."

"That's very generous of you."

Mrs. Armstrong laughed again, the tinkling sound almost musical. "My husband spoils me beyond measure. I believe it's only fair I pass along my good fortune to the people I care about."

Katie felt her cheeks heat, a little awed that Mrs. Armstrong included her among the people she *cared about*.

"Now, then." Mrs. Armstrong stood, straightened her skirt, fluffed her hair, then gave Katie a broad, delighted smile. "Let's have a look at what you've accomplished since my last visit."

The fitting went well. The client's enthusiastic pleasure in the unfinished garments bolstered Katie's confidence, and, with considerable excitement, Mrs. Armstrong set the date and time for their next consultation. "I'm looking forward to it with all eagerness."

"As am I," Katie admitted.

Just as they moved back into the main living area, the front door swung open, and Bridget sailed into the apartment, humming an unfamiliar tune, a ladies' magazine dangling from her fingers.

Brief pleasantries were exchanged, and then, as Bridget disappeared into the bedroom, Katie showed Mrs. Armstrong out of the apartment.

After shutting the door behind her very happy client, she pressed her back against the hard wood, pleased the fitting had gone so well. She and Mrs. Armstrong were of a like mind, something Katie hadn't expected.

Her stomach growled just then, alerting Katie to the fact that she'd yet to eat her supper. Concern for her aunt, though, won out over her own hunger.

She found Jane resting in her room. The older woman had lost her glow. It could've been a trick of the light, but Katie feared otherwise. "Have you eaten?"

"Bridget made me a bowl of soup before Mrs. Armstrong arrived." Slight crescents of shadows showed beneath her eyes, and even as Katie adjusted the pillow behind her head, Jane drew in a ragged breath.

"You had a rough day," Katie said decisively, a lump forming in her throat.

"Not as bad as some. I enjoyed my visit with your friend."

Katie didn't doubt her aunt's claim. She'd seen the color in her cheeks, as well as the happiness in her countenance. But a single look at the exhausted eyes now and a dozen simultaneous thoughts shuffled through her mind, pinpointing one clear course of action: ease her aunt's pain.

Unfortunately, there was no cure for a weakened system. Jane had survived a disease that had killed so many. That she had a few bad days was better than the alternative.

After ensuring that the older woman was resting comfortably, she went in search of her cousin. She still had hours of sewing ahead of her. But it was time for a candid talk with Bridget.

She found the young woman in the room they shared, standing before the mirror. A magazine was propped on the dresser, opened to a page with a picture of a pretty woman. Bridget's fingers moved quickly as she worked her hair into a similar hairstyle as the model's.

Eyes on her reflection, Bridget greeted Katie, then added, "I take it all went well with Mrs. Armstrong."

"It did."

"Want to tell me why you were late?"

Not particularly. Yet Katie found herself unburdening herself anyway. "I had a run-in with my supervisor."

Bridget's hands paused over her hair. "Again?"

"I was late this morning." Katie worked her feet out of a pair of worn ankle boots and sat on the edge of her bed. "I stopped to help a child."

Hands lowering, Bridget turned her back on her reflection. "You are too good, Katie. I fear your kindness will be the end of you."

Katie bristled at the unfair criticism. "I prefer to think it will be the making of me."

Bridget sighed. "That's a ridiculously naïve way to look at life."

Two days ago, Katie would have agreed with her cousin. But tonight, she would not allow regret in her heart. She'd done the right thing, saving a child.

"The important thing is that I still have a job. And a private commission that needs my immediate attention." Hoping that was the end of the discussion, Katie grabbed a garment out of the basket and set it atop her lap.

Bridget continued staring at Katie. After a moment, she moved to the mirror and went back to styling her hair. "Will you check on Mam in a few hours?"

Katie felt a tiny confused frown form in the spot between her eyes. "You're going out?"

Eyes focused on her reflection, Bridget pulled a handful of her hair off her face and then secured it in an artful arrangement at the crown of her head. Long dark curls tumbled down her back in a waterfall of shiny black silk. "Regina invited me to a party."

"In her apartment?"

Bridget nodded absently. The bulk of her attention was on accenting her hair with a few randomly placed crystals affixed to pins. "Her brother just got a new job with some big construction company in Brooklyn, and they've invited a few friends over to celebrate."

At least Bridget would be in the building, Katie thought.

"That sounds like a good time." Katie had no idea what else to say. She wondered who would be at this party. Bridget seemed to be working extra hard with her appearance.

"I'm sure it'll be fun." Bridget sounded both pleased and excited, almost like her old self, which was a far cry from the cynicism that usually clung to her like a second skin.

An answering smile curved Katie's lips. She liked seeing her cousin happy. The young woman carried too much sorrow of late. Katie understood the helplessness that came with watching a parent's decline.

Even in the dim light of the room, Bridget was uncommonly pretty, many would say beautiful. Her features were stunning from every angle. Her profile, perfection—the sort of defined lines and swooping angles that would make an ivory cameo weep in green-eyed envy. Her complexion, as white and smooth as the carved silhouettes.

Men had always liked Bridget's looks. Even as a young girl in Ireland, she'd had her share of admirers. By thirteen, Bridget had learned the art of conveying her disinterest without issuing an insult.

Was she as successful now that she went out of her way to gain male attention by highlighting her looks and voluptuous figure? Katie couldn't help but fear that Bridget was courting trouble in her job. No good would come from dancing on the street corner with the express purpose of luring men inside a gambling den.

"I wish you would join your friend at the department store." Katie knew she was belaboring the point, but she couldn't seem to stay silent on the matter. She worried about her cousin and feared something bad would happen if Bridget continued down this path.

"You know why I can't quit my job."

Money. Every decision seemed to come down to money. Choices were for the rich. "Surely the pay at Bergdorf Goodman is comparable to what you earn at the club."

"Not even close. And besides, that particular retailer rarely, if ever, hires girls from Ireland." Bridget's tone remained even and calm, except for the hint of disgust that colored the last word.

"Regina is from Ireland."

"She told them she hails from Boston."

"They believed her?" Regina sounded as Irish as Bridget.

"She affects a snobby Bostonian accent to perfection." Turning from the mirror, Bridget demonstrated. "Good morning, miss. How may I assist you?"

"How did you change your voice like that?" Each vowel was flat and carefully enunciated.

"Regina taught me. I expect I'll be out late this evening." She placed another pin in her hair. "Don't wait up."

Katie was still gawking at her cousin when Bridget made a final adjustment to her elaborate hairstyle and exited the room without a backward glance in her direction.

Katie followed after her. She moved too slowly, however, and was rewarded for her snail's pace with the soft click of the apartment door closing firmly in her face.

Well. Katie sighed in resignation. That was certainly a succinct end to their conversation.

A ferocious ache settled between her eyes. The prospect of returning to her room, and the hours of sewing that awaited her, was exhausting. She had no real choice in the matter. Money was a powerful motivator.

Katie would eat a quick supper. Then, she would sew. She would sew all night. She would sew until she expired from the exertion. Sew, sew, sew. Only then, once all her work was complete, would she fall into a dreamless sleep.

Another sigh rustled in Katie's throat. She simply had no desire to pick up needle and thread. Instead, she paced. And worried. About Bridget. About Aunt Jane. About money, and Shannon, and then, of course, about money again, all of which made for an unproductive ten minutes.

Katie ordered herself to stop dawdling and get to work.

Pivoting on her heel, she froze mid-spin when a knock sounded at the door. Odd, Bridget must have rushed out so quickly she'd forgotten her key. Or perhaps it was Regina or some other neighbor.

Unspeakably glad for the interruption, Katie hurried across the floor, yanked open the door, and got the shock of her life as her gaze connected with silvery-blue eyes the color of midnight starlight.

"I, oh, it's . . ." Katie drew in a sharp breath. "Good evening, Ty."

A slow smile spread across his handsome face, the expression so brilliant that it nearly blinded her. "Good evening, Katie."

An avalanche of emotion crowded inside her head. She could hardly breathe, could hardly make sense of the moment. Just looking at the man did strange things to her insides. There was something reassuring about his presence. Even more confounding, she got the sense that he liked her, really liked her.

And, oh, how she liked him. She liked him a lot. So much.

Too much.

As a child, she'd secretly fantasized about meeting a handsome man who would lavish her with attention and spoil her mercilessly, as her father did her mother. Katie thought she'd set the fairy tale aside. She thought she'd learned the danger of loving too much. But Titus Brentwood looked very much like the man she'd once dreamed of meeting.

His stance was full of masculine confidence that put her immediately at ease. He'd taken off his hat and now held it in his hand. In the other, he carried a small suitcase that looked familiar. Where had Katie seen that piece of baggage?

Though only seconds had passed since she'd opened the door, it felt like an eternity. She couldn't stop staring.

His dark hair was disheveled, as if he'd shoved his fingers through it more than once. Stubble darkened his jaw, adding to the image of a man who had more important things to do than worry about his appearance. He also looked like he could handle himself in a fight. Why that mattered, Katie couldn't say.

Helpless against the pull of him, she leaned slightly toward Ty.

A clock from inside the apartment marked the hour, seven distinct chimes. Seven o'clock? Why was he standing on her doorstep so late in the day? She opened her mouth to ask, but then she noticed a shift in the air behind him. "Oh, you're not alone."

"I have brought along my new friend, someone I know you'll want to see." Instead of making introductions, he simply stepped aside.

The shadow morphed into the beloved form of Katie's sister.

"Shannon." Hand flat against her heart, Katie fell back a step. Restraint shattered. Calm evaporated. Welcoming speeches died on her tongue. The only emotions left were shock and relief and joy—complete, heartrending, breath-robbing joy.

Katie ached at the core of her being.

"Oh, Shannon!" She all but soared across the threshold, into the hallway, and, sobbing now, yanked the girl into her arms. "Oh, my dear baby sister. Welcome to America."

Chapter Eleven

Ty, still holding Shannon's suitcase, watched Katie and her sister from his vantage point tucked in the corner of the hallway. He hardly recognized himself in his reaction to the two women laughing. Without realizing it, he'd taken a step closer, pulled toward the happy reunion by some invisible force.

What a picture they made, the very essence of sisterly love. The happiness radiating off them was contagious, and he found himself wanting to bask in their excitement.

With an angelic smile, Katie stepped back from her sister, hands still on Shannon's shoulders. A steady stream of emotions advanced across her expressive face as she turned her head in his direction. She was pleased with him.

He was rather pleased with himself.

He loved the way she looked at him, as if he'd accomplished a miracle. In that moment, Katie O'Connor was the most beautiful sight he'd beheld in a long time, perhaps ever. Some unacknowledged wall deep within him came tumbling down, and the empty crevices of his heart filled to overflowing.

She made him feel like a man worth believing in. Ty allowed himself to imagine that he was capable of great things. Not the man he once was, but someone even greater.

Still smiling, Katie released her sister and came to stand before him, her wide, wondering eyes shining with unmistakable pleasure. Ty had put that look on her face.

Everything about her was warm and pleasant and soft, the balm to his wounded soul. She glowed like a flame, and like a moth lured to his doom, Ty was drawn to her wealth of rose-copper hair pinned atop her head.

"Oh, Ty. I . . ." A flush of color spread high on her cheeks. "I don't know how you did it, or what promises you had to make, but . . ." She launched herself into his arms. "Thank you."

His breath caught in his chest. He adored the way she felt against him, the way they fit so perfectly together, magnets pulled home.

"You're very welcome."

He should set her away from him. Anyone could see them.

Even knowing this, he pulled her closer and held her against him for longer than was wise. He felt a tremor run through her, and his hold tightened even more.

This was bad. Ty knew it deep in his soul. He was going to hurt this woman. He hurt everyone he cared about eventually.

"Thank you," she whispered again. With her cheek pressed against his shirt, her words were muffled yet clear.

Ty had performed countless surgeries and never once received this sort of gratitude. There was a lesson here, one his brain couldn't quite capture. Charmed out of his wits, he held Katie a bit tighter, wanting this moment never to end.

"Oh, for God's sake." A young, exasperated voice came from somewhere behind Katie. "Can we please move this touching display inside before someone sees you two?"

The irony that the voice of propriety came from Shannon O'Connor was not lost on Ty. With a trace of amusement making his heart light, he set Katie away from him and prepared to say his goodbyes. He had no business being in the middle of this family reunion. He'd facilitated, and now his job was done. Katie would want time alone with her sister.

"I'll leave you to—"

"No, Ty. Don't go yet." Katie clutched at his hand. "Please. Come inside with us."

Giving him no chance to argue, she tugged on his hand, easily guiding him forward.

"I want to hear every detail of how you managed to free my sister from her confinement. I can't imagine what you had to do." She barely paused for breath as she dragged him into the apartment. "You must tell me everything."

As her rapid chatter flowed over him, something inside Ty released. It was like this whenever he was in Katie's presence. He became a different man, wanting to keep this woman all to himself and damn the consequences.

As Ty crossed the threshold, hand clasped with Katie's, he felt an inexplicable flourish of warmth, a renewed happiness similar to what he'd experienced on the ferryboat yesterday.

He had a consuming desire to be more than just Katie's friend. It was an impossible wish, one that would never come to fruition. She was sweet and innocent, and he would destroy all that made her special if she let him in her heart.

Getting a bit ahead of yourself, Dr. Brentwood?

He nearly laughed at himself. But his chest was too tight, and something in him was changing. He couldn't keep up.

Once inside, Katie let go of Ty's hand and reached around him to shut the door with a soft snick. He glanced around. Despite the peeling wallpaper and shabby furniture, he felt a sense of homecoming spread through him. Love resided in this tiny home.

Taking a moment to calm his racing thoughts, he set Shannon's suitcase down on the floor and took a more detailed look around the apartment.

Since there was no foyer to speak of, he stood in the cramped main living area. Craning his neck to peer around a rickety, trifold room divider, he took in the kitchen, nothing more than a stove, a table, and three straight-backed chairs. The two other rooms, one on his left, the other on his right, he assumed were bedrooms.

Ty couldn't imagine four women living in this tiny space. In truth, he couldn't imagine *two* women living here.

"Now that you're here"—Katie took her sister's hands in hers—"let's have a good look at you."

Shannon remained still under her sister's inspection.

"You seem quite healthy."

Shannon gave her a watery smile.

"You're positively glowing." Katie glanced at Ty, her brows knit together. "I can't imagine why she was detained."

Ty felt his lips twist at a sardonic angle. "Can't you?"

The woman, after all, had assisted a midwife. She'd told him the story yesterday evening as they'd walked from the docks.

Katie's scowl deepened. She let go of her sister's hands and gave her another thorough assessment. She focused on Shannon's midsection for several beats, then returned her attention to the girl's face.

For her part, Shannon held steady under her sister's scrutiny, her eyes locked on a spot just over Katie's right shoulder. She didn't move, barely breathed, but it was only a matter of time before the truth was revealed.

Ty saw the exact moment understanding dawned. Katie whipped her head toward him, back to her sister, back to him. Cocking his head at a sympathetic angle, he gave her an apologetic grimace.

She opened her mouth, but the sound of shuffling feet heralded the entrance of an older woman.

This was, Ty concluded, Katie's aunt. He took in the pucker of her forehead, the twitching fingers at her waist. Her grayish skin, combined with the thin, brittle hair and pinched mouth gave the appearance of chronic illness. Weakened system, Ty decided, probably the lasting effects of a virus or bacterial disease.

"I thought I heard voices. Oh!" The older woman caught sight of Shannon, and her hand flew to her heart. "My sweet baby girl. I can't tell you how worried we've all been."

Shannon, who'd grown passive ever since Katie had begun her inspection, finally showed some emotion again, in the form of a shaken sigh. "I confess I was a bit worried myself."

"Well, you're here now." The older woman opened her arms in quiet invitation. The girl rushed to her aunt, her eyes bright with fresh, happy tears.

She glanced at Ty over the older woman's shoulder. Her green eyes regarded him with quiet resignation, as if she'd accepted that she couldn't hide her secret from her family much longer. He gave her a nod of encouragement.

After only a slight hesitation, Shannon seemed to give herself up to the emotions of the moment and really let go, sobbing all over her aunt.

The scene was quite poignant, and, once again, Ty felt he didn't belong in the middle of this intimate reunion.

The older woman drew back and placed a hand on Shannon's cheek. "I'll make us some tea, and you'll tell me all about your horrible ordeal. It would appear the women in our family can't make it through the registration process without a few bumps along the way."

"It wasn't too terrible," Shannon admitted. "I was only confined for a day and a half, though it could have been much longer. I have Dr. Brentwood to thank for my newfound independence."

She gave Ty a lovely smile. In that moment, she looked very much like her sister.

The older woman tracked the younger's gaze. Her face crumbled into a frown.

Katie made the introductions. "Aunt Jane, this is Dr. Titus Brentwood. Ty, this is my aunt, Jane Sullivan."

"So," Jane said, hands on hips. "You are the man I've heard so much about."

Ty was silent with surprise. That he'd been a topic of conversation in this home was so unexpected that he couldn't help but wonder what was said.

By the twinkle in the older woman's eyes, he assumed Katie had been complimentary. Something like dread settled in his gut as he waited for the older woman to continue. She clearly had much more to say.

"It would seem, my dear boy"—she came to stand before him, her hand lifting to pat his cheek in a motherly fashion—"you are my family's own personal savior."

Savior. Ty did not like the word.

Or perhaps he liked it too much.

Savior. He rolled the choice of phrase around in his mind. This wasn't the first time he'd been described in such lofty terms. The society papers had been full of praise: *Dr. Titus Brentwood saves lives by executing dangerous surgical procedures.*

They'd been wrong about him. Ty was no savior.

Jane took his hands, the ones that had killed instead of healed, and smiled up at him with happy tears brimming in her eyes. "I owe you my sincere gratitude."

He pulled his hands away. He could not allow this kind woman to misunderstand the situation. "I merely did what any man would do, given the circumstances."

"We both know that isn't true."

Ty shifted, uncomfortable under this woman's appreciative smile. Even at the height of his success, he hadn't liked being praised, at least not in person. It was one thing to read accolades in newspapers and journals, quite another to receive verbal praise.

Accomplishing something no one else could, that had been the reward Ty sought. The drive to be immortalized in print and spoken of in awe among New York's finest homes because he was the best of the best, that had been his desire. And his downfall.

"I must go," he said, wishing to be anywhere but in this house with these smiling, grateful women.

"I thought you might stay for a cup of tea," Jane said.

Ty raked a hand through his hair with exaggerated roughness. "I'm afraid that I have another engagement this evening."

Not entirely true, but not a complete fabrication either. Shannon's discharge had taken longer than he'd expected, requiring a bit of finesse on his part and a lot of signatures on official documents. All of which had kept him away from the clinic all day.

The older woman was not to be discouraged. "I cannot persuade you to stay even for one cup?"

Ty held firm. "I'm sorry, no."

"Very well. You will come another time?"

He forced a light, easy laugh. "You may count on it."

Smiling now, she turned to her niece. "Katie, dear, why don't you see our guest out while Shannon and I make tea?"

"Of course."

Katie moved toward him while the other two women began the short trek to the kitchen. They were nearly there when Shannon broke away from her aunt and rushed back to stand before Ty.

Worrying her bottom lip between her teeth, she shifted from one foot to another. He raised a questioning eyebrow.

Impulsively, the girl stepped forward and drove her face against his chest. Her arms came around his waist, and then, after a moment of hesitation, she tightened her hold and actually clung to him.

"Thank you," she mumbled into his chest. "You have no idea what your lack of censure means to me."

It had never occurred to Ty to judge this young woman. He'd committed his own list of offenses out of pride. Whereas Shannon's actions, regardless of the unintended consequences, had been prompted by love. How could Ty find fault in that?

He gave her a comforting squeeze. "You're going to be fine."

"I will be," she agreed, keeping her voice low enough for only Ty to hear. "When Liam arrives."

Not if, but when.

Such youthful confidence. Such utter faith in another. Over the girl's head, he glanced at Katie, who was knuckling a stream of tears away from her cheek.

Catching his eyes on her, she smiled. That smile, he thought, so full of certainty. Certainty in him, in his abilities. That silent vote of confidence was more potent than any sip of brandy. This woman was intoxicating, lovely, and he wanted to see her again.

It would be better for them both if he didn't.

"Goodbye, Dr. Brentwood."

He glanced at the younger of the two O'Connor women and easily found his smile. "Take care of yourself, Shannon."

"I will." She approached her sister, said something low, then joined her aunt in the kitchen.

Ty kept his gaze trained on Katie, her gratitude still strong on her face as she escorted him out of the apartment and into the empty hallway. She left the door slightly ajar.

Katie clearly trusted him enough to linger in the darkened corridor. But she didn't understand who he was, who he *really* was. No, she saw him through the filter of what he'd done for her sister. He may have helped Shannon today, but he'd hurt people in the past and could never outrun what he'd done. Not with good works. Not with brandy. And not because a good woman like Katie O'Connor believed in him.

That didn't mean he wouldn't continue atoning for his sins. It was only in reconnecting with Katie O'Connor that he realized how far he still had to go toward redemption. Long days of serving the poor had taught him restraint, and he thought he'd conquered the worst of his selfish desires.

But no.

Case in point, he was moving toward Katie, stopping at a spot close enough to smell her clean, flowery scent, with a host of unsuitable thoughts battling his resolve.

Her aunt had called him a savior. Why did Ty get the feeling that Katie was the savior? His savior.

He wanted to kiss her. He wanted to escape into the sanctuary of her arms. But she deserved better. Whatever sliver of goodness that might have been in him had been destroyed in a matter of minutes.

"Ty." Katie reached out her hand.

The silent call was too much to resist. Helplessly, he pressed his palm to hers and drew her close. He inhaled the scent of laundry soap and lavender.

With his free hand, he lightly fingered a tendril of hair hanging low over her forehead and smoothed it into place behind her ear. He recalled the last time he'd done that, on the ferryboat, and found himself smiling.

Katie smiled back. "What you did for my sister, oh, Ty, it was too much."

Not nearly enough, he wanted to argue.

"I cannot find the words to thank you properly."

"You've already said them."

He could stay, under the pretense of giving Katie instructions for her sister's care. But the woman had assisted a midwife. She would know what to do without his help.

There was only one thing left to do. Let her go.

Let her go.

The command was both a literal order and a figurative one. He continued holding on to her hand.

"What you did for my sister—"

"I didn't do it for your sister." He placed a fingertip beneath her chin and eased her head back. "I did it for you."

The wonder in her eyes was a living, breathing thing. A pang of tenderness clutched in the center of his chest, pounding like an ache.

He wanted to drag Katie into his arms, to hold on to her and feel her flush against him. He liked her scent; the soft floral mix soothed him.

So calming, this woman before him. And despite his best efforts to remain unmoved, a sense of homecoming washed over him once again. He leaned forward, not sure why. Well, yes, actually, he knew why.

He managed to stop his pursuit.

Katie took up the gauntlet he hadn't known he'd set at her feet. Eyes still locked with his, she took a minuscule step toward him.

They were nearly touching now, and Ty didn't have it in him to move back. He was aware they stood alone in the hallway, with no eyes watching them.

"Tell me what I can do to repay you for your kindness."

"I want nothing from you."

Not precisely true. He wanted things from her he had no right claiming.

Let her go.

He slowly lifted his hands in the air, palms facing her in the universal show of surrender. Looking everywhere but at Katie, he put distance between them in a rush of movement.

She refused to give him the space he required. Much as her sister had done, she swooped forward and wrapped him in a tight embrace. "You are a dear, dear man," she whispered. "I'm honored to know you."

Caught in a whirlwind of emotion, Ty closed his eyes.

"So very honored," she reiterated, then shifted her stance, the move drawing her lips to his bare throat. The delicate feel of her breath reminded him of mist sweeping over moonlight. His resistance crumbled.

Ty knotted his hand in a loose fist in her hair. The sounds of Shannon and her aunt speaking to one another inside the apartment were far away, a world away. A lifetime away.

"Katie." He buried his face in her hair, reveling in the silky feel against his cheek.

She lifted her head to stare into his eyes. The soft glow of the dim hallway lighting defined the angles of her face, the fullness of her lips.

Her pull was too much.

Ty felt his head lowering. Lowering. Lowering still. Just a hair more, and her sooty lashes fluttered closed.

He was doomed. Yet what a lovely way to go, he thought, and went down without a fight.

Chapter Twelve

Katie tensed as Ty's mouth closed over hers. She'd expected him to kiss her. She had not expected him to be so gentle. He made no demands, nor did he give her any silent promises. He was almost tentative in his approach, the crush of his lips as light as silk rubbing over satin.

Not sure what else to do, Katie answered with cautious pressure. A rush of confused pleasure flooded her. This was her first kiss, and her mind was in a jumble of conflicting messages.

Push him away. Pull him closer.

Stop.

Keep going.

Her stomach went light. Her head grew dizzy. Something like hunger swept through her, an empty, gnawing feeling that wasn't altogether terrible. She should be scandalized, kissing a man in the shadowed corridor. She felt emboldened.

As the pressure of Ty's lips became more urgent, a heady, delicious feeling took hold of Katie, one that resembled falling.

She clutched his shoulders. It was either hold on or slump into a heap of quivering sensation at his feet.

She'd never thought kissing could feel like this: exciting, a little frightening, and so very, very wonderful. The press of Ty's lips became stronger still, more earnest. He was offering a portion of himself to her, asking her to heal him, as if she were the balm his hurting soul needed.

She was thinking too hard. Who needed any of this to make sense? Katie was tired of everything making sense.

Feeling was all that mattered.

She lost herself in sensation.

Wanting more, she slid her arms around Ty's neck, enjoying the feel of hard muscle encased in a perfectly tailored wool suit, if a bit frayed at the edges. She'd never been this close to a man.

"Ty," she whispered against his mouth.

He abruptly pulled away.

Thrown off balance, Katie staggered toward him. He reached out and steadied her. Hands still on her shoulders, he looked as mystified as she felt, his gaze traveling slowly over her face, not pitying, not censorious, more of an appraisal, as if he sought an answer to some unknown question. Any words Katie had intended to say vanished under the intense scrutiny.

At last, she found her voice. "I have my balance now."

His hands dropped away, and he broke his silence only after briefly clearing his throat. "I'm sorry. I should never have kissed you, mere feet away from your aunt and sister. It was inappropriate and—"

"No, Ty. Please. Don't." A wild rush of heat raced across her cheeks. All her skin had become too tight for her body. "Don't apologize."

"I took advantage of your gratitude."

Feigning to relax her posture, Katie met his gaze and, in all seriousness, said, "I rather thought it was I who took advantage of you."

His expression changed in the length of a breath. He looked stunned and slightly taken aback by her outrageous declaration.

Then, eyes twinkling, he gave in to his humor with a low rumbling chuckle. What a wonderful laugh he had. The sound was mesmerizing. Deep, throaty, and terribly masculine.

"You continually surprise me, Katie O'Connor. And before your scowl digs any deeper, I meant that as a compliment."

Bottom lip caught between her teeth, Katie looked away. Desperate to steer the conversation away from herself, she said, "I know I've said this already, several times, in fact, but thank you, Ty. Thank you for rescuing my sister. Seriously, thank you."

"Once was enough, sweetheart."

Sweetheart. Did he know how the endearment filled her with confusion? There was joy and a dull ache in her heart that she couldn't find the right words to describe. Best she didn't try. Best to keep the focus on her sister. "Will you tell me how you managed to get Shannon off the island?"

He seemed to consider his answer. "I performed my own exam and discovered she'd been misdiagnosed. She wasn't sick after all. At least, not in the way the previous doctor assumed."

How circumspect he was being. "You simply declared her healthy and they let her go?"

"It was a bit more complicated than that."

"How complicated?"

He lifted a shoulder, dropped it again. "I had to call in a few favors."

"It was probably more than a few. Will there be any repercussions?"

Up went the shoulder again. "Nothing I can't handle."

Staring into Ty's face, Katie saw no trace of concern or self-congratulation. Either he didn't understand the depths of her gratitude or he was just that altruistic. Was giving of himself such a part of his nature that something as monumental as freeing a woman from detainment—and possible deportation—was just another act of kindness for him?

Nothing was ever that simple, and no one was ever that good. Something else had driven Ty's actions today. Katie wasn't selfish enough to think it was solely because he liked her.

She would probably never know the full truth. Still, he'd acted on her behalf, and for that she was genuinely appreciative.

Although she had a pretty good idea what had caused her sister's symptoms, she still found herself asking, "Was Shannon seasick?" *Oh, please, let it be so.* "Was that the explanation for her detainment?"

"She was not seasick, as I predict you have already deduced on your own."

One sentence. That was all it took for Katie to accept the truth. Well, that and the look in Ty's eyes. Not sympathy or even pity, but a sort of certainty that came from extensive medical training.

When she continued staring at him, he asked in a quiet voice, "Shall I tell you what ails your sister?"

"There's no need. She's pregnant." Her sister, her *baby* sister, was carrying a man's child, and Katie couldn't feel anything but guilt, so raw and palpable it ate away at her composure. "This is all my fault."

She was surprised at the calmness of her tone, when all she wanted to do was howl in agony.

"You weren't the one who put the child in her belly."

Ignoring the remark, she shook her head in defeat. "I should have never left her in Ireland."

"It's not your fault."

Oh, but it was. "If I had been there, I could have protected her from making this mistake. How she must hate me for leaving her alone and vulnerable, open to a man's nefarious advances. What have I done?"

Katie was pulled back into Ty's arms again. She struggled and shoved against him, but he held on tight. When he gently guided her head to his shoulder, the fight left her, and she gripped his shirt in her fists.

"Don't do this to yourself." He set her slightly away from him. "I saw no signs of resentment on your sister's part, hidden or otherwise. She doesn't blame you."

"I blame myself."

"Do you think your presence would have stopped her from forming a tenderness for the young man?"

"Yes. No." She sighed. "Perhaps. Maybe." She sighed again. "I don't know." She gave a hopeless little laugh. "I don't know anything anymore. I don't even know the boy's name."

"It's Liam. Liam Gallagher." Shannon's voice, coming from inside the apartment, was pitched at a dreamy, girlish level.

Katie swung open the door and gaped at her sister. "The father of your child is Liam. *Liam Gallagher?*"

"That's what I said."

Katie felt her throat thicken with dread at the defiant gleam in her sister's eyes. Shannon had never been defiant before. Apparently, the girl had changed. No, not a girl. A woman. A woman carrying Liam Gallagher's child.

Not Liam. Anyone but him.

It was too terrible to contemplate. Shannon had not, as Katie hoped, become involved with a ruddy-faced boy her same age. That would have been bad enough. But no. Oh, no, Shannon had to fall for a full-grown man who was several years older than she was.

It was no secret Liam liked women. And they liked him.

Of course women liked him. He was charming, handsome as sin, a silver-tongued rogue with years of experience in winning women's hearts. Katie couldn't remember a time when the man wasn't surrounded by a handful of pretty girls vying for his attention.

What had Shannon been thinking, getting involved with such a notorious flirt?

"Oh, Shannon." She couldn't keep the disappointment out of her voice. "Of all the men you could have fallen for, why him?"

A mutinous expression crossed her sister's features, reminiscent of Bridget's face whenever they discussed her job in the Bowery. "Don't you dare judge me, Katie O'Connor."

"I wasn't judging you." *Very much.* "I was judging him."

How could she not, under the circumstances? Liam was older, presumably wiser, but he'd knowingly taken advantage of a sweet, innocent girl at least six years his junior.

"I see you have much to discuss with your sister." Ty's voice came from somewhere behind Katie. "I'll leave you to it."

She barely had time to swivel her head in his direction before he was gone.

Ty had left the apartment so abruptly she hadn't had the chance to say a proper goodbye. Katie realized with a wave of chagrin that she would probably never see him again. Her last image of the man would be him staring into her eyes with a rueful frown.

A burst of longing shot through her, reminding her how desperately she wanted a husband and children of her own. She secretly craved security and love, and a happy, stable relationship. They would be a family, a real one, where everyone felt loved and special in their own right.

If Katie closed her eyes, she could almost see herself sitting with Ty by a fire he'd built, a laughing toddler bouncing on his knee.

She was being ridiculous, fanciful. Nothing would come of wishing for such a dream with a man like Ty. With *any* man, for that matter.

Katie's life had never been hers, not completely, certainly less so now that her aunt was too ill to work a regular job and her cousin's endeavor put her in harm's way on a daily basis.

Then there was Shannon. Katie's sister was carrying Liam Gallagher's child. Her mind kept circling back to Liam and how the man was nowhere in sight to do his duty.

That, Katie thought as she dropped her gaze to Shannon's midsection, was what came from falling in love.

* * *

For the next hour, Katie found herself biding her time while Aunt Jane insisted on welcoming Shannon to America over a cup of tea. Katie kept silent for most of the conversation, taking the opportunity to pull together what she would say when she and Shannon were alone.

In silent agreement, they didn't tell Aunt Jane about the baby. There would be time for that later.

Katie endured not one but two cups of tepid tea while Shannon regaled their aunt with gossip from their village. In turn, Jane told her niece about a time during her early days in America when Bridget had mistaken a local policeman for a cowboy. "She kept asking him to say howdy, which he flatly refused to do."

Listening with only half an ear, Katie studied the two women. Both looked tired, Aunt Jane more so than Shannon.

One of Katie's goals was to relieve her aunt's burdens. She wasn't sure she was succeeding, and that bruised her heart. She silently vowed to do better. Getting her out of the tenement house with its stale air and crowded conditions was her first priority. Shannon's arrival would help with that, at least. The girl was with child, not ill. She should be able to work during most of her pregnancy.

Aunt Jane stood. Smiling wanly, she placed a hand on Shannon's shoulder, the other on Katie's. "I'm so happy to have my sister's girls with me, together, at last." The dull light in the kitchen emphasized the purple shadows beneath her eyes. "Maggie would be pleased to know you are with me here in America."

The words had a bittersweet effect on Katie. To her way of thinking, the move to this country was supposed to have been the beginning of a new life, a fresh start for her and her sister.

At least she and Shannon had a place to live. And they had family, the most precious commodity of all.

Gaining her own feet, Katie pulled her aunt into a gentle hug. "I know I've said this countless times since you opened your home to me, and now Shannon, but I'm going to say it again. You are a blessing, Aunt Jane, a true and wonderful blessing."

"You, my sweet girl, are the blessing," the older woman whispered in her ear. "You do too much, and I pray one day you will receive your just reward."

"What a lovely thing to say."

Stepping back, Aunt Jane swiped at her eyes. "You look so much like your mother. I miss her every day."

"I miss her, too." Katie reached out to squeeze her aunt's hand with gentle pressure. "We lost her too soon."

"Oh, aye, that we did." Eyes misty, Aunt Jane busied herself saying good night to Shannon. "There, now. We'll talk more in the morning."

"I'd like that very much. I have so much more to tell you."

"I look forward to hearing every word."

Katie and Shannon fell silent as the older woman left the room.

Shannon kept her gaze averted, suddenly engrossed in the contents of her teacup. When she continued looking down at the smooth amber liquid, Katie decided the tension in the air wasn't going away.

"I'd like to hear about your"—she searched for the proper word—"relationship with Liam."

Shannon studied the teacup as if committing the flowery pattern to memory. "What do you want to know?"

"How did you two meet?"

She lifted her head. "He came into the apothecary shop."

Though her eyes brightened for a moment, Shannon quickly fell back into her somber mood. There were secrets in the girl's gaze, and a strange sort of hollowness that Katie recognized. She'd seen that same look in their mother's eyes after the death of her husband.

Katie drew in a shaky breath, forced down the suspicion that Shannon was hiding something, and reached for her sister's hand. "I'm sorry things didn't work out between you and Liam."

"But they did work out." Shannon yanked her hand free. "We are engaged."

"And yet, you traveled to America alone." Katie gentled her tone. "That can't mean anything good."

"You're reading too much into his absence." Shannon's expression turned thunderous. "I will ask you to stop making assumptions before you hear the entire story."

It was a reasonable demand, but Katie hated the misery she saw in her sister's eyes. "All right, tell me. Why isn't Liam with you?"

"He missed the boat. And before you say something to malign his character, it was an accident."

Katie very much doubted that. "Are you absolutely certain Liam didn't miss the boat on purpose?"

Shannon shook her head. Katie had no idea whether it was in direct response to the question or because she was greatly disappointed Katie had dared to ask it. She hated upsetting her sister like this.

"You must have wondered during the crossing."

"Not once." Her voice hitched ever so slightly. "Liam would never abandon me willingly."

Katie's heart ached for her sister. "You seem certain. Help me to understand what happened."

"Oh, Katie. You can't know how awful it was to see him racing up and down the docks, shouting out my name. The devastation on his face matched what I felt deep in my soul. Liam promised to catch another ship as soon as he could."

The earnestness in the girl's manner told its own story. Shannon believed every word she spoke.

"How will Liam find you once he arrives in America?"

"He has this address. He's probably already on his way as we speak. I trust we will be reunited soon."

"You have put a lot of faith in a man who's never shown the least bit of interest in—"

Shannon banged her fist on the table, the unexpected anger rendering Katie speechless. "Why can't you accept my word that Liam is a good man?"

It was a fair question. "Because sometimes the people we believe in most are the ones who let us down."

"Liam will never let me down."

And yet, he had already done just that. "He is twenty-four years old, Shannon. The age difference alone gives me cause for concern."

"Our mother was ten years younger than our father."

Exactly. "Look how that turned out."

"Our parents' marriage was the stuff of legend in our village."

Was that how Shannon saw it, as some sort of fairy tale come to life? Katie refused to concede the point. "Our mother was too dependent on our father. She loved him too much."

"There is no such thing as loving too much." The mutinous expression was back on Shannon's face. "What our parents shared was good and true and . . . and . . . romantic."

Katie blinked in mild horror. Shannon couldn't possibly think their mother's blind devotion to their father was *romantic*? Not when that devotion had killed her.

"I always dreamed of finding a love like theirs. And I have." Shannon sighed and her eyes went dreamy. "With Liam."

"Oh, Shannon." Katie drew in a shuddering breath and did her best to make her face impassive. "What if you're wrong? What if he fails to live up to this image you have of him in your mind?"

"He won't fail me."

A silent clash of wills began in earnest between them. Shannon leaned across the table until they were practically nose to nose. Refusing to back down, Katie held her sister's gaze.

"I find your attitude toward the man I love sufficiently hypocritical." Shannon sat back, looking quite satisfied with herself. "Especially considering your relationship with Dr. Brentwood."

Katie felt an unpleasant rush of guilt as Shannon's words sank in. "Ty is a friend."

"Right, friends. Except friends don't kiss the way he kissed you."

"How did you know about—" Katie shook her head. "Never mind. It doesn't matter. What matters is that you're assigning more meaning to a kiss that, in all likelihood, was nothing more than a tender, and very final, goodbye."

Shannon smirked, youth shining in her eyes. "That kiss looked more like hello to me."

"I don't like what you're implying. Ty is a gentleman."

"And Liam isn't?"

"I didn't say that." *Out loud.*

Sniffing indelicately, Shannon shoved away from the table, the move so quick the legs of the chair scraped out a groaning protest. "Your judgmental attitude speaks loudly enough."

Well, when she put it that way. "One of us is with child and one of us is not," Katie pointed out. "I think the facts speak for themselves."

"You might be older, but you don't get to control this situation, Katie. Not this time."

Katie looked directly at her sister's stomach, opened her mouth to speak, then clamped her lips shut. Flinging accusations wasn't the answer. She wasn't really angry with Shannon.

Liam Gallagher, however, had earned Katie's fury.

The situation must seem like a nightmare to her sister. Shannon loved Liam, and she clearly thought he loved her in return. No matter how it had happened, she'd been separated from him in a very frightening manner.

"I know how scared and alone you must feel," Katie said softly, the sorrow she felt sincere. "And here I am making matters worse. I don't mean to condemn you."

"But you're doing just that. You're condemning me because I fell in love. You're jealous." Her voice was filled with resentment, but her face . . . it paled to almost white. "You wish Liam had fallen in love with you instead of me."

Stricken by the venom in her sister's voice, Katie rose and made her way to the other side of the table. She laid a hand on the girl's head.

"You're wrong. I don't want your man." She stroked the silky curls as she had when seven-year-old Shannon had fallen out of a tree. "Try to understand, little sister. Everything I have done has been to protect you."

"I don't need your kind of protection."

Katie had no ready argument. Shannon was right. She hadn't protected her sister. For all intents and purposes, she'd abandoned her. Liam wasn't the only guilty party.

"You came to America without me," Shannon accused.

"I left you with family."

Shannon snorted. "You could have waited until we had the money for both of us to travel together. But no, you had some big delusion in your head that if you arrived first, you would be able to send for me right away. In reality, it took you three times longer than you planned."

Shannon was right, about everything. Katie had been naïve and impatient and, most of all, terribly selfish. Her plan had seemed so simple, so doable. In reality, she'd left her sister vulnerable, in the care of an uncle who saw her as nothing more than another mouth to feed.

Katie drew in a slow breath of air, remembering Shannon's face when she'd said that final goodbye. The choices Katie had made, no matter how sound they'd seemed at the time, had harmed her sister in ways that she could never take back.

"Do you have any idea how lonely I was after you left?" Shannon's voice was small, her gaze lowered.

"I thought I was making the right decision for us both."

Shannon's head came up. Raw pain swam in a pair of light green eyes so like her own. "What do you think about your decision now?"

"I should have never left you behind."

"Well, you did." Spite returned to her voice. "Now you don't get to be self-righteous or reproachful about what occurred in your absence."

"I'm sorry." Katie heaved a sigh and returned to her chair. "You have every right to resent me."

"I don't resent you." Shannon reached across the table and squeezed her hand. "I have no regrets about what happened with Liam. I love him, Katie. And he loves me. He will come to America. Wait and see, he's going to prove you wrong."

"I hope that he does." Katie felt humbled by her sister's certainty. Shannon was so sure of her man, so completely full of faith in him. Even in her condition, she was still sweet and untouched by the terrible realities of life . . .

Surely, Katie wasn't envious of her own sister, as Shannon had claimed? She clicked her tongue, impatient with herself. "Will you tell me about the man you fell in love with?"

Chapter Thirteen

In the calm after the emotional storm, Shannon settled back in her chair. This was her chance to convince Katie that Liam was a good and honest man.

She would not waste the opportunity.

In a halting tone, she told Katie how she and Liam had met, about their romantic whirlwind courtship and his mother's disapproval when he'd told her he planned to marry Shannon. She ended the story with their plan to run away to America and the series of events that had led to her boarding the ship ahead of him.

To her credit, her sister listened without interrupting. It was a good sign, one that had given Shannon the confidence to keep continuing with her tale.

"That must have been dreadful for you."

Shannon didn't know what she heard in her sister's voice. Not condemnation, precisely, but not encouragement either. Katie was withholding judgment until she heard the entire story.

That would have to be good enough.

"Liam will find me, and we'll get married as planned." Shannon felt the need to reiterate that point, as much for herself as for Katie.

"Shannon, look at me."

Katie's hand moved in her direction. Not wanting her sister's touch, not even on her sleeve, Shannon shifted out of reach.

Drawing back, Katie sighed. "I don't want to scare you, but there are hundreds of thousands of people living in this city, many of them on this very block."

"Surely, you're exaggerating."

"For an entire year, Ty and I have been living and working blocks away from one another, and our paths have never crossed. Not even once."

"Liam will find me," Shannon whispered with less force than before. Even to her own ears, her voice came out garbled and full of the first strains of doubt. "He has the address to this building."

"Shannon." Katie reached for her again. This time, the move was too quick, lightning fast, and Shannon was caught. Her fingers were linked together with her sister's, cementing her to the spot. "You seem confident he'll board another ship soon. But what if he doesn't?"

Ignoring the twinge of doubt, Shannon smiled widely. "He will. He said he would."

After a short pause, Katie seemed to switch tactics. "If you are so certain he loves you—"

"He does."

"Then why didn't he marry you before you and he, before you, that is, before you"—Katie glanced at Shannon's stomach, looked quickly away—"were intimate?"

"It's all Mrs. Gallagher's fault. Liam's mother didn't approve of me. She said I was too young to know my own mind." Shannon let out a rough breath. "But she was wrong. I knew then, as I do now, exactly what I want, and who."

"Liam should have married you, especially once he knew you were carrying his child."

"He doesn't know."

Katie raised her eyebrows. "You didn't tell him?"

"I didn't know myself until Dr. Brentwood informed me. Isn't it wonderful?" She pressed a hand to her stomach and sighed dreamily. "I'm going to have Liam's baby."

Katie's brows went higher. "You're an unmarried girl of eighteen, carrying the child of a man who didn't have the decency to marry you before he took advantage of your innocence."

Shannon felt her cheeks heat at her sister's even tone. The admonition seemed so much worse when spoken in such a matter-of-fact manner. She couldn't fault Katie's concern. She knew her sister loved her. But she was wrong about Liam. "The situation isn't as dire or as scandalous as you're making out."

"Shannon—"

"Liam and I will marry as soon as he makes his way to America."

"You mean, *if* he makes it to America."

"Of course he'll make it. He made a promise, and he always keeps his promises. It's what I love most about him." Shannon didn't wear his ring yet, but she had the locket he'd given her when pledging his love to her. She wanted to reach for the piece of jewelry tucked beneath her dress, but feared the gesture would lead to questions she wasn't up to answering.

Some things were private between a man and a woman.

Katie made an impatient sound. "Once again, I feel the need to caution you."

"You've cautioned me enough for one night."

"There is no guarantee he'll make it into the country. The registration process is ruthless. You know this, Shannon. Or are you forgetting your own experience of the past two days?"

As much as she wanted to shy away from the memory, her sister's words brought forth an image of the scowling immigration official. "Liam is strong and healthy. He'll make it through the medical inspection."

"I don't doubt that." Katie softened her voice, but her resolve remained in the way she leaned forward and commanded Shannon's gaze with an unbending look. "But he could be denied entry for a dozen other reasons."

"Such as?"

Katie lifted her hand and began ticking off the list on her fingers. "He could be pronounced mentally unfit. Or the inspectors could decide they don't like his looks and deem him a potential public charge. He could be—"

"You've made your point."

"Have I?"

"Yes."

Apparently, Katie wasn't through. "He could fail to answer the inspector's questions satisfactorily and be deported on the spot. He could be harmed on the journey over."

"Why are you saying these terrible things? What's happened to my sister? When did you become so cynical?"

Katie snatched in a sharp breath. "I like to think I've become less naïve."

"You used to always look on the bright side. Truth be told, you were rather annoying with your sunny disposition. I miss that sister."

Something sad came and went in Katie's eyes. "You must be realistic. As much as you want to believe Liam will arrive soon, I urge you to prepare for the worst."

Shannon gnawed on her bottom lip, not sure what to say to that. *Prepare for the worst.* As the words slowly sank in, time seemed to stop. Her stomach performed a fast, painful roll, and she thought she might be sick. No matter how many breaths she took, she couldn't seem to wrestle her thoughts into submission.

It was all Katie's fault, putting these doubts in her head. "You don't understand what it is to fall in love. How much it changes you."

"Actually, I do understand, all too well. I saw firsthand what love did to our mother."

Apparently, Katie's memory of their parents' marriage was vastly different from her own. At the moment, Shannon simply didn't have the energy to continue arguing with her sister. The tension between them, combined with fatigue, left her numb. She tried to stand, but her knees weakened, and she had to reach out for balance.

As if on cue, a wave of queasiness washed over her. She felt the color drain from her face and had to swallow several times to keep from heaving.

"I've got you." Katie's arm wrapped around Shannon's waist. How had she moved so fast? "Lean on me. Good. Now, breathe slowly. That's it. Nice and measured. The queasiness will soon pass."

"I . . . I know." Her voice was just a whisper as she cringed at the exhaustion consuming her. She would soon have a baby to care for. She must be strong.

Even as the thought swam in Shannon's brain, Katie pulled her close in silent sympathy. Shannon could not stop the flood of tears that seemed to come and go as randomly as her moods.

Katie tightened her hold around her waist, reminiscent of the caring older sister Shannon remembered.

"You need rest." The sympathy in the words was from another time, when Katie took care of Shannon's every need. "Let's get you into bed."

"I'm so tired," she admitted hoarsely. Yet weariness hadn't stolen her will to fight. Out of pride, she attempted to stand on her own, only to promptly stumble again. An overwhelming sense of lethargy crept over her. "I'm not sure I can make it on my own."

"Together, then." After brushing gently at her tearstained cheeks, Katie wedged in beneath Shannon's arm to support the bulk of her weight. "We don't have very far to go, only a few dozen steps. Think you can manage that?"

"Of course."

"Good girl."

Shannon found herself staring into the familiar eyes of her loving, protective sister. "I've missed you, Katie."

"I've missed you, too. Now"—she adjusted her stance—"let's get you to bed. Shall we?"

"Let's." To Shannon's relief, they hobbled out of the kitchen as a single unit.

Chapter Fourteen

For the next couple of weeks or so, life fell into a pattern. Katie didn't see Ty again. Though tempted to stop by his clinic to express her gratitude, she never marshaled the nerve. Her job at the factory, meanwhile, became more demanding. Her own fault.

She'd arrived late to work yet again after she'd stopped to help a little girl who'd fainted on the streets. As before, Katie's supervisor had not been happy and continued to keep a hard eye on Katie, looking for ways to reprimand her.

Bridget continued her dangerous occupation as a tambourine girl, regardless of Katie's arguments. The tension between Bridget and her mother grew thicker by the day. Aunt Jane would eventually discover her daughter's dishonesty.

Katie wasn't looking forward to the blowup that would follow. At the moment, however, she was more concerned about Shannon, who was no longer the happy girl Katie remembered.

As days turned into weeks with no word from Liam, the girl grew more difficult, more despondent. Her nausea had gotten better, but Katie still worried. Shannon refused to leave the apartment for more than a few minutes at a time, and never ventured farther than the front stoop.

Missing Liam was harming Shannon's health, and nothing Katie said or did seemed to help matters. The girl was suspended in a strange sort of limbo, her mood swinging from hopeful to surly to hopeful again. She never spoke a word against Liam, and her belief in him never wavered.

A part of Katie admired the girl's devotion to her beau. Another part despaired over the lasting effects of such blind loyalty.

Just thinking about Shannon's situation made a growl lodge in her throat. Katie knew she should be sewing instead of worrying about her sister. She couldn't afford to get behind. They needed the extra money, more than ever now that Shannon was with child. Katie wasn't sure how far along her sister was. It was hard to estimate with a first pregnancy, and with Shannon refusing to expound on her relationship with Liam—well, besides the girl's unbending belief that he loved her and would arrive in America any day now—Katie simply couldn't be certain of anything pertaining directly to the baby.

Sew, she ordered herself.

She paced the main living area instead, taking fast, tight circles around the room. Not more than thirty minutes ago, she'd tucked Shannon into her own bed much as she'd done when her sister was still a small child. As she had every evening since arriving in America, the poor girl had fallen into an exhausted sleep almost as soon as her head hit the pillow.

They'd had a rough reunion. At least she and Shannon had come to a tenuous truce, so long as Katie didn't mention Liam's absence, which became harder and harder to do. Shannon attempted to put on a brave face, and her defense of Liam was admirable. But there was sadness in her.

Katie knew she caused much of her sister's despair. But no matter how hard Shannon argued in his favor, Katie didn't trust Liam Gallagher.

She heard the clock on the mantelpiece ticking, the rhythmic sound working in time with her footsteps. The exhausting day had caught up with her. She switched direction.

Stretching her arms overhead, she went to the window and stared blindly at the street below. Her fingertip absently traced the wood-grain sill. Standing here, alone, with only the ticking of the clock to keep her company, she felt the weight of responsibility pressing in on her.

What am I going to do?

It was hard to accept Shannon's situation. Liam represented everything Katie didn't want for her sister. But, oh, how she wanted the man to prove her wrong, for Shannon's sake. If she was honest, there was no denying the joy that lit her sister's eyes whenever she spoke of her fiancé. Deep inside Katie, something quivered, a small twinge of . . . jealousy?

Perhaps. Not for the man himself, but for the ability to love without fear, without the emotion suffocating her. Katie could not lose herself for the sake of one man. Too many people counted on her.

What would it be like to share her burdens, though, to know she wasn't alone in the trials of life?

Sighing, she leaned her head on the window and shut her eyes. A mistake. An image of Ty played across her closed lids. She would never forget the look in his gaze right before he'd kissed her, as if she were the only woman in the world. It seemed hours ago, not weeks.

Katie swallowed around the knot in her throat.

Shoving away from the window, she resumed her pacing. She'd made another two circuits of the room before relenting to her need for sleep. As she curled up on the sofa, she promised herself she would work extra hard tomorrow evening.

She fell into a restless slumber and was barely aware of Bridget's entrance. At the sound of the door clicking shut, she mumbled a warning to her cousin not to wake Shannon.

"I know, I know," Bridget whispered. "Any word from Liam?"

Eyes still shut, Katie frowned. "None."

The cushions dipped slightly as Bridget sat on the edge of the sofa and gave a frustrated sigh. "Should we try to contact him?"

"I've considered it, on more than one occasion." Opening her eyes, Katie pushed herself up to a sitting position. "Unfortunately, I'm not sure where he is, and even if I knew, I'm not sure Shannon would appreciate my interference. Whenever I mention sending a letter to Liam's home in Ireland, she works herself into an agitated fit."

The girl was hiding something about her relationship with him, some detail that made her hesitant to send word about the baby.

When Katie suggested they wait a few more weeks to send a letter, Bridget responded with a noncommittal "Hmmm," then headed off to bed mumbling something about stubborn cousins. Katie didn't ask which cousin she meant. *Probably both of us.*

She woke the next morning with a foggy memory of the conversation and a renewed determination to provide a safe, loving home for Shannon and her unborn baby. Liam or no Liam.

Decision made, she went to check on her sister, found her still fast asleep. And alone. Glancing at Bridget's empty bed, Katie worried her bottom lip between her teeth. As was her custom, her cousin had left before the sun rose. Not because she needed to be at work, but to continue the ruse that she had honest employment. It was anyone's guess what the woman did with her time between leaving the apartment and reporting to work at the gambling den. Bridget had to be exhausted with all her comings and goings.

Bridget thought she was fooling her mother. Aunt Jane was far cagier than that. It was only a matter of time before all Bridget's lies were revealed.

There would be an argument.

But not today. No, not today. And for that, Katie decided to be grateful. An hour later, with Shannon in Aunt Jane's care—and Aunt Jane in Shannon's care—Katie exited the tenement house prepared for another long day at the factory.

She stepped into a wall of noise and feverish activity on the street. Already on shaky ground with her supervisor, she'd left earlier than she did most mornings. Still, she increased her pace.

Her breath fogged in front of her. The air was surprisingly frigid for the mild spring they'd had, and yet also stifling.

There had to be three dozen pushcarts already set up for business. Even at this early hour, the crowds wove through the great mass of peddlers. Vendors offered almost anything for sale on these streets: shoes, boots, hats, tobacco, demijohns, paint, even musical instruments. Fresh vegetables and fruit were also available, as well as potato cakes and other prepared foods.

Katie turned west onto Hester Street, a beehive of sights and sounds. Laundry hung from every available roof overhang, balcony, and protruding ledge, waving in the wind like ghosts. A particularly large pushcart, nearly twice the size of all the others, had three men selling oysters.

Taking in her surroundings, Katie once again marveled at how her route to work took her but a few short blocks away from Ty's clinic on Henry Street.

Had they crossed paths and never known?

It was possible.

A newsboy ran past her and hitched a ride on a carriage, yelling, "Extra! Extra!" He probably hoped to direct attention away from other young boys selling the same stories.

Katie heard the tromp of feet coming from behind her, right before a pack of ragtag boys sped past her with frenzied aggressiveness. A street gang, she realized, and she attempted to step out of the way.

The largest boy, clearly the leader, barreled right into one of the others and, using momentum from the collision, slammed the child to the ground. The other boys—who could've been between only eight and twelve years old—circled the victim, shouting and kicking. The fallen boy curled into a ball, covering his head and eyes.

Someone had to help him. Katie looked around. Despite the panicked wails coming from inside the circle, she seemed to be the only one concerned.

"Stop," she shouted. "You're hurting him!"

The beating continued.

Katie broke into a run.

The boy managed to get to his hands and knees, scrambling unsuccessfully to gain his feet. The leader kicked him in the ribs, again and again and again.

Katie arrived at the edge of the pack, hesitated while she took in the violent scene. She knew better than to insert herself into the middle of a vicious fight. But she couldn't stand by and do nothing.

The leader landed a blow to the boy's midsection. The child howled in pain and collapsed onto his belly. Just as Katie reached forward, sunlight glinted off a bloodstained knife twirling in the leader's right hand.

Forcing herself to remain calm, Katie pivoted in several directions, searching desperately for someone to aid in her quest. "Help," she shouted, furious at the unfair odds. Five against one. "Someone help! A boy has been stabbed!"

The sound of footsteps brought great relief. Two burly men with fierce expressions had answered her call. Katie remembered seeing them manning the pushcart of oysters. Their third partner must have stayed behind.

No longer alone, Katie shoved at the gang of boys. Frantic to get to the child moaning on the ground, she all but lifted one of the smaller kids out of her way.

With the help of the men, she managed to create a small opening in the tight circle.

Her eyes fell on the leader, the dagger still clutched in his hand, blood dripping from the blade, blood from the little boy writhing on the ground.

Katie's outrage sounded in her sharp intake of air. Both boys looked in her direction. She kept her gaze locked on the one holding the knife.

His face was cast in shadows beneath the brim of his floppy hat. Their eyes met briefly, his black and furious, hers surely as angry, and then the two men were stepping in front of her, a third sweeping out to her left. In one voice, they demanded the boy put down the knife.

Eyes feral, he spat out a series of profanities.

"Drop it, now."

"Nobody gets to tell me what to do." He whirled in a fast, tight circle, stabbing blindly into the air. He didn't hit anything or, thank God, anyone. One of the men yelled at him in sputtering Italian, which seemed only to infuriate the boy further.

As if recognizing the odds had shifted out of his favor, he searched frantically for an exit. Turning right. Then left. He spotted a hole in the circle and took off at a dead run. He kept going, legs pumping madly on the ground, screeching out words Katie didn't recognize. More profanities, she assumed. He never broke stride or looked back to see what damage he'd done or if the boy he'd stabbed was even alive.

The rest of his gang scampered after him.

With his compatriots hard on his heels, he jumped in the air and caught the lower rail of a balcony. Arms and feet working in tandem, he climbed up and up. And up some more.

The rest of the boys scattered in various directions, some following the same route as their leader. Others headed into the shadowed alleyways, looking like frightened rats seeking higher ground in a storm. They clamored for the dark, moving quickly as if a good dose of speed could remove them from the ugliness of their world.

Hands curled into fists, Katie swung back to their tiny victim. He was moving, perched precariously on hands and knees, his right thigh bleeding profusely. He paused mid-crawl, shuddered violently, then collapsed to the ground, face flat in his palms. He was breathing hard, sobbing softly. A tough kid, but incapable of battling the pain he suffered.

Katie drew her own shuddering breath and gauged the situation with a single glance. The boy's right pant leg had been torn at a jagged, vertical angle. Blood poured out in a steady stream, indicating the blade had been very sharp. The wound needed tending immediately. That was assuming the one on his leg was the only cut. The boy could have multiple injuries.

Katie had never stitched a stab wound before, but she'd never come across such a vicious scene in the middle of a crowded street either. She would do what must be done, but not at the risk of sewing infection into the leg. First order of business was to staunch the flow of blood while she checked for other cuts.

Heart in her throat, Katie sank to her knees. The crowd was growing, new gawkers joining the others.

Closer now, she could see the cut went deep. She would have to apply pressure to the wound with her gloved hand and conduct a search. It wasn't the best or most sterile of solutions, but time was of the essence.

She reached for the boy's leg. Eyes wild with fear, and probably the beginning of shock, he scrambled away from her. In an attempt to calm the child and slow his heart rate, she spoke softly. "I'm not going to hurt you. I'm here to help."

People pressed in from all sides. The lack of air washed away her concentration.

"Stand back, please." She drew in a breath and gritted her teeth so hard her jaw hurt. She must stop the blood flow.

"Aiden!" The name came from somewhere high above Katie's head, wrapped in ragged concern.

The child responded with a bitter sob, his shoulders trembling. Katie used his momentary distraction to move in close enough to place her hand over the wound.

"Let me through," came an order in a thick Irish brogue that reminded Katie of home. "That's my son, Aiden Kelly. My son. My son!"

Even as the frantic voice lifted over the others, Katie could feel the onlookers shifting to let the man pass.

By the time Mr. Kelly was kneeling beside her, she'd performed a brief inspection of the boy's condition, though she had not yet been able to determine the full range of his injuries.

"What happened?" he demanded.

Without taking her eyes off the child, Katie gave a brief account of what she'd seen, explaining the attack by the gang of older boys.

"Where is he hurt?" The father's panic and worry threatened to steal her focus.

"He has a bump on his head," she said, unsure how severe. "He was stabbed in the leg. There could be other injuries, a broken wrist, but he won't let me help him."

He stared at her. "Who are you?"

"Katie O'Connor. I trained with a midwife, but rest assured, I have tended similar injuries as your son's."

As though he hadn't heard a word she'd said, the father shot his gaze back to his son, over to the gathered crowd, then back to his son again.

"His wounds need tending, especially the one on his leg." Urgency made her words come out in a fast staccato.

The father eyed her bloodstained glove. He frowned. Gulped. Gulped again. Then finally—*finally*—he spoke to his son in a mixture of Gaelic and English.

Aiden shook his head in denial, soft sobs slipping from his mouth. Katie felt her jaw clench as a jolt of pity for the young boy washed through her.

At last, the father gave her a short nod. "You may take care of him now."

Katie lifted her hand. Almost immediately, the blood began flowing again. She applied pressure once more.

The boy's father, a sturdy man who looked to be in his late thirties, sucked in a hard breath. "Can you fix him?"

Katie didn't know. She'd only trained a few years with the midwife, who'd insisted on conducting most of the care herself, using Katie only as an extra pair of hands to fetch supplies. Although she'd helped other injured immigrants in the year since she'd been in America, the gash on Aiden's leg was long and deep and oozed blood so thick it was nearly purple.

At least she knew what to do about that. It wasn't the best idea, but would have to do until she could get the boy off the street. After a quick glance at the spectators, she pointed to a man in a well-made suit. "Give me your belt."

His eyes widened. He started shaking his head, but before he could protest, Katie narrowed her eyes at him so that he understood time was of the essence. "I need to make a tourniquet. To quell the bleeding."

The man stood straight at the tone of command in her voice, as did the others in the crowd. Within the blink of an eye, she had the belt in her hand.

"Thank you," she said, a light sigh escaping her as she went to work.

The little boy moaned.

"You're being very brave," she cooed.

The boy's eyes fluttered and closed.

His father sucked in another breath. "Is . . . he dead?"

Katie could see the rise and fall of Aiden's torso. "He's still breathing." She set her hand on his chest. The boy's breath came in snatches.

Someone from outside the ring of spectators spoke. "Let me through. I'm a doctor."

Katie glanced in the direction of the familiar voice. At the same moment, the crowd parted and there stood Ty.

The man's timing was impeccable.

He looked like an avenging angel. Tall. Dark haired. Broad shouldered. Dressed in a nondescript white shirt, sleeves rolled up to his elbows, black pants, and a matching waistcoat, no jacket. He carried the same small black bag he'd had with him on the ferryboat.

He shouldered through the bulk of the crowd, his gaze shifting over the scene, taking note of the injured boy first, his worried father, then swooping across Katie. The only sign of recognition came in a slight widening of his eyes.

Then he was back to measuring the situation.

Negotiating the final few feet, Ty dropped to his knees beside Katie. He set the medical bag down next to him. "Tell me what I'm dealing with."

She gave him a quick summary of what she'd witnessed, how she'd been only partially successful in staunching the blood, then concluded with, "I was just about to tie off the flow with a tourniquet."

"Let's hold off on that a moment." The sharp planes of Ty's face tensed, and his mouth pressed into a tight line. Reaching in his bag, he pulled out a pair of scissors. Instrument poised over the bloody pant leg, Ty locked his eyes on Katie.

Snared in that powerful stare, her lungs constricted.

"Speak to him, Katie. Keep him still." His eyes said the rest. If the boy jerked or kicked out, he could make the injury worse.

Jolted into action, Katie leaned over the boy.

With quick, decisive moves, Ty made a perfect cut along the pant leg, starting at the knee and stopping at the upper thigh.

Never taking her attention off the boy, Katie repositioned herself so that she could look into his small pale face without hindering Ty's progress.

Glassy eyes stared back at her.

She swallowed down a gasp. Aiden was terribly young, no more than six, maybe seven years old. He had curly black hair and big brown eyes. He looked like innocence itself.

What had he done to bring on the wrath of an entire gang? She glanced at Ty. He gave her a solemn grimace.

She quickly looked back to the injured child. His eyes were ringed with pain, tears wavering on the edges of his lashes. Instead of giving in to them, he gritted his teeth and released a shaky sigh.

"You poor thing." Katie touched his cheek softly, then brushed the sweaty hair off his forehead with her fingertips.

As though her tenderness gave him permission to give in to the pain, the tears spilled from his eyes. "It . . . it hurts," he gasped. "Real bad."

Katie stroked her hand along his hairline. "Dr. Brentwood is going to make it all better."

Shutting out all thoughts but this small, helpless child, she returned her attention to the doctor's face. "Isn't that right?"

The sun chose that moment to break through a slit in the fast-moving clouds, casting the aristocratic angles of Ty's face in a bold stream of light. "I'll do my best."

The boy let out another shaky sigh.

Ty cut his gaze back to Katie. "Let's get to work."

She nodded.

Ty set aside the scissors and peeled away the blood-soaked fabric. The cut was long and deep and would need stitches.

But the boy was alive, and Ty was here.

"It's going to be all right," Katie whispered to Aiden, knowing he and his father weren't the only ones who needed to hear the words.

Just as both visibly calmed before her eyes so, too, did Katie.

Chapter Fifteen

While Katie calmed the patient, Ty's thoughts morphed into one undeniable realization: she'd stopped to help an injured boy. Instead of fleeing the unpleasantness of the situation and the potential danger to herself, she'd run straight into the fray for the sake of an innocent.

Even now, as she soothed the boy's nerves and explained to his father what Ty was doing, compassion blazed in her eyes.

What eyes. What depth of emotion.

He'd missed her.

Now was not the time to tell her so.

Ty flicked his gaze to the stab wound. It was deep, filled with dirt, and wouldn't stop bleeding. His first reflex was to pull in a sharp breath. Instead, he detached. Separated emotion from logic. And focused on the boy's injury, only the injury.

Blood soaked the pant leg, turning the light brown cloth such a deep red it was nearly black.

"The wound needs stitches." At least a dozen.

"Will . . . will it hurt?"

Ty's chest pinched tight at the sound of the boy's anguish.

Before he could answer, Katie linked her fingers with the child's. "I want you to concentrate on me, Aiden." She waited for him to turn his head toward her. "Dr. Brentwood is going to have a final look at your injury, and then we'll get you patched up."

He sucked in big gulps of air. "I . . . I'm scared."

"I know," she said, barely above a whisper. "But you're being very brave."

Ty wanted to tell them both that everything would be fine, but he couldn't make such a promise. Stab wounds could be life-threatening. If improperly treated, further blood loss, shock, or, worst of all, infection could result.

"You're nice," the child announced. "I like you."

Ty felt his lips twitch. The boy was clearly smitten with Katie. He knew the feeling.

"Why, thank you, Aiden. I like you, too." Leaning toward the boy's ear, she began singing softly in low, hushed tones in a language Ty didn't recognize.

Her voice was pitched in a rich, smoky timbre. Pure velvety warmth crept from the ancient-sounding song, threatening to transport Ty to another place, another time.

As Aiden's leg relaxed under his touch, Ty felt the restlessness that had become a part of him release as well, momentarily relinquishing its grip on his soul. He knew the sense of peace wouldn't last, but for the moment, it was enough to focus his mind on the task at hand.

He studied the long, nasty gash running from mid-thigh to inches above the knee. He didn't see any indication of a break.

Katie's singing became more of a low, lyrical humming. She turned her gaze toward the injury as well. To her credit, she didn't flinch.

Impressive.

Ty had seen trained doctors fail to maintain their composure so well.

He directed his attention to the boy's father. "The wound needs stitches," he repeated. "We'll have to move your son—"

"No hospital. You treat him here."

"Not on the street." Ty held firm. "It's too unsanitary."

The father seemed to waver between holding fast to his demand and helping his son.

"You can use my shop." The offer came from a man shoving his way through the edge of the crowd. He was dressed impeccably in a fine suit, much like a banker would wear, or one who made his living as a tailor. Confirming Ty's suspicions, he added, "It's the haberdashery behind you."

The man pointed to a storefront over Ty's left shoulder.

"That'll be fine." Ty looked back to the child. "Aiden, before we move you, I want to make sure you haven't broken any bones."

The boy squeezed his eyes shut, shuddered, then told Ty to get on with it in a very grown-up voice.

"This might hurt," Ty warned.

At his words, Katie fell silent. Ty willed her to resume her impromptu musical. Instead, she gently stroked the child's hair along his forehead. "The doctor will be careful."

"How do you know?"

"I was his patient once."

"Really?"

"We met on Ellis Island."

"I was there once."

While Katie engaged Aiden in conversation about the immigration station, Ty took the opportunity to check for broken bones. "Tell me if it hurts when I press on your leg."

The child ignored him. "What's your name?"

"I'm Katie."

Ty moved his fingers along the boy's kneecap, found nothing alarming, and continued probing.

"Katie," Aiden said, his face scrunching into a frown. "That was my mother's name."

Was. No wonder the father was frantic over the incident. He'd lost his wife and was now forced to watch strangers take care of his son.

"I'm sure she was a lovely woman."

Soft little-boy sobs followed the statement. "I miss her."

"I miss my mother, too."

"You kind of sound like my mam. She used to sing to me every night before she tucked me in to bed."

Ty finished his exam by searching for any obstruction or object lodged in the wound. There was considerable dirt that would have to be removed, but nothing large enough to prevent moving the boy.

Satisfied, Ty hopped to his feet and lifted Aiden into his arms. "Let's get you off the street."

"Miss Katie," the boy wailed. "Don't leave me." Struggling in Ty's arms, Aiden reached out to Katie, who was still bent on the ground, gathering up Ty's medical bag.

"I'm not going anywhere." She stood, then hurried up to Ty and took the boy's outstretched hand. "I won't go until you're all patched up."

Ty didn't doubt her word, but he wondered if Katie would be late for work in the process. Would that pose a problem for her?

Probably. And yet, she'd made the promise anyway.

Ty repositioned the child in his arms.

Aiden's father fell into step next to Katie. The haberdasher led the way into his shop, then directed them to a room in the back.

Ty took a cursory look around. He hadn't worked in such rudimentary conditions before. Even when he'd opened his clinic, he'd started with all the proper tools and equipment. He would have to improvise.

The room had two tables, each filled to overflowing with bolts of fabric, spools of thread, and other notions. Working fast, the owner and the boy's father cleared off one of the tables. Katie continued to chat with the boy.

"I'll be right back." The owner disappeared behind a red velvet curtain. He soon reentered with an armful of clean linens and set them on the center of the now-clear tabletop.

"I will also need a large basin of fresh water," Ty told him, allowing his training as a surgeon to take over. "Several needles, a spool of thread, a cup, and some salt if you have it."

"I do."

"What about alcohol?"

"I have a bottle of brandy."

Brandy. It had to be brandy. Ty shut his eyes a moment, breathed through an uncomfortable twinge at the base of his skull. He expected the craving to gnaw at him, to send him shaking. He felt nothing but calm focus. "Bring the brandy and an additional cup as well."

Once again, the owner disappeared into the other room. He returned carrying the requested items.

"Katie," Ty said without looking at the woman. He found looking at her distracted him. "I need your assistance."

She stepped forward.

He set Aiden on the table and picked up a clean cloth, handing it over. "Staunch the blood with this. Apply as much pressure as the boy can stand."

It took her five full minutes to gain control over the bleeding. In the interim, Ty mixed a small portion of the salt into a cup of water.

After removing debris from the wound, he warned Aiden, "This will burn."

The boy gave a shuddering sigh.

Ty had his father hold the boy's leg as he irrigated the wound with the mixture of fresh water and salt.

A crash from upstairs had the haberdasher shaking his head in resignation. "I better check on that."

After sharing a quick look with Ty, the man left the room.

Katie smiled after him. "What a nice man."

Ty swallowed back an unexpected kick of jealousy and rummaged through the items the haberdasher had set on the table, focusing on the needles. Twelve would suffice, but just to be on the safe side, he counted out fifteen. "Katie, I assume you're a competent seamstress?"

His voice must have come out harder than he'd planned, because she took a sharp step back and eyed him with a healthy dose of wariness, or perhaps insult. "I'm a finisher at the Fleur Factory."

Right. He remembered now that on the ferryboat, she'd told him her skill with a needle had earned her the position over girls who'd been there longer.

"You'll continue to assist me." He spoke over her gasp. "I'm going to make simple interrupted sutures, knotting and cutting them off one at a time."

She slid a quick glance at the angry wound. "What do you need me to do?"

"When I finish each stitch, you'll take the used needle from my hand and replace it with a clean one, already threaded."

"I can do that."

"We'll work as a team."

Because the procedure would be painful, so much so that Aiden would need holding down, Ty waited for the haberdasher to return and addressed both him and the boy's father. "I need you to keep the boy still."

Their eyes widened in instant, horrified understanding.

"Don't let him thrash about. Keep his hands out of our way and his legs from kicking us."

The men each placed a hand over one of the boy's knees and the other on one of his too-thin arms.

"Hold him higher," Ty instructed. "Just below the shoulder so his body can't buck up off the table. That's right." He sterilized the needles in the brandy, then nodded to Katie. "Let's get started."

She returned his nod, made the sign of the cross, flexed her fingers. Nodded again.

Watching Ty thread the needles, Aiden whimpered from his position on the table. “Is this going to hurt, Miss Katie?”

“I’m afraid so.”

Good, Ty thought as he watched her trail the back of her fingertips down Aiden’s cheek. She told the boy the truth.

“You must remain very, very still,” she added. “The less you move, the quicker this will be over.”

Aiden squeezed his eyes shut and took a deep, shaky breath. “Do what you must.”

The adult words were completely at odds with the childish hiccupping that followed. Ty placed the threaded needles in a neat row atop a clean piece of linen, then instructed the other two men, who remained in position on either side of the boy.

“Keep your touch light,” Ty told them, “and only increase the pressure if necessary.”

Katie leaned forward and placed a kiss on the boy’s head. “We’ll be done before you know it.”

The lingering scent of soap and lavender brought a vague sense of peace on the edges of Ty’s mind.

He shut it down.

Katie met his gaze with honest trepidation in her eyes. No coyness. No pretend confidence.

He gave her a heartening smile. “Let’s begin.”

She nodded.

“Steady,” he told the father.

Ty pinched the edge of the cut with his left hand and, with a firm thrust, dipped the first needle into the boy’s skin.

Chapter Sixteen

Katie's hands might've been shaking, her heart pounding, but she handed needles to Ty as efficiently and quickly as possible. Aiden didn't flinch during the suturing process, but his lips thinned each time Ty sank the needle into his skin.

"Only one more to go," Ty encouraged. "You're doing fine."

Katie wasn't sure if he was talking to her or the child. She'd assisted the midwife in tense situations and sewn her share of stitches in garments, thousands upon thousands, but she'd never performed a suture on human skin. The task went far beyond her capabilities.

Ty's hands moved with the grace of an artist. The long tapered fingers were so beautiful, Katie thought as she watched him pull the thread through Aiden's skin. He was a healer, his skills almost poetic. Katie wanted to weep, but she didn't understand why.

Surprised by the direction of her thoughts, she swallowed back a sigh and focused only on the task before them. He tied off the final knot and handed her the bloody needle.

"There," Ty said, sweeping the back of his hand across his forehead. "All done."

"That . . ." The little boy's bottom lip trembled. "Wasn't so bad."

The tear tracks down his face told a different story.

The realization that she'd been party to hurting a child, in spite of the necessity, weighed thick in her throat, making her breath come in ragged spurts.

Seeking reinforcement, or at least a nod of approval, she glanced at Ty. He paid her no attention. Head lowered, he blotted the remaining blood off Aiden's skin and then wrapped strips of linen over the wound. It wasn't until he finished the task that he looked at her directly.

She sucked in a quick breath of air. The eyes that stared back at her were a troubled blue.

What sort of inner strength did it take to administer healing when it caused such pain? Certainly, it had to be a difficult life Ty had chosen for himself. Lonely even. Katie felt a sudden urge to offer some show of comfort to Ty, a kind word at least. But he turned away and began giving Aiden's father instructions on how to care for the wound.

"Keep it dry and clean. Replace the bandage daily for the first week, making sure to look for signs the healing process is going well."

The father looked at Ty with an imploring expression. "How will I know if it's going well?"

"The real question is how will you know if it isn't healing properly. If you see significant swelling or redness around the cut, or thick discharge, or smell a foul odor, you'll want to bring him to my clinic." Ty rattled off the address on Henry Street. "If all goes well, you will still want to bring him in next week so I can determine when to remove the stitches."

The father heaved a sigh. "What's the best way to wrap the bandages around his leg?"

Ty explained, demonstrated, then said, "If you stop by the clinic this afternoon"—he quickly gave the address again—"I'll give you a salve that will help the cut heal. I'll also lend you a supply of clean bandages."

The offer was very generous, and Katie felt a pang of yearning in her chest. Needing to do something, *anything* but stare at the man's rigid back, she whisked Aiden into her arms. He wrapped himself around her like a monkey.

"Poor baby," she whispered, rubbing his back in slow, soothing circles. "It's over now."

Sniffling, he wiped his nose on her shoulder. "That really hurt."

"I know, darling."

He clung harder to her neck. "I don't ever want the doctor to do that again."

She tightened her hold, too. "I don't blame you."

The chiming of a clock indicated the top of the hour. The workday was under way at the factory. "I'm afraid I have to go now." She set him away from her.

The child's eyes grew wide as saucers. "But I want you to stay."

"I have a job waiting for me."

Aiden started whimpering, breaking Katie's heart in the process. She nearly relented, but his father stepped in and said, "Let her go, boyo. We don't want the nice lass losing her job, now do we?"

"No, Da."

The man pried his son loose from his grip on Katie. "Thank you for tending my boy."

"I'm glad I could help." She glanced at Ty. "Goodbye," she said, including each of the room's occupants in the farewell.

Turning wearily to the door, she heard Ty call out, "Katie, wait."

She paused in the doorway, looked back over her shoulder. He gave her the warmest of smiles as he approached, leaving her unbearably touched and unsure of herself. She realized she was staring and turned away, her gaze falling on the busy streets beyond the shop.

Standing very still, she absently counted the sound of his footsteps, her mind scrupulously active, ticking over possibilities of what he wanted to say to her. Would he thank her for her assistance with Aiden, or perhaps praise her for her steadiness under pressure? Ask to see her again? Remark on the kiss they'd shared last time?

He drew alongside her. "Let me hire you a carriage."

"Oh." *That* wasn't what she'd expected. "I'm perfectly capable of walking."

"You're already late."

"Not much more than an hour." It might as well be an eternity. A vague sense of despair attacked her previously good mood.

"Is it possible you'll lose your job over this?"

Not for the first time, Katie had an uncanny sense that Ty knew more about what was going on in her mind than he should. "Yes," she conceded.

"Then please accept my offer. I won't take no for an answer."

They walked outside. It was a lovely day. The morning's chill had slid away with the mist, the sun a dazzling orange marble in the blue, blue sky. A woman with laughter in her voice called after a child, urging, "Hurry up." Down the lane, a stray dog scratched at the ground.

Ty reached up his hand to hail a carriage. While they waited, he asked after her sister.

"She's fallen into an exhausted sleep every night since her arrival in America," Katie said. "I predict it will take her a bit more time to recover from her journey."

"I don't doubt it."

A carriage arrived. Before guiding Katie into it, Ty said, "I have a request."

She reached for a calm that didn't exist. What could this man possibly want from her? She wished he would kiss her again. A flush spread high on her cheeks at the thought. She lowered her head, willing the moment gone. "What do you need?"

"I'd like you stop by the clinic on your way home from work."

An invisible blade of excitement sliced through her at the request. A group of girls rushed past, laughing, and turned to glance over their shoulders at Ty. Their youth and exuberance reminded Katie of her sister. Just this morning, she'd vowed to put Shannon first. "I should probably—"

"It's important."

"Then how can I possibly refuse?"

One of his eyebrows rose in a way she was coming to think of as distinctly his. "Is that a yes?"

"It's a yes."

"Excellent."

He handed her into the carriage after that, though he said not another word. He did give her a brief smile, right before he shut the door between them.

* * *

Katie entered her place of employment ten minutes later. The carriage ride had gone quickly and without incident, and she'd spent the time thinking about Ty's odd request.

Now, as she discarded her hat and gloves in the area designated for finishers, she had to contain her excitement, her hope, as she made her way to her work station in the dressmaking room.

The creak of pedals needing oil and the hum of sewing machines hard at work filled the air. In an attempt to avoid notice, Katie moved quickly to her station, all but gliding across the factory floor. In her haste, she almost tripped over a pile of scraps littering the path she chose.

No one took any notice of her as she entered the dressmaking room. The other finishers, mostly women but a few men, were too caught up in their individual tasks to give a greeting. Not that they would have spoken to her if she'd arrived on time. Talking was not allowed on the job; neither was humming or singing.

At least, Katie thought in relief, the managers were still in their morning meeting. A small victory, to be sure.

Again, she wondered what Ty wanted to discuss with her that was so *important.* With her mind sweeping over possibilities, she took her seat at a table situated close to the window. Feeling the heat from the pressers on the other side of the room, she pushed a curtain of hair away from her eyes and picked up the top garment from the pile at her station.

Working quickly, yet with great care, she checked each seam, made corrections where needed, then focused her attention on the tattered hem on the right sleeve. That would have to be redone.

Hand-sewing was hard on the back, strained the eyes, and required exacting concentration. Katie was paid only ten dollars a week for her efforts, two dollars more than the workers who manned the sewing machines. The children were paid even less but were required to work the same ten-hour shifts, six days a week.

Katie thought of Aiden Kelly as she made a series of tight stitches. She couldn't help but remember the way Ty had sewn up the wound on the little boy's leg. He'd been patient and efficient, and had given Katie clear directions. They'd worked well together, as if Ty had been suturing wounds with Katie's assistance for years.

"Miss O'Connor, a word, if you please."

Wincing at the angry tone, Katie felt her hands still over the dress. Her late arrival had not gone unnoticed after all. She should have known better than to hope otherwise.

Her hands shook ever so slightly, and she urged herself to remember that although she didn't regret why she was late, she was in the wrong. She completed the next stitch, very much like the one Ty had made on Aiden's leg, then drew in a small breath and set aside the garment.

Heart full of dread, Katie followed her supervisor through the cluttered room. They wove around tables and pressing machines, finally stopping once they were out of earshot of her fellow workers.

Even in the stingy light thrown off by a lone wall sconce, Katie was able to decipher Mrs. Zephyr's scowl. The woman was draped in a drab gray dress and equally uninspired shoes, and her rust-colored hair looked like it might have corroded onto her head. Her starched collar matched her rigid stance. She stood so straight, her shoulders so far back, that Katie was amazed her spine didn't snap in two from the tension.

When Katie forced her gaze to meet the other woman's, the frosty expression and pursed lips reminded her of the immigration officials she'd encountered at Ellis Island.

Mrs. Zephyr wasted no time getting to the point. "Miss O'Connor, you are late again. This is two days in a row and the fifth time this month."

"I know. I'm sorry. It couldn't be helped." An empty excuse, she knew, having made enough of them in the past few weeks. They came too easily these days. This insight into her flaws was upsetting, and Katie attempted to stand as straight as her supervisor.

"Am I to assume the cause was another child in need?"

Katie shook her head at the skeptical tone. "A young boy was stabbed on the streets. He was hurt rather badly."

At the other woman's stone-cold silence, Katie lost her battle to keep the desperation out of her voice. "I couldn't leave him bleeding in the streets."

"Oh, but you could have. Most definitely, you should have. New York City is a modern city, Miss O'Connor. The ambulance services are very efficient."

"The boy was an immigrant."

Her argument went ignored. "The city has more than a few hospitals that cater to the poor."

"His father doesn't trust hospitals."

"That is not my problem. Nor should it have been yours. You made a choice today, Miss O'Connor, and now I must make one as well."

Katie braced for what was to come.

"As I said before, you are one of my best finishers. Perhaps even the best. However, I cannot continue to disregard the rules on your behalf. Nor can I continue to turn a blind eye to your failings."

Blind eye? The woman was like a predator, constantly circling Katie, never missing a single mistake. For some reason, she'd taken it into her head that Katie was a problem.

You have given her cause.

Katie wasted no energy on regret. *I have no regrets.* She repeated the words over and over in her mind, even as she knew they weren't completely true. Helping Aiden had been the right thing to do, but at what price? Her job?

Clarity came like icy wind. Even at the cost of her job, Katie wouldn't have walked away from the injured boy. It wasn't in her nature. She would find another job.

Expression pinched, Mrs. Zephyr continued spelling out Katie's ongoing transgressions, mostly her penchant for helping the sick—not only her aunt, but those on her way to work. Just last week, she'd been late returning from her break because a worker, a girl of thirteen, had shut her finger in a door, drawing blood, and Katie had bandaged the wound with a strip of linen from the scrap heap.

Mrs. Zephyr's mouth continued moving, words spilling out in a familiar tirade. But Katie couldn't catch them all, not in a way that mattered. Just one here, another there: *your duty . . . your future . . . your position now in question . . .*

A thread of perspiration trickled down her back. Katie forced herself to nod at what she assumed were appropriate intervals, silently begging this was just another chance for her supervisor to spill her wrath and not the end of Katie's position at the factory.

Wishful thinking on her part.

They'd had nearly this same conversation just yesterday, as well as a week ago and three days prior to that. It wasn't that Katie didn't value her job at the factory—she did—but she didn't have it in her to ignore someone else's pain, not a coworker's or a child's. Still . . .

What have I done?

Mrs. Zephyr's voice came back to her.

"You received your final warning yesterday. You were told to arrive on time or forfeit your job. You have given me no other choice. It is with great sadness that I must inform you that your services are no longer needed. There." The woman heaved a purposeful sigh. "It's done."

Momentary horror rendered Katie speechless. The woman had just fired her and had the gall to act as though it had been a difficult task. Perhaps it had been challenging. *You are one of my best finishers.*

Katie took great comfort in knowing Mrs. Zephyr would have to find a comparable seamstress to replace her. She drew in a deep breath and let it shudder past her lips. "I understand."

Why wasn't she more upset?

She'd just lost her job and the money that came with it. Yet her mood was strangely light, as if a weight had been lifted from her shoulders. But . . . she *needed* this job.

"I require you to finish out the week while I search for your replacement."

It took every ounce of patience for Katie to stand under Mrs. Zephyr's lifted eyebrows, looking as if she dared Katie to argue over the unfair stipulation. She felt relief and frustration at once. Relief that she had a job for a few more days, and frustration that she couldn't begin her search for another job immediately.

"Although I am not releasing you until the week's end"—Mrs. Zephyr paused for emphasis—"you have left me no other choice than to dock your pay for the hour you were late."

The number she recited was the equivalent of a full day's work.

"Now get back to your station."

Katie gaped as the woman moved onto the factory floor, weaving through the rows of sewers, seeking her next victim.

Mrs. Zephyr's lack of compassion wasn't completely unexpected. Her dislike of immigrants was legendary, though inexplicable. She might be a natural-born citizen herself, but her parents had arrived in America a few months before she was born.

For one fleeting moment, Katie's instinct was to walk out and start looking for another position right away. After all, she wasn't technically receiving wages for her work. Then again, a week's salary—minus one day—was better than no pay at all.

No, as much as she wanted to walk out now, it wouldn't be wise to do so.

Katie returned to her work station. Hands in her lap, she scanned the hard concrete floor at her feet. She'd brought this on herself. She would have to inform Bridget and Aunt Jane she would be out of work soon. Bridget would say she was better off. Katie could practically hear her now: *I say good riddance. That job was beneath you, anyway.*

Aunt Jane would worry about money. What a wretched turn of events.

Something changed inside Katie at that moment. A small shift, but a decisive one. This wasn't a terrible twist of fate. She was skilled and young and hardworking. She would find another job. Surprised by a fresh spurt of excitement, of the possibilities that spread before her, Katie smiled.

She had connections. Katie knew better than to let pride keep her from turning to the people in her life who had the power to help her. She could approach Mrs. Armstrong. Surely, the woman knew of a position that would suit Katie's skills. She would query her friend the next time they met.

And then there was Ty.

They'd worked well together. He'd asked to see her again, immediately following the workday. Perhaps he would offer her a position at the clinic and—no, she would not allow herself to wish for something that had little chance of coming to pass. Then again, why not?

Why not embrace hope as she had when she'd first arrived in America? Why not take control of her destiny? Suppose Ty didn't offer her a job; that didn't mean she couldn't ask him for one. And if that didn't work out, then maybe he knew someone else who would employ her.

Katie told herself all would turn out in her favor and then concentrated on believing it.

Chapter Seventeen

Later that afternoon, when respectable businesses were shutting down for the day, Ty found himself addressing the aftereffects of a vicious fight that had broken out in a bar a block from the clinic.

Two battle-weary ruffians had shown up outside the clinic, with injuries ranging from minor in one case to a potentially serious head wound in the other. Neither had come willingly, the man with the head gash proving even more reluctant than his friend with the broken arm.

Head Wound had refused to cross the threshold, his fear evident in the heated Italian spewing from his lips as he argued with the owner of the establishment where the fight had taken place. Broken Arm had added his opinion.

Frustrated, the proprietor threw his hands up in the air. "I got them here. Getting them inside is on you."

He was gone an instant later.

Ty had been forced to use all his persuasive skills to talk the injured men into trusting him enough to let him have a look at their wounds. The language barrier hadn't helped his cause, nor had the alcohol consumption that had clearly played a role in the fight. The battered men were as stubborn and headstrong as any Ty had met in the Bowery.

What made matters worse was that his only knowledge of their native language was from his sporadic attendance at the opera.

Before Ty resorted to humming a few lines to find the words he wanted, Sebastian Havelock had come to his rescue. The British doctor was fluent in four languages, Italian being one of them.

Ty knew French and Latin, neither language at all helpful with the people he served in the Bowery. Most of the newly arrived immigrants spoke German, some Italian, Russian, and, as was becoming more and more common, Yiddish.

Even Sebastian didn't speak Yiddish, though he'd begun lessons with his landlady in an effort to conquer the basics. Ty's fellow doctor was an interesting, complicated individual.

His first impression of the young man had been months ago, when Sebastian had arrived on his doorstep asking to volunteer.

Welcoming the help, Ty had asked for the doctor's credentials and information regarding his formal education. Havelock had answered without hesitation, starting the verbal dissertation with "I studied at Cambridge."

The earnest young man had gone on to tell Ty, without a hint of bragging in his voice, that he'd graduated top of his class from the prestigious university and then reiterated that he wanted to help out at the clinic as much as his schedule would allow.

When Ty pressed for a reason, Sebastian admitted his motivation wasn't completely altruistic. "I accepted a position at New York Hospital. I want to study infectious diseases and believe your clinic, with its unique location, will prove the perfect place for me to expand my education outside the usual channels."

The argument had been sound, but London had equal pockets of impoverished areas.

When Ty had asked "Why come to America?" Sebastian's eyes had gone dark.

"I know what it means to be poor and without resources." His voice curdled with emotion. "As a boy, I watched my mother die of appendicitis when no qualified doctor would take her case."

Not exactly an answer to his question. Ty changed tactics. "How did you end up at Cambridge?"

"Scholarships."

Ty had looked into the other man's thoughtful gray eyes that peered out from behind wire-framed spectacles and seen secrets. He'd also seen strength of character. Clearly, there was more to the story, but Ty didn't need to hear the particulars. Sebastian Havelock was sincere in his desire to serve the poor. He was also qualified.

Of course, wanting to serve the less fortunate and being faced with the reality of what that entailed were two different matters entirely. Ty had accepted Sebastian's help, expecting him to last no more than a week.

Yet three months had come and gone, and the young doctor was still showing up to volunteer his time and expertise. Ty had no complaints. In truth, the man was a godsend.

Sebastian was dedicated, hardworking, and often appeared disheveled and hastily arranged, as if he were constantly running behind schedule. His hair never sat quite as it was meant to, due to his constantly shoving splayed fingers through the black curls.

This afternoon, Sebastian had arrived just as Ty had nearly given up convincing the Italian men to accept medical treatment. Dressed in his customary black pants and clean white linen shirt, the young doctor had taken in the scene with one fell swoop.

With an intense expression, he greeted the reluctant patients in English, then quickly switched to Italian. Soon both injured men were inside the clinic. Unfortunately, it took considerably more persuasion to steer them deeper into the building and then into an examination room.

Ty and Sebastian tackled the head injury first, set the broken bone next, then addressed the minor cuts and bruises last. As they worked in silence, Ty let his mind wander back to his first patient of the day.

Aiden Kelly had been a tough little boy, and frustratingly tight lipped about the reason the gang had targeted him. Ty wished Katie had stuck around a bit longer—he was convinced she would have been able to coax the information out of the child. She had a way about her that made others relax their guard. She was also efficient, capable, and smart. She'd been able to anticipate Ty's needs while he sewed up Aiden's leg, often before he'd voiced them.

Ty, or rather *the clinic*, could use a woman with her skills. Now all he had to do was convince her she belonged with him, or rather working with him at *the clinic*.

Sebastian stayed behind to clean up the room while Ty walked the two men out. Neither had money to pay for their care, something that happened too often. Most of Ty's patients were unable to compensate him for his services. Thankfully, the clinic had a generous benefactor.

Alone on the front stoop, Ty took in the activity around him. Men in shabby suits and women with worn faces herding unruly children strode busily past. The overall scene was one of despair, people working hard but never quite getting ahead. There were some who would do anything—anything at all—to feed themselves and their families. Others still had their pride and drew the line at illegal activity.

Ty breathed in. The day was dry and mild, but the promise of rain scented the air. He was about to go back inside when a familiar form turned the corner and headed his way.

His breath stalled in his lungs. Silhouetted against the red-and-orange smudge of sunset, Katie O'Connor looked like a luminous woodland sprite with the eyes of an angel.

Ty was ridiculously happy to see her.

She looked equally pleased to see him. But her uncertain gaze told him she was worried about this meeting. In hindsight, he realized he should have been more forthcoming with his reasons.

Dismissing his guilt, he allowed himself to disappear into the satisfaction of watching the beautiful young woman approach.

She stopped in front of him, and he said her name in a whisper. "Katie."

"Hello, Ty."

She was light and goodness. That explained his visceral reaction, the filling of his lungs, the speed of his heartbeat, and the blood pounding in his ears. Her easy, unassuming manner, the calm, womanly air she carried with her, called to the restless part of his soul. She was meant to be the heroine of a story.

Her story, he wondered, or . . . his?

She smiled and deep inside him something came alive, as if a part of him had been half slumbering and half waiting to be nudged awake. Ty knew that he would never be the same for knowing this woman. He'd known it since their eyes first met across the crowd of new arrivals on Ellis Island.

Even after all this time, Ty still recalled the odd pitch of his stomach, the same sensation he experienced now.

"I believe you called this meeting," Katie said when he'd failed to speak.

"So I did." He stood taller. "Won't you come inside?"

"I'd like that." Her smile widened, and Ty's heart missed a beat. Neither of them moved toward the clinic's entryway.

But then Sebastian joined them on the stoop, moving to stand between them, evidently unaware of the moment he'd interrupted.

"Miss? Are you in need of medical care?" Sebastian quickly assessed Katie in the clinical, semidetached way they were taught in their first year at medical school.

There was nothing personal in his manner, no flicker of anything inappropriate, and yet Ty felt the stirrings of something primitive inside him, something like jealousy or perhaps even possession. *Mine.* The word echoed in his mind, shocking him with its intensity.

Katie's voice broke the spell, and Ty wanted to bask in the sweet Irish lilt. "No, I . . . I am well. I"—she peered around the other man and connected her gaze with Ty's—"I have come to discuss something important with Dr. Brentwood."

"I see." Sebastian stepped aside, using his hand to open the door wide enough for both her and Ty to pass through.

Katie looked around after she stepped inside, then said to Ty, "I trust everything went well with our patient after I left?"

Our patient. She was already thinking of them as a team. Ty liked that. What he did not like was how the question had Sebastian's eyebrows lifting.

Ty ignored him. "I patched Aiden up, but your guess is as good as mine as to how he's faired since his father took him away."

"But"—she shot a wary glance at Sebastian—"surely, he picked up the salve and extra bandages you promised to give him."

"Not yet." Ty stifled a sigh. "But the day isn't quite over."

"I . . . well, no." Those sea-green eyes flicked up to his, and for a moment, they were unguarded. Ty saw the confusion in their depths, the sorrow and disappointment for a child she hardly knew, and it took his breath away because he understood each of those emotions on an elemental level. "There's still time."

The staring began again.

Sebastian cleared his throat. "I'm afraid we haven't been properly introduced."

"This is Katie O'Connor." Ty swept his arm in a small arc. "Katie, this is Dr. Sebastian Havelock. He volunteers at the clinic a few days a week."

All charm and teeth, Sebastian executed a short elegant bow more suitable for the ballroom than the Bowery. "A pleasure, Miss O'Connor."

The smile Ty had always thought solely for him was now given to the other doctor. "You're from England. I hear it in your voice."

"Worcestershire, to be precise. I recently arrived in America."

Katie stared at him, as if trying to picture this man as a fellow immigrant. "Did you go through Ellis Island?"

"I'm afraid not." Sebastian grimaced apologetically. "I traveled in first class."

For a moment, she simply looked at him, her face calm, but Ty could see a flicker of wariness in the tightening of her lips. "First class," she repeated. "Of course."

She watched the young doctor differently now, her shoulders tightening, her gaze a bit distant, as if she'd pulled up an invisible shield to keep herself apart from the other occupants in the room, Ty included.

Not that he blamed her. First class meant privilege and special treatment. Only passengers in steerage had to go through the registration process at Ellis Island. Katie had been one of many because she'd been too poor to purchase a first- or second-class ticket. The thought made something in Ty's heart contract.

"You're from Ireland," Sebastian said, now smiling kindly in a clear attempt to settle her unease.

She nodded her head slowly. "I grew up in a small village twenty miles outside of Cork."

"Ah, Cork." Sebastian's voice held a hint of longing. "A beautiful city, if ever there was one."

"You've been there?"

"Indeed, I have. I attended a festival with friends a few years back. I quickly discovered I'm a great fan of Celtic music, art, and food."

This seemed to be the right thing to say. Katie's guard dropped, and she conversed with Sebastian about her homeland with a lighter, calmer air in her manner.

Ty only half listened as she spoke of her small village. It was a world where poverty existed but was far different from what lived outside his door.

"For much of my childhood, I didn't know I was poor. We had the basics and that was enough."

Wondering if that was true for the people of the Bowery, Ty glanced out the window. Did they not realize they were poor? A woman carrying flowers in a basket on her head peddled her wares, crying out the cost, now half the price they had been earlier that morning. A beggar sat on the corner, hand outstretched, his feet covered with shoes that were nothing more than scraps of tattered leather.

These people seemed to know they were poor, too poor to live elsewhere. Hardworking immigrants shared space with prostitutes, thieves, and cutthroats. And with the latter came starvation, despair, abandonment, and disease.

So much unmet need, Ty decided. Helplessness besieged him at times. Good intentions went only so far. The small dent he made was minuscule and more often than not insignificant. Even the ones he helped, or the people that loved them, like Aiden's father, didn't give him their full trust.

Though Ty had given Katie cause to believe Mr. Kelly would come for the salve and bandages, Ty himself held out little hope. Would Aiden's father eventually come if the boy's wound didn't heal? That was the much more imperative question.

Ty resurfaced at the sound of Katie's soft laughter. Her face was lit from within. What had Sebastian said to bring her such joy? Ty knew the man had hidden depths of caring and was an example of complete integrity. He'd be a perfect match for a woman as good and kind as Katie.

An unpleasant sensation rushed through Ty. It took him an instant to recognize—with some irritation—that he felt jealous. Again.

The direction of his thoughts had him scowling, torn by guilt and a selfish need to admit, if only in the privacy of his own mind, that he'd become impatient with his own rules. He'd strictly forbidden close relationships, especially with females, and yet he could no longer deny that he craved more than a solitary life of sacrifice. He was tired of being alone.

When Sebastian cleared his throat again, Ty realized he was still scowling. A headache had started behind his right eye.

"I should go," Sebastian said. "I'm overdue at the hospital."

"At this hour?" Katie asked.

"I have a meeting with the chief of surgery about a patient." He clasped her hand. "I hope to see you again, Miss O'Connor."

She smiled, looking completely at ease now. "I'd like that."

Sebastian gathered up his medical bag and checked the contents. Seemingly satisfied, he picked up the rest of his belongings, and goodbyes were said. Then, with another smile and a nod in Katie's direction, the young doctor exited the clinic.

That left Ty and Katie. Just the two of them. Alone. With no one to stand in as a buffer.

Katie tilted her head and studied him with wide-eyed intensity, reminding Ty of a small bird contemplating flight. He swallowed, wondering why he was so reticent to state his business. He knew he was making the right decision. Would she agree?

He eased into the conversation. "How is your sister settling into the tenement house?"

Katie looked at him oddly. No wonder; they'd had a similar conversation just this morning. "Well enough, I suppose, considering her condition."

"How is her health?" he asked, realizing he should have made this query earlier. He knew why he hadn't, because he didn't want to worry about the girl. *She isn't Camille.* There was no reason to think her pregnancy or the subsequent birth of her child would prove problematic.

Still, a sense of foreboding made the muscles of his shoulders knot up.

"Aside from the exhaustion I mentioned this morning, she has all the typical symptoms of pregnancy." Katie hesitated a second, giving Ty the impression she meant to say more.

When she remained silent, he filled the conversational void himself. "And what of your aunt?"

"She worries about my cousin, and that steals her strength. I'm sure you can guess why she frets, but she seems happy to have Shannon for company. The two get on well, and, honestly, now that I think about it, I would say Aunt Jane's health has rallied a bit now that she isn't alone for so many hours during the day."

"I'm sure that's a relief."

"Very much so." Katie's eyes met his, proud and penetrating with concern for her family.

This brave young woman faced more than her share of challenges, yet she persevered without complaint. Her inner strength awed him. "I trust you arrived at the factory this morning without incident."

She lowered her head. "I ran into a bit of trouble."

"What sort?"

Lips pressed together, she glanced up and took a moment to look around the clinic. Ty followed the direction of her gaze, taking in his world, one of medicine and science, from her perspective. The inky stillness of the room and the sharp scent of iodine didn't present the most appealing of impressions.

The contents of his portable medical bag lay on a table beside the now-empty case: a heating iron and tourniquet, sponges, and plasters. The small surgery box that had been housed inside the larger bag sat open, revealing a stethoscope, scissors, lance, forceps, and a cutting knife, all the necessary tools of his trade. And on one wall were shelves containing books and vials of medicines in powder, liquid, and pill form.

"You mentioned having trouble at work," he prompted when Katie continued her silent inventory.

The question seemed to render her momentarily mute. In truth, she remained silent so long that Ty wondered if she would answer him at all.

She exhaled and moved to the shelves. "I arrived late by more than an hour." Her fingers touched a row of glass bottles. "My tardiness was in clear violation of the rules of my employment."

"You were sacked."

He heard her slow inhale. "I'm afraid so, but with the stipulation that I can finish out the week."

"Is that usual?"

Her shoulders lifted, fell back into place. "I don't know, but I need the money, so I didn't argue."

Katie had put her job in jeopardy this morning because a child needed her. Ty wanted to touch her, to stroke her cheek and tell her she would prevail. Tell her that he would help her fight her demons. "I should have sent you away sooner."

She stepped to the table of instruments, bending at the waist to get a better look. "I wouldn't have gone," she assured him. "I find it impossible to ignore someone in need. My cousin says it's my greatest weakness."

That was absurd.

"Your cousin is wrong." He went to stand beside her, careful not to touch her, though his fingers vibrated with the need to feel her warmth against his palm. "Caring for the welfare of others, at the expense of your own comfort, is not a weakness. It's one of your greatest strengths."

She lifted her gaze from the table. "I have lost my position at the factory."

"Would knowing that ahead of time have changed your behavior this morning?"

"I have asked myself that question a hundred times since my supervisor informed me I was out of a job." A tiny self-deprecating smile played at her lips. "I would still stop to help that little boy."

Ty glanced down at her, so beautiful, so full of compassion. She made him think of silver linings at the end of a long, dark year.

Time to make his offer. "I believe I have a solution to your problem."

"Which one?" Her lips curved in a wry smile. "I seem to have so many these days."

"Your sudden loss of wages." He swept his gaze over her face, and some of the knots in his gut unraveled. "Katie O'Connor, I would like to make you a proposition."

Chapter Eighteen

For the second time since entering Ty's clinic, Katie was struck speechless. If she wasn't mistaken, the good doctor was about to offer her a job.

She shifted her stance and tried to focus on his face, not the fact that her heartbeat had picked up speed or that she was experiencing a flash of insight. She felt as though she were standing at a crossroads, where one path led to uncertainty and the other to a life-altering situation.

"What sort of proposition?" She tried to keep the twinge of excitement out of her voice.

"I . . . or rather, *my clinic,* needs a nurse. I'd like to offer you the position."

Her excitement turned to despair. "I can't accept. I have no formal training."

He waved off her argument with a sweep of his hand. "You were a midwife's apprentice in a small village, where you no doubt assisted in procedures besides birthing babies."

"Actually, yes, that's true." The man was very astute. "But will my limited experience be enough?"

"I would wager you're more seasoned than any young woman fresh out of nursing school. What do you say, Katie? Want to come work at the clinic with me?"

Oh, she did. She really, really did.

What a joy it would be to work in a real medical clinic, serving the sick and needy, to pursue a calling in her life that went beyond herself.

But she had to think beyond her own driving need to reach for a higher purpose. She had to think about her family, something she'd failed to do earlier this morning when she'd helped that small boy. "How much would you be able to pay me?"

"What were you making at the factory?"

Too afraid to hope, she didn't blink, not once. "Ten dollars a week."

"I'll pay you twenty-five."

Now she blinked. Twice. Twenty-five dollars a week was a lot of money. No, not what Bridget made at the gentlemen's club, but more than Katie could ever make at a factory. "Can you afford that much?"

"That's my concern, not yours."

"When would you need me to start?" Was she really considering this?

"Immediately."

"Can I have a day to think about it?"

Reaching out to her, he laid his hand on her sleeve. Something inside her shifted under the touch. "You can have two."

Her lips twitched at the lighthearted response.

"Katie, this is a sincere offer." His hand dropped away. "The people living in this neighborhood need medical care, but as you saw for yourself with Aiden's father this morning, they don't readily trust American doctors."

"No, they don't," she agreed, surprised to hear her calm tone when so many ugly emotions churned just under the surface.

Good medical care was within reach for many, yet they denied themselves out of fear. She could help with that.

"I want this clinic to be a safe place of healing." Ty pierced her with a penetrating look. "Everyone deserves equal and fair treatment."

"I couldn't agree more."

"Having one of their own inside this building, having *you*, Katie, that will go a long way in alleviating their fears."

Katie nodded. What Ty said made sense.

"I see you're seriously considering my offer."

Why deny the truth? "I am, yes."

"Then as much as it pains me to do this, I'm now going to play devil's advocate and give you several reasons to walk out of this building and never come back."

His words were so unexpected her chin jerked, just a little. "Why would you want to do that?"

"This neighborhood is dangerous, Katie, full of unsavory characters with ugly intentions, especially when it comes to pretty young women."

Katie carefully stripped her voice of emotion. "I'm aware of that."

"I am committed to treating everyone in need. I turn no one away." He paused, lifting his eyebrows in challenge. "Do you understand what I'm saying?"

She nodded her head and remained tactfully silent.

"In the past month, I have treated prostitutes with venereal diseases, drunks, men and women enslaved to opium, three thieves, and two cutthroats bent on killing each other. And those were some of the tamer cases."

He was exaggerating to make a point. Wasn't he?

"Many of my patients are crass, crude, and would steal from their own mothers."

The chill of his words sat heavy in the room between them. Katie understood Ty's tactics. She even understood why he felt the need to be so blunt. He wanted to make sure she knew what she was getting herself into.

She knew. Of course, she knew. "If you're trying to scare me off, it isn't working."

He continued mapping out the worst-case scenarios.

She tilted her head and considered him while he spoke. His expression was unreadable, but there was a spark at the back of his eyes, something that looked like hope. She cut him off midsentence. "You are only making a stronger argument for me to say yes to your offer."

He continued as if she hadn't spoken. "Beggars with lice crawling all over them will come looking for a handout. You will be exposed to infectious diseases, including syphilis. Have you seen the ravages of that particular malady?"

Wasn't he a shining beacon of hope? Katie attempted to keep her expression bland. "I have."

"Many will die in your care, regardless of how hard you work to keep them alive."

There he went again, being all rosy and full of cheer. What Ty didn't know, what she'd hardly known herself until he'd made his fortuitous offer, was that helping people was all Katie had ever wanted to do with her life. Out of sheer survival and the need to provide for her family, she'd set aside that dream.

This was her chance to reach for it again and change the course of her life forever, all while being paid more than double her current salary. And to think, she was being offered the job for the very reason she'd lost her other one.

That's what the priest at her church called Providence.

"Carry on if you must, Ty. But you can say nothing that will dissuade me. My decision is made."

She'd never spoken truer words. For although Katie knew working at the clinic would be challenging, some days worse than others, she also knew she would relish all aspects of her duties. She would learn. And she would grow in her skills.

Sadly, patients would die, as he'd warned her, but many would survive. Even thrive. This was her calling.

"I'll take the job."

Shaking his head, he crossed his arms over his chest. The lines around his eyes seemed to cut deeper. "I insist you take the full two days to consider your answer."

A surge of impatience flooded through her. "I want the job, Ty. I can start work three days from now."

His gaze traveled over her face, as if seeking something in her expression that hadn't been said in her words. She watched several unidentifiable emotions chase across his face and wondered what he was thinking. "Take the time to think over your decision, Katie. In the meantime, you should head home." He took her elbow in a light touch. "I'll see you out."

Unsure whether to laugh or weep at his abrupt manner, she let him escort her to the door. He tugged it open, then stepped aside to let her pass. "I'd offer to see you home, but—"

"I'm quite capable of seeing myself home. Besides, you need to remain here in case Aiden's father shows up."

"I would hate to miss him."

"I would hate that, too." She edged closer to the threshold but didn't cross over. Far-off thunder made the air quiver. Katie cast an eye to the horizon. Rain was coming. "How long will you wait for Mr. Kelly?"

"All night."

"Truly?" That seemed a bit excessive. If Aiden's father hadn't come to the clinic by now, he probably wasn't coming at all.

"I live upstairs," Ty explained.

An obvious choice, Katie decided, glancing to the ceiling. She studied the peeling plaster a moment, then lowered her head. "That must be terribly lonely."

"I don't mind the solitude."

She wasn't sure she believed him.

He reached out. She did as well. Their hands brushed, but then they stopped abruptly, both frozen mid-reach. Katie yanked her hand back first, losing her balance in the process.

Ty grasped her shoulders.

Drawing in a tidy breath, she smiled shyly up at him and thought of their kiss. But then he released her and took a small step back, moving carefully, maybe even a bit reluctantly. Something was happening between them, something Katie couldn't define and didn't want to try. Putting a name on it would make it seem somehow . . . less.

"Katie." Her name sounded like an apology.

"Oh, Ty." She placed her hand on his chest. Warmth spread up her arm.

Slowly, their smiles faded, first his, then hers.

There was nothing left but more staring.

* * *

Ty wanted to kiss Katie. The last time he'd taken her into his arms had been glorious. So glorious that it had been disastrous. A moment not to repeat.

And so he told himself to keep his distance. He ordered his feet to take a step back.

He remained right where he was. He liked the feel of Katie's palm on his chest. The gravity of the moment danced a shiver up his spine.

But Ty had committed himself to a life of servitude, one that called for a monk's existence. That was all he wanted. It was all he deserved. Helping the poor was his one chance for atonement, and if he failed here, he would be nothing.

Some wrongs needed more than forgiveness to correct. Apologies were just words. And if there was one lesson Katie had already taught him, it was to think of others above himself.

Smoothly assuming control over his thoughts, he wiped them away with a swipe of his hand across his mouth.

"Goodbye, Katie," he said. "I don't want to see you at this clinic for another three days. If, at that time, your decision still stands, your presence on this doorstep will be your answer."

There was a slight pause as she digested his dismissal. Eyes filled with disappointment—in him, yet again—she removed her hand from his chest.

Ty expected to feel relief. It didn't come. For, instead of letting her hand drop, she brought her warm palm to his face and cupped his cheek. "Goodbye, Ty."

Head high, she walked out the front door. She didn't look back, didn't pause to smile over her shoulder. She simply left him staring after her.

The sense of loss that sliced his heart was one more thing he must grow to accept. Just another part of his penance.

As if pulled by an invisible force, he went up the stairs and straight to the bottle of brandy, now as empty as his soul. To say he regretted tossing out the amber liquid was a gross understatement.

With a growl, Ty threw the bottle across the room. The glass shattered into tiny pieces, like the fragments of his life.

He collapsed into a wingback chair and, after leaning his head back, settled in for a good brooding session. He wouldn't sleep tonight, but he sensed The Dream would haunt him anyway.

A knock sounded on the clinic's door.

Ty immediately thought of Katie. She'd come back to him.

He clambered down the stairs and, coming to his senses, stared at the slab of wood. Katie wasn't on the other side. She couldn't be. He'd told her not to return for three days' time.

Perhaps she'd come back for further clarification of her job duties. Or maybe she wanted advice concerning her sister's care. Had Ty grown so absorbed with his own redemption that he'd missed an opportunity to help a friend?

He closed his eyes, mourning the lost chance.

It's not too late.

Well, it would be if he continued scowling at the door while Katie was on the other side waiting for him.

The knock came again, louder and more insistent. Perhaps Aiden's father had come at last. Ty was across the room in seconds.

With a fast yank, he wrenched open the door.

He blinked, bemused. Neither Katie nor Aiden's father stood on the threshold. It was a young man, lanky in build and dressed in a crisp suit that hung loose on his thin frame. A film of sweat covered his face. Behind him on the street, a familiar carriage awaited. The fact that this man was here instead of the clinic's benefactor was not a good sign.

Ignoring the jolt of apprehension, Ty opened the door a fraction wider. "May I help you?"

"Are you Dr. Titus Brentwood?"

"I am."

"I have a letter for you, sir." The young man's Adam's apple bobbed, and if Ty wasn't mistaken, his pupils had dilated in the last two seconds, a clear sign of nerves. "Mr. Temple insisted I place it directly in your hand."

Ty reached out, bracing himself for what was sure to be bad news. He'd feared this day would come, but he'd hoped not quite this soon.

Edwin Temple was a wealthy man of business, a family friend, and a well-known philanthropist. He'd fallen ill a year ago, and his son, Josh, had taken over much of his responsibilities.

Josh and Ty had been friends since childhood. But Josh was also a friend of Camille's husband, Shepherd Huntington III. Josh hadn't held Camille's death against Ty—at first—but like many of Ty's friends, he'd distanced himself soon after the tragedy.

Ty reached for the letter with the steady hand of a surgeon. Recognizing Josh's handwriting, Ty feared that something terrible had happened to Edwin. Not only had the older man become a friend, one of the few who'd shown Ty unconditional support, but he was also the clinic's sole benefactor.

Ty had a substantial inheritance left to him by his grandfather, but during the dark weeks after Camille's death, his father had put the bulk of the money in a trust fund that he controlled with an iron fist. *For your protection,* his father had argued.

But Ty had known that was only partially the reason.

William Brentwood wanted his son to return to his old life. Until Ty obeyed and became a surgeon again, he was cut off. The threat hadn't worked to change his mind. Nor had the lack of access to his own money mattered. Until now.

"Mr. Temple told me to wait for your response."

Ty nodded, refusing to let any of his inner thoughts show on his face. He ripped open the envelope and read the words that signaled the clinic's ruin. There was no personal missive, no explanation as to why Josh had written the letter instead of Edwin.

Ty read the words again.

This letter is to inform you that the Temple Foundation is suspending funds to your clinic indefinitely. The enclosed check is the last.

Ty considered the amount. Now that he'd hired Katie, it was only enough to keep the clinic running for a month, maybe two if Ty economized in his personal spending.

What then?

Defeat knifed straight through his middle, but he soldiered on, keeping his face expressionless as he invited the courier inside to wait while Ty penned his response.

Though he'd been expecting something like this, the blow, when it came, nearly knocked the breath out of him. This wasn't about him, Ty reminded himself, save for the grief he felt for an old man with an altruistic heart, whose son had taken over his business and now his charitable foundation.

By making this personal between himself and Ty, Josh was hurting not only his father but also the people Ty served. The people Edwin Temple had been devoted to most of his adult life.

Ty didn't blame his former friend.

He blamed himself.

The repercussions of one bad decision kept coming, harming people that came into his sphere. It could have been worse, he told himself. Josh could have cut off the funds immediately.

Ty still had up to two months to resolve the problem. That wasn't much time, but enough.

There was a simple solution, of course. He could go to his father and ask him to relinquish control of his trust fund. But should William Brentwood refuse, Ty would have to find another benefactor, perhaps several. That meant entering the world he'd left.

A fitting punishment.

Chapter Nineteen

As one week had turned into two and now approached three, Shannon's optimism faded, her mood growing gloomier with each sunset. When yet another morning dawned, no different from all the others, she spent the majority of the day in bed, something she'd been doing more and more since arriving in America. She alternated between sleeping and crying and, when her worries nearly overwhelmed her, praying. She hated giving in to such weakness, but it couldn't be helped. Her heart was full of fear for the man she loved.

Where are you, Liam?

She'd been in America for almost three weeks—three!—and no sign of him, not a word. No letter, no telegram, nothing.

He'll come and prove Katie wrong, she told herself, hurt and disappointed by her sister's lack of faith in her choice of fiancés.

After several attempts to talk to her through the closed door, Aunt Jane left Shannon to wallow in her misery.

Flat on her back, with tears leaking from her eyes and pooling into puddles on her pillow, she stared up at the ceiling above her head. The peeling plaster turned into a big ugly blur. Liam would come. Katie was wrong to make Shannon question his loyalty.

Sighing, Shannon rubbed her hand over her forehead and left it there to cover her eyes. Liam hadn't walked away from her, from them, not intentionally. Shannon knew it as sure as she knew her own mind, and there was nothing anyone could say to convince her otherwise.

There was still hope, she reminded herself. Liam simply had to board another ship destined for New York. If he hadn't done so yet, he would soon. Sooner than soon. He would write of his plans and send the letter to this address. Shannon needed only to be patient.

She'd never been very good at patience.

A thick blanket of despair fell over her. She let it come, let it consume her. For five entire heartbeats. Then she scrambled out of bed, lowered to her knees, and took her pain to her Heavenly Father.

By the time the sun began its descent toward the horizon, Shannon was feeling a little less sorry for herself. She would not allow fear to hold her in its sinister grip.

She desperately wanted to rely on faith instead. She just wasn't sure she knew how. Perhaps she needed wise counsel. Thus, when her aunt knocked on the door and suggested she come out and eat something, Shannon wiped her eyes, padded across the floor in her bare feet, and let the woman in the room.

Aunt Jane wasted no time yanking Shannon into her arms. The icy numbness that had surrounded her heart thawed ever so slightly.

"My dear, dear girl." The older woman set Shannon away from her and narrowed her gaze over her swollen red face. "Your ordeal on Ellis Island must have been truly terrible to leave you traumatized for so long."

"You think I'm still upset about my detainment?"

"What else could it be?"

Through the haze of her tear-soaked brain, Shannon realized it was time to tell her aunt the truth. Assuming, of course, that Aunt Jane hadn't figured it out on her own. Bridget had seen the truth almost immediately. But when she'd confronted Shannon late one night after everyone else had gone to bed, her cousin hadn't judged her. She'd even agreed to keep Shannon's condition secret from her mother.

In a surprising show of support, Katie had done the same, allowing Shannon the chance to reveal the delicate situation to the older woman when she was ready. Shannon had yet to find the right moment. Though she didn't regret her actions, she didn't want Aunt Jane thinking less of her. Or Liam. Having Katie question his integrity was hard enough.

Gathering the words in her head, Shannon went to look out the window. The setting sun had turned the sky a pretty pink washed in gold. She reached for the locket. The symbol of Liam's love for her gave her courage.

Releasing the necklace, she placed her hand on her stomach, breathed in deeply, and said, "In Ireland . . . I fell in love with Liam Gallagher."

"Gallagher? I know his mother."

"Then perhaps you know how possessive of him she can be."

"Oh, aye." Aunt Jane shook her head. "Quite unhealthy, I always said. Am I to assume she didn't approve of her boy getting involved with you?"

Shannon sighed. "She hates me."

"There, now. That woman has the heart of a snake. I wouldn't take it personally."

How else was Shannon to take it, if not personally?

"She did everything she could to break us up. That's why Liam and I decided to run away together." She shoved at her hair. "We're engaged. Did I tell you that?"

"No, you didn't."

"Well, we are." She couldn't keep the defensive note out of her voice. "We should be married by now, but nothing has turned out as planned. Least of all that I'm . . . I . . ." She reached for the locket again and stroked it for strength as she drew another breath. "I'm carrying Liam's baby."

Aunt Jane's shocked gasp was the exact reaction Shannon had feared. She lowered her head in defeat. "You think less of me."

"Not at all. My dear sweet child. You aren't the first young woman to find herself caught in the family way out of wedlock."

Hope spread heat to her limbs. "You don't think I'm a terrible sinner?"

"I think you are a young woman with a big heart who loves deeply and passionately."

Shannon released the locket and, for her own sake as well as her aunt's, said, "Liam and I should be married by now."

"I know all seems lost." Aunt Jane approached her and touched her back, her voice but a whisper and, thankfully, full of the compassion that Shannon craved. "But know that you won't have to raise the child alone. Your family will stand by you."

Shannon appreciated the sentiment, but it was clear her aunt had misunderstood the situation. "Liam didn't abandon me."

The hand on her back flexed. "Then why are you crying?"

"Because I haven't spoken with him in weeks. And I'm frightened he won't be able to find me here. And because Katie has put doubts in my head." The anger in her voice surprised her, but now that she'd unleashed the dark emotion, she couldn't pull it back. "Why would she do something like that?"

Her aunt gripped her shoulders and gently turned her around. "Your sister loves you."

Shannon waited until she was certain she could speak without her voice breaking. "Then she should have faith in me and my choice of fiancés. I wouldn't be with a man who didn't love me to distraction, the way our father loved our mother." She paused. "Katie claims I'm being naïve."

"Are you?"

"Liam loves me. Why is that so hard to believe?" She couldn't keep the frustration out of her voice. In truth, she didn't even try. "Am I not worthy of a man's love?"

"Of course you're worthy. I'll thank you not to think otherwise. You are a beautiful, loving soul meant to be treasured."

Liam had used nearly the same words the night they'd made love. "He treasures me."

"Yet he isn't here with you now." Aunt Jane held her gaze. "Can you tell me why?"

"Mrs. Gallagher must have gotten to him."

"Shannon." The older woman drew her to a chair and applied gentle pressure on her shoulders until she sat. "I sense Mrs. Gallagher isn't the only reason you've been crying all afternoon." The eyes of wisdom stared out of the weathered face. "Tell me what you're afraid of."

"I'm not afraid."

Aunt Jane simply stared at her. Then, in silence, she went to a dressing table, picked up a hairbrush, and returned. As the older woman pulled the brush through her niece's hair, Shannon was reminded of her mother but even more of Katie, the big sister she'd missed as much as her parents. She closed her eyes and let a sense of peace wash over her.

With each stroke, she became a little less combative and a bit more honest with herself.

Perhaps it was time to admit that, maybe, a very tiny part of her *was* afraid. "I don't want to be left alone again."

Her aunt's hand paused, then just as quickly resumed brushing. "Again?"

"Like I was when Katie came to America." Cowardice came with the words. Shame. Fear. Doubt. Shannon felt the weight of each emotion in the pit of her stomach.

She could stop her story there. Leave the rest unsaid. But she continued.

"I wasn't prepared for the depth of my loneliness. I hadn't realized how much I depended on Katie, not only as a sister but as a companion and a confidante."

Aunt Jane nodded in understanding. "It's the way of sisters in our family."

Was it? Shannon had been young when her aunt had left Ireland shortly after her husband died, barely six, and she couldn't remember if her mother had been close to this woman. She seemed sincere.

Nevertheless, how did she describe the pain, the hollow feeling of loss when the one person she'd counted on most had up and abandoned her? "Every morning after Katie left for America, I would wake up with a dark sense of despair. There were days I didn't think I would survive. Oh, Aunt Jane, I never want to feel that sort of loneliness again."

"I'm sorry, dear, so very sorry you went through that." Her aunt hugged her from behind. "Have you told your sister any of this?"

Shannon gripped the arm swung loosely around her neck. "My first night here, when we argued about Liam. She was devastated."

"I'm sure she was. Your sister loves you very much."

"I know."

"For the past year, she's spoken of nothing but sending for you. It has been her life's mission."

"I know." Which made it impossible for her to resent Katie.

If anything, it made her love her sister more. While Shannon had been struggling with bitterness and sorrow, Katie had been working to reunite them. She'd written weekly—long, chatty letters that were a welcome distraction from Shannon's feelings of isolation.

She squeezed her eyes shut, hating the tears stinging behind her lids.

The brush paused briefly, then stroked through her hair again. "Do you think your loneliness drove you into the arms of your young man?"

She'd asked herself the same question during the boat ride to America. She'd looked deep into her heart for the answer. "By the time

I met Liam, I was over the worst of it. No, loneliness didn't play a part in my falling for him. I love him with the heart of a woman." She fiddled with the locket around her neck. The smooth edges against her fingertips brought her clarity. "I miss him so much. I ache for him."

Her aunt set down the brush and came around her chair.

"Listen to me. You don't ever have to worry about being alone again." She knelt in front of Shannon and took her hands. "God forbid, if something prevents your young man from marrying you, know that your family will help you raise the child."

Shannon took great comfort in that, yet she shook her head. "Liam will come for me."

"Time will tell." Jane stood. "In the meantime, I want you to promise me something."

"I'll try."

"If you ever feel lonely or afraid or lose hope, I want you to come to me. Please, I beg you, don't suffer alone. Will you promise me that?"

Shannon drew in a shuddering breath. "Yes."

"Wonderful. Now, my dear." Her aunt drew her to her feet. "I want you to go wash your face, and, once you're feeling more yourself, we'll get some food in you."

"I could eat."

Later, with her aunt resting in her room, Shannon was left with nothing but a basket of mending and her riotous thoughts.

Telling her aunt about the child she carried had been a wise decision. The older woman had taken the news in stride and pledged her support. It was more than Shannon could have hoped for.

Surprised, happy, and, yes, missing Liam dreadfully, she set aside the basket. Perhaps a bit of fresh air would erase her melancholy.

Her thoughts turned troubled as she made her way out of the apartment and down the first flight of stairs. She hated the doubts that wanted to creep into her mind, little nagging threads of dismay that had begun sometime during the journey across the ocean, though she would never admit such a thing to Katie.

Shannon knew she was a pretty girl, but she was shy and didn't make conversation easily. She hadn't wanted money or a big, fancy house. She didn't have a penchant for lace and ribbons, like other girls. No, Shannon had dreamed of only one thing. Falling in love with a wonderful, caring man who loved her in return.

Liam was everything she'd ever dreamed of, and more.

Halting on the second-floor landing, Shannon briefly gave in to a bout of queasiness and leaned into the solid strength of the wood-paneled wall. She allowed exhaustion to steal over her.

Most of the time, she was able to control the nausea, but sometimes, when she thought of Liam and the sight of him running along the docks in Cork, fear for his safety manifested itself into a physical pain so acute she had to swallow back bile.

Closing her eyes, she forced herself to breathe through the worst of her nausea. As her lungs worked, her mind reviewed her time with Liam. It would be wrong to say they fell in love during their secret meetings. In truth, they'd each fallen that first day he'd entered her uncle's apothecary shop and had consummated their feelings rather quickly, both regretting the rush, if not the deed itself.

Shannon's hand went automatically to the locket Liam had given her the night of their lovemaking, along with his promises.

He would prove her sister wrong. Preferably before Shannon's stomach expanded.

Shoving away from the wall, she continued down the last flight of stairs. Liam's baby was growing inside her, becoming his or her own little person, bigger and stronger every day. The night they'd created the child had been the most special in Shannon's young life, far exceeding her imaginings.

Afterward, when their breathing had calmed, he'd held her against him, smoothing strands of her hair from her face and whispering against her ear. "I will never love anyone but you."

Shannon had promised Liam the same, meaning every word despite the newness of their relationship.

He hadn't appeared surprised by her words, but his arms had tightened around her. "You're mine, Shannon O'Connor. I'll find a way to make you my wife."

"I believe you, Liam Gallagher."

He'd smiled then and pulled her even closer, making all sorts of vows that would take him a lifetime to fulfill.

The thought of that night made her shiver with happy memories.

Smiling softly, Shannon exited the tenement house and sat on the top step. Though dusk was upon them, and day had nearly surrendered to night, the streetlamps illuminated the world beyond the apartment building.

So, she thought, looking around with interest. *This is America.* The sheer volume of sights, sounds, and smells enthralled her. She'd never seen so many people in one place.

Well, except for her time in steerage. But that had been different. The people there had lived in a sort of suspended existence.

Here, on this massively populated lane, they moved at a mind-boggling pace. The street was like a river of chaos, noise, and activity rushing through the city. Men, women, and children were all over the place, moving fast and furiously, shouting and laughing.

Their energy was contagious, and Shannon's insides performed a gleeful roll. This was another kind of romance, vastly different, and yet as compelling as what she shared with Liam.

People moved every which way, a sea of hats, scarves, wool-panted legs, and swishing skirts. Horse-drawn carriages rattled past. Pushcarts lined both sides of the street. A man of indeterminate age turned to look at her with raised eyebrows.

Shannon ignored him.

"Get your cabbage here," shouted a vendor close enough for her to see his hair was black underneath his floppy hat.

A little dizzy now, Shannon closed her eyes. She was unable to tell if the air had grown hot or if the jolt of sickness came from inside her. She leaned her head in her hands and breathed through the nausea. The baby was really making his—or her—existence known this evening.

This light-headedness was a strange and somewhat frightening sensation. Why wouldn't the sickness go away?

A hand rested on her shoulder with the barest of touches. "Shannon, are you feeling ill?"

Katie's soft whisper barely broke the silence, yet Shannon sprang away from the sound as if a shot had fired overhead. She opened her eyes in time to see her sister's remorseful frown highlighted in the glow of the streetlamps.

"You startled me."

"I realize that." Katie moved closer and put her hand on Shannon's shoulder again. "Dear sister, I hate seeing you sad."

Shannon felt her mouth fall open, and a soft puff of air came out. "I'm not sad." Despite her best efforts, her voice broke, making her denial as hollow as her heart.

"You're beyond miserable."

Abruptly, Shannon's tattered control broke, and the tears she thought had dried up hours ago returned full force. Trying to discreetly rub away the liquid collected at the corners of her eyes, she forced a smile. "I don't know what's wrong with me. I can't seem to stop crying."

"You're with child," Katie said softly, lifting her hand from Shannon's shoulder. As she sat down on the step, an expression of big-sister adoration came across her face. "I should think that explains the rush of emotions."

Feeling a bit like her old self, Shannon pitched her voice at a teasing tone. "I suppose you would know."

"I would." Katie's smile almost reached her eyes. Almost, but not quite.

Shannon disliked the strange distance that had settled over her and Katie—nothing she could put her finger on, just a subtle shift in their relationship. They were both being so careful with each other, and a new stiffness stood between them, as if they were working very hard to return to their natural closeness but couldn't quite get there.

Even the way Katie looked at her was different, still affectionate and loving, but also concerned she wasn't fully capable of taking care of herself. After a year of living practically on her own, Shannon was cast in the role of little sister once again. She didn't like it. Even though she understood Katie's side of things. She still didn't like it.

"You have to stop worrying about me," she said. "I'm going to be all right."

"I know you are."

They shared a tight smile.

Katie bumped shoulders with her. "Do you want to hear *how* I know?"

"Not particularly, but I'm sure you're going to tell me."

Katie laughed. "You're my sister. First. Last. Always. Nothing and no one will keep me from standing by your side."

A little of the awkwardness disappeared, and, despite herself, Shannon was moved by Katie's support.

Now Katie was crying, too. Reaching for her, Shannon draped her arm across her sister's shoulders and tugged her against her side. They sat that way, neither speaking, the chaos of the streets acting as background music to the moment.

Shannon had forgotten the strength of her love for Katie, of the bond they shared. This was the sister who'd made her laugh, made her feel safe, and promised to stick by her, come what may. Which left them precisely where they'd been before Katie had left for America.

Family. Sisters. Best friends.

First. Last.

Always.

Chapter Twenty

Two days after receiving Josh's letter, Ty rounded the corner of Forty-Fourth Street. His feet ground to a halt in front of the Harvard Club. The sun shone directly overhead from a cloudless sky. The unmarred perfection was a mockery to the mess he'd made of his life.

But this errand wasn't about him. The people Ty served needed him to set aside his pride and think of them, only them, not the mistakes he'd made. He studied the building, knowing his hesitation was nothing more than a stalling tactic. If he wanted to secure a new benefactor for the clinic, then he must regain entry into the most exclusive homes in New York City, especially the one he'd grown up in.

The Harvard Club was the place to start. Neutral territory. The private club for some of the most influential men in the city—the country—nay, even the world, his father included among them.

The traffic on the street continued moving behind him. Men, women, and children passed him by on the sidewalk without looking his way or breaking stride; just another moment in another day like any other.

That wasn't the case for Ty. He hadn't stepped inside this club in well over a year. Built in the neo-Georgian style of architecture, the building's façade reminded him of the gates at Harvard Yard. As he took in the stately splendor before him, he was transported back to his college days, to simpler times, when his only goal in life was to earn the necessary degrees to become a great surgeon.

Finished stalling, he climbed the steps leading to the entryway. He nodded to the doorman wearing the requisite crimson-and-gold livery.

"Good afternoon, Dr. Brentwood." Though the man clearly recognized him, the voice showed no sign of shock as he opened the door and stepped aside to let Ty pass.

"Thank you."

The moment he entered the building—and stepped into a world of wood, leather, and cigar smoke—the year of self-imposed exile seemed to fall away. Ty had spent many afternoons, and more than a few evenings, in these stately surroundings. He'd read in the library on the second floor, a snifter of brandy in his hand. He'd played cards and billiards in the designated areas, eaten excellent meals in the private restaurant, fallen asleep in an oversized chair when he'd overindulged. And . . .

He didn't miss any of it.

I don't belong here anymore.

The thought should have come as a surprise. All Ty felt was a sort of numb acceptance.

He paused at the edge of the cavernous Harvard Hall, now filled to capacity with club members lounging in fat leather chairs. Some read the morning papers. Others conducted business deals; a few napped. The hallmark of tradition was everywhere he looked. Even the roaring fire snapping and popping in the large marble hearth was more for show than to ward off any chill.

Ty moved to stand in the shadows pooling at the feet of an oversized potted plant. Although a few interested stares followed his progress, most took no notice of him. It was, Ty thought bleakly, the reception he'd expected, neither hot nor cold, mostly indifferent. His own doing, he thought. Gaining invitations to parties could prove harder than he'd hoped.

So be it.

He changed direction, heading toward a group of men he'd rowed with in college.

Halfway to his destination, his attention was drawn to a familiar form crossing the hall. Shoulders back, head high, clad in an expensively tailored suit, Dr. William Brentwood moved with the physical grace and confidence of a man who knew his place in the world.

Ty took in his father with an objective eye. Though he'd passed his sixtieth birthday four years ago, his austere features were still striking, free of the ravages of time that struck most men his age.

"Son." They shook hands. "It's good to see you."

The easy demeanor surprised Ty, as did his reaction to the older man. "It's good to see you, too, Father."

Reality chipped away at the anger he'd harbored in his heart. Until this moment, Ty hadn't realized how much he'd missed his father, his hero, the man he'd measured his own successes and failures against. He'd forgotten other things as well, the camaraderie of like minds, the sharing of stories from the operating room, family holidays, his father and mother laughing by the fire in the years before she'd died, his brother organizing the lot of them into different poses for yet another one of his experimental photographs.

Ty hadn't just abandoned his life's work. He'd abandoned his family. It required a great deal of willpower not to buckle under the guilt. The disappointment in himself. Somewhere in the past twelve months, he'd become his own worst enemy.

"Are you here for lunch?"

Ty hitched his shoulders in a slight shrug. "I have no firm plans."

"Then dine with me."

The metaphorical olive branch was too tempting to resist. "I'd like that, thank you."

They were settled in their seats before either of them spoke again. They discussed the weather, politics, even religion, but each avoided any talk of medicine or the hospital or what Ty had been doing in the months since they'd last met.

It wasn't until their meals were sitting before them, untouched and growing colder by the second, that Ty broached the reason for his appearance at the Harvard Club. "I received a letter from Joshua Temple. He's pulling his father's support from the clinic."

With visible effort, his father cleared his face of all expression.

But just as he parted his lips to likely deliver a lecture, Ty continued, "I will find another benefactor."

His father frowned. "Am I to assume that is the reason for your presence here today?"

"Yes."

"Then you haven't come to your senses, as I had hoped."

"My work at the clinic is important."

"Your work at the hospital is equally so." Ty knew his father wasn't being intentionally callous toward the poor, though his words could be interpreted as such. William Brentwood had a deep concern for those less fortunate than he was and had taught both of his sons to care deeply for the needy. But the man also had an active dislike for wasted talent.

As was the case in the past, he had no problem voicing his feelings on the matter now. "Titus, Son, you have a calling to perform surgery. Your skill and proficiency are unmatched. Many aspire to what comes naturally to you. Few, if any, will achieve your brilliance with the scalpel."

Ty confronted his father's observations with silence. He'd heard this same argument a dozen times, a hundred.

"It is your privilege and responsibility to use the gift God has bestowed on you."

Ty felt his temper rise. His father spoke in platitudes, as if his decision to walk away from surgery was nothing more than stubborn pride.

"To whom much is given, much is expected."

In that, at least, they agreed. It was the perfect opening to return the conversation to the important matter at hand. "If I let the clinic fail, who will serve the sick in the Bowery?"

"Any number of doctors can take over for you. Come home, Son." Ty heard the longing of a father in the other man's voice, and ruthlessly suppressed any reaction to it. He would not be swayed by sentiment.

"I'm committed to the clinic."

"Very well, then." His father sat back in his chair. "I'll financially support your little endeavor myself, if that's what it takes."

"And if I refuse to return to surgery? Will you rescind your offer of support?"

His father's silence was answer enough.

"Will you constantly hold money over my head?" Ty asked in a frustrated hiss.

A swift wash of color darkened his father's face. "We both know this isn't about money."

Now Ty sat back, his posture deceptively relaxed, but inside, his heart burned with surprising bitterness. His father was right. It had never been about the money. It was about so much more. Respect. Pride. Honor. Pain. "That's not what you said a year ago."

"I was wrong to put conditions on your choice."

His choice. As if there'd been a choice to stay or go.

"I killed a woman."

"You lost a patient on the operating table."

"It's one and the same."

His father shot him a long look, which Ty met evenly. "They are two very different things. Until you recognize the truth in that, perhaps you aren't ready to come home."

Hearing the dismissal, grateful for it, Ty stood. He would not beg. With or without the money that was rightfully his, he would find a way to keep the clinic open.

He turned to go, paused at the sound of his name on his father's lips. "I have one final thing to say."

Ty glanced over his shoulder.

"Whether you remain stubborn for a day or another year, when you return to the life you're meant to live, and return you will, know that I will welcome you with open arms."

* * *

The two days that Ty had given Katie to think over his job offer came and went in a flurry of activity. Katie had finished her tenure at the factory, the time a gray-and-white blur in her memory. Each minute had played out like the one before, each hour as tedious and exhausting as the last, each day seemingly endless.

One moment stood out in the haze of all the others. Early in the morning on the day following Katie's visit to the clinic, when Bridget had already left for work and Katie was about to exit the apartment herself, a knock had come at the apartment door. A young boy had come delivering a telegram for Shannon.

"It's from Liam," her sister squealed. "I knew he would contact me. I knew it!"

Katie was equal parts happy for her sister and incredibly frightened. Love like that had the power to make the rest of the world disappear. It made a person reckless and blind to the other person's faults.

Hands shaking, Shannon lowered her head and read the telegram. Her excitement vanished in stages, morphing into something darker.

"I don't understand." A frown marred her smooth forehead. "It's simply not possible."

Katie exchanged a worried glance with her aunt.

The older woman carefully approached Shannon. "What does your young man have to say?"

Shannon looked up, her eyes glassy.

"Liam's journey has been delayed." The frown dug deeper, the confusion now sharing space with a hint of outrage. She lowered her head again and seemed to take a moment to reread the telegram. "Mrs. Gallagher has taken ill."

Aunt Jane looked once again to Katie. "Oh, dear."

"It's just like that old dragon to pull something like this. I knew she didn't like me, but this is, it's just . . . evil." The word crackled like a struck match in the chill that had fallen over the room. "Liam doesn't feel comfortable leaving Ireland until his mother recovers."

There was new frustration in Shannon's voice, and Katie's heart broke for her. She thrust out her hand. "May I see the telegram?"

Shannon yanked the paper out of her reach. "He's still coming. It says so right here." Lip caught between her teeth, she turned slightly away and read Liam's words aloud. *"Once Mother is well, I'll board the first ship to America."*

Head down, Shannon shifted the paper from one hand to the other, turning it over onto its back and then face up again. She studied the black type as if it would somehow magically transform into a different, more pleasing message.

"He'll come," she whispered, pure grit in the words.

While her niece pored over the telegram, Aunt Jane took Katie aside. "Do you think he's sincere? Will he come for her?"

Katie cast a worried look in Shannon's direction. "I simply don't know."

"I have no idea what to say to the girl."

"Let me try." With a deep sigh, Katie considered at least a dozen ways to confront the situation.

Carefully, Katie told herself, *proceed carefully.* "Perhaps you should write Liam and tell him about the baby."

Shannon was shaking her head before Katie finished speaking. "That's not something I dare put in a letter."

"Will you write him at all?"

"Of course."

"What will you say?"

"I'll tell him I'm sorry for his mother. I'll keep it light and tell him I miss him and can't wait to see him again."

"Shannon, you might want to consider—"

"Don't finish that sentence. I won't hear a single word against Liam." She screwed her eyes shut and took a long, deep breath before cracking them open again, first one, then the other. "He said he would do anything—anything at all—to be with me. He will come. I'll keep saying the words until he does."

Katie made the conscious decision to relent. For now. The risk to their fragile relationship wasn't worth further agitating the girl. Yet. It wouldn't be long before they would know whether Liam's promise had been given in earnest. He'd sent the telegram, which spoke well enough of his commitment for now.

Still, Katie worried things weren't as happy between the young lovers as Shannon wanted to believe. Again, Katie told herself, time would reveal all.

And so, after choosing to avoid an argument, Katie had reluctantly left for the factory, torn between frustration and concern for her sister's mental state.

Apparently, she'd been right to worry.

According to Aunt Jane, Shannon had spent the rest of the day working herself into a lather. She'd alternated between worrying that Liam would never get away from his *controlling mother*, and fretting that something terrible would happen to him on the ocean voyage over. She'd eventually exhausted herself and didn't have the strength to come out of the bedroom to eat.

"I hate seeing you so sad," Katie said on returning home that night. She sat on the edge of the bed. "Maybe a change of scenery will help. Perhaps it's time we find you a job."

"You want me to leave the tenement house? No." Her sister stared at her in horrified panic. *"No."*

"You're pregnant, Shannon. Not ill. You can work." Katie used her calmest voice, displayed her most understanding manner. "It won't hurt the baby."

"But. But." Shannon sat up, knuckled an errant curl off her face. "I can't leave here."

"You can."

"Not *all day*."

"Having something to do, someplace to be, will help make the wait for Liam go quicker. And besides, Shannon, we need the extra money."

"Now wait just a minute." Shannon climbed hastily to her feet, jammed her fists on her hips. "You told me you've decided to take the position at Dr. Brentwood's clinic."

An image of Ty insinuated itself in her mind. Katie refused to let the man distract her. "Well, yes, that's right."

"You said he's going to pay you more than double what you made at the factory."

"Again, that's right."

"Then I don't need to work," Shannon said, mutiny written all over her face, "because you'll be making enough money for the two of us."

Katie couldn't quite stifle her impatience. She'd had a long day at the factory. Her supervisor had seemed determined to make Katie work three times as hard as the other finishers. Punishment, Katie supposed, for leaving, even though her exit was Mrs. Zephyr's decision. The woman couldn't know about Katie's new job, and yet . . .

None of that was important at the moment. Shannon was making herself sick with worry, practically immobilized by fear. Katie had to think of something to get her sister's mind off her troubles.

"Shannon." Katie spoke over a surge of emotion that felt as much like defeat as annoyance. She hardly recognized the person her sister had become. Where was the girl who couldn't wait for the next adventure? "Why won't you leave the tenement house?"

"What if . . . ?" Shannon dipped her head and drew in a quivering breath. "What if Liam shows up and I'm not here?"

Katie fought back a sigh. "I'm sure Aunt Jane will entertain him until you come home from work. She's very good at—"

"No. I won't do it. I can't. I can't risk missing him. I must be here when he arrives. I won't listen to another word about leaving this apartment. I won't."

Now the girl was being irrational. It was no different than talking to Bridget about her job. The experience was just as frustrating, just as fruitless.

And much like arguing with her cousin, there were so many flaws in Shannon's thinking that Katie didn't know where to begin. But then her sister lifted her head. There was real fear in her face, and her hands shook as they clutched at Katie's arm. "Please don't make me leave the apartment. Let me stay until Liam arrives."

Concerned for her sister's mental state, Katie had again relented, promising herself to bring up the topic again once Shannon was better rested.

Unfortunately, she and Shannon had nearly a repeat of the conversation the next morning and the morning after that, their stalemate coming no closer to a resolution. At this rate, Shannon would worry herself sick, which would not be good for her or the baby she carried. The thought came with a sharp pang of defeat.

It was now the day Katie was to begin work at Ty's clinic, and she sighed for what must have been the tenth time in so many minutes as she looked away from her sister's set expression. Her gaze landed on the stack of sewing awaiting her attention.

Of course. *Of course.*

Why hadn't she thought of that sooner? Of the two of them, Shannon had always been the better seamstress. Katie went to the table. She traced her finger across one of Mrs. Armstrong's unfinished gowns.

Gazing at the garments, she said to Shannon, "If you insist on staying inside the apartment all day, you'll grow comatose from boredom."

"I'm willing to take that risk."

Stubborn to the end.

Very well.

"I could use your help." Katie shook out the gossamer pink silk, a perfect complement to Mrs. Armstrong's dark hair and alabaster skin. "This dress is nearly complete, but I'm not fully satisfied with what I've done. It's the bodice. Something's missing. I can't figure out what it needs."

To Katie's relief, Shannon joined her at the table and concentrated on the dress in question. "It needs additional decorations here"—she pointed to a spot just above the waistline—"and here," she said, indicating the sleeves. "Tiny rosettes in white, lavender, and blue would look lovely."

Indeed. "All excellent suggestions, but Mrs. Armstrong is coming by tonight for a fitting after supper. I won't have time to sew on rosettes before she arrives."

Shannon looked at her dubiously. Then, making a face, she reached for the gown. "I suppose I could work on them while you're at the clinic."

"That would be such a help. You truly don't mind?"

She lifted a delicate shoulder. "Not at all."

Katie released an exaggerated sound of appreciation. "Thank you. You have no idea how much this means to me."

A rueful smile crossed Shannon's lips. "Laying it on a bit thick, don't you think?"

Katie gave her a mock look of surprise. "Who, me?"

Her lips curving at the edges, Shannon took the dress and sat on the bed. She studied the garment with the eye of a master seamstress. "Would you mind if I made a few other alterations? Nothing substantial, just a gather here and a tuck there."

"I would be thrilled. Go ahead, Shannon. Unleash your creativity. And, no, before you say it, this time I'm not overstating my enthusiasm."

Katie left the apartment ten minutes later, her steps lighter than in the previous few days. It was nice to see her sister a little less sad and not so obsessed with Liam. Better yet, Shannon's talent with a needle and thread would produce a finished product far grander than what Katie could have created on her own.

The day was unseasonably warm, the sky only slightly overcast. At another time, on another day, and in another place, Katie would have stopped to admire the collection of clouds. She loved looking for shapes, especially the ones that reminded her of animals, like the one in the east that almost, if she squinted, had taken on the form of an elephant.

Smiling, Katie let her thoughts drift over what lay ahead. Her mind wanted to linger over the image of Ty offering her the job, and his quiet desperation when he'd spoken of his patients.

Despite what Shannon thought, even with the higher salary Ty would pay Katie, money was still an issue. Aunt Jane's health wasn't getting any better, and once Shannon's baby was born, that would be one more person in an already overcrowded apartment.

They really could use another person contributing to the household expenses, if for no other reason than to move the entire family into a larger living space.

Passing off the extra sewing to Shannon was only a temporary solution. The sooner the girl could contribute on a more permanent basis, the better. Katie wasn't overly fond of Shannon working at a garment factory, but what other prospects were there for an eighteen-year-old Irish immigrant?

With nothing but her depressing thoughts to keep her company, Katie allowed herself a moment to wallow as she made her way down the seemingly endless street. Lined with crumbling tenement houses, it was one long and terrible stretch of deprivation. She walked past characterless buildings with tired-looking façades, sure signs of the despair that lived within their walls.

At the street corner, she reminded herself that the situation for her family wasn't dire. She and Bridget had jobs. They also had time before the baby arrived, at least six months, possibly seven, or maybe only five. Katie could only estimate and not with much accuracy. First pregnancies were difficult to gauge from symptoms and weight gain alone, and Shannon was stubbornly tight lipped about the date of conception.

Liam Gallagher owed a full accounting of his behavior when he arrived. *If* he arrived.

Katie's stomach sank at the thought. *That man better not break my sister's heart.*

The streets were crowded this morning, no more than any other day, but Katie suddenly felt suffocated by the sheer numbers packed in the small space. The poor were everywhere, competing for jobs with long hours and ridiculously low pay.

As Katie pushed through the milky morning light, she was more determined than ever to make a move uptown, or perhaps across the river to Brooklyn, where there was less chaos and despair.

Today, Katie reminded herself, was her very own new beginning, the start of a new job and one rather large step in her quest for a better life.

As if to add its encouragement, a bold ray of sun escaped like a finger through a crack in the clouds. The clinic came into view. Katie quickened her steps and stopped at the sight of a familiar form standing on the front stoop.

Her heart soared. Ty was waiting for her. That was her first thought, followed by a happiness so profound that she had to stop walking to regain her lost breath.

A dark, wistful longing she hadn't experienced since childhood speared through her heart, leaving a vague sense of dissatisfaction. Not sure what to do with her hands—with the unexpected yearning she didn't want—Katie remained very still and forced her mind to clear.

She had no room in her life for dreams abandoned years ago. Her family depended on her, and Dr. Titus Brentwood could not be allowed to divert her attention. One problem with that—his very presence was a distraction.

As if sensing her eyes on him, he turned his head.

Something flashed in his gaze, something like delight. He was happy to see her. Katie watched as he slowly blinked, and the pleasing glint was gone, replaced by the serious expression she was growing to think of as part of his medical persona. He gave one firm nod in her direction. It was his only greeting, but Katie felt her cheeks heat with pleasure.

This man was special, and not merely because he'd been the first man to kiss her. He cared about the people he served. That wasn't always the case in this neighborhood.

Face impassive, lips pressed in a straight line, he motioned her forward.

Katie answered the call without hesitation, adoring the feel of his eyes on her. A light breeze kicked up, the air pleasantly cool on her face. "I didn't expect a welcoming committee."

"A pitiful showing of one."

"One is enough," she said, smiling now.

He returned her smile. "I assume your presence means you've decided to take the job."

"You assume correctly."

"I'm glad."

The sun slipped from behind the clouds and bathed him in light. Her heart dipped, and she could feel the blush creeping up her cheeks.

Eyebrows cocked, he asked, "Shall we get started?"

She nodded.

He stepped back, reached for the door, then swept it open with a flourish that reminded her of a circus ringmaster introducing the main attraction.

Once inside the clinic, she followed Ty to a wooden coat stand. He took off his jacket and rolled up his shirtsleeves. His forearms were muscular and, oh, what splendid hands he had, capable of fixing damaged people.

She glanced up to his face.

Expression bland, he stood like a sentinel, straight, with his eyes level. "We're low on supplies, so I'll need you to take an inventory of what we have plenty of and where we're short. I won't be able to replenish everything at once, so we'll have to improvise at times."

He smiled with a quiet apology in his eyes that caused her breath to catch. Ty was such a good man, and yet distant. There was something profoundly solitary about him. Even his smile seemed to somehow isolate him further.

"Not to worry." Compassion scraped her words raw. "I know how to make do with very little."

"It's a lesson I'm still learning."

Her smile wobbled. His remark was yet another reminder of the difference in their situations. For once, Katie was the one with a set of skills he didn't have. It seemed absurd.

"I thought I would be the student, but it looks like there's something I can actually teach you."

"Katie."

"Yes?"

It felt like years passed before he spoke again. "You mustn't be nervous." Ty covered her hand with his, his glance sincere, spurring her heart into a faster beat. "You and I, together, we're going to make a difference in this neighborhood."

Her heart lifted and sighed at the certainty in his voice.

"It's my greatest hope."

She was quite unable to look away from him.

"Ours will be a strong partnership," he said.

"I'm counting on that."

"As am I." The smile he gave her brought to mind thoughts of forever and happily ever after, and Katie had never been so scared in her life. She couldn't fall for this man.

She couldn't fall for any man. Even as she told herself this, her heart constricted with a whirlwind of emotions she'd never felt before.

As she tried to breathe through the pain, her mother's words came to her: *If love doesn't hurt a little, if loving a man doesn't make you question your previous thoughts about everything that came before him, then he isn't the man for you.*

Why had that memory come to her? Why now? Katie didn't want her mother's brand of love. She knew how it ended. In heartbreak.

Fighting to regain her composure, she stared at the ceiling as if utterly fascinated by its chipped, dull gray paint.

She was saved from further contemplation when the door swung open and Mr. Kelly rushed into the clinic, carrying his white-faced son.

Chapter Twenty-One

Ty stepped forward, immediately taking in the boy's condition. Pale, sweating profusely, his color turning a sickly green. His eyes were shut, making him look as if he were sleeping peacefully. But his chest rose and fell in a restless cadence that indicated a different diagnosis.

Before Ty could ask, Mr. Kelly said, "He fainted on the way over."

"How long has he been feverish?" Ty asked, his hand flat against the boy's forehead.

"Two days."

How could Mr. Kelly wait so long to bring the child to Ty? What had the man been thinking, letting his son's condition worsen, when Ty had given him the address of the clinic?

Blood slammed through his veins, and he had to battle the reflex to scold the sick boy's father. Even one day of neglecting an infection could prove the difference between life and death.

No use upsetting the man, Ty told himself. *No use.*

He completed his initial exam in tight-lipped, stoic silence. At the sight of the original bandage covering the wound, Ty's frustration came out in a ragged sigh.

Instead of asking why Mr. Kelly hadn't changed the plaster or, barring that, brought Aiden to the clinic to have it done, he leaned in and sniffed. The unpleasant odor wafting off the wound had him reaching for the boy.

The father pulled back, clearly unwilling to hand over his son.

Grasping for his last scraps of patience, Ty grazed a hand over his chin and spoke with deliberate precision. "Please put your son on the examination table."

When Mr. Kelly continued to hesitate, Ty put a real sense of urgency in his voice. "It's imperative I check the wound for infection."

The signs were there. He just needed confirmation. Then he could treat the problem.

"Mr. Kelly." Katie placed her hand on the man's shoulder. "Give Aiden to Dr. Brentwood. He'll treat your son with the same gentleness and care he did once before."

The tension visibly seeped from the father's body, and, with Katie leading the way, he moved to the exam table, then set the boy on top with a worried frown.

While Ty washed up and put on a sterile apron, Katie cooed softly to the child.

"Aiden, sweet boy." She swept her fingertips across his forehead. "Can you hear me?"

The child surfaced at the sound of her voice. "Miss Katie? How . . . how did you get here?"

"I'm afraid it's the other way around, dear." She leaned over the prone form. "Your father brought you to me."

"I guess that's just as good." He gave a tentative smile, then curled up and let out a pitiful moan.

Ty took his place at the table opposite Katie. "Aiden, can you tell me where it hurts?"

"My leg."

"Anywhere else?"

"Just my leg. It feels like someone put a flame to it and won't let up."

"I'm going to have a look at the wound."

"Okay. No, wait." The boy grabbed Katie's hand and held on as if his life depended upon the connection. "Okay, now I'm ready."

Ty swallowed past the lump in his throat. The picture the two made was more mother and son than nurse and patient. He could see Katie as a mother. She would kiss away all the hurts and hug away all the sorrows.

The beating of his heart went wild, thudding heavy and uneven against his ribs. Ty shifted his stance and reached for the bandage he'd applied to the wound three days ago. The skin was hot to the touch, and, even before he lifted away the scrap of linen, Ty could see the red streaks progressing away from the wound.

Hand poised on the bandage, he exchanged a look with Katie. She reapplied herself to the task of keeping the boy calm.

Ty pulled away the linen, his expression never changing. It was precisely as he'd feared. The wound had become infected. The skin was swollen, the color an angry red. There was also considerable discharge of a thick yellowish liquid from the wound itself.

Now that he knew what he was dealing with, Ty worked quickly. He applied iodine to sterilize the infected area, then took his time cleaning the wound. While he worked, Katie kept the boy still and the father calm.

When all that was left was to bandage the leg again, Ty called the father forward. Again, he had to fight the urge to lecture the man. "You were right to bring your son to me."

Mr. Kelly's shoulders relaxed.

"I cannot stress enough that you must keep the wound clean at all times, change the dressings regularly, use the salve Katie will give you, and whatever you do, avoid direct exposure to the cut from dust or other debris."

The man shielded his eyes with his hand. The resulting shadow curtained his expression, but Ty saw the strain in his flat, grim mouth. "You're saying this could have been avoided if I had done what you told me to do the first time."

Smart man, also a worried father wallowing in guilt over failing his son. It wasn't necessary to add to Mr. Kelly's suffering.

"Katie will send you home with the necessary supplies to take care of the wound. If Aiden continues to have a fever, or the wound doesn't heal, or it continues to smell foul, bring him to me at once."

"I understand."

Ty saw that he did. "Even if the wound appears to be healing, I want to see Aiden again in a week."

The boy perked up. "Will you be here, Miss Katie?"

"You may count on it."

"Then I'm happy I got stabbed. Well, not really, but kind of, sort of." The response, as well as the grin, belonged to a child caught in the throes of first love.

Ruffling his hair, Katie laughed, a delicate, airy sound that lightened the atmosphere considerably. For reasons Ty couldn't understand, his heart lurched.

The rest of the morning went quickly. They treated five patients, three with minor cuts and contusions, one with a broken finger, and one complaining of abdominal pain that Ty, after extensive investigation, decided was caused by food poisoning, an all too common ailment due to the neighborhood's unsanitary conditions.

Katie was giving instructions to the victim of food poisoning when Sebastian arrived with a bag of supplies donated from the hospital. That was his claim, at any rate. Ty suspected the other doctor was the donor, but save from calling the man a liar, there wasn't much he could do. He would, however, bring up the situation with the Temple Foundation. He owed Sebastian the truth.

But not now.

Now, he introduced Katie to Sebastian again, but this time with the addition of her job duties. "She'll be assisting us here at the clinic."

This seemed to surprise the other man. "You're a nurse?"

Her face went blank, like a switch had been turned off, but then her smile returned and she said with quiet confidence, "Not yet."

Things got busy after that when an elderly woman with heavily accented English came into the clinic complaining of chest pains.

The work was consuming and required all of their focus. Ty nearly forgot about the letter from Josh Temple. It was just as well. Neither Ty nor Sebastian had a break until the end of the day.

After putting Katie to work restocking the shelves and making a list of what they lacked, Ty requested a word with the other doctor in his office.

Sebastian sank in the lone chair facing Ty's desk. "I must say, old fellow, I thoroughly approve of your new hire. Katie O'Connor is the perfect addition to the clinic. She's dedicated, meticulous, and, like I said, an excellent hire."

Though he'd expressed nothing more than simple admiration for the woman's work ethic, the other doctor sounded as smitten as little Aiden.

Ty adjusted his smile to one of polite indifference. "You think she's worth twenty-five dollars a week?"

"Twice that. But it's not what I think. It's how the patients respond."

Ty agreed.

"She has a way about her." Sebastian made a vague gesture with his hand as if he couldn't quite come up with the quality he meant to attribute to Katie. "She puts people at ease, especially the frightened ones. And she charms even the most cantankerous. She really is rather remarkable."

Yes, she was.

Ty was trying very hard to forget just how remarkable. He had nothing to offer a woman like Katie, not anymore. Maybe he never had. Vanessa had deserved better, and so did Katie. He would end up hurting her. Not intentionally, but—

"You wanted to speak with me about another matter?"

Right. He rummaged in his desk and fished out Josh Temple's letter.

Leaning forward, hand outstretched, Sebastian took the paper. "What's this?"

"Read it first, then we'll discuss its contents."

Worry shadowing his eyes, Sebastian whistled softly. "Well, the man is certainly succinct."

"That's one way of putting it."

Eyebrows cocked, Sebastian gave him back the letter. "What are you going to do now?"

"The only thing I can, given the situation." Making a sound of impatience deep in his throat, Ty returned the letter to his desk. "Find another benefactor."

"That won't be easy."

"No." Jaw set, he allowed a short humorless laugh to glide through the word. "It won't be."

Ty didn't immediately share the details of his disastrous meeting with his father at the Harvard Club, or the fact that he had yet to secure an invitation to any of the homes once open to him without question. He knew he had three options at his disposal. He could do nothing and simply leave the clinic in the hands of fate. It would either flounder or thrive. Or he could approach his father again, hat metaphorically in hand, and agree to whatever terms would restore goodwill between them.

Perhaps you aren't ready to come home. No, he wasn't. Nor was he prepared to perform surgery again, which left him with a single choice.

The one he'd already decided upon yet hadn't seen through at the Harvard Club. Ty would reach out to his former friends and acquaintances and get himself back on the list for parties given by the matrons of society. "I have a plan."

He laid it out for Sebastian.

"You don't seem very happy about returning to that world."

"I have my reasons for resisting, as you well know."

Sebastian nodded. "Guilt is a powerful motivator or, in this case, a detractor."

The other man would know. Soon after hiring the Brit, Ty had given him a brief history of the clinic's beginnings, including his personal reasons for leaving a promising career in surgery. It had seemed only fair to let the other doctor know what kind of man he would be working with.

Encouraged by Ty's openness, Sebastian had shared more of his own history and how he'd failed to save his mother from a butcher posing as a doctor, finishing in a philosophical voice: *We each must seek redemption in our own way.*

Indeed.

"You know I'd offer to reach out to my connections," Sebastian said now, "but I've been in the country for barely six months. My social circle here is relatively small. And most of my friends are, like me, just starting out in their chosen professions. None of us have the sort of funds you need to run this place. Still . . ." The other man opened his hands, palms forward in the universal show of surrender. "If you acquire the invitations, I will happily attend the functions."

"Happily?"

Sebastian shrugged. "Close enough."

Ty knew the man's offer to help was given in all seriousness. One thing he'd learned over the past few months was that Sebastian Havelock had a highly developed sense of duty. He would attend the parties if Ty requested it of him.

But no, Ty was the one with the connections and this was his clinic, his responsibility.

Besides, he'd hidden from society long enough. "I appreciate the offer, but this is something I have to do myself."

"You will want to borrow one of my suits."

"This one is fine."

"That may have been true a year ago. But you've put some wear on it, old fellow."

"Quality can withstand a little wear," Ty argued.

"The jacket is wrinkled beyond repair, and you're missing a button there." The man closed one eye and pointed to one of the lapels. "The hem is frayed on the left trouser leg as well."

Ty looked down, noted that Sebastian was correct. "How did you know that? I'm sitting behind a desk."

"I noticed it this morning. Take it from someone who knows, you will squeeze out more money from your rich mates if you look as though you don't need it."

"You make a valid point."

"Where will you start?"

"I'm still working on that part of my plan."

"What about your father? He's the most renowned surgeon in the world. His connections must be legendary."

Clearly, the other doctor had no idea what he asked of Ty.

"You could use me as the catalyst, a way to open that door, if you will." Sebastian turned thoughtful, rubbing his chin, the sound of day-old stubble scratching against his palm. "I could talk up the clinic, and, selfishly, I would relish the opportunity to mine your father's brain, for scientific purposes, of course."

Familiar irritation flared and, with it, acceptance. Ty's father was widely known for his groundbreaking techniques. It stood to reason that a gifted young doctor like Sebastian would want to meet the man in person. "I'll arrange an introduction."

It was the least he could do.

"Well, now I *have* to help you court new donors." The other man stood. "We aren't going to lose the clinic. I won't let it happen, and neither will you."

Of all the words the other doctor spoke, one stuck out: *we.* When had Sebastian become emotionally invested? Probably around the same time he'd started showing up on afternoons in addition to their original agreement of three mornings.

A second of silence passed between them. It was then that Ty heard the sound of skirts swishing. He glanced to the doorway.

Katie hovered on the threshold, a tiny frown pleating the small space between her thin eyebrows. Her eyes smoldered with a dozen questions.

Ty swallowed around the knot in his throat. How much of the conversation had she heard?

Too much, he decided, if her lack of direct eye contact was any indication.

"I've finished restocking the shelves and have made a list of the items we're running low on." She lifted the small piece of paper she had clutched in her hand. "I'll just leave it on the table next to your medical bag."

Her voice was full of the efficiency Sebastian had mentioned not more than five minutes ago, but her face had paled to milky white.

She turned to go.

"Katie, wait." Ty shoved to his feet. "Let me walk you home."

For a moment, he thought she might argue. Or worse, actually agree to his offer. And then, when they were alone, push him for answers about his past.

Ty worried that if she did press him, he would tell her every sordid detail of how he'd come to opening the clinic. He would tell her the truth.

He would tell her that Dr. Titus Brentwood was a killer.

Chapter Twenty-Two

Katie looked from one doctor to the other, wishing she'd waited to deliver her list by five minutes. She hadn't wanted to overhear their conversation, but she had. And now she couldn't look either man in the eye.

She'd worked with each of them and had thought she'd known them. She'd thought that although they were young, they were also educated and highly skilled.

All of that was true. Still. It never occurred to Katie that they served the people of the Bowery out of guilt as much as dedication. She felt all achy inside, as if she carried a portion of their burden merely because she'd heard the tail end of their conversation.

She lowered her gaze as Ty approached her. He'd offered to see her home. She wasn't sure that was a good idea. Her curiosity was too strong. She would ask him questions she knew he didn't want to answer.

"I'm perfectly capable of walking myself home."

"I insist."

Dr. Havelock joined them at the door, his face grave. "I'll take care of this."

The doctor pulled the list free from her fingertips, looking as awkward as Katie felt.

He was a handsome man, in his late twenties, perhaps, with dark hair and a heavy, intelligent manner, but with the sort of smile she'd learned was bestowed freely under most circumstances. This was not one of them. The smile he gave her was one of regret, the sort that tried to mask an unpleasant situation with polite indifference.

"Until tomorrow," he said without inflection.

Katie nodded. "Tomorrow."

There was nothing more to say to the young doctor. She remained silent while Ty helped her into her coat and escorted her outside, and then all the way until they were nearly upon Orchard Street. It was a glorious evening, warm but not hot. The sun had begun its lazy descent. Shadows lengthened at her feet, the late-afternoon light just beginning to burnish the buildings with gold tones.

Heaving a heavy sigh, she drew to a stop.

Ty did the same. Surprisingly, he was the one to speak first. "I'm scheduled to work at Ellis Island tomorrow."

"I thought you only volunteered on Fridays."

"Usually that's true. But I'm filling in for Dr. Anderson. I'll be gone all day." His expression turned alert, watchful. "You'll be comfortable working with Dr. Havelock, alone, without me there?"

Katie heard something in his voice that gave her pause. She was on full alert now, breathing faster, aware of every sight, sound, and smell with sharp-eyed clarity. "You don't trust Dr. Havelock?"

"On the contrary, I trust him implicitly. The question is, do you?"

She thought for a moment. While she found the doctor easy to work with, she'd rather assist Ty. An odd sensation swept through her at the thought, part confusion, part longing. And . . .

Ty had asked her a question. "Yes, I trust him."

"Then I won't insist you stay home."

He would let her stay home if she felt uncomfortable with the other man? He would do that for her?

Of course he would. Ty was protective by nature. And yet, his concern for her also seemed more than that. It was personal.

She felt a furious drumming in her heart, an anticipation that had been building in her since they'd shared a bench on the ferryboat.

With a shaky hand, she touched his sleeve, closed her fingers over the material. "You're paying me too much to stay home for half a day, much less a full one." Ah, yes, here was her opening. "Speaking of money, I'm sure you know I overheard part of your conversation with Dr. Havelock. I didn't mean to eavesdrop."

The muscles beneath her hand went very still. "What part did you hear?"

A fresh spurt of disquiet tickled her throat as an awful thought occurred to her. "I know you can't afford to pay me twenty-five dollars a week."

"I never said that."

"Not in so many words." The memory of what he had said sent too many questions scrambling around in her brain, like moths to a streetlamp. "You and Dr. Havelock need to find new donors for the clinic, and that means money is tight."

"I'm not letting you go." The way he said the words made her think he needed her. Katie wanted him to need her. She wanted to be his center. His helpmate.

Oh, my. She was in deep.

"Why do you need new donors, Ty? What happened to the others?"

"It was one donor, a lone benefactor." His eyes were so grave beneath those thick lashes. "His son made the decision to pull funding after one last payment."

"I'm sorry."

He swallowed a few times, and she realized he didn't know how to respond. She dropped her hand, and they continued toward her tenement house.

"Did the man's son give you a reason?"

"He didn't need to expand. I know why."

There was such resignation in his voice that Katie found herself stopping again. "Will you tell me?"

"It's a long story, best saved for another day."

She sensed there would never be a good time to hear the sad tale, and so she pushed. Just a little. She took his hand, linked their fingers. "I'm a good listener."

He straightened his shoulders as if taking on a weight. "I'll tell you, but not here, in the middle of the street."

"How about there." She pointed to the front stoop of 223 Orchard Street. Not ideal, nor the most comfortable or even the most private, but they would be away from the main flow of traffic. And most people at this hour were too busy hurrying home to notice a man and woman sitting on the steps of a run-down tenement house. If Bridget arrived home from work, unlikely but possible, well, then Katie would send her cousin inside the building with a meaningful glare and a promise to join her soon.

The fast-flowing traffic whooshed by, the noise constant—people coming and going, merchants striking deals as they negotiated prices in polite arguments, and sometimes not so polite.

Katie and Ty sat, neither speaking right away. As one minute turned into five, Katie realized she would have to be the one to start the conversation. She snatched a quick fortifying breath and forged ahead. "You mentioned your father is a famous surgeon, and although you offered to introduce Dr. Havelock to him, I got the sense you were resistant to doing so."

"My father and I aren't close. We once were, but now there's tension between us. He insists I'm wasting my training working in the Bowery."

"There's great honor in serving people less fortunate than yourself."

"He wouldn't disagree with you, but he claims my calling is not at the clinic."

The grim twist of his lips puzzled her. “I don’t understand. Are you saying your father looks down on the poor?”

“Not at all. He’s a dedicated philanthropist, well known for funding causes that forward reform in all parts of the city.”

“Now I’m thoroughly confused. Why would he claim the clinic isn’t your calling?”

“Hundreds of doctors can work with the poor, but only a few have my skill and my . . . hands.” He lifted them as he spoke, then turned them over palms up, frowning, with an expression so sad it made something inside her ache.

“You’re a surgeon.” How had she not seen that sooner? The signs had been there, in the way he’d sewn up Aiden’s leg with careful precision, each stitch an exact replica of the one before.

“I’m not a surgeon. Not anymore.” Hands still in the air, he swept his eyes over her face, his features unreadable. “I’ll never operate again.”

“What happened?”

“A woman died on my table.”

Not that Katie knew a lot about surgical procedures, but she knew enough to ask, “Was it the first time you’d lost a patient?”

Surely, that would explain why he seemed so devastated.

“No. There are always risks. But this patient wasn’t just any woman. Her name was Camille, and she was my friend’s wife. She’d miscarried twice before.”

As Ty told Katie the story of the third pregnancy, the baby’s breech presentation, and the procedure he’d insisted on performing, she didn’t move, didn’t speak, afraid if she did she would break down and weep for Ty, for his friend, and for the woman he’d unsuccessfully tried to save with a cesarean section.

“I told them the operation was the only way to save the child. It was the truth. But there were unforeseen complications even before I made the first incision.”

“What went wrong?”

"The baby's heartbeat was dangerously slow. I could barely hear it with the stethoscope, which told me time was running out for the child. By the time I opened Camille's belly, he was already dead. The cord was wrapped around his neck, and Camille . . ." Ty turned his head in Katie's direction. "She died moments later."

From the way he looked at her, Katie knew Ty was expecting her to be outraged. She wanted to sob for him instead, to mourn the woman he'd lost on his operating table.

Katie's first instinct was to defend Ty's actions. Not with false words but the truth.

"You made the right decision, Ty. The cesarean section was the only way. I've witnessed the birth of breech babies. The complications are too many to count. Even if the midwife—or doctor," she added with a meaningful look, "manages to turn the baby, the delivery rarely ends well."

"I should have never operated on her, or maybe I should have opened her sooner. Either scenario puts the blame firmly on me."

Oh, Ty. Her heart bled for him.

Katie drew in a few quick breaths. From the age of seven, she'd wanted nothing more than to help people. She'd originally aspired to become a nurse, knowing the odds were against her ever achieving such a dream. It was only in her later years, after she'd begun assisting the village midwife, that she'd dreamed of becoming something even more.

What would it be like, she'd often wondered, to be a doctor? Or when she was feeling especially fanciful, she'd imagined herself a surgeon. With the knowledge and ability to save lives with her own two hands.

She'd hardly allowed her mind to embrace such an unlikely notion. When she did, it was only in the vaguest of terms. What she'd never contemplated was the cost that came with the job. It had never occurred to her, not once, that in the process of saving lives, she would risk taking them instead.

The burden Ty carried was massive, and Katie worried for him, more than was good for either of them.

"Shep blamed me for his wife's death, as did many of our friends."

Katie tried another couple of breaths. She looked into Ty's eyes, saw the sense of failure in their depths, shimmering in the tears that formed but didn't dare fall. She was lost for an answer to his pain.

"People who knew us both chose sides." He frowned at something beyond her shoulder. "Most of them aligned with Shep, rightfully so. He was the one who'd suffered the loss."

Ty had suffered a loss as well. Katie couldn't be the only one to see that. "Surely, not everyone turned against you."

"A few stayed loyal. My father and brother have never lost faith in me." He moved slightly away from her, keeping his face blank as he said, "And my fiancée stayed true. To this day, her faith in me has never wavered."

"You're"—emotion clogged her throat, tightened in her stomach—*"engaged?"*

But that couldn't be right. He'd kissed her. And held her close, not in the way a man engaged to another woman should.

"Vanessa and I aren't engaged. Not anymore."

Not anymore. The same words he'd used to describe his career as a surgeon, spoken with the same lack of inflection.

"Vanessa did nothing wrong. She was a rock. Even when our friends sided with Shep, she stood by my side. When my father pushed me to return to surgery, she pushed as well, for all the reasons my father gave but with more grace. She said one mistake shouldn't define my future."

Katie wanted to dislike the woman but found she couldn't. She'd recognized Ty's potential. Katie would be wise to do the same, to consider that his calling in life might not be the clinic. "Vanessa sounds wonderful. Why aren't you still engaged?"

"She broke things off when I insisted on living in the Bowery, among the people I serve."

"I'm sorry."

"Don't be. We parted amicably. I wasn't the man she'd agreed to marry. My priorities had changed. *I* had changed, and there was no going back to what I'd been. She wanted security and a life of privilege. I could no longer give her either."

"You wanted to serve the poor. There's nobility in that."

"I want to serve the poor, yes, but I also seek redemption. I save lives in the name of the one I lost. That's selfish, not noble."

This man had lost so much: his friends, his family, his fiancée. All because he'd insisted on performing a procedure that often proved fatal. "How long has it been since you last saw your friend—what was his name—Shep?"

"Not long after I killed his wife. Mutual friends threw a dinner party and invited us both. They probably thought it was a good idea to force us into the same room together. They were wrong. To say the evening ended badly would be a gross understatement."

His response had Katie's stumbling heart slamming against her ribs.

"You aren't a killer," she said, her hand coming to rest on his arm. His muscles were coiled like a spring.

"I pushed for the surgery. I knew the risk, but in my conceit, I thought the odds didn't signify. I convinced Shep surgery was the only way to save his baby." He buried his face in his hands, hissed softly. "I failed my friend. I failed Camille. I can't stop thinking I should have saved her."

"Listen to me, Ty. The baby was breech, the umbilical cord wrapped around his neck. You didn't kill your friend's child, or his wife. You tried to save the woman and her baby."

"I didn't do enough. Or maybe I did too much."

"The odds of survival were stacked heavily against them. You have to know that."

The tense, quiet stare he gave her accomplished what words couldn't: *I want redemption.*

Oh, Ty.

She leaned forward. "I'm going to ask you something, and I want you to think very carefully before giving me your answer."

As she leaned in closer, she focused intently on one aim: to help this man see the truth of what happened, the full truth, not his distorted version. "If you hadn't operated on your friend's wife, if you had given up after failing to turn the baby, would he now blame you for not trying hard enough to save his wife and child?"

Ty blinked, his face the very picture of bafflement.

"Allow your mind to go back to the scene," she urged softly, "to the moment when you realized you wouldn't be able to turn the baby. What was your first thought?"

He shut his eyes. "If I don't act quickly, both mother and child will die."

"Why did you think that?"

There was an unusual look on his face now, a frown not only of concern, but also of powerlessness. "The fetal heartbeat had dropped. I couldn't hear it with the stethoscope. Neither could the nurse."

"And your friend's wife? How was she faring?"

"Her pulse was also low. She'd gone limp on the table." He opened his eyes and turned a look of despair Katie's way. "Camille was going to die no matter what I did. She had uncontrolled bleeding at the separation of the placenta. I was too late."

Katie gasped. A hemorrhage. The poor woman had bled to death.

"If I had operated on her sooner—"

"You may have still been too late."

He pressed his lips together in a grim line.

"You did everything you could, Ty."

"It still wasn't enough." Katie heard the rough honesty and the deep code of ethics that ruled him. "All my training and reading and attendance at lectures by the best doctors in the world, and, when it came down to it, I couldn't perform a simple delivery."

Katie had never considered that her expertise could exceed Ty's. She'd come to believe that he knew everything there was to know about medicine. Yet she said, "That's where you're wrong. There is nothing simple about childbirth."

"You're right, of course. What I meant was that I've performed some of the most dangerous surgical procedures, many rarely tested. A cesarean section should have been nothing in comparison. I should have—" He stopped, shaking his head in self-deprecation. "And that's the sort of arrogance that led to Camille's death."

"Being confident in your skills is not arrogance."

Mouth still flat and grim, he balled a fist and stared down at it. "You shouldn't be so easy on me."

"And you shouldn't be so hard on yourself."

Still looking at his hand, he flexed his fingers, closed them into a fist again. "Why are you defending me?"

"You lost a patient." *And so much more,* she thought. "You left surgery, and, setting aside my opinion on that, instead of letting sorrow cripple you, you made a new life for yourself. One that involves sacrifice that most men from your world would never embrace."

"Not for the right reasons." He swiveled his head to look at her. "Like I said, my motives are selfish."

"Perhaps they were at first," she allowed, her heart tripping over itself at all his fierce attention focused on her. "But I don't believe that's true anymore."

His eyes narrowed. "You think you know what's in my heart?"

"I know you've stuck with it for a year. I know people in the Bowery have access to medical care previously unavailable to them."

"I picked the easy route, where my skills are hardly tested."

"Taking the easy route doesn't necessarily mean you've chosen the wrong path." Though Katie feared, in Ty's case, it *was* the wrong one.

"You know nothing of my life." Something dark came and went in his eyes. "I have not lived entirely above reproach."

She very much doubted that. How much hard living could he do? "Have you frequented saloons, gambling houses, and opium dens on a regular basis?"

"No."

"Have you stolen what didn't belong to you?"

"No."

"Have you denied treatment to someone in need?"

"*No.* Of course not."

She swallowed a smile at his obvious outrage.

"I have done none of the things you listed, but if I was to speak plainly, I would say that I have spent too many nights in the past with a glass of brandy in my hand."

A weight settled in Katie's stomach. She glanced to the sky stacked with clouds that had taken on the colors of sunset and attempted to reconcile her mind with an image of Ty overindulging in alcohol. She couldn't.

Looking at him, she saw the eyes of a consistently sober man, and so she said, "I have never seen you suffering the consequences from a night of overindulgence."

"I haven't had a drink since the night our paths crossed on the ferryboat."

With something close to wonder, she fought to keep her breath from clogging in her throat. "You're a good man, Titus Bartholomew Brentwood. Never doubt that."

As she made the declaration, something shifted inside her. Could it be? Was she . . . ?

Dear God, it couldn't be true.

She wasn't falling in love with Ty. Was she?

Doomed, she thought, holding his gaze without blinking. She didn't want this. The feelings in her heart were bold, astonishing. And although Katie couldn't quite fathom how or why, they rang true.

No. No, no, no. She wanted nothing—*nothing*—to do with this kind of love. It was too possessive, too poisonous, and thoroughly consumed its victims.

How could she have let this happen?

Somehow, when she hadn't been paying attention, she'd condemned herself to the very fate she'd fought against ever since her mother had died in her arms.

* * *

Although Ty had argued with himself nearly every night in the dark loneliness of his current life, fully convinced his reasons for opening the clinic were self-serving, he now realized his motives had been far more complicated. He'd thought his life had morphed into an existence defined by loss, but that wasn't wholly accurate.

With Katie sitting beside him, the truth unfolded in his mind as if it had been waiting for a final push.

He liked serving the poor. Liked the fact that he made a difference. Liked that he served where others refused. It wasn't about skill. Service was about desire and heart. And right now, all he could think was that Katie O'Connor, with her quiet beauty and compassionate nature, was the one who'd led him to this revelation.

The monumental consequences struck him. The future that stretched before him no longer seemed so bleak, because this woman believed in him.

She thought he was a good man, one of noble character. She truly believed Camille's death was an unfortunate turn of events, not the mistake of an egotistical man trying to prove he was the best of the best.

Maybe Ty could be the man she thought him to be. Maybe, just maybe, for the sake of this woman, he could manage to overcome his past.

Lingering doubt twisted in his heart, freezing the breath in his lungs. But then he stared into Katie's eyes. There was acceptance in her face, a kind of peace that was a part of her very nature. Knowing this woman had changed him from the inside out.

In that moment, he believed he was worthy of the forgiveness he sought, that redemption was within his grasp.

"Katie." He spoke her name only once. She spoke his in return. And then, they were silent again.

Mildly aware of one moment turning into two, he took her hand and, together, they rose to their feet. She felt the shift in their relationship. He knew she did by the way her breath quickened and her eyes softened with unbearable tenderness. He saw healing, friendship, and more.

He shouldn't do it.

He shouldn't kiss her. Not here. Not in the view of a hundred strangers. He moved his hand up her arm, stopping just under her elbow. The little catch in her breath told him he could press his lips to hers and she wouldn't push him away.

He pulled her closer, and she relaxed against him. And for that brief moment, all was right in the world.

"Ty? Ty Brentwood? Is it really you?" A female voice came at him from mere yards away, startling him as if someone had tossed a glass of cold water in his face.

Ty took a step back from Katie and, slanting a glance in the direction of the well-dressed woman alighting from a horse-drawn carriage, found himself confronted with his past.

A chance meeting, on the steps of a nondescript tenement house nestled in a Lower East Side neighborhood, and the carefully constructed life Ty had built for himself teetered on its rocky foundation.

The woman completed her ascent up the stone steps with a smile on her face, a bundle of inexhaustible energy.

"Oh, my stars, Titus Brentwood, it *is* you." Surprised delight sounded in every word. "Ben and I were just talking about you the other day. What an odd, wonderful, fortuitous coincidence that you should be standing on this stoop, today of all days."

Ty had decided to reach out to old friends, and here stood the wife of one of the best he'd ever had. He hadn't believed in coincidences until now. For, surely, the woman hadn't sought him out.

An avalanche of emotion crowded inside his head. He could hardly breathe, could hardly make sense of the moment. With great effort, he managed to push words past his frozen lips.

"Hello, Ellie." Even as he greeted her, his mind reeled. Eleanor Armstrong. Ben's wife. Vanessa's closest friend. Here. "You're looking well."

Ellie had always been a striking woman, her features flawless, her skin a creamy alabaster. Her eyes were as dark as her hair, the irises nearly the same color as the pupils, a symmetrical, matching set perfectly aligned beneath arched eyebrows.

Ty seemed to remember that she came from humble beginnings, but he couldn't recall the particulars. Not that her simple roots had mattered. Her beauty had made her the darling of the season three years ago. Every man of Ty's acquaintance had vied for her attention. Only one had turned her head, Benjamin Armstrong. Ben. A successful businessman and doctor who also happened to be Ty's former colleague and one of the few people who'd stood by him after Camille's death. Ellie had been another.

Memories—some good, many of them not so good—threatened to rob him of the calm he desperately sought.

Cocking her head at an attractive angle, Ellie glanced briefly at Katie, who seemed rendered speechless by their exchange, then returned her attention to Ty. By her wide, unassuming smile, it was easy to tell that his old friend was pleased to see him. "I must say. You're looking much happier than when we last met." She gave his arm an affectionate pat, pat, pat. "I'm glad."

In an attempt to honor her candor, Ty responded in kind. "I apologize for my behavior. I left rather abruptly, without thanking you for the invitation. It was badly done of me."

"I'm afraid none of us were at our best that evening."

Her words brought him immediately back to the night in question, when Ty had made the final break from his former world. Ellie and Ben had requested he attend a small, intimate dinner party at their home.

He'd accepted the invitation before knowing that Shep had been invited as well. His friends had meant well, clearly hoping that by putting the two men in the same room, they would somehow heal their rift.

From start to finish, the evening had proven a disaster. Accusations were made. Words were said that couldn't be taken back. And that was before the second course had been served.

Sweat broke out on Ty's face at the memory. He had to resist the urge to hook his finger beneath his suddenly too-tight collar and tug it away from his neck.

"Ben and I have longed for news of you. But, Ty." Ellie's brows pulled together in a delicate frown that managed only to add to her stunning looks. "I don't understand. Whatever are you doing here, on the steps of the tenement house Ben inherited from his father? You couldn't have possibly known I would be here."

"I escorted Katie home. The streets can be dangerous at this hour." Ty regretted the words as soon as they left his mouth. He shouldn't have exposed Katie to . . . he wasn't sure what he'd exposed her to. Not reproach. Ellie wasn't that sort of woman.

"So, you two do know one another." She glanced at Katie, back to Ty, then back to Katie again. "And here I was making this meeting all about me." Ellie gave a tinkling laugh as she swung her gaze once more to Ty. "I insist you tell me how you know this lovely girl."

Katie chose that moment to leap into the conversation. "I'm working as Ty's assistant."

"He's fortunate to have you."

Katie's cheeks turned a becoming pink. "What a kind thing to say."

"It's nothing but the truth." Ellie gave Katie a winsome smile, her eyes full of affection. Katie's responding grin was equally congenial.

Their ease with one another spoke of friendship, which wasn't all that surprising, Ty realized. Both women were generous of heart, kind spirits who cared for the people in their lives.

He was still pondering their connection when Ellie shifted her attention back to him. "I wasn't aware you owned a garment factory."

"I don't."

She angled her head. "Yet you hired Katie?"

Ty shifted from one foot to the other and opened his mouth to explain, but once again, Katie beat him to it. "I work at his medical clinic in the Bowery."

"You opened a medical clinic in the Bowery. How absolutely wonderful." The silky tone had a delighted note underneath. "Although, I daresay, Ben won't think so. He would much rather you teach him everything you know about surgery."

A chill ran up Ty's spine. For a third time, Katie spoke in his stead. "The work Ty is doing at the clinic is invaluable."

"I have absolutely no doubt."

Ty stared straight into Katie's glittering eyes. Her expression had grown fierce. A woman on a mission, determined to defend him and his choices.

He fell a little in love with her in that moment, a dangerous prospect, one that wouldn't turn out well for her.

What if he fell all the way in love with her?

There had to be a way to forestall the inevitable. But he couldn't make his mind work properly, not with Ellie's curious gaze bouncing from him to Katie, measuring, gauging, putting the puzzle pieces together.

He knew exactly how to distract her. "Now that we've established how I know Katie, the question, Ellie, is how do you?"

Chapter Twenty-Three

While Mrs. Armstrong talked, Katie watched Ty closely. In a futile attempt to remain calm, she shifted her stance. The new position did nothing to eliminate her unease. She feared she was about to lose what little progress she'd made with him.

To make matters worse, she was filled with a confusing mix of feelings. Jealousy, for one, because Ty had known Mrs. Armstrong in his former life and they'd been friends. Good friends, by the informal way they spoke to one another. Clearly, she and her husband had been among the few people who'd stood by Ty.

That was a point in the woman's favor.

However, knowing it was a source of shame for him to have failed so dramatically as a surgeon, if only in his own mind, Katie also felt a sense of protectiveness—and a stirring of antagonism. There was something wounded in Ty's eyes that Mrs. Armstrong's unexpected presence had rekindled.

Katie wanted to offer him comfort, to smooth away that haunted expression on his face, but she simply didn't know how. She was in over her head, drowning in uncertainty and powerlessness. Ty had opened a portion of his very soul to her, sharing his deepest shame only moments before confronting someone he'd known when the event had occurred.

She knew the situation couldn't be easy for him. With Mrs. Armstrong on his left and Katie on his right, he was, quite literally, standing between his past and his present.

"As I said," Mrs. Armstrong continued, "upon the death of his father, Ben inherited this building and three others on this block. Two more one block over."

"That doesn't explain how you and Katie know one another."

"I was getting to that." She gave him a slightly scolding pat on his arm.

The gesture brought a slight tilt to his lips. And just like that, jealousy took precedence over the other emotions in Katie's heart. Mrs. Armstrong was at her best, full of charm and upper-crust manners.

"Katie and I met a few months back," the other woman said. "Not long after Ben discovered he owned the tenement houses. We'd both heard horror stories of the living conditions down here, thanks in large part to your brother's heartrending photographs." Pausing, she moved to address Katie directly, her smile firmly in place. "When Ben decided to tour the properties and see for himself if the rumors were true, I insisted on tagging along. We'd planned to sell the buildings, but have changed our minds. Instead, we want to make further improvements."

"That's good to hear." A portion of her antagonism vanished, and Katie found herself returning Mrs. Armstrong's smile.

This woman had stood by Ty, and she seemed generally happy to see him. If Katie hadn't already liked her from their previous encounters, she certainly had every reason to now.

"So, you met Katie during that initial tour," Ty said.

"Not then, no."

Ty simply looked at her.

"I am taking a rather roundabout way to get to my point." She released a breezy laugh at herself. "I met as many tenants as I could that first day, Katie's aunt among them. While Jane Sullivan and I shared a cup of tea, I noticed a pile of women's garments in various stages of completion. I'd seen similar pieces in other units, but none as beautiful or as well made."

The look she gave Katie was one of complete respect. Katie seized the moment and interjected herself into the tale. "Mrs. Armstrong commissioned me to make her a few dresses for a series of upcoming occasions. She is here today for a final fitting."

Ty's expression never changed as he looked from one woman to the other. "Is that . . . typical?"

"No," they said in unison, smiling again at one another.

Ty smiled as well, and he cupped Mrs. Armstrong's hand neatly between his palms. "It's good to see you, Ellie. I mean it. I should have said that right off. My only excuse is that you took me by surprise."

"I'm quite certain that I did."

He released her hand. "My sincere apologies."

"You were a beast to disappear as you did, without a single word to let us know you were all right." The woman's soft, faintly amused affection was unbearable to watch. "But I forgive you."

His stance instantly relaxed. "Please give Ben my regards."

He gave one firm nod, a sort of abbreviated bow. Any second now, he would take his leave.

Mrs. Armstrong didn't give him the chance. She laid a hand on his arm, looked into his eyes. "Perhaps you should contact Ben yourself. I know he would enjoy hearing from you."

Ty turned thoughtful, a bit reluctant, but after a moment of silent contemplation, he said, "Perhaps I'll do just that."

His response reminded Katie about the conversation she'd overheard between him and Dr. Havelock. He planned to return to his old world for the sake of acquiring a new benefactor. How could Katie fault him for that? But once he returned and found he was missed, would he wish to stay?

"Wonderful. Ben will be so pleased. Perhaps I could coax you to come by the house one evening next week."

The silence that followed this request seemed to last an eternity.

"Please, Ty. It would only be the three of us. Or"—she paused—"you could bring Katie with you, if that would make you feel more comfortable."

Katie opened her mouth to object. There was no reason for her to accompany Ty to this woman's home. She didn't belong in that world.

And Ty doesn't belong in yours.

His presence was only temporary. Katie knew that now, understood it on an elemental level.

"Please don't say no," Mrs. Armstrong said to Katie, then turned and addressed Ty once again. "I'd very much like to hear more about your clinic. If not dinner next week, then some other time in the near future."

"I'll think about it. Goodbye, Ellie. I'll contact you soon."

With a preoccupied glance, he said goodbye to Katie next. A moment later, he'd melted into the crowd, another form bobbing in the sea of humanity.

Katie bit her bottom lip. The force of feelings rushing through her made her want to weep with frustration, helplessness—and hope.

She wanted to be a part of Ty's life—oh, how she wanted that—but she didn't really know the man. Not the complete man, not the part of him that had been a brilliant surgeon, who moved in circles that included sophisticated women like the one standing beside her, staring after his retreating form.

Katie took a hard breath and made herself say what was on her mind. "I don't think it would be a good idea for me to accompany Ty to your home. You see, Mrs. Armstrong, he and I—"

"Call me Ellie."

Katie blinked, feeling flustered and embarrassed. "I don't know that I should."

"Of course you should." The woman linked her arm in Katie's, making them a unit. An illusion.

"We come from two different worlds," Katie was quick to point out, speaking not only about the two of them, but also about her and Ty.

"Not so different. Actually, you and I have quite a lot in common."

"I don't see how."

"I grew up in a small town out west. You grew up in a small Irish village. We are also two women who share a love of fashion and a mutual friend."

"You are very . . . persuasive."

"It's one of my more endearing qualities. Now, come. We have much to discuss. And I have dresses to try on." She guided Katie into the building with the confidence that came from ownership. "I'm quite desperate to see what you've created with those lovely hands of yours."

The woman's easy manner went a long way to quieting Katie's nerves. Ignoring the little flutter in her stomach, Katie told her about Shannon's expert assistance. "My sister is a remarkable talent. You won't be disappointed."

"Now you've piqued my curiosity even more, and I find myself wishing to race you up the stairs in all eager anticipation."

"I'm half tempted to join you."

They laughed in tandem. Nevertheless, they made the climb at a relatively sedate pace.

After introductions were made, Katie and Shannon helped Ellie into the first of the commissioned dresses—the pink silk with the rosette embellishments.

Breathing slowly, she turned in a circle, studying the dress in the mirror from every angle. She twirled again, a happy grin on her face, her dark eyes sparkling with appreciation. "It's simply the prettiest dress I've ever worn."

"I'm glad you like it." Nearly limp with relief, Katie moved in behind the woman and began checking the fit.

While Shannon worked on the hem, Katie tugged at the seams on the bodice, placing pins in strategic places. They worked in silence and managed to finish nearly at the same moment. As one, they stood back and checked their handiwork.

"It really is a stunning dress," Shannon murmured, her voice full of the pride that came from a job well done.

They helped Ellie out of the first dress and into the second. When Katie went to work securing the buttons at her back, Ellie made a request. "Shannon, would you be a dear and make me a cup of tea?"

Shannon turned a questioning eye in Katie's direction. No wonder—Ellie had turned down the offer of tea when they'd begun the fittings. Katie nodded at her sister, knowing Ellie's sudden desire for tea was nothing more than a ruse to get Katie all to herself.

Her suspicions were confirmed when Ellie called after Shannon. "Take your time, dear. I prefer a strong brew."

Once they were alone, the other woman's gaze filled with silent inquiry. "Have you known Ty long?"

Katie fought to hide her dismay over the blunt question beneath a calm smile. "Yes and no."

"Well, now I'm thoroughly intrigued."

Why was Ellie so curious? Was she seeking fodder for gossip? Katie turned the problem over in her mind. This woman cared about Ty, that much was evident. Her feelings blazed real and true, giving Katie confidence that she truly considered Ty a friend and was possibly even worried about him.

Deciding to trust this woman, Katie told her about meeting Ty on Ellis Island in his official capacity.

Mouth agape, Ellie pressed the palm of her hand to her heart. "How extraordinary."

Katie explained about the risk he'd taken on her behalf, not only with her, but also with Shannon.

"I had no idea it was so difficult to get into this country."

Katie flushed. "There are reasons for the rules."

"Of course there are, but I have to wonder how many deserving immigrants weren't as fortunate as you." She shook her head. "I suppose we'll never know. The important thing is that you and your talented sister made it here, and we have Ty to thank for that."

"We do."

"And you have stayed in touch ever since that fateful day?"

"Our paths crossed again only recently." She told Ellie about the ferryboat ride, and then their teamwork sewing up Aiden Kelly's leg. "Ty offered me a position at his clinic that very day."

"It's all so fascinating. I am more determined than ever to tour the facility."

"It's not a facility." Katie described the clinic and the difficulties Ty faced, withholding his financial troubles. That wasn't her story to tell. "Gaining the trust of the people in the neighborhood is slow, which was one of the reasons Ty hired me."

"That's brilliant. You smooth the way, so to speak, since you are one of them."

Since you are one of them.

The words cut deep, leaving a gaping hole where her stomach used to be. Though she probably didn't realize how hurtful her words sounded, Ellie had just put Katie firmly in her place.

"What's wrong, Katie?" There was sympathy in Ellie's gaze, a quiet understanding that would have soothed Katie's distress if she didn't know how impossible the situation was. "I've said something to upset you. Won't you please tell me what it was?"

The sincerity of the question startled her. Katie realized she was on the verge of crying. She could not answer for fear of losing control. Her eyes drooped, nearly shutting before she fluttered them open again. "It is nothing."

"Oh, it's something." Ellie took her hands and squeezed gently before releasing them. "I've upset you and I really must know why."

"It's not what you said, precisely. You merely pointed out that I'm an immigrant. And Ty . . . is not."

"Do you have feelings for him?"

Katie felt the familiar race of her pulse. She shrugged a shoulder, wanting to tell this woman nothing, yet needing to tell someone—anyone—everything. Why not Ellie?

"I care about him, I admit. He's a good man. But it's all so hopeless."

"Ben and I come from different worlds. Katie, if a man truly cares for a woman, he sees past her background."

"Nothing could come from an attraction between Ty and me."

Ellie paused a moment, her head cocked at a curious angle, before asking her to explain. And when she made the request, she spoke as if she and Katie were the oldest of friends, accustomed to sharing their most troubling secrets.

Katie confessed it all then, telling Ellie about her parents' legendary love and her mother's death so soon after her father's.

"Tragic," Ellie agreed. "It's also a testament to their love."

"You sound like my sister."

"I knew I liked that girl."

"But, don't you see, I'm not of a romantic disposition. I haven't been since childhood." It was one of the ways she'd willfully distinguished herself from Maggie O'Connor. "Ty deserves a woman who can love him without reservation, with her whole mind, body, and heart."

"I think you just might be that woman."

Hadn't Ellie been listening? "My vow to avoid turning into my mother has become a habit. One I'm afraid has become so ingrained in my nature, I can't remember a time when it wasn't a part of me."

Ellie's face filled with quiet purpose. "I think you're on the verge of breaking free."

Katie bit her lip. A sob lodged halfway up her throat, sticking in the same spot as her lost hope. She wanted to love Ty, but not at the expense of herself.

"Since you've been so forthright and honest with me," Ellie said, "I feel it's only fair that I do the same." Turning away from the mirror, she fiddled with the lace Shannon had added to the cuffed sleeve. "I have a confession to make."

The splash of guilt in Ellie's voice didn't escape Katie.

Stunned with an inexplicable sense of things about to go very badly, very quickly, Katie wrapped her arms around her waist and waited for whatever news her friend wished to impart. "I'm listening."

"I didn't meet Ty through my husband. I met him through my closest friend, Vanessa."

A bolt of alarm shot through her. Katie knew that name. "You're speaking of Ty's fiancée."

Ellie hesitated, but only briefly. "His *former* fiancée."

Discounting the spurt of anguish that swept through her at the knowledge Ty had loved another woman, enough to ask her to become his wife, Katie told herself that she was sorry he'd lost so much with one surgical procedure gone wrong.

Unlike Ellie, she was not a persuasive person. Worse still, she'd revealed the contents of her heart to this woman, Vanessa's *closest friend*. Katie felt foolish and ashamed. "I have put you in a tough position."

"Not at all. I hope . . . that is, Katie . . ." She paused. "May I speak freely?"

Katie nodded.

"No one was happier to see Vanessa call off her wedding to Ty than I."

After a moment of numb shock, outrage struck. Anger on Ty's behalf squeezed Katie's chest with a tight fist, clenching, clenching, until she couldn't inhale. "Ty is an honorable, decent man," she ground out. "The best I have ever met."

"Oh, dear, I didn't mean to imply he was anything but wonderful. What I meant to say was that Ty and Vanessa weren't a good match.

They never really suited beyond a few superficial commonalities. I adore them both, but they would have been miserable as husband and wife."

"I . . . don't know what to say."

"Then let me do the talking. And perhaps this time I won't muck it up." She drew a step closer. "You, Katie, suit Ty. And I believe he suits you."

If only that were true. If only Katie could let herself love him and not have her feelings overwhelm them both. If only . . .

If only . . .

"Take away all the trappings of your situation and his, ignore the outlying details that brought you together, and simply look at Ty as a woman would look at a man on the most primal level. Do that, Katie, and you will see that I'm right about the two of you."

Was that hope soaring in her heart? She knew better than to give in to the emotion. Ty would heal one day. He would return to his true calling, and Katie would lose him. But not yet. "You've given me something to think about."

"Excellent. Now." Ellie spun around to face the mirror once again. "What are we going to do about this neckline? It's a bit too severe for my taste."

Happy to return to more comfortable ground, Katie moved in behind the other woman and went to work on the dress.

Chapter Twenty-Four

Shannon paced outside the closed bedroom door, her mind a riot of thoughts and emotions. She was beyond pleased that Mrs. Armstrong loved the dress she'd worked so hard on—truly, she was—and she was gratified that the woman preferred the extra little details she'd added to the gown. But, really, what could she possibly want to say to Katie that required Shannon out of the room? The request for tea had clearly been an attempt to dismiss her without offering offense. Shannon had been hurt nonetheless.

The reflex to interrupt came fast, strong, and too powerful to deny. But deny it she did.

Shannon was young, not ill mannered.

Shooting a hard glare at the shut door, she continued her one-woman vigil. She strode back and forth across the frayed rug at her feet. She'd been at it for fifteen minutes when the baby moved.

Laughing softly, Shannon set her hand on her stomach and whispered, "I can't wait to meet you. I hope you look just like your father."

The child rewarded her statement with another quickening.

A slow smile curved her lips. "So fierce, little one. Just like your mother."

Feeling bolder, Shannon approached her eavesdropping as she would a particularly difficult seam, with ruthless focus.

She pressed her ear to the door. If she remained perfectly still and held her breath just so, she could hear most of the conversation through the poorly insulated wood.

Katie was telling Mrs. Armstrong how she'd met Dr. Brentwood a year ago on Ellis Island and how he'd rescued her from certain deportation. *Yeah, yeah*—Shannon rolled her eyes—*old news.* She pushed away from the door, made two more circuits around the perimeter of the room, then gave in to temptation once again.

Now, Katie was admitting she had feelings for Dr. Brentwood. Shannon snorted. More old news.

What wasn't old news was that it seemed Mrs. Armstrong knew the good doctor personally. At last, they were getting somewhere. Shannon pressed up against the door. If she could get a little closer . . .

Just when things were getting interesting, the front door opened, heralding Bridget's arrival home from work. Next came the sound of her cousin's feet moving across the floor. Shannon was too absorbed in the conversation on the other side of the door to acknowledge Bridget with more than a brief wave over her head.

What was this? Dr. Brentwood had a fiancée? Correction, a *former* fiancée, and Mrs. Armstrong happened to be close friends with the woman?

"Shannon, what on earth are you doing?"

"I'm making tea for Mrs. Armstrong."

"Right. Don't know how I could have missed something so obvious."

"Not even mildly amused," Shannon said without looking back at her.

Bridget's hand closed around her arm. "Come away from the door, little cousin."

With her ear still pressed against the wood, Shannon tried to shrug off Bridget's grip. "I can't leave now. They're just getting to the good part."

"Stop eavesdropping." Bridget tugged on her arm. "It's rude."

A minor battle ensued. Bridget, four inches taller than Shannon, soon gained the upper hand. Eventually, size won over determination. Shannon, her chances of hearing anything else ruined, was forced to step away from the door or risk alerting the occupants on the other side of her nosiness.

Annoyance had her spinning around in a flurry of skirts and bad attitude. The sight of her cousin's face made her gape. "What happened to your eye?"

Pink crawled up Bridget's neck. "I sort of fell into a man's fist."

Shannon's eyes narrowed. "That can't have been pleasant."

"This is a true statement." Sighing softly, Bridget reached up, touched the swollen skin beneath her eye, then winced.

"You had trouble at work."

"Another true statement." Bridget glanced over her shoulder.

Shannon followed the direction of her cousin's gaze, which lingered on Aunt Jane's bedroom door. It was her turn to wince. Aunt Jane was a wise woman. One look at Bridget's face and her cousin's lies would be exposed.

Perhaps it was for the best. Risking her safety wasn't worth the extra money Bridget earned at her job. Her cousin had lost objectivity, and now she would have to confess all. No hiding that eye.

"What happened, Bridget?" Shannon sensed this story was even better than the one unfolding in the bedroom. "You have to tell me everything."

Seconds ticked by before her cousin slid her attention back to Shannon.

"Not here." She hitched her chin to her left. "In the kitchen. I'll show you how to make tea properly. Your way isn't very efficient."

At least her cousin's sense of humor hadn't completely disappeared. Shannon fell into step beside Bridget without a single argument.

Bridget's eyebrows shot up, not exactly an attractive look with the red eye quickly turning green. By morning it would be fully black. "What? No more eavesdropping?"

"I've been reformed."

"So quickly?"

"What can I say? You're a good influence on me."

"I beg you, little cousin, don't ever emulate me." Bridget's features were set and determined, as severe as the black cloak she had yet to discard.

After helping her cousin out of the garment, Shannon sat at the table, waited for Bridget to do the same, then said, "So? What happened?"

"The police raided the club." Bridget's voice was barely above a whisper as she spoke, and all the more chilling for the soft, bleak tone. "Oh, Shannon. I made a terrible mistake that cost the club both patrons and money. Sounding the alarm is the most important duty I have and one of the reasons I get paid so well. I failed and I have no excuse."

"It can't have been *all* your fault."

"Perhaps not." Drumming her fingers on the table, Bridget fell silent. Her eyes grew dark and turbulent. "I was arguing with Declan instead of keeping a good lookout. The police were already entering the building before I noticed their presence."

"You weren't arrested yourself?"

"Declan dragged me away before they saw me."

"You don't mean Declan Kennedy, as in Regina's older brother? The neighbor who lives across the hall? The big one, with all those muscles and the handsome face so pretty he looks like a fallen angel?"

"That's the one." Bridget made a face. "Although your detailed description is entirely too flattering for the odious man."

"What was he doing in the Bowery?" From everything Shannon knew about the man—which, admittedly, wasn't much—Declan

Kennedy was a hardworking Irish immigrant set on getting out of the neighborhood as quickly as possible. "He doesn't seem the type to drink or gamble *or* loiter outside a gentlemen's club."

"That's because he's not." Bridget folded her hands together on the table and studied them as if the answer to all her problems resided there. "The man is a veritable saint."

"Then what was he doing outside the club arguing with you?"

"Causing trouble, that's what." She blew out a hiss. "He'd shown up specifically to lecture me about the *error of my ways*. Apparently, he's decided to be my self-appointed guardian angel."

"He certainly looks the part, all stoic and tough and manly."

"Don't defend him. As big and bad as he looks, Declan has the patience of Job. Until he's pushed." Bridget let out a slow breath, head down, gaze still locked on her clenched fingers. "I seem to be very good at pushing him."

A terrible, horrible, awful thought occurred to Shannon, and she felt sick to her stomach. "Bridget. Please tell me Mr. Kennedy isn't the owner of the fist that you *accidentally* fell into."

"What?" Bridget's head whipped up. "Good God, no. Declan would never raise his hand to a woman."

"Then who hit you?"

"It happened before Declan showed up. A patron got a little out of hand and . . . anyway"—she curled a tendril of black hair around her finger—"that's not important."

Shannon disagreed, and she sensed Mr. Kennedy would side with her if he were sitting in the kitchen with them.

"One look at my face, or more specifically, my eye, and Declan went all protective and possessive on me."

"Did he now?" That sounded awfully romantic to Shannon. She suddenly missed Liam very much. Longing filled her heart as she reached for the locket around her neck.

Bridget's expression still showed frustration, but there was a very slight softening in her tone. "If the police hadn't shown up when they did, I believe Declan would have gone into the club and imparted a little Old Testament vengeance on my behalf."

A low-lying resentment simmered in the words, but also something else. Appreciation, perhaps.

Well, well. Despite her obvious irritation with Declan Kennedy, Bridget liked the man. Shannon liked him, too. "He reminds me of Liam."

"Who does?"

"Declan."

Bridget folded her lips into a fierce frown. "Then you're better off without him."

Shannon felt the color drain from her face.

"I'm sorry, Shannon. I didn't mean that."

Too late. The words had been spoken.

"I'm not better off without Liam." She could feel her skin burning with outrage. "He's the best thing that ever happened to me."

"Of course he is."

"I miss him." Clutching at the locket, she fought back an onslaught of tears. "Oh, Bridget, I miss him so much."

"I'm sure he'll show up soon."

Shannon angled her head in surprise. "Since when are you so certain?"

Bridget didn't quite hold Shannon's gaze. "I believe he'll come because . . . because *you* believe it."

"Good answer."

"I know. Anyway." Bridget shifted in her chair, the tightness returning to her shoulders. "Not only do I have to do some quick talking to keep my job, now I have to figure out a way to hide my black eye from my mother."

"No," came a voice from the doorway. "Now you have to stop lying to your mother about your job."

Bridget's face went deathly white. "Mam." She climbed hastily to her feet. "You're supposed to be resting in your room."

"And you, Bridget Constance Sullivan, are supposed to be working at the garment factory, sewing buttons onto gentlemen's coats."

Knowing when it was time to retreat, Shannon slipped out of the room with soundless footsteps.

Neither woman took note of her departure. Bridget, the dear girl, was about to face a reckoning, and, in Shannon's estimation, it couldn't have come a moment too soon.

Chapter Twenty-Five

One month later, after an especially long day at the clinic, Katie woke with a start.

Mind in a muddle, she shoved up onto her elbows and looked around the darkened room. Still unused to sleeping on the sofa, even after all this time, she couldn't make out the shapes swimming before her.

Impatient for her eyes to adjust to the weak light, she rubbed at them, wondered at the time. The heat was unbearable, and she could hear the distant rumble of a thunderstorm. But that's not what had woken her.

Bang, bang, bang.

An insistent knock sounded at the door, giving Katie another jolt. She squinted at the clock on the mantle. Ten minutes past midnight. Who would come at such a late hour?

She pushed to her feet.

At the same moment, Bridget stumbled out from her bedroom, her hair a black waterfall of wild tangles cascading down her back.

She looked exhausted, as if she'd had a restless few hours. More like a restless few weeks. Now that the lies about her job had been exposed, Bridget seemed worse rather than better. Her relationship with her mother was practically nonexistent, and, worse still, she refused to quit her job. She seemed determined to destroy her life.

Wasn't truth supposed to set a person free? It had only made matters worse for Bridget.

"Who's making all that noise?"

"I don't know." Hurrying to the door, Katie pressed her cheek to the wood and called out, "Who's there?"

"It's me, Regina. From across the hallway." An unmistakable note of fear rang in her voice. "I, we . . . it's your sister," she said to Katie. "She needs you."

Shannon.

Katie threw open the door. "Where is she? What's happened to her?"

"There's no time for explanation. You need to come quick."

Bridget drew up alongside Katie. "I'm coming with you."

"What about Aunt Jane?"

Bridget glanced over her shoulder. "If all that banging didn't wake her, I say we let her sleep."

"Agreed."

"Hurry," Regina urged from the hallway. "Shannon's sick, really sick. I found her on the washroom floor."

Fear struck like a fist.

The sound—was that retching?—stopped Katie cold. No, not retching. A woman was sobbing.

Katie rushed ahead of the other two women, calling out her sister's name. A moan was her only response.

"Shannon?"

There was a pause, followed by a series of coughs and sniffles. "I'm in here," came the weak reply.

Katie rushed in the direction of her voice. When she got to the end of the hallway, she halted at the sight of her sister crumpled on the floor of the communal washroom, a gold locket pressed in her hand, her head resting on her folded arms. "I want Liam."

"Shannon." Katie's tone remained even, though she wanted to cry out in helpless agony.

She'd hoped Regina had been exaggerating when she'd claimed her sister was sick. But Shannon's hair was in wild disarray, and what little Katie could see of her face was an entire shade lighter than freshly fallen snow.

"Oh, Katie." From her position on the floor, Shannon drew in a ragged breath. "I don't feel so good."

"Where does it hurt?"

"I'm having fierce stomach pains." She tugged at the locket around her neck. "I want Liam."

"Shh." Lowering to her knees, Katie reached out to her sister. Her shaking fingers petted Shannon's head in slow, gentle strokes. "Deep breaths, baby sister."

Not good. Not good. Her voice was too full of her fear.

Katie shifted her weight from her knees to her heels. The very edge of fear had her rocking back and forth. "How long have you been sick?"

"Thirty minutes, maybe a little longer." She took several slow gulps of air. "You said the sickness should have passed by now."

Trying not to alarm her sister, Katie told a slight fabrication. "It will, once the baby grows a bit bigger."

"I'm quite impatient for that day to come."

As am I, Katie thought, hating to see her sister in such agony. She did a few quick mental calculations from several starting points, unable to determine the date of the baby's conception and, thus, the source of this sickness. Shannon was either still early in her pregnancy or farther along than she'd indicated whenever Katie had pressed her about the date of conception.

Shannon eyes went glassy, and she bent into herself. Katie lifted the pot by her feet just in time. Shannon finished with a series of dry heaves.

"Lay your head on my lap," Katie ordered, quickly shifting her position so that Shannon had to lift her head only a few inches.

Even that appeared to be too much trouble. Shannon collapsed with a sigh, her hair falling forward and curtaining half her face.

"The nausea," Katie asked, "is it the same as before?"

"Slightly worse."

"Only slightly?"

"All right, much worse." Pressing a limp hand to her mouth, Shannon rolled onto her back. "It's . . . oh, Katie, you don't think something's wrong with my baby?"

"Blood," Bridget hissed under her breath, indicating a wet stain on Shannon's skirt about the size of a child's fist.

Katie told herself not to panic. A little spotting was normal. *That's not a little spotting. And my sister is farther along than she's led me to believe.*

Casting her cousin a quick worried glance, Katie leaned forward and lifted Shannon's tangled mass of mahogany curls. "Is your stomach cramping?"

Shannon lifted her head, dropped it just as quickly.

"Terribly." She swiped the back of her hand across her mouth and struggled to sit up. "The pain woke me, and I was having such a pleasant dream about Liam. I'm fine now." She seemed to force a smile, the edges around her mouth pulled tight with tension, as if she could will herself well. "See, all better."

Katie exchanged another glance with Bridget, then looked over at Regina. "Is Declan home?"

She nodded.

"Do you think he'd be willing to do me a favor?"

As if on cue, Declan Kennedy poked his head in through the doorway. "Did someone say my name?"

The Irishman was tall and big-framed, with amber hair. His wintry-blue eyes were full of concern. He glanced briefly at Bridget, an odd look on his face, then returned his attention to Katie. "What do you need me to do?"

"Will you fetch Dr. Brentwood?"

Declan's eyebrows pulled together. "I don't believe I know the man. Does he live in the building?"

"He lives on Henry Street, above a medical clinic." She gave him the address. "Please, Declan, I urge you to hurry."

She was speaking to his back.

The sound of his footsteps echoed as his feet gobbled up the stairs in a lightning-quick staccato. Even from five floors above, Katie heard the front door slam behind him but a moment later. She shared another look with Bridget.

"How are you feeling?" she asked Shannon.

"Better." This time, Katie believed her. Shannon's breathing had evened out, and she wasn't nearly as bent over as before.

"Are you still cramping?"

"I . . . no, I don't think so."

Katie glanced at her cousin, then to Regina. "We need to move her somewhere more comfortable than this hard floor."

They worked quickly, taking great care not to jostle Shannon any more than absolutely necessary to return her to the apartment. Once they had her settled on the sofa, Bridget procured clean water and fresh linens, then retreated to the kitchen with Regina to await Ty's arrival.

Left alone with her sister, Katie placed a cool cloth across Shannon's forehead. She was reminded of the one and only time her mother had cooled her brow in a similar fashion. Katie had been six years old and contracted a severe case of influenza. Mam had cared for her with such tenderness, gently massaging her aching limbs, singing lullabies to her, making her feel special and loved.

Katie did these same things to Shannon now, talking to her as if she were far younger than her eighteen years. "I love you," she whispered, pressing a kiss to the edge of her cheek.

A soft snore was her only response.

* * *

Ty fell into step beside Declan Kennedy. Moving at a clipped pace, they turned onto Orchard Street shoulder to shoulder. Fog slithered at their feet. Weak moonlight, aided by the streetlamps, silvered the trees and splashed a pale glow over the buildings.

Declan was a man of few words, which worked out well for Ty since he wasn't in the mood for conversation. He took a few furious strides, then cast his companion a glance.

After Declan had introduced himself as Katie's neighbor and insisted Ty call him Dex, he'd explained that there'd been an incident at the tenement house. Then he'd grown quiet, leaving Ty with a hundred terrible scenarios playing out in his head.

"Katie's been hurt?" he'd demanded when the man failed to give him more information.

Ty's legs became unsteady beneath him until Dex assured him, "She's quite well. It's her sister, the one that arrived from Ireland a couple months ago."

As the words sank in, Ty let out a shaken breath. Finally able to control the surge of excess emotion, he asked, "What's wrong with her?"

"I don't know." The other man's gaze fastened on him with dark intensity. "But Katie was insistent I fetch you at once."

They'd left the building soon after that.

Fortunately, Ty had been unable to sleep. With only his thoughts to keep him company, he'd been fully alert and prepared to treat the young woman.

Unfortunately, he'd wasted precious time gathering up items he might or might not need to treat her.

Both grim, neither man spoke as they entered the tenement building. They maintained their silence as they commandeered the first set of stairs—far quicker, Ty noted, than the last time he'd entered this building. The night he'd liberated Shannon from Ellis Island.

Much had changed since that fateful day, especially his relationship with Katie. Ty remembered the look of gratitude and awe in her eyes and was pierced with a tenderness so acute it made him want to weep. The emotion was soon followed by a burst of panic.

What if he couldn't help her sister?

What if he failed Katie like he'd failed Shep?

He rolled his shoulders as if he could shrug off the uncomfortable thought. The sound of his heels striking wood reverberated off the walls like hammers to nails. He glanced at the man beside him.

Who was Dex to Katie? The man wore what Ty thought of as the typical immigrant's uniform: black pants, muslin shirt, and a driven, almost hungry expression.

Ty had seen a similar look in his own mirror not more than two hours earlier.

As they rounded the corner and then tackled the second flight of stairs, Ty broke his silence. "Tell me what I should expect when we reach the top floor."

The Irishman pressed his lips tightly together. "I already told you what little I know."

Ty doubted that. People tended to know more than they realized. "Did you see the girl?"

Dex's steps faltered. "I got a brief glimpse of her."

"Then you know more."

The other man stiffened as if Ty had insulted him.

Returning his gaze evenly, Ty pulled Dex to a halt on the third-floor landing. "Tell me exactly what you saw in that brief glimpse of the girl."

His mouth flattened into a thin line. "Shannon was lying on the washroom floor."

"Had she fainted?"

"No, she was awake and moaning softly. The sound was gut-wrenching." He looked up at the ceiling, his mind clearly on the memory. "Katie was on the floor with her. Far as I could tell, the girl was sick to her stomach. But before that, when I was in the hall looking for my sister, I heard someone gasp out something. I don't know what. I didn't quite hear what she said. I thought she said *blood*, and maybe, yeah, that's what she did say, because then I heard my name and Katie sent me to find you straightaway."

Shannon could be losing the baby.

The memory of Camille's final hours materialized despite Ty's efforts to hold it back. She'd gripped his arm, sucked in a pain-filled breath, paused for endless seconds, then choked out her plea: *I can't lose another one.*

Ty shuddered. "All right." His voice came out tinny, as if rubbed with gravel. "That gives me a good idea what I'm dealing with."

"Will she be okay?"

"I'll know more once I see her."

They resumed their climb up the stairs and finally arrived at the fifth floor.

Ty gathered his bearings, then set out for Katie's apartment. The other man fell into step beside him. But when Ty turned right, Dex went left. "I'll be in the apartment across the hall if you need me."

"I'm sure someone will bring news once there's any to share."

"Appreciate that."

Alone now, Ty continued his pursuit. The sound of his breathing filled the empty hallway, the even cadence a mockery of the trepidation he felt. He flexed his neck to relieve the knots that had formed there, then checked the time on his pocket watch. One o'clock in the morning.

He lifted his hand, rapped lightly.

A familiar voice called out for him to come in.

Features twisted in a frown, he entered the room and then shouldered the door closed behind him. Tonight, he refused to accept another defeat.

Chapter Twenty-Six

Katie glanced up from her position on the sofa and connected her eyes with Ty. For a still moment, his return stare held her prisoner. She couldn't figure out why his shoulders were bunched as he pushed away from the door, or why, when he looked down at Shannon, he became tenser still.

And then she remembered about his friend's wife, so his reluctance made sense. She wanted to ease his pain, but she also wanted him to ease hers by telling her Shannon was going to be all right.

He said nothing.

His rumpled dark hair had a wild appearance, as though he'd run his fingers through it so many times that the ends now stuck out permanently. Declan must have roused him from his bed, but the look did nothing to detract from Ty's appeal.

This is the man his future wife would see, Katie realized, feeling a moment of envy toward that unknown, faceless woman.

He moved through the room at the slow, steady pace of a graceful jungle cat. A day's worth of scruff on his well-defined jaw gave him a dangerous edge. Katie had no problem remembering how, when he'd walked her home from the ferryboat, he'd forestalled a troublesome encounter with that pack of ruffians with a single glance. He was a healer, yes, but also a protector, and she couldn't take her eyes off him as he closed the distance.

Tell me everything's going to be all right.

He didn't say the words, but he looked every bit the competent doctor here to make everything better. Katie swallowed a sob of relief.

His eyes moved to Shannon, and a small frown creased his brow. Crouching beside the sofa, he ran his gaze over Shannon's prone form. Quiet. Speculative. The only sign of emotion showed in the tightening of his jaw when he noticed the rust-colored bloodstain.

"Shannon, can you tell me where it hurts?"

She blinked up at him with large eyes. "My stomach."

"Are you nauseous?"

"Yes, but not like before. It's . . . different. I don't know how to explain it. I started feeling cramps. That's never happened before."

"When was that?"

"About an hour ago."

"Was it a constant cramping, or did the sensation come and go at intervals?"

"I don't know. Both, maybe?"

Ty glanced to Katie, gave a short jerk of his head. She slid out from under her sister and then knelt beside him. "Tell me what to do."

"I'm going to give your sister a thorough examination, and I need you to help me."

Before Katie could respond, Shannon squeaked, "Will it hurt?"

"It may feel a bit uncomfortable." His gaze tracked around the apartment. "I need to wash up before we begin."

Bridget showed him to the kitchen. Katie heard her introduce him to Regina; then Shannon clutched at Katie's hand and all other thoughts but her sister disappeared.

"I'm afraid."

Katie was, too, but admitting that would only upset her sister further. Working through a panicked sweat, she squeezed Shannon's hand and forced a calm she didn't feel into her voice. "Don't worry. I'll be right here the whole time."

Proving he understood the potential for embarrassment, Ty returned from the kitchen and called back for the other two women to stay put until he summoned them. Then, with the efficiency Katie had come to expect from him, he opened his medical bag and began the examination.

He started simply, checking Shannon's pulse, listening to her heart. With Katie's assistance, he completed the more awkward portions of the exam with a sensitivity she appreciated and was certain her sister did as well.

His pause, a mere beat in time, alerted Katie to the exact moment Ty discovered the cause of Shannon's cramping. And in that time, Katie noticed three things: Ty's breathing hitched, his hands shook, and his eyes executed a slow, guarded blink.

An instant later, he slid a look at Katie and smiled, though his smile appeared forced.

"You did great, Shannon."

Clearly sensing something was wrong, Shannon lifted onto her elbows. Eyes wild with fear, she asked in a quivering voice, "Am I losing the baby?"

Ty kept his gaze averted. "Your baby is fine."

"Oh." She collapsed into a prone position once more. "Oh, thank God." The girl's tears of relief came in racked sobs.

Undone by Shannon's reaction, Katie smoothed a hand over her sister's hair. She cooed encouraging words, kissed her forehead, moved to her temple. The sobbing only increased, as if all the tears the girl had forbidden herself to shed during the exam now spilled out of her.

Katie shot Ty a helpless plea.

"Let her cry it out," he suggested. "The release will do her good." He swept a hand across Shannon's forehead, the soft touch almost parental. "Rest now."

Aunt Jane appeared in the room. "I heard crying. Is someone ill? Shannon . . . oh, you poor, poor dear."

The older woman hurried across the room and pulled Shannon into her arms before Ty could tell them what he'd found.

As he assured them all again that Shannon wasn't losing the baby, Katie allowed herself to let go of her own worry.

Perhaps that moment of grief she'd seen in him had been for the woman and child he'd lost, not for Shannon and her baby.

"Shannon," Ty said in the same soft tone he'd used before, "I'm going to have a quick word with your sister in the hallway, and then I'll come back with a few instructions for the days ahead."

Curled up in Aunt Jane's arms, the girl nodded.

Ty reached out and patted her on the shoulder, smiling gently. The gesture was so full of kindness that Katie felt an ache in her chest. Straightening, Ty then casually held out a hand to Katie, and her heart made a quick extra thump before she allowed him to guide her out into the hallway.

Once they were alone, Katie saw the concern return to his eyes. A lump rose in her throat. She pushed it down with a hard, silent swallow. "You saw something."

Rubbing a hand over his face, Ty rolled troubled eyes in her direction. "The placenta is lying unusually low and has become inserted in the lower uterine segment."

Katie's pulse thundered in her ears. Absently, she shoved at her hair, found her forehead was lightly beaded with sweat. "Is it completely covering the cervix?"

"No."

Thank God.

"A small portion probably sheared off and caused the bleeding."

Vicious fear clogged Katie's throat, stealing the words out of her mouth. She swallowed again, started over. "Will the baby be okay?"

Before answering, Ty studied her face for an endless moment. The look in his eyes warned her she wasn't going to like what she heard.

"The placenta hasn't shifted so far down that it's covering the cervix completely. However—"

"It can continue to move lower." She'd seen it happen.

"It's not out of the realm of possibility. If that does happen, and the baby shifts into a breech presentation—"

"Let's not go down that road just yet."

Hand shaking slightly, Ty speared splayed fingers through his hair. "At this point, I'm hopeful Shannon will have a normal delivery, so long as the bleeding doesn't get any worse. I'm going to recommend complete bed rest."

Katie was just about to make the same suggestion.

"Katie." His voice held both support and a hint of caution. "The situation isn't dire."

Yet. The unspoken word hovered in the air between them.

"You trained with a midwife. I'm sure you've seen this before."

"I have, and it doesn't always have a happy ending." Dejection spread through her limbs.

"Keep an eye on the placenta. If the organ moves any farther down, or Shannon's bleeding becomes heavier, you'll want to take her to the hospital."

That wasn't what Katie wanted to hear, but she knew it was wise advice. "Understood."

A line of consternation drew Ty's eyebrows together. "Shannon is young and healthy. The odds are in her favor."

"Yes." But for how long? If the placenta covered the cervix, all sorts of terrible complications could arise.

He strode over to her, his lips twisted at a determined angle. "I don't want you to worry. I'm going to make sure your sister gets the best care possible."

"I believe you."

He opened his arms in silent invitation.

Her control unraveled, and she launched herself into his embrace. With his arms wrapped around her, she felt warm and cared for and safe.

"Oh, Ty," she said in a low tone. "I'm so scared for my sister."

"I know, sweetheart."

Cheek pressed to his chest, she took two slow breaths, letting each out in a quick burst. Something had been bothering her since she'd found Shannon on the washroom floor. "I haven't seen a placenta move into the lower segment of the uterus early in a pregnancy."

"It would be impossible. The isthmus of the uterus doesn't unfold until the third trimester."

Katie knew this. But hearing it spoken aloud, in such a matter-of-fact, clinical tone? She let out a disappointed sigh. "My sister is farther along than she's led me to believe."

"It would appear so."

Oh, Shannon, why didn't you trust me with the truth? Katie knew, of course. Her initial reaction to her sister's involvement with Liam had created a level of distrust that had yet to be fully repaired.

"Thank you for coming in the middle of the night," she said to Ty, all but clinging to him now. "I know how hard it must have been for you."

His answering flinch said more than words. "It wasn't easy, but you needed me, Katie."

"I did."

He tightened his hold, and for one blissful moment, she let his strength seep into her.

Eventually, she shifted in his arms and glanced up. At the look in his eyes, a dozen simultaneous thoughts shuffled through her mind, coalescing into one pure moment of clarity: Ty was a man she could count on.

Reaching up, she touched the fresh crop of bristle on his jaw that hadn't been there when she'd left the clinic earlier that day. Unable to resist, she lifted onto the tips of her toes and pressed her mouth to his. It was a brief kiss, only a quick meeting of lips before she lowered back to her heels.

The creak of a door opening had them jumping apart.

"I should check on my patient." His voice poured warmth over the icy fear that had taken up residence in her heart ever since Regina had woken her up.

Katie followed Ty into the apartment. Neither of them spoke of the kiss she'd given him. Not while he prescribed constant bed rest for Shannon. Not when the two of them helped move the girl to the bedroom.

And not when Katie walked Ty to the door.

But just before she said good night, something flashed in his eyes, an aching hunger that held her captive.

He crooked his finger.

Dragging air into her lungs, Katie answered his silent call. Two steps later, she stood close enough to catch a whiff of his familiar scent. He smelled wonderful, like soap and cedar and man.

"Good night, Katie."

She opened her mouth, praying something brilliant would come out, but nothing came to mind. He took advantage of her hesitation and pressed his lips to hers. The kiss was as brief as hers had been, and so absolutely perfect that all she could do was stare after his retreating back.

"I'll see you at the clinic later," she called after him.

He answered without turning around. "Yes, you will."

For the rest of the night, Katie sat on the bed with Shannon, her sister's head in her lap, the long red tresses draped over her knees. As she smoothed a hand over Shannon's hair, Katie knew a moment of genuine hope.

The girl's condition wasn't without concerns. But Ty would make sure that Shannon received the best medical care available. She was going to be all right. The baby was going to be all right.

Katie was going to be all right, too.

For the first time in months, she allowed herself to look toward the future without the prejudice of the past. To consider a life free of fear and worry. To believe a happy ending was possible not only for her sister, but for herself.

She didn't know what was happening to her, or why her perspective was changing. But she knew Ty was at the center of it all.

Chapter Twenty-Seven

More than a month after ordering strict bed rest for Shannon, Ty left the clinic in the capable hands of Sebastian Havelock and went on an errand that amounted to swallowing his pride. He'd thought through his options, considered using the telephone, but the delicacy of the upcoming conversation required a face-to-face meeting. He hired a carriage to take him uptown, his destination the corner of Sixty-Third Street and Fifth Avenue.

The day was hot, oppressively humid, and he wished he'd worn a lighter suit. Ty didn't own a lighter suit. With no new benefactor on board yet, money was tight at the clinic.

We both know this isn't about money. Said the man with the overflowing coffers, Ty thought sullenly. He knew he wasn't being fair. If he erased the clinic from the equation and considered his father's concerns objectively, then, no, the situation wasn't about money.

The sun hung low on the horizon, suspended in that eerie moment when day surrendered to night. Patches of waning sunlight shared space with the creeping shadows of dusk.

Wanting time to organize his thoughts, he exited the hired carriage two blocks from his destination and took off with purposeful strides.

Once he turned onto Fifth Avenue, his destination loomed a half block ahead. The large three-story structure built in the Italian Renaissance palazzo style was a standout among the other buildings. The house's façade was made from Indiana limestone and rare materials imported from Europe.

Ty entered the foyer of the grand mansion that had been his home since boyhood, and he paused. He caught the welcoming scent of beeswax and the perfume of fresh flowers arranged in vases on the tables flanking the entryway. The blend of rose, jasmine, and lavender reminded him of the past, of surer times, of home.

A moment of revelation buckled his knees, the kind that came out of nowhere as a subtle whisper, all the more shocking for its unexpected arrival.

I shouldn't have stayed away so long.

He became very still, his feet immobile, his lungs unable to draw breath. It was as if a curtain had been drawn back to reveal the mistake he'd made by abandoning the only world he'd ever known. A mixture of grief and shame sat heavy on his heart, reminding him why he'd turned his back on the people who cared the most. Still . . .

This is my home.

A part of him would always belong here, in this house, in the world that had created the man he was today. He was becoming someone new, no doubt about that. The future that had once been so set in stone, so entrenched in his very nature, looked different now. And that wasn't a bad thing.

However, by denying his own personal history, by turning his back on the very people and things that had made him who he was, had Ty crippled his chance for redemption?

Perhaps not crippled, but he'd certainly hindered the process.

He unexpectedly burst into a cold sweat, and his fingers curled into a fist, as if he could hold on to something already lost. Fumbling for the handkerchief in his jacket pocket, he found the scrap of linen and swiped it across his forehead.

With his emotions better under control, he trudged forward. Reaching the central hall, he paused again and took in the high ceilings and double staircase that led to the second floor.

This time, the sensations that spread through him were happier, less gut-wrenching. Everywhere he looked, he saw his mother, even though she'd been dead for well over a decade. The luxurious furnishings were gracious, with an eye for comfort over the excess usually found in mansions along this strip of New York.

"Good evening, Dr. Brentwood." The family butler materialized by his side, his expression as dry and bland as toast. "May I take your hat and coat?"

Ty blinked at the other man, his agitation slowly dissipating inch by restrained inch. There was something reassuring in the butler's self-possession and blank stare, the same expression Ty had witnessed a million times over his lifetime.

"Thank you, Miles." He handed over the requested items with a smile. "Is my father at home?"

"He's in his study with your brother. Would you like me to announce your arrival?"

"Not necessary. I know the way."

The butler stood in his path, still blank-eyed and unemotional but for a slight tick in his clenched jaw.

Ty knew that look. The cadaver-thin man, with the shock of white hair and matching eyebrows, had been serving this home since before Ty was born. "Was there something you wanted to say to me?"

The butler glanced to his feet, then to his left, then back to Ty. The brief chink in his ramrod steel armor spoke volumes. "Welcome home, sir. You have been missed."

Touched by the words, Ty grinned at the older man. "Thank you, Miles. I've missed you as well."

"Perhaps you would consider coming around more often in the future."

"Duly noted."

"Very good." With stone-faced precision that would make a statue weep with envy, the butler disappeared in the direction he'd come.

Anxious to get this long-overdue reunion behind him, Ty took the stairs at a jog. Hearing two distinct voices coming from the second-floor study, he moved quickly toward the sound.

Ty paused at the threshold and took in the scene. His younger brother, Gabe, and their father were bent over a table, where a row of photographs had been lined up side by side. The men were similar in height and build, indistinguishable from Ty's own physique. Watching them interact was like looking in a mirror at his past and future selves. The twinge in his chest left Ty momentarily incapable of announcing his presence.

The last remaining beams of afternoon sunlight shafted through the tall windows, casting bars of warm gold over the blue-and-green pattern of the carpet. Ty inhaled the scent of leather, cigars, and brandy.

He was too far away to make out the photographs on the table, but by his father's disturbed expression, he had a good idea of the subject matter.

"Son," his father began. "I understand you want to bring attention to the dismal living conditions of the poor in this city. I just hadn't expected to feel so aggrieved from a series of photographs."

Gabe's posture stiffened. "That's rather the point, Father. The pictures are meant to tell a story."

"This is not art."

"It *is* art."

"Art is supposed to make the viewer feel good."

Gabe sighed in a way that told Ty he'd had this discussion with their father before. "Not always."

"Your mother and I raised you and your brother to be socially conscious, but I have to wonder." The older man picked up one of the photographs, studied it with a grim twist of his lips. "Is this exposition of raw hopelessness and despair the most effective route?"

Gabe took the photograph in question, studied the image, then set it back on the table. "Newly practicable casual photography is supposed to elicit a visceral response from the viewer."

"Is your end goal practical or theoretical?" At Gabe's questioning gaze, his father expanded, "Do you hope only to gain a reaction with these gut-shredding images, or is there a specific point?"

"They are a call to action."

This, Ty decided, was the prompt he'd been waiting for.

"If Gabe raises awareness for social reform in the eyes of even one person of influence," he said, entering the room and crossing to where his father and brother stood in stunned stillness, "then he will have made the most of his art."

The two men held silent, clearly taken aback by Ty's sudden appearance in this home after over a year of self-imposed exile.

Then a slight smile traced its way across Gabe's lips, and to Ty's surprise, he laughed. "The prodigal returns and at precisely the perfect moment. I can always use reinforcements when defending my work, especially to Father." Gabe moved to embrace Ty in a backslapping hug. "Welcome, Brother."

His father, coming around a bit slower than Gabe, took his turn hauling Ty into his arms. "You came sooner than I expected," he said in a low, choked voice. "It's good to see you, Son."

No judgment, no platitudes, only warmth and welcome.

After their meeting at the Harvard Club, or maybe because of it, this was the homecoming Ty had never expected and certainly didn't deserve. He had to clear his throat to speak, and even then, his voice was husky. "It's good to see you, too, Father."

"Are you back for good?"

Ty had known the question was coming. He'd come here knowing. He tried to smile, but it proved an impossible task. "I'm back. But not perhaps in the way you hope."

His father set his jaw, the disappointment evident in the pinched lines around his eyes, and Ty saw in the older man's gaze the strain of the past year. Strain Ty had ignored at the Harvard Club. Strain he'd caused, not only through his failure in the operating theater, but by deserting his family and friends.

He attempted to explain in terms that would make sense to his father, something he'd failed to do at the Harvard Club. "I'm not the doctor or the man I once was."

"That's not to say you can't be again, in time."

Ty appreciated his father's unwavering support, but every time he thought of walking into New York Hospital, every time he considered operating on a patient, he was carried back to that tragic day with Camille.

"You have a natural talent bestowed on you straight from Almighty God." A new spin on the same old argument, and yet Ty couldn't find it in him to hold the words against his father. Not when he looked into eyes that held both anticipation and longing. "It is your privilege and your responsibility to share your skills with the world."

It wasn't fair to either of them to give false hope. "I can't guarantee I will ever be able to perform surgery again, not like before."

"Answer me this. Do you miss your former life, Titus? Do you miss surgery?"

Every hour of every day. But Ty didn't trust his skills anymore. People's lives depended on his unwavering confidence. Why couldn't his father see that? Why must he persist in misunderstanding?

"Everyone is called to serve in his own way," Ty said, sidestepping a direct answer to his father's question, wishing for once, just this once, the older man would hear the truth in his words. "No one route is better than another. You, Father, have a philanthropic heart and the gift of giving. Gabe uses his artistic talent to push for social reform. I simply want to provide medical care to the poor."

"You can't help everyone."

No, he couldn't. That didn't mean he wouldn't try.

"I have one more question," his father said, lowering his head. But not before Ty saw his father's desperate need to win him over. His father had never been able to hide his emotions from his sons—from the world, yes, but not from his sons. "Are you fulfilled, Titus?"

Ty wasn't looking for fulfillment, not anymore. He only wanted forgiveness. That was enough. It had to be enough.

He stood at a fork in the road of his life, unsure what route he would take, knowing only that decisions would have to be made.

When he said as much to his father, in less than elegant phrasing, the older man's response took him completely by surprise. "It required great courage to come here and lay yourself bare. But you're wrong, Titus. You *are* the man you always were, but also . . . more. Whether you pick up another scalpel or walk away from medicine altogether, I'm proud of you, Son."

The unconditional words struck him to the core. He hadn't known he'd been waiting to hear them until now.

Ty had to glance away a moment and compose himself. He'd worked hard to redeem his failure. Every day, every single day, he climbed out of bed and convinced himself that what he did mattered, that every difference he made in the life of an immigrant was one step closer to reaching his goal of salvation.

To hear his father say he was already there? It nearly brought him to his knees. Although he was feeling a bit cornered, and his heart was beating extremely fast, he was fairly certain he kept his face expressionless.

"Well, now that Father has sufficiently built up your ego, let's move on to the portion of the evening where we celebrate your return over a hearty meal and a glass of spectacular port."

Ty had nearly forgotten Gabe was in the room. Appreciating his brother's attempt at lightening the mood, he said, "While I wouldn't say no to a good meal, I'd like to look at your photographs first."

"I was hoping you'd say that." Gabe gestured him forward.

Ty studied the images, impressed with the faithful representation of the ravages of poverty on its victims. His brother had captured the hopelessness of the poor. But more than that, Gabe had captured their hearts.

"These are good."

"Only good?"

"Stellar, actually. I see the misery, but I also see the tattered dreams, not bright and shiny but not dead either. And in this one"—he pointed to a photograph of a small child staring straight at the camera—"I don't see brokenness, I see innocence and hope for the future."

Gabe laughed. "Guess I'm better than I thought, or you're more insightful than I previously understood."

"Maybe it's a little of both," their father said, his eyes shining with parental pride.

Ty returned his attention to the photograph.

The scruffy little boy with the big eyes reminded him of the child he'd stitched up in the haberdashery. He liked Aiden Kelly and secretly enjoyed the way he kept randomly showing up at the clinic, not only to moon over Katie but also to follow Ty around. *I want to be a doctor one day, just like you.*

Ty had never been good with emotion. Or, more to the point, he'd never been good with *feeling* emotion. He preferred logic and reason to sensation. Surgery had suited his reserved personality, as had his volunteer position at Ellis Island.

Sometime along the way, he'd learned to see the individual as well as the disease. Knowing Katie had changed him. Not just knowing her, loving her.

Ty drew in a sharp breath. He *loved* Katie. He could lie to himself and say his feelings for her had grown over time, as he'd gotten to know her, as he'd watched her blossom at the clinic. But that wasn't the truth. He'd fallen for her that very first day on Ellis Island.

Love. It was a beautiful, overwhelming, stunning feeling. He let the emotion settle over him, seep into his limbs, and in the darkest recesses of his soul, the healing began in earnest.

Katie had reached a part of him no one had ever touched, a part he'd kept hidden even from himself. The question still remained: What was he going to do about her?

He would know more when he saw her again.

His father came to stand beside him and studied the photograph a moment. He touched another, then moved on to the next. "These are the people you serve at your clinic."

Ty exhaled and tipped back his head to stare at the ceiling, marshaling his thoughts. This conversation was the reason he'd come tonight, to explain why he'd abandoned his father's world, *his* world.

Ty had left for the wrong reason, though he was only beginning to understand that now. He'd been raised in privilege. He'd never known want until he'd lived among his patients, in their own neighborhood. "Look at these photographs, Father. Take in the need, the despair, but also see the hope." Ty set down the picture of the young boy. "The poor in this city have the right to medical care. Not just any medical care, good medical care."

He said the words simply, the truth of them evident in his voice and the photographs spread out on a table worth more than an immigrant's yearly salary.

"Why you, Titus?"

He blinked. "I've told you why."

"To atone for Camille's death."

"At first that was true. But my motivation has morphed into something bigger than myself. I've lived among these people." He swept his hand in an arc to include the images staring up at them. "I know many of them personally. Serving them has become as much a part of me as my hair and eye color."

His father nodded, drew in a hard breath, then nodded again as if he'd come to a conclusion. "While I still believe you are meant to be a surgeon, I was wrong to give you an ultimatum. I meant what I said at the Harvard Club. I will support the clinic with my own money, if that is what you want."

Ty had come here to make amends. He had not expected his father to apologize or to renew his offer. He addressed the first, put off answering the second. "I understand why you felt the need to force the issue. At the time, you were right to be concerned. I left surgery for the wrong reason." He swallowed the last of his pride and admitted, "I'm a stubborn man."

"You get that from your father."

They shared a warm laugh. Gabe joined in, and now it was time to address his father's offer of financial support. "While I appreciate your offer to fund the clinic, I would rather do so with my own money."

The hesitation lasted only a second, but Ty felt it in the marrow of his bones.

"If you fail," his father said, "you may well become a pauper."

True. "My patients are worth the risk."

Another hesitation, longer and more pronounced, and as Ty watched the other man closely, he recognized the fatherly pride in his eyes. "I admire your commitment."

The rest of the evening was spent in conversation and easy camaraderie. His father told stories of their childhood that brought back memories, the good ones, the ones Ty had tucked away with the bad. A mistake he wouldn't make again.

Before he left, his father informed Ty that he would meet him at the bank the next morning and release his trust fund back into his name. "Do with the money as you see fit."

Ty arrived home that night a rich man once again, not only in money. But in relationships restored.

* * *

Katie sat at the dinner table with the other women in her family, minus one. Bridget had yet to arrive home from work. It was half past seven in the evening, which made her well over an hour later than usual.

"You have to eat something, Aunt Jane." Shannon nudged the bowl of untouched stew a few inches closer to her aunt. "No good will come from making yourself sick."

"I'm not hungry."

"A bite, then. We'll take it together." Shannon lifted her fork and waited for the older woman to do the same.

Katie felt a small smile cross her face as she watched her aunt and sister eat a small portion of the stew. The two had become close recently. Proximity certainly had something to do with it. Both were trapped in the apartment all day.

They were also both lonely and sad, though neither would admit such a thing out loud.

Katie wanted to weep in frustration. While Aunt Jane seemed to be slightly better for the connection, her color returning if not completely restored, Shannon had lost her glow. The inner light that used to define her had simply disappeared as she seemed to turn further inside herself, often preferring her own company to that of others. There were days when even Aunt Jane couldn't convince the girl to come out of the bedroom.

Not that Aunt Jane was any less despondent.

Ever since she'd confronted Bridget about her job, the older woman had . . . faded. There seemed to be no other word for it. Her hair hung in limp threads. Her eyes had grown dull. And her face—it was as if all her natural animation had retreated behind the mask of a dozen new lines.

Katie sighed. She told herself to stay silent, but she couldn't. She just couldn't. "What can I do to lighten the mood at this table?"

Two pairs of eyes stared at her.

"You're both so glum. I wish there was something I could do to make you smile. Or at least alleviate your worries." She turned to the older of the two. "Would you like me to talk to Bridget?"

"I've tried. It won't do any good." Aunt Jane looked at her with haunted eyes. "The more I push her to quit her job, the more determined she seems to keep it. I don't know what I was thinking, confronting her like I did."

"You were thinking she needed help."

As if mere talk of her cousin could call her home, the front door opened and closed. A moment later, the object of their discussion appeared in the kitchen, looking nothing like her usual self.

She posed in the doorway, as if making certain all eyes were on her. Katie couldn't form complete sentences. Her cousin's transformation was that complete. No longer a tambourine girl, but an elegant woman dressed in a lightweight green-and-ivory linen dress.

The bodice was cinched at the waist, the skirt slightly trained. A stylish lace collar covered her entire neck, the delicate lattice pattern repeated in the three-quarter sleeves that fell to a spot just below her elbows. She'd arranged her hair in a full and wavy Gibson Girl pompadour and looked simply wonderful. Katie wondered how her cousin had managed to leave the house looking so put together. Probably in the same way she'd disguised the costume she wore as a tambourine girl, with heavy cloaks, subterfuge, and stealth.

Or perhaps she'd changed at Regina's apartment. Katie was on the verge of asking for an explanation when Bridget sashayed over to her mother. Reaching inside a hidden pocket in her dress, she pulled out a small box wrapped in glossy white paper and tied with a pretty red ribbon. "This is for you."

Aunt Jane blinked at the gift as if she didn't know quite what to do with it.

"Go on," Bridget urged, smiling softly at her mother, a look of deep love and affection in her eyes. "Open it."

Hands shaking, the older woman tugged at the ribbon, then carefully peeled away the wrapping paper. She stared at the contents—a small vial the size of a man's thumb filled with dark amber liquid.

"What is it?" Shannon and Aunt Jane asked in tandem, the younger leaning over the table to get a better glimpse.

"It's French perfume," Bridget informed them in the Bostonian accent she'd demonstrated for Katie months ago.

Aunt Jane's eyes narrowed. "Who gave you French perfume? A man?"

"No one *gave* it to me. I earned it. It's my bonus for selling more of these little gems"—she plucked the bottle from its nest and twirled it around in her fingers—"than any other salesgirl at Bergdorf Goodman."

Aunt Jane made an aborted movement, as if she'd meant to stand and then changed her mind. "You . . . you took a new job?"

"Two weeks ago today."

Confusion and relief shared equal space on Aunt Jane's face. "Why are you only just telling us now?"

"I wanted to say something right away, but I wasn't certain it would work out."

Aunt Jane nodded in understanding. "You didn't want to get my hopes up, only to disappoint me."

"You may officially get your hopes up." Bridget beamed at her mother. "Apparently, I'm very good at selling perfume to wealthy New Yorkers. I'm a natural."

"Oh, Bridget, darling." Aunt Jane's eyes filled with tears. "I'm so proud of you."

"I'm rather proud of myself." The young woman kissed her mother's forehead, shot a winsome grin at Katie, winked at Shannon, then plopped in the empty chair. "So. What's for supper?"

Chapter Twenty-Eight

Two nights after reconciling with his father, an incessant pounding in his head woke Ty from a deep slumber. Groggy, eyes gritty, he stared at the cracked plaster above his head, trying to gather his bearings. Peace enveloped him.

Instead of dreaming of Camille and his failure, Ty had dreamed of Katie and the life they would have together. Once he convinced her to take a leap of faith on him. On them.

You don't deserve her.

He would, one day, because he couldn't go through life without her in it. No matter what else he sacrificed, Katie was the one thing he wouldn't—couldn't—lose.

They would have a pack of children, dark-haired boys with Ty's drive and commitment to excellence, pretty little girls that looked just like their mother and had her kind, giving heart. Their home would be filled with peace, hope, and love. Lots of love. And if it took the rest of his life, Ty would teach Katie that love didn't have to end in tragedy.

The banging became loud and persistent.

"Dr. Brentwood. It's Dex. Declan Kennedy. Open up. Katie sent me to get you. It's her sister again."

Ty was out of bed in an instant, dragging on a pair of black trousers first, a linen shirt next. "One moment," he yelled down the stairwell.

The knocking stopped.

Ty finished dressing.

A minute later, he was down the stairs and throwing open the door to the sight of Katie's overwrought neighbor.

"Shannon went into labor."

At least a month ahead of her due date, Ty estimated, based on the increased activity of the fetus as well as Shannon's other symptoms that he'd witnessed recently, including muscular spasms in her lower extremities and a slight coordination disorder. Not the best of news, and they were wasting time while Ty calculated the days in his head.

"Let's go." Ty started in the direction of Orchard Street.

The Irishman stopped him. "Wrong way." By the tense set of Dex's mouth, Ty knew he was in for more bad news. "They took the girl to the hospital."

Heat threaded through him. The situation was serious, then. "Which one?"

"New York Hospital."

The site of Ty's greatest failure. He wallowed in a fit of dread for the span of two seconds. Then, he hailed a cab.

While they waited for the carriage to pull in closer, he demanded, "Tell me what you know."

"Katie made me memorize exactly what to tell you." Dex took a deep breath. "She said the placenta has moved down and is now fully covering the cervix." The man swallowed audibly. "I assume you know what that means?"

"I do." Heart bleak, Ty climbed into the carriage, waited for the other man to join him.

They rode to the hospital in silence, then parted ways at the entrance—Ty to discover more about Shannon's condition, Dex to sit with the family.

"Tell Katie and the others that I'll come with news as soon as I know something."

Dex bobbed his head.

Ty increased the length of his strides, as if he could outdistance the emotions nipping at his heels. He was met in the surgery lobby by Dr. Benjamin Armstrong.

His former colleague looked composed, capable, and faintly relieved. The other doctor approached him, expression warm, open palm leading. Ty blinked, something inside him squeezing. The knowledge that this man had stood by him through the worst days of his life cut through the remaining scraps of his restraint. A moment's hesitation, nothing more, and then he shook the outstretched hand.

And that was that.

His self-imposed time of exile melted away. He was back to being colleagues, and friends, with this man.

"We'll talk more when we aren't facing a medical emergency," Ben said. "But you should know that Ellie told me she ran into you a while ago."

Ty tried to smile, but it seemed an impossible task. "We crossed paths on Orchard Street."

"Where, apparently, you agreed to give her a tour of your clinic in the Bowery."

"What can I say? Your wife is very persistent." Drawing in a quick, reedy breath, Ty spread his hands. "She wouldn't take no for an answer."

"That's my Ellie." Ben smiled fondly, clearly just as smitten with his wife as the day they'd met. "You know she's going to pester you until you fulfill your promise."

"Actually," Ty said, taking his own leap of faith, "I'd like both of you to come by. Name the day and time, and we'll make it happen."

"Don't think I won't. Now"—Ben shifted his stance—"let's talk about Shannon O'Connor. I understand you have a personal connection with the patient."

"Her sister assists me at the clinic. I've examined Miss O'Connor on two separate occasions, the first earlier in her pregnancy, the second more recently."

"Then perhaps you're aware of the situation with the placenta."

Every muscle in Ty's back coiled. It was *painful* to care, to wish Shannon could have the easy delivery she deserved. "It's the reason I suggested bed rest."

"Very wise." Ben rubbed his chin. "With the baby now in a breech position, a cesarean section is their only option for survival."

Ben's unemotional words coursed through Ty, revealing the dire nature of the situation in simple life-and-death terms.

"Assuming the family agrees to the operation, I'd like to assist with the surgery," Ben requested.

Ty became aware of a fine quiver running through his hands, a constant hum of nerves. The circumstances were too familiar, the stakes too high. Shannon and her baby might not survive a cesarean section. The thought made his heart contract. "I want you to do the surgery."

"I've never performed the procedure, while you have. It makes sense for you to take the lead."

Ty's throat closed on a rush of anguish. "Aren't you forgetting something? My previous patient died by my hands."

"Camille didn't die because of the surgical procedure. Her prognosis was grim. Time was of the essence. Despite the outcome, you made the right decision. I've never doubted that. You shouldn't either."

Ty's gaze narrowed onto his friend's face, the words difficult to hear over the roar in his ears.

"Ty." Ben clasped his shoulder, squeezed. "Miss O'Connor deserves the best chance at surviving the operation. That best chance, my friend, is you."

Ty's heart began to pound, and his legs weren't quite steady beneath him. What the other doctor claimed was true. Ty was one of the few surgeons in America who'd attempted a cesarean section. Most considered delivering babies to be the job of a midwife. The procedure wasn't even taught in some medical schools.

He was in an impossible position. If he refused to perform the procedure, Shannon and her baby could die.

But if he did operate, Shannon and her baby could die.

Ty glanced at his hands. They were steady. *Camille didn't die because of the surgical procedure.*

All this time, he'd called himself a killer. Katie had disagreed. His father had reframed the scenario from a surgeon's perspective. And now Ben was showing similar support.

He could do this. He would do it. Not to prove his worth as a surgeon, or so he could rise to unprecedented heights within his profession, but to save a young woman and her unborn child.

"Where is the girl's family?"

"In the waiting area."

Ty moved fast and decisively. He took three steps and, pausing at the door, shot over his shoulder, "Prepare the patient for surgery, Dr. Armstrong, while I talk to the family."

Orders given, and trusting they would be followed to the letter, Ty pushed into the waiting room. He sought and found Katie sitting hunched in a chair, her head resting on her cousin's shoulder. Her aunt sat on her other side, clutching her hand.

Declan Kennedy paced in the small area opposite the trio, his eyes glued to Bridget Sullivan's face. A tortured expression came and went in his gaze before he made his way to the young woman.

Leaning over her agitated form, he whispered something in Bridget's ear. Whatever he said made her shoulders instantly relax. Eyes shining with an emotion that looked like appreciation, she patted the seat beside her. Declan sat in the offered chair, took her hand, and said nothing more. His presence seemed to be enough.

With no time to waste, Ty advanced on the family.

Katie must have heard his approach, because she hopped to her feet and strode across the room before he took his second step.

She looked up at him and placed her palm on his cheek. "Thank you for coming."

Ty saw her trust in him, the trust he wasn't sure he had in himself. How many times had he almost broken free of his past, only to be dragged back, sometimes willingly, sometimes not?

Why had he expected this time to be any different?

Because this time he wanted something different, something within reach, something he'd never really wanted before. In a life that had been filled with privilege and success, he wanted to save a young woman for all the right reasons, and none of the selfish ambition that had driven him before walking away from his calling.

Unable to stop himself, he pressed his forehead to Katie's and sighed.

"It's bad, isn't it?"

He honored her with the truth, relaying the details Ben had given him moments earlier. "A cesarean section is her only hope."

Words he'd used before, just as real as when he'd spoken them to Shep, the need to make his case equally strong. "Do I have your permission to perform the surgery, Ben?"

"You are the only man I trust with my sister's life."

"Katie," he said, pulling her against his violently pounding heart. "I won't let you down."

It was a vow he had every intention of keeping.

"I know you won't."

Bolstered by her confidence in him, he left her with her family and went through the rigorous preparations for surgery, scrubbing away germs on his hands and forearms. Arms bent at the elbows, palms facing him, he shouldered into the brightly lit operating room. The familiar odor of chemicals scented the air.

Ty swept his gaze over the room, across the lamps and reflectors and onto the table of instruments and washbasins.

"Everything's ready, Doctor."

He nodded to Ben and then the two nurses. Lastly, he allowed his eyes to settle on the patient, her body covered with a white sheet pulled all the way up to her chin.

A whimper slid from her lips.

Ty moved in closer so she could recognize him beneath the cap and surgeon's gown he wore. "Hello, Shannon."

Tears of panic slipped from her eyes. She reached up and grabbed his bicep with a surprisingly strong grip. "Please, Dr. Brentwood. I don't care about me. Save my baby."

The same request Camille had begged of him, given with the same dose of fear.

"I'm going to do everything in my power to save you both."

This time, he silently vowed, he would follow through on his promise.

"Let's begin."

Chapter Twenty-Nine

Katie sank heavily in a chair close to the door Ty had disappeared behind. Nothing she had ever experienced as a midwife's assistant had prepared her to watch her sister crumble into a heap of howling pain. Or to witness the blood.

So much blood.

One of the neighbors had tracked down an ambulance while Katie had attempted to keep Shannon calm. The trip to the hospital was a blur, as were much of the events of the past two hours. The only moment of relief had been when Ty had held her in his arms.

She trusted Ty. She believed in him, more than he probably believed in himself. That was all right. Her faith was strong enough for them both. Ty would save Shannon and her baby. Katie would allow her mind to dwell on no other outcome.

Moments passed, or perhaps it was hours. Katie was only vaguely aware that Bridget and Declan Kennedy conversed in hushed tones on the other side of the room. They alternated between glancing in her direction and whispering to each other, but they seemed to understand that Katie didn't want to join the conversation.

She could hear her pulse drumming in her ears and, desperate for a distraction, concentrated on counting each sporadic beat of her heart. The tactic worked for a few seconds, but then her mind swam out of the calm and the panic returned, a rabid gnawing in the pit of her stomach.

As if to taunt her, the memory of Shannon's pale, frightened face came at her like a sharp pain in her chest. It was a good time to pray. And so Katie prayed, chanting the same words over and over in her head. *Save my sister. Save my sister.*

Fist pressed to her heart, Katie let the words echo in her mind. *Save my sister.* She felt her eyes closing. But then, the distinct sound of heavy muslin rustling over silk had her snapping her attention to the open doorway.

A woman dressed in a dark cloak entered the waiting area.

"Ellie?" Katie jumped to her feet, unable to hide her surprise. "I don't—Ellie!"

What was her friend doing at the hospital at this ungodly hour? It made no practical sense.

"Oh, honey, I came as soon as I heard the news about your sister's surgery." The other woman tossed the cloak's hood away from her face and, divesting herself of the garment, strode across the room with fast, clipped steps. She took Katie's hands and squeezed gently. "You must be beside yourself with worry."

Katie was worried, of course she was worried, but she was also confused. "I don't understand. How did you know to come to the hospital?"

"Ben telephoned the house." She tugged Katie into a fierce hug, then let her go. "He's aware of our friendship and thought to inform me that you'd brought your sister to the hospital. I knew I had to come at once."

That was all well and good, but Katie couldn't seem to make her brain function properly. "Ellie?"

"Yes, dear?"

"How would your husband know I brought my sister here?"

"Ben happens to be the surgeon on duty tonight." Manner gentle, she guided Katie to a chair, applied light pressure to her shoulders until she sat, and then settled in the empty chair beside her.

Katie recognized the sincerity staring back at her, and she was reminded how much she liked Ellie Armstrong. "Thank you for coming."

"It's what friends do for one another." She didn't say more. She didn't need to.

A comfortable silence fell over them, and Katie began to relax.

"I'm going to make myself useful," Ellie said. "Let me see if I can rustle us up a pot of coffee. Or perhaps"—she angled her head—"you'd prefer tea?"

Katie didn't want anything to drink, but the others might. Thinking mostly of her aunt, she nodded. "Tea would be lovely."

"Then tea you shall have." Ellie leaned over and pressed a light kiss to Katie's cheek. "Shannon is going to come through this just fine. Ty is an exceptional surgeon. And with my husband in the operating room with him, well, your sister couldn't be in better hands."

Katie drew comfort from Ellie's confidence. "I'm going to concentrate on believing you."

"You should. I'm almost always right about these things." Smiling softly, the other woman stood. "I'll be back shortly."

Alone with her frenzied thoughts, Katie stared down at her feet. Even so, she could sense her aunt stand up and then move to sit in the empty chair Ellie had recently vacated.

Katie kept her head lowered. "I can't help thinking this is partially my fault. I didn't watch her closely enough. I missed a sign, some indication that things weren't going well."

"Sweet girl, you have cared for your sister with the love and attention of a mother. Because of your diligence, her baby stayed safe and warm in her belly weeks longer than any of us believed possible." Aunt

Jane patted her arm. "And now that your talented young man has taken over, all will be well."

Katie's head jerked up. "Ty's not *my* young man. We are only friends."

"Katie." Aunt Jane ducked her head in an attempt to capture Katie's gaze. "You must know he's in love with you."

For a moment, Katie actually felt her heart freeze in terror. Her hand covered her mouth as she stared at the older woman. Ty couldn't be in love with her. He'd never said the words, though his actions revealed the depths of his feelings for her. Was that the same as love?

She simply didn't know. "It's hopeless," she muttered.

Ty belonged in this world. He would discover the truth once the operation was over and Shannon cradled a healthy baby in her arms.

"What if I love him too much?" There. She'd voiced her deepest fear aloud. "What if my love consumes us both, until neither of us can breathe or think rationally and only sick, toxic need remains?"

"You aren't your mother."

Katie desperately wanted to believe her aunt.

"Maggie was always clingy and unnaturally dependent on others. Even as a child, she couldn't bear to be left alone for any length of time. Your father enjoyed being the center of that kind of obsession. In that, at least, they were well matched."

A symphony of conflicting thoughts played in Katie's mind, robbing her of a good response. She looked at her aunt, a little dazed.

For a moment, hope sliced through the ocean of her doubt. She started to thank her aunt for giving her something to think about, but two people entered the waiting area, and Katie forgot what she'd meant to say.

Regina Kennedy had come to keep vigil with the rest of them. Except she wasn't alone. She'd brought a visitor with her. Katie's breath caught. Bridget gasped.

Declan jumped to his feet.

"Who is that with my sister?"

"I'm not certain," Bridget said, holding him back. "But I believe that's Liam Gallagher. The baby's father."

It was, indeed, Liam.

But how . . . why . . . when?

Katie's silent questions were answered when Bridget added in a low voice, "I sent him a letter when she arrived, and then another the night Dr. Brentwood put Shannon on bed rest."

Aunt Jane, too, confessed, "I sent one as well."

And so he'd made the trip.

Because of the baby? Or for Shannon?

Katie didn't have a chance to ask what the women had put in their letters before Liam caught sight of her and started toward her, his long strides eating up the distance between them. The closer he came, the easier it was to see he had a weary expression on his face and hard, suspicious eyes.

Katie's return stare was equally challenging.

This man had taken advantage of Shannon's innocence and then left her to deal with the consequences. He was here only because he'd been summoned.

He stopped inches from Katie. She held his stare, only half aware that Ellie had returned carrying a tray laden with a teapot and several cups. As if sensing she'd interrupted a tense moment, the other woman nodded to Katie, then retreated without uttering a word.

"Where's my fiancée?"

Katie wasn't the least intimidated by the angry tone.

"Why are you here, Liam?" she asked, aware she sounded a little angry herself. "Why now?"

Rough, grave eyes bore into her. "I was told Shannon was ill and needed me. I came as soon as I could."

He made no effort to explain himself, which did not endear him to Katie. But when she looked closer, she saw the strain shadowed in his eyes.

He journeyed all the way to America, she reminded herself, *and endured the registration process at Ellis Island.*

A man didn't make that kind of gesture without caring a great deal.

"Tell me what's wrong with Shannon."

Katie glanced at Liam's escort, who'd been standing beside him in silent watchfulness. "Regina didn't tell you?"

The woman lifted her hands. "Not mine to tell."

No, Katie supposed not. It wasn't really hers to tell either, but some things couldn't be helped. If Liam had come even a day earlier . . .

He's here now. "Shannon is in labor."

"She's . . . wait, what?" He leaned closer. "Shannon's pregnant?"

"Yes, and now the baby's coming."

He seemed to do some mental calculations. "The baby is early."

"By at least a month. There have been a few other complications as well." She explained the situation in quick, concise language.

Liam blinked, and Katie saw actual tears form in his eyes. "She should have told me about the baby."

"In her defense, she didn't know until she arrived."

"Why didn't she tell me in her letters? I would have never allowed my mother to—" Breaking off, he slipped his hands into his pockets and wandered the room, his handsome face full of despair. Regret.

Katie knew the look when she saw it. Liam was overwrought and had been dealt several rough blows at once. All the terrible thoughts she'd had about this man and his intentions toward her sister seemed petty when confronted with the very real sight of his agony.

This man loved her sister.

Sucking in a hard breath, she crossed the room and reached out to touch his sleeve, the gesture full of an acceptance she hadn't felt before tonight.

He turned empty eyes in her direction. "I can't lose her."

In retrospect, Katie shouldn't have been surprised by this man's devotion. Shannon was worth every ounce of Liam's love. Katie should have trusted her sister's judgment. She should have known Shannon was smart enough to recognize when a man was telling the truth and when he was playing her for a fool.

"Shannon is going to pull through this." Remorse filled Katie's voice. "She's in good hands, the best in the city."

A flicker of hope flashed in Liam's dubious expression. "You trust the doctor?"

"With my life." She meant every word. Katie trusted Ty's abilities totally and completely.

But did she trust him with her heart?

* * *

Ty stayed with Shannon until he was certain the bulk of the anesthesia had worked its way out of her body. Since making the initial incision in her lower abdominal region, he'd left her side only once, just long enough to discard the surgeon's gown and to scrub away the blood from his hands and forearms.

Now, as the nurses cleaned up the baby and the orderlies waited to take the girl up to her private room—a luxury Ty had personally arranged—he watched her still form with a sense of satisfaction.

The surgery had been a success. Shannon and her baby would suffer no lasting effects from their frightening ordeal.

Glancing at his hands, now clean and as steady as they'd once been, Ty knew a moment of absolute clarity. He hadn't needed redemption. He'd needed forgiveness. Not from others, but from himself.

He would always mourn the loss of Camille on his operating table, and he accepted that his friendship with Shep would never be fully restored, but Ty was a surgeon. Saving lives was his calling. He wouldn't abandon the clinic—it was too much a part of him now—but he would continue to hone his surgical skills and keep up on the latest medical advances.

He would continue to save lives, and, yes, he would lose some, too.

A soft groan sounded from the table, diverting Ty's attention. He glanced down at the prone form. Shannon looked small and unbearably innocent, as if she were a fairy-tale princess caught under some wicked witch's spell. Unlike those fanciful stories, she would open her eyes soon and meet her baby for the first time.

Ty had yet to tell her family the good news. Not until the girl awakened. Still, he was anxious to assuage their worries, especially Katie's, so he spoke Shannon's name softly, once, twice.

Her eyes flickered opened.

The sense of relief that spread through him nearly brought him to his knees.

Smiling for the first time since Declan Kennedy had shown up on his doorstep, he moved a step closer to the table. "Welcome back, Shannon O'Connor."

She blinked. "I went somewhere?"

"In a manner of speaking."

"Oh, but I don't . . ." Her forehead creased in confusion. "I don't think I like traveling."

He chuckled, thinking of Katie's penchant for seasickness. "It must be a family trait."

"Mmm, must be." The girl closed her eyes, strained to open them again, but didn't quite win the fight. "My . . ." She tried again, had minor success. "Baby?"

"Healthy."

"Thank you." Her eyelashes fluttered closed.

"Rest now," he urged gently. "I'll come check on you once you're settled in your room."

She responded with a low humming sound of agreement.

Ty entered the waiting area moments later. A hush fell over the assembled friends and family members.

After a sweeping glance across the room, Ty noticed two things: there'd been an addition to their numbers, and Katie had distanced herself from the others. Her pretty green eyes showed signs of fatigue, but she was also alert. And shoving away from the wall she'd been propped against.

A rush of love and affection hastened through him. It would take a lifetime to get used to his reaction to the mere sight of her. Two lifetimes. He would pledge his love to her this very day.

But first, he had to relieve her anxiety.

He started in her direction.

The newcomer, a tall, lean broad-shouldered man with ginger-colored hair and formidable self-possession, fell into step beside Katie. The three of them met in the middle of the room.

Ty spoke directly to Katie. "The surgery was a success."

"Oh, thank God." She looked ready to leap into his arms. Ty began opening them to receive her, but she froze midway, cleared her expression, and asked in a calm, controlled voice, "And the baby?"

He presented the same diagnosis he'd given Shannon. "Healthy."

Katie, reaching out to the man beside her, clutched the stranger's arm and let out a relieved whoosh of air. Her gesture didn't seem overly familiar, didn't speak of an intimacy between the two, but the contact seemed to push her companion into action.

He stepped forward, going nearly toe to toe with Ty. "I want to see Shannon." The heavy Irish brogue was a perfect accompaniment to his ginger hair and ruddy complexion. "Take me to her, now."

The demand had Ty studying the stranger more closely. He appeared about the same age as Katie, perhaps a little older, but that's where the similarities ended. He was not family. That left few alternatives. "You are . . . ?"

"Shannon's fiancé."

Ty had suspected as much.

"Ty," Katie said. "This is Liam Gallagher. He arrived from Ireland just this morning."

With introductions made, Ty answered the man's request. "I'll take you to Shannon now." He directed Liam to follow him. "Katie, are you coming?"

"Liam should see her first."

Ty didn't think he could love Katie any more than he did in that moment. The concession was so like her. She was sacrificing her own peace of mind so her sister could reunite with her fiancé in private.

Ty's gaze lingered on her. Loose strands of hair fell in an enticing array around her face. She tucked one of the strays back in place. Another found a way to tumble loose. Captivated, he grinned into her beautiful sea-green eyes.

Her return smile reached inside his heart, and he found himself wanting to sweep her away from this place and pledge his love to her in words and kisses and all the other intimacies a man and wife shared. He wanted Katie to be his wife, as soon as humanly possible.

"I'll be back."

"I'm not going anywhere." Her expression was open and warm as she spoke. No artifice, no pretense. She always looked at Ty like that, as if she were seeing him, the man, not the doctor, not the surgeon.

Outside of his family and a select few others, no one really saw past the outer trappings to the inner man. He liked how knowing that Katie was part of that group warmed his heart and made him feel less alone in the world.

Katie was his future.

He would not let her slip from his life.

But first . . .

He turned to Liam, who was practically vibrating with impatience. To his credit, the man contained the edginess behind a composed façade. "Come with me."

Liam did so without hesitation.

Katie's aunt stopped them at the door. "Thank you for saving my niece."

"It was my honor." Truly, saving Shannon O'Connor's life, and that of her baby, had been a privilege. Ty had found fulfillment in the simple act of serving where he was most equipped. Blessed in the doing, as his father would say.

"Dr. Brentwood." The older woman glanced briefly over her shoulder, straight to the spot where Katie still stood. "May I offer you a quick word of advice?"

Ty gave a short nod.

"Not all women become their mothers."

He lifted an eyebrow at the cryptic remark.

"Katie will need reminding of that when you speak with her again."

The explanation baffled him even more. He wasn't quite sure what to say.

"I have great faith in you, my boy." She leaned in, and her voice dropped so low he was forced to bend over to hear her final words. "Don't let me down."

"I . . . uh . . ." Ty paused, searching for a reply.

"No need to respond." Her eyes bright with emotion, she patted his arm, then moved away to stand with her daughter and the Kennedy siblings.

As he mulled over the woman's odd piece of advice, Ty escorted Shannon's fiancé to the third floor. Something told him not to dismiss Jane's words, yet he set them aside for further contemplation at another time.

"Your fiancée may be confused," he warned the other man. "An aftereffect of the anesthesia. Don't be alarmed if she seems disoriented or can't focus on your conversation or falls asleep in the middle of a sentence."

Liam digested this in silence. Ty took the opportunity to study the determined look in his eyes, the hard set of his jaw. "Will she know me?"

"Possibly not, at first. Once the medicine wears off, then yes."

"I understand." The fierceness in his gaze dissipated. "Is the baby in the room with her?"

"One surefire way to find out." Ty opened the door, then stepped aside to let the nervous new father pass. The last thing he heard as he shut the door behind Liam Gallagher was the man's soft-spoken greeting.

"Shannon, my love . . ."

Chapter Thirty

The moment Ty returned to the waiting area, Katie let out a noiseless sigh. There he stood, in the doorway, larger than life, a man in charge of his domain. He'd always turned heads, commanding attention wherever he went. But now, he seemed more compelling, more himself, a man comfortable in his own skin, fully and completely whole.

And the way he looked at her . . . *Oh, my.* Her knees went a little wobbly. He fixed that smile on his face, the one he reserved solely for her. Her heart erupted with infinite amounts of gladness and wistfulness. The latter emotion sent her hands shaking. The air in her lungs shifted, expanded, then settled in her throat.

He motioned her forward. She was powerless to do anything but answer his call. He was hers. *Mine,* she thought, realizing she'd been thinking of him as hers for some time now, long before Aunt Jane had deemed him her *young man*.

She still had a few feet to go. His scent invaded her senses. He smelled of soap and spice, a pleasant counterpoint to the harsh chemicals of the sterile hospital.

"Katie." His smile relaxed and his look became soft. "Come for a walk with me."

How could she refuse? Yet she didn't dare agree, not with that look in his eyes. A look that said he wanted to pledge his feelings to her. "I don't think that's a good idea. Shannon will be awake soon, and she—"

"Will want time alone with her fiancé."

Ty was right, of course. Shannon and Liam deserved privacy for their long-overdue reunion. "I suppose a bit of fresh air would be nice."

Taking her hand, he led her to the exit with leisurely strides. Once outside, he continued strolling at an easy pace.

They walked in silence, the early-morning air brisk but bearable. Sometime in the past hour, evening had given way to dawn. Threads of pink-tinged light stretched across a sky peppered with rooftops and frothy clouds, creating a romantic feel to the moment.

Katie chanced a peek at the man walking beside her. A furious flash of emotion ripped through her. She loved him, and desperately wanted to build a life with him. The extent of her longing scared her.

Ty slowed, then stopped at the edge of a small park, seemingly caught in a moment of indecision. His gaze circled the perimeter, then landed on an empty bench. "I want to tell you about the conversation I had with my father. Let's sit."

She didn't want to sit with him. She definitely didn't want to participate in another intimate conversation. Every detail of every moment they'd shared up to this point was already branded in her memory. Adding to the reservoir would make letting him go hurt that much more.

But let him go, she would. He was meant for great things. A woman like her would only hold him back.

Even knowing the pain that awaited her, she agreed to his request, albeit reluctantly. "All right, but only for a moment."

He guided her to the bench, but instead of sitting beside her, he prowled to a tree, stripped off a low-hanging twig, and proceeded to pluck away the leaves. Every line of him was taut with tension. If Katie didn't know better, she'd think Ty was nervous.

"Tell me what happened with your father."

In a halting tone, he explained about the two separate conversations he'd had with his father, starting with the first at the Harvard Club. "He offered to fund the clinic himself. With conditions."

"The same as before?"

He sent her a sardonic glance that wasn't all that hard to interpret. "Yes."

Katie's heart took a hard tumble. "So you operated on Shannon to save the clinic."

"No. *No.*" He strode to her, a tortured expression in his gaze. "Katie, you must know I would never put your sister's life in danger, not even for the sake of the clinic."

She did know that. *She did.* It had been wrong of her to suggest otherwise. "I'm sorry. I'm tired. Not thinking clearly. I didn't mean to accuse . . ." She placed a hand over her face, dropped it into her lap. "I'm sorry."

"It's all right. It's been a tense evening for all of us." He stooped before her, placed his hands on her knees. "More recently, my father made his offer to fund the clinic again, this time without conditions."

"That's wonderful." She braided her fingers together in her lap to keep them from shaking. "Did you accept?"

"I told him no."

"But . . . why?"

Ty straightened, then turned to pace the small area in silence. Eyes shining with resolve, he came back to stand in front of Katie. "I told him I want to use my own money."

Of course that's what he'd said, she thought, realizing how well she understood this man. She blinked up at him, experiencing a delightful sense of peace, knowing he was indeed everything she'd always thought him to be. Good and generous, true and honorable.

"He agreed to my terms."

"Oh, Ty." The sun broke free, a ball of orange fire above the horizon, gilding him from behind. The sight of him covered in the dawn's morning light knocked thought from her mind.

He was really quite something—handsome, talented, skilled, determined to do what was right. *I love you.* The words clawed up her throat, begging for release.

I love you.

Katie wanted to scream the words for anyone, everyone, to hear. "I'm proud of you," she said instead. "Not only for rescuing the clinic, but also for saving my sister. It couldn't have been easy, performing that procedure after what happened the last time."

"It wasn't easy, no. And yet, without my previous experience, I wouldn't have known exactly what to do this time."

Katie experienced a myriad of contradictory emotions. She was both pleased and sad. Good had come from bad; life had come from loss. Her sister had benefited at the expense of another woman.

"You, Katie, you were the defining factor in my success."

She hadn't realized he was still talking. She reviewed what he'd said. "I didn't do anything."

In fact, she'd never felt more useless, relegated to waiting for news of her sister in a hard wooden chair.

"Your belief in my ability gave me the confidence to walk into the operating theater." Ty's gaze slid away from the tree, locked with hers. His blue eyes lit with appreciation. Tossing aside the twig, he came to stand beside her. "You have changed me, Katie. Knowing you has made me a better man."

"No, Ty." She couldn't allow him to misunderstand what had happened to him over the past months. "Your strength of character was always inside you. I merely shined a light on what was already there."

"My sweet, beautiful, darling girl." He took her hands and gently pulled her to her feet. "Before you came into my life, I was half dead inside. I was racked with guilt and barely surviving one day to the next."

"Oh, Ty." She drew his hand to her face, sighed into his palm. "What matters is the man you are today."

"Katie." He said her name in a low growl.

The moment his lips closed over hers, she was lost. *I love you.* The words echoed in her mind again.

He drew back, a look of wonderment in his eyes.

Had she said the words aloud?

No, he'd been the one to say them. "I love you," he repeated.

"No, don't say that. Please, anything but that." The emotions surging through her brought a bone-deep urgency to run.

"Katie, look at me." He pressed his palm to her cheek. "You love me, too. No, don't argue with me. I'm not wrong about this."

"No," she agreed. "You're not wrong."

"Say the words, Katie." He pressed his lips to her temple, smoothed his hand over her hair. "I want to hear you say the words."

Her whole body trembled, and she thought she might be sick. The sensation was not unlike what she'd experienced on the journey to America. "I'm afraid."

The admission came from the depths of her soul and sounded as shattered as she felt.

"Tell me what scares you most about loving me."

"I'm not afraid of loving you." She shoved out of his embrace. "I'm afraid of loving you too much."

He only blinked at her in response.

Katie was going to have to tell him about her mother. The prospect made her edgy.

Regulating her breath, she put another foot between them, raising a hand to keep him from closing the distance.

"My parents had the kind of marriage people in our village envied, but it didn't translate into a happy childhood for Shannon and me. My mother and father were so deeply in love, they had little time for anything but one another."

Ty listened without interrupting.

"My father died, and my mother grieved so deeply she never recovered. She died a broken woman three months later." Katie beat the worst of the memories back and, lifting her chin, finished her tale. "Her love for my father killed her."

"That's not love. That's obsession."

"Precisely," she said. "Now you know why I can't say the words. Why I won't allow myself to feel the emotion behind them."

His eyes widened, then softened, then filled with surety. "You aren't your mother, Katie."

"What if you're wrong? What if I'm exactly like her?"

Ty's arms went around her. "You aren't your mother," he repeated. "You're too strong, too focused on helping others. The woman you described was wholly focused on herself and her own need to be adored."

Katie wanted to believe him. But she was the product of the two people who'd made her, half her father and, God help her, half her mother.

I will not become my mother. I will not.

"Your work is too important to take a chance on someone like me," she said. "You need a woman in your life that will lift you up and share your burdens, not one who will demand all your time and attention."

"I need *you*, Katie. You are the essence of my heart, my helpmate, the woman who will share in my life and my work. Think of what we can do together. The possibilities are endless."

The picture he painted of their future was compelling, a dream she'd never allowed to materialize fully in her mind. But Katie couldn't take the leap. She loved Ty too much.

She pulled away from him, distancing herself emotionally as well as physically. "We have a busy day ahead. You're due at Ellis Island, and I need to check on my sister, then head over to the clinic."

"All of that can wait until we settle this." He reached for her, a tender, open gesture that tugged at every want and need she'd ever experienced, both real and imagined.

"There's nothing more to say."

His hand dropped to his side. "This conversation isn't over. We're meant to be together. You know it. I know it. Even your aunt knows it."

"What does Aunt Jane have to do with us?"

"Let's just say she's on my side." The warmth in his gaze was her undoing. If Ty had shown the slightest hint of anger, or even need, Katie would have been able to end things right then. She would have had the strength to tell him there was no future for them.

Instead, she delayed the inevitable. She kept the door to her heart slightly ajar with a single sentence: "Can we put this discussion on hold until later?"

He looked prepared to disagree.

"Please, Ty."

"Until later, then. But, Katie, we will finish this discussion, and when it's over, I will pledge my life to yours. While you, my dear, beautiful essence of my heart, will pledge your life to mine."

That's what scared her most.

"No, Ty. When this discussion is over, you're going to walk away and I'm going to let you."

* * *

Shannon woke, disoriented, her mouth dry as dust, her face moist with tears. It was so hard to concentrate when every thought had to battle through the fog in her brain. She'd had the sweetest dream of Liam coming to her in the middle of the night. "Shannon, my love, I'm here and nothing will separate us again."

His whispers had seemed so real, soft and beautiful in her ear. *Oh, Liam.* She reached for the locket he'd given her. The warm metal against her skin gave her comfort, as if he was with her now, and all was well.

The moisture on her cheeks might have been caused by tears of joy if not for the pain in her stomach. She felt as though someone had cut her open and ripped her insides out.

The dull, throbbing, persistent pain wouldn't release its grip on her midsection. She ached everywhere, in her bones, in her throat, in places she hadn't known could hurt. She wanted to howl in agony, but even that was too much effort, so she settled her head back on the pillow and moaned softly.

Her sense of time and place was jumbled in her head. She cracked open one eye, then another, then slammed them both shut.

The light was too bright. It hurt her head. But that made no sense. The apartment in the tenement house was dimly lit.

Where am I?

She opened her eyes again, took in the white bedding, the white gown she wore. Pain morphed immediately into panic. She'd seen this sterile white room once before.

The hospital on Swinburne Island, she realized, unable to keep the fear at bay.

No, it couldn't be. *Please. Dear God, no.*

She cried out.

"Shannon." A hand came to her forehead, swept her hair away. "You're safe, darling."

She lay very still, forcing herself to stay calm until events fell into some semblance of order. Her heart stopped beating too fast, and she slowly slid out of the nightmare. She was in a hospital, but not the one on Swinburne Island.

This room . . . it smelled of Liam.

But he wasn't in America. He was back in Ireland with his mother, and Shannon had gone into labor without him.

She remembered it all now. The pain in her belly, the fear on Katie's face, the agonizing trip to the hospital, Dr. Brentwood's final words before everything went dark: *Let's begin.*

Shannon fought to subdue the feelings of loss and powerlessness, to remember a time when she'd harbored dreams of happiness and forever with the man she loved. She clutched at the hand hovering over her.

"Where's my baby?" She struggled to sit up. "I want to see my baby."

"She's right here."

She. Shannon had given birth to a daughter.

"She's as beautiful as her mother." The voice was from her memory, the same one that had whispered promises of forever in her ear. "Meet our daughter. She's perfect. Ten fingers, ten toes. She has her mother's eyes and her father's healthy set of lungs."

Liam stepped into her line of vision, a bundle in his arms.

"Liam." Shannon's breath hitched in her throat. "Oh, Liam. Is it really you?"

"Aye, my love. It's me." He bent to kiss her cheek with the same tenderness she'd relived in her dreams every night since losing him.

Liam was here. He was here! And he was holding their baby.

Shannon burst into tears, a messy explosion that tore at her belly. Liam stared at her in alarm.

"Shannon. Oh, God, you're going to hurt yourself." With one quick, careful swoop, he set the baby in the bassinet and returned to her side. "It's going to be all right. You'll be better soon."

He mopped at her face with a handkerchief he'd fumbled out of his jacket. Sitting on the bed, he continued soothing her with his words and his touch. "Are you in pain?"

"A little," she admitted. "But it's better now that you're here."

His hand stilled, and he cleared his throat as though trying not to suffocate on emotion. "We're together now." He stroked her wet cheek with the pad of his thumb. "You're mine, Shannon. I'm never letting you go again."

"Oh, Liam, how I've missed you. I love you so much."

"I love you, too." He pressed his lips to her forehead, her temple, her lips, lingering long enough for Shannon to sigh with pleasure.

"I never lost hope you would come," she whispered.

Guilt brushed across his features. "I should have been here sooner."

"What kept you so long?" She tried to keep any accusation from her voice, unsure if she succeeded. Her head still felt light, foggy, as if she were looking at him through a sheet of water.

"Like I said in my letter, Mother took ill, or so I thought." Dark emotion swarmed his words. "It was all a ruse. She is perfectly well, and as mean as ever. She vowed that if I chose to come to America, virtually picking you over her, then I would no longer be welcome in her home. I tried to reason with her. I told her it didn't have to be her or you, that I could love you both, but she would hear none of it."

Shannon saw the agony in him, and she knew he suffered. "I'm sorry."

"I'm not." His scowl matched the anger in his voice. "The choice was easy. You are my heart, Shannon, my life, my future."

"Oh, Liam." She hugged him fiercely, refusing to let him go. He didn't try to pull away.

They clung for several minutes, until a snuffling sound reminded them of the other occupant in the room.

Liam stood. "Want to meet our daughter?"

"More than I want air."

He laughed, then retrieved the squirming bundle and set her in Shannon's arms. As she took in the skinny arms, the pretty round face, and cheeks that felt like velvet against her lips, restraint shattered. Calm evaporated. Well-thought-out speeches died on her tongue. The only emotions left were tenderness and love. Painful, heartrending love for this beautiful child she and Liam had created together.

Shannon looked up and saw the tears of joy in his eyes. "She's beautiful."

"She is," Liam said with his gaze locked on Shannon. "Like mother, like daughter. What are we going to name her?"

An impossibly tiny hand that looked like a miniature star closed tightly around her finger, as if the infant claimed Shannon as her own. Touched, she stroked and cradled her precious baby girl. "I haven't thought what I want to call her."

"Well, I have." Liam gave her the lopsided grin that had won her heart. "What about Margaret Katherine, after your mother and sister, the two women who made you who you are."

"I love that." Eyes stinging, she kissed the tiny forehead. "Hello, Margaret Katherine Gallagher, I'm your mother."

Liam copied her movement, placing his lips in the same spot as Shannon had. "I'm your father. Your mother and I are going to be very good parents. We'll make sure you grow up in a loving, happy home and have the freedom to make choices for yourself."

Shannon feared her heart might explode with happiness. "I suppose this means I have to make an honest man of you."

Liam choked out a low laugh. "Is tomorrow too soon?"

Her answer was a kiss, longer than the one he'd given her, and completely inappropriate within view of an infant.

Shannon couldn't think of a more perfect beginning for their life together.

"We're going to have a good, solid marriage, Shannon O'Connor, soon to be Shannon Gallagher. I vow to be a good father to our children and the devoted, adoring husband you deserve."

She wasn't naïve enough to believe they weren't in for some rough patches. Love would carry them through, though, and as they added to the family they'd already begun, Shannon would cherish this moment when they'd reunited on the soil of their new homeland.

"Welcome to America, Liam."

Chapter Thirty-One

Katie came to her senses precisely two hours after Ty had left for Ellis Island. Up until that moment, she'd done everything in her power to push him out of her mind, to no avail. During every minute of his absence, she hovered on the verge of tears, knowing she couldn't lose him.

Not knowing how to keep him.

What am I going to do?

The question plagued her, leaving Katie restless and edgy. She'd never wanted anything so much as to spend the rest of her life with Ty. She wanted to work by his side, love him with all her heart, and bear him a houseful of children.

Both Ty and her aunt had told Katie she wasn't her mother. Her head believed them. Her heart still grappled with childhood bitterness and fear. She knew she would be a slave to the past if she didn't take a leap of faith.

The final moment of revelation occurred when she stepped into Shannon's hospital room and found her sister curled up with Liam on the hospital bed, their newborn baby nestled between them. The three of them presented a single unit, the perfect expression of happily ever after. The embodiment of love and family, as it should be.

Katie had let fear drive her for too long.

No more. No. More.

She slipped out of the room before being noticed. Aunt Jane met her in the hallway. "I can't tell you how relieved I am that Shannon's young man turned out to be faithful and true."

The words reminded Katie of something the older woman had said earlier. "Did I hear you and Bridget both admit to sending letters to him?"

Aunt Jane showed not one single speck of contrition. "I knew his mother when I was a girl," she explained. "Mean, nasty, selfish creature—traits she never grew out of. The boy needed a nudge out of the nest. I gave it to him."

Katie shook her head in awe. "Remind me never to get on your bad side."

"You could never get on my bad side." The older woman patted her arm. "You're a good girl, Katie O'Connor. You deserve the best life has to offer."

"What a lovely thing to say."

They shared a quick hug. Katie stepped back and eyed her aunt as a thought occurred to her, something Ty had said in the park. "Aunt Jane, did you speak with Ty earlier?"

Suddenly fascinated with the toe of her left shoe, she shrugged. "I may have given him a word or two of advice."

"About me?"

She looked up, her gaze full of motherly love. "You deserve happiness, Katie. That man makes you happy."

Yes, yes, he did. "I love him."

The words were surprisingly easy to say.

"I know, dear. So stop wasting time talking to an old woman." Her aunt took her by the shoulders and spun her in the direction of the exit. "Go find your man and tell him how you feel."

Katie didn't need to be told twice.

If she hurried, she could time her arrival just as the ferry was taking on passengers for another trip to Ellis Island.

Forty-five minutes later, Katie stood at the railing, watching the Battery disappear in the mist. Though the waters were relatively calm, the crossing was no less a nightmare for her than the last time she'd traveled to the immigration station.

I was not made for sea travel. She pressed her nose into the wind, desperate for the cool air to relieve her suffering.

Happy to put the miserable voyage behind her when the ferry finally reached its destination, she disembarked ahead of the majority of her fellow passengers, with resolve in every footstep. Eyes cast on the imposing building that had brought her both joy and pain, she set out to find her man in the crowd of immigrants.

Her search proved blessedly short. She'd barely entered the area near the Kissing Post when Ty exited the immigration station, his face full of grim determination, a man on a mission.

She moved directly in his path. "Hello, Ty."

His feet came to a grinding halt. "Katie?" He sauntered toward her with his long-legged stride, a smile lifting the corners of his mouth at the sight of her. "I didn't expect to see you here."

She looked up at him, trying to keep herself firmly rooted to the spot when all she wanted was to vault into his arms.

"I didn't expect to be here. But now that I am, I thought we might finish our discussion. You know, the one about our future together."

"Let me get this straight. You came all the way to Ellis Island, on a *ferryboat*"—he looked pointedly at the vessel bobbing in the sea—"so we could discuss our future?"

"I wanted to make a grand gesture, and . . . oh, boy." Her stomach took a hard dip to port. "I need to sit down."

Ty took her hand and guided her to an empty bench. He sat beside her, searched her gaze, then brought her hand to his lips. "You're seasick."

"Just a little queasy. It'll pass."

"I'm a doctor. I know these things. You're seasick," he repeated with quiet understanding, and no small amount of awe. "You put yourself through certain suffering because you wanted to make a grand gesture."

She closed her eyes and breathed through a wave of nausea. "Is it working?"

"Look at me, Katie."

She opened her eyes.

"It's working." Hope kindled in her chest, then ignited into a flame when he brought her hand to his lips once more.

"I love you, Ty." The declaration came far easier than she'd expected. So easy, in fact, that she felt the need to say the words again. "I love you."

"Marry me. We love each other. We're good together. You make me a better man, and I'd like to think I challenge you in a similar way."

"You do, Ty, in so many areas of my life."

"Marry me, and we'll change the world together, one patient at a time."

Katie was desperately tempted. But she gave him one last chance to change his mind.

"Be certain, Ty. I couldn't bear it if you sacrificed your future as a surgeon and then grew to resent me for it."

"You're thinking too small. There's no reason that my choice has to be one route over the other." His smile broadened, giving him a boyish look that had her heart stumbling over two distinct beats. "I can perform surgery, volunteer at Ellis Island, and continue at the clinic on a regular, albeit limited, basis."

She angled her head. "How would that work, exactly?"

"We'll hire another doctor to serve at the clinic, perhaps more than one." He ran a finger over her temple, brushing a strand of hair off her face, then tucked it behind her ear. "I can't guarantee smooth waters all the time. We'll have our share of choppy seas to navigate. But we'll make it work. Together, we can do anything, Katie. I believe it. Do you?"

"I do," she said, feeling a surge of emotion for this man, her partner, her friend, the love of her life. "You asked me a question earlier. Would you mind repeating it?"

He took her hand. "Katie O'Connor, will you let me love you, with all my heart, until my last dying breath?"

"That wasn't exactly the question I meant."

"Patience, sweetheart, there's more to be said." He shifted, moving to stand before her, then dropping smoothly to bended knee. "Will you be my partner at work, my companion at home, and the mother of my children?"

Still not the question she was hoping for, but he'd asked for her patience and so she waited for the rest.

"I love you, Katie O'Connor. Will you do me the honor of becoming my wife?"

At last. *At last!*

For a moment, she was too choked up to speak. Feeling nervous pangs in her stomach, she wrapped her arms around his neck and pulled him close. "Yes, Ty. Yes to it all. I will be your partner, your companion, and the mother of your children. Yes, I will be your wife."

Grinning, he pulled her to her feet. "Come." He kissed her on the lips, once, twice, a third time that lasted entirely too long for propriety. "We have a life to begin."

"We do, indeed." Katie didn't even mind that the first leg of their journey involved another stomach-churning ferryboat ride.

About the Author

Photo © 2012 Caroline Akins / One Six Photography

Renee Ryan is the author of twenty-four inspirational, historical, and contemporary romance novels. She received the Daphne du Maurier Award for Excellence in Mystery/Suspense in the Inspirational Romantic category, for her novels *Dangerous Allies* and *Courting the Enemy*. She is the secretary for Romance Writers of America. Ryan currently lives in Omaha, Nebraska, with her husband and a twenty-six pound cat many have mistaken for a small bear. For more information about Renee's books, please visit www.reneeryan.com.